ITEM **028 556 014**

KT-232-393

THE
NEW
ORDER

CHRIS WEITZ

ATOM

First published in the US in 2015 by Little, Brown and Company
First published in Great Britain in 2016 by Atom

1 3 5 7 9 10 8 6 4 2

Copyright © 2015 by Chris Weitz

The moral right of the author has been asserted.

A CIP catalogue record for this book
is available from the British Library.

ISBN 978-1-9074-1182-3 (paperback)
ISBN 978-1-4055-1832-1 (eBook)

Printed and bound in Great Britain by
Clays Ltd, St Ives plc

Papers used by Atom are from well-managed
forests and other responsible sources.

 MIX
Paper from
responsible sources
FSC **FSC® C104740**

Atom
An imprint of
Little, Brown Book Group
Carmelite House
50 Victoria Embankment
London EC4Y 0DZ

An Hachette UK Company
www.hachette.co.uk

www.atombooks.co.uk

For Leila and Genny

JEFFERSON

THE GODS LEAN out of their machine and wave at us from the sky.

A loudspeaker pronounces, "PUT DOWN YOUR WEAPONS NOW."

The Islanders have been told to defend the lab. They raise their guns and fire, making little pockmarks appear on the gray skin of the beast, around the bold black letters that say US NAVY.

The soldiers duck their heads back in, and the snout of a machine gun swivels down toward us and coughs fire. The kid nearest to me and Donna turns from a person into a chaos of blood and meat.

The rest of the Islanders take off for the safety of the lab. More of them get churned up by another volley from the chopper. Donna and Brainbox and Peter and Theo and Captain and I have hit the ground, prostrate and helpless, like we're worshipping a volcano.

Later, we are disgorged from the belly of the helicopter the moment it lands on the massive rectangular slab that tops the carrier, itself as tall as a midtown office block. Crowds of sailors, arrayed in brightly colored jumpsuits, are anting all around us. As our guards pull us away from one another, words are swamped in the sound belched from the rotors and the engines of the jets crouching everywhere. I barely have a chance to look at Donna before we're rushed off the deck and down into the metal labyrinth of the ship.

I shout her name, but nothing gets out.

I wake up to the buzz and the dim light of the fluorescent panel. There's no clock in my cell and no window to the outside, so I can't say if it's day or night. Now and then I hear, through the hull, the clatter of boots or the braying of a Klaxon, but if there's a schedule, I haven't learned it yet. In this humming metal box, I've lost my circadian rhythm and float around in time like a ship with shattered masts, out of sight of land. I ghost through memories, mind disordered and thinking shot.

Pictures in my head. There's Washington Square, a green postage stamp (remember those?) in the gray circuit board of Manhattan. In the mind's bird's eye, just as it ever was. But as I zoom in, clicking the plus sign on my mental Google Map, wrongs emerge like blotches on the city's complexion. There's a garbage fire. There's a pile of corpses. Cars wrenched out of their courses and abandoned, looking like they've been played with by a giant three-year-old. (Was that God—a giant toddler? Or had he just gifted the earth to a friend's kid, a spoiled little demiurge, and gone off on pressing business in another galaxy?)

Down at street level, behind the makeshift walls enclosing the Square, the tribe would be going about its business, scavenging for food and fuel and wondering whatever happened to me and my little band. And dying.

In some kind of amphibious loading dock, I'm hosed down with a greenish liquid that bubbles and scums and pools at the grates. Frog-marched into a shower by two marines in hazmat suits, their eyes wide with fear of the Sickness. Sopping, I'm held in restraints as medicine is given and blood taken.

A week of quarantine, and I'm thrown in the brig.

Again, I take in my surroundings. A cube of metal painted oily gray, with a brushed-steel toilet and sink occupying one corner and a narrow bunk opposite. A stout metal door with an inset Plexiglas slab, duct-taped blind from the outside.

It's like Beckett but worse. No sun shines on the nothing new.

I can't see out, but I'm pretty sure they can see in, since they keep the lights on, poisoning my sleep. They're watching me, and listening, too, no doubt. I look around for beady camera lenses no bigger than an insect's eye.

And then, the rap of a metal baton on the door, a call of "clear the hatch!" and my interrogator slips in, lifting a folding chair over the threshold. He's out of hazmat, as are the rest of them. Looks like they're satisfied that their cure works as well as ours.

"More?" I say.

"Just a few questions," he says. It's what he always says.

Is there something I don't know that I know? The voice that always drones away inside my head, sometimes like a pesky little brother and sometimes like a strict parent, and sometimes like someone I think of as "myself," recites a sort of ditty, with the insinuating logic of a kid's nonsense verse: *There are known knowns. These are things we know that we know. There are known unknowns. That is to say, there are things that we know we don't know. But there are also unknown unknowns. There are things we don't know we don't know.*

"What do you mean by that?" says the interrogator. I didn't realized I had spoken the thought.

"Why haven't we landed? You know there are people dying, right?"

He doesn't answer. But one of my guards in quarantine told me

4

that the *Ronald Reagan* keeps its massive self just over the edge of the horizon from land, just out of sight of the Island.

"Aren't you going to run out of fuel?"

To my surprise, he actually answers this one. "This is a nuclear-powered ship," he says. "We can stay at sea for twenty years at a time." He smiles. I realize it's his pride in the ship that made him talk.

Maybe, with America gone, it's all he has to call home.

I try another. "Are we the only ones left? Are you the only adults who don't have the Sickness?"

My guess is that the carrier is a little floating city-state in a sea of death. Or maybe there are other ships at sea, a water-bound quarantine that's protected them from the Sickness. Beyond that, how could the adults have survived? The Sickness decimates everything.

No, says the teacher in my head, it does worse than decimate. The word *decimate* originally referred to the Roman custom of punishing legionnaires. They would select, by lot, one out of every ten soldiers in a legion that had mutinied; and put them to death. Discipline through terror.

What the Sickness did was worse. All the little children, all the adults gone. The Sickness, like an advertiser, respects the teen demographic.

"I thought you might like some extra dessert," he says by way of changing the subject. He holds out a foil-sealed cup of fruit salad. He's been trying to train me with these doggy treats for a week now, like he wants my memory to sit up and beg.

I take the plastic cup. It's still cold from the refrigerator. Even if the ship could stay afloat for twenty years, they couldn't feed everyone aboard, could they? I once saw a documentary about carriers that said the biggest ones had crews of thousands. How long could they survive off the ship's stores? They'd need fresh supplies.

If I can talk to Brainbox, maybe we can figure it out. I bet Box is vacuuming information in, no matter how hard they try to keep him in the dark. Or rather, no matter how hard they try to keep him in the dim. Like the low fluorescent light, the interrogators feed the mind a numbing trickle of illumination, enough for it to think there's nothing more to know.

Back at Plum Island, when the helicopter had done its deus-ex-machina thing, hanging in the sky fat and ungainly as a bumble-bee, I had hoped for a lot better. I guess after everything we'd been through, I'd reckoned on a hero's welcome. A slap on the back, an ice-cold Coke, a you've-done-good-son-now-the-nightmare-is-over, a slice of pizza? Instead, questions, like a shitty episode of *Law & Order* on permanent replay.

"Why did you fire on the helicopter?"

I say, "We didn't fire on the helicopter. *They* did."

"Who?"

"The Islanders. I mean, the kids who lived on Plum Island."

"You're not one of the kids who lived on Plum Island?"

"No. We're from Washington Square. And Harlem."

"All right, why did the kids who lived on Plum Island fire on us?"

"I don't know. Ask them, if there are any left."

"What about the bodies we found in the lab?"

"That'd be the Old Man—that is to say, the *adult,* I guess. He was a scientist or something. Biowarfare. And the girl would be Kath. She was...kind of one of us."

"What happened to them?"

"The Old Man killed Kath. He was using us as lab rats. He injected her with something that brought the Sickness on quicker than usual. He did the same thing to me, but he and Brainbox figured out the Cure, and I beat it. Well, you know that, I guess."

"And what happened to the old man?"

"I told you."

"Remind me."

"I killed him. Or...Brainbox poisoned his medicine. Then I finished him off."

"How?"

"I...strangled him."

The Old Man was going to murder us all. I don't think about killing him, not much.

I ask, "Are the others alive?"

His face shows nothing, not even the shadow of an answer he's not giving. "That's enough for now," he says, gets up, and shuts the hatch as the marine with the M4 carbine glares at me.

I return to my bunk, sprawl on my back, and think about Donna. Then I think about thinking about Donna. I've been trying to keep the thinking about her at bay, since I figure nothing good can come of it. I have no way to see her, or talk to her, or touch her. And I have the

7

strangest feeling that things had gotten about as good as they could get, that night on the tugboat *Annie* before we were taken captive by the Islanders. Almost that it had been *too* good. That there's an inverse relationship between how beautiful something is and how long it lasts. Sunsets, orgasms, soap bubbles.

Then I reflect on how perverse I am. Then I remember explaining the difference between *perverse* and *perverted* to Donna on a cool autumn morning at the Square before It Happened, and what the "imp of the perverse" is. Then I remember Donna called me the imp of the pervert. And again the seawall that keeps Donna out of my head fails, and I am drowning in loneliness, and I begin to rebuild it with melting bricks of ice.

So I think about thinking about thinking about Donna. And as I do, I turn over the cup of fruit salad in my hands. And I see that there's an expiration date stamped onto the bottom. They usually ink it out, along with any other lettering on the sad little packaging, as though they want to starve my eyes. But someone got slapdash, and the black ink underlines the date rather than obscuring it.

The use-by date is—from what I can figure—a month into the future. Which means that it was manufactured after What Happened. How is that possible?

DONNA

IN BETWEEN ALL the Ask Me Anythings and Up Close and Personals administered by Ed the Interrogator and the medics—suddenly I'm like some fricking celebrity with a bigger entourage than Beyoncé or something—I let myself just float on the feels.

It's as good a way as any to pass the time, I figure. Yeah, it'd be more fun to have some DVDs or whatever, but this is just old-school entertainment. First they had channel surfing and then they had Web browsing and now I just use my memories to pass the time.

I've got to say, it leaves something to be desired.

It's fun enough to go all gooey over Jefferson and remember what happened and how we fell in love and everything, but I wouldn't mind having a magazine or two. I mean, you can only do so much replaying a memory in your mind before you realize that each time you retell it to yourself you're changing the details just a little bit. So after a while, like, say, fifty thousand times conjuring up that first kiss in your head, you realize that all the little substitutions—maybe he held me like that instead of like *that*, wouldn't it be better to remember our first kiss from a third-person perspective, like in a movie, rather than with his face looming up to me—have added up to a big fake. Like that lame joke my dad used to tell about Paul Revere's original ax, with the ax head replaced and the handle replaced.

This is the thing about solitary confinement: It makes your mind eat your mind. So I'm downright happy when my interrogator arrives.

Me: "Hi, Ed, what's the word?"

I've taken to calling him Ed, because he *looks* like an Ed. Round-faced, soapy skin with razor burns, and a little paunchy, with the same buzz cut as the rest of them.

Ed: "Good morning."

So it's morning. What should I do today? Maybe a little staring at the wall followed by some nail biting? Then a bit of almost going mental before lunch.

Me: "So, Ed, have you thought about my request? Run it up the flagpole? Is that what you navy guys call it? A flagpole? Or is it a 'vertical banner-attachment interface' or something?"

Ed: "We're considering it."

There's the teensiest note of flirtation in the way he says that. I can tell that Ed is on his best behavior, and definitely a company man, and for that matter that he doesn't give two shits about me per se. But I can also tell that he's ever so slightly perving out on me. I stack it up to a shortage of women in the navy and a dash of creepy power-imbalance fetish. I am, after all, at his beck and call, his own little Princess Leia in the detention wing.

He offers me fruit salad. Which I take, while wishing he had a bit more to offer by way of swag. I suspect the fruit salad is calculated to make me indebted to him in some sort of wanky, pop-psychology way, but, fortunately, I am also cultivating a hearty strain of contempt to counterbalance it. I'm not all defiant and take-nothing-from-your-tormentors. I'm more use-every-angle-you-can. Which doesn't mean I'm, like, flashing my tits (such as they are) at him or anything. I'm just not refusing little morale boosters like peaches in syrup and brand-x Oreos. Anyhow, I've asked him for something cuter to wear than the outfit they gave me, which is a baggy blue camouflage. What would you call the color? Sunset Bruise, maybe? Asphyxia? It reminds me of the Uptowners, with their whole paintball/paramilitary look, and I hate it. I've asked for a bunch of other crap, too—makeup, an iPad, fashion magazines, Ugg boots, newspapers, tampons.

See what I did there? I asked for a bunch of dumb shit that any teen girl might want, like there hadn't been a global apocalypse and nobody had anything better to do than read *In Touch* or whatever. But in among all the garbazh was something that could actually tell me what the hell is going on, like a newspaper, if they still had those. Hey, it's worth a try. I can tell from Ed's condescending 'tude that he thinks I'm pretty much a waste of gray matter, so I figure I might as well play down to his expectations and see if he slips up.

As for the tampons, well, that one was for real, which is a heck

11

of a thing. See, ever since the Sickness hit, nobody was having babies or periods or anything associated. But, for better or worse, since getting on the USS *Solitary Confinement,* reboot! The system is up and running again. Which, yay, I guess? Part of me is all I Am Woman, and part of me is kind of pissed that the one perk of the apocalypse is out the window.

Ed: "I can do the, uh...sanitary, uh...supplies." (Ed's as thrown as any dude by Lady Situations.) "As for the rest, well, a lot depends on your cooperation."

It's hard to get your hooks into Ed—he doesn't act like he feels bad for keeping me cooped up, or recognize that simple human decency might require that he tell me a thing or two about what's going on. At the same time, he doesn't do the game-playing, head-tripping thing that interrogators in old movies and TV shows do. Instead there's a sort of fatigued persistence, like a beleaguered substitute teacher running an endless quiz.

Ed: "I still have just a few questions."

Just a few questions. True enough if "a few" means hundreds, thousands, often redundant and occasionally bizarre.

Ed: "Let's go back to the days before the electricity went out. You said that you were on a field trip at the UN on the day that the Conference on the Viral Crisis began."

Me: "Yeah, for, like, fifteen minutes, before they shut down the trip."

Ed has been rounding on this question again and again over the last few days, so much that I can tell it's important. He tries to hide it

in a smoke screen of bullshit questions like "what did your diet con-
sist of?" But he's got this ridiculous tell, which is that his leg starts
bouncing up and down when he really cares about an answer. Little
does he know that I used to watch the World Series of Poker on TV,
all those pale, misshapen, bedraggled bros trying to put one over on
one another while madly suppressing every emotional indicator their
bodies were trying to give out.

So, like any decent poker player in this situation, I keep my hand
to myself.

Ed: "Did anyone ever talk about what happened to the
president?"

Me: "No, nobody gave a shit about what happened to the president. They were too busy trying to find food. What happened to
the president, anyway? Did he make it? If not, who's the president
now?"

Ed half sighs, then stops himself and begins the long loop
around to the same question, his leg coming to rest.

Ed: "You told me that you and your friends formed a sort of
gang? For mutual protection?"

Me: "Not a gang. A tribe. That's what we called it."

Ed: "What's the difference?"

Me: "A gang sounds like it's a bunch of dudes doing something
against the law. But there was no law. Or, if there was, we were it."

Ed looks unconvinced.

Me: "Look. Everything has broken down. No authority. No parents, no cops, no schools, no government, no nothing. If you don't

band together with other kids, you're just a random, and that means that anybody can prey on you. You ever read *Lord of the Flies*, Ed? Bunch of fancy-pants English schoolkids stuck on a desert island? Bullying, dancing around the fire, kill the pig, et cetera? It was like that but with automatic weapons."

Ed: "Okay. Tell me more about your 'tribe.' How many people?"

Me: "Two hundred, more or less. Less now, I guess, since people are probably still aging out."

Ed: "From the Sickness."

Me: "*Yeah*. Or violence, or starvation. But mostly the Sickness. I only made it because of what Brainbox and the Old Man came up with in the lab. How did you guys make it? If you have a cure, Ed, you have to give it to my friends. You have to take it to New York. Kids are dying."

Ed: "Like your friends in Washington Square."

Me: "Yeah, but there's more than us. Thousands. A lot of them are assholes, but still."

Ed: "You mean your tribe has enemies?"

Me: "Sure. There's the Uptowners. There's the Ghosts at the library—they're cannibals. There's—"

Ed: "What do you mean by 'cannibals'?"

Me: "What it sounds like. They eat people. They cook them first, I'll give them that much credit. Smelled pretty tasty, actually, until you found out what it was. My stomach was growling. Kind of makes you think differently about people and animals and...and everything."

14

Ed doesn't say anything. I shake off my little Existential Horror Moment.

Me: "But, hey, whatever floats your boat, right?"

Ed: "But you say there was no central authority. No one tribe predominated?"

Me: "No. There were a bunch. Some were stronger than others. The Uptowners had plenty of guns. They had a good chunk of the island. The kids from Harlem might take over soon, though. They were making guns? With three-D printers?"

Ed: "Three-D printers."

Me: "Yeah. Melting down LEGOs and using computers to, like, extrude plastic AR-15s. They're really smart. And pissed off, on account of, you know, centuries of oppression and unfairness and stuff?"

Either Ed has a great memory or somebody is recording this, because he never writes anything down, even though I can tell from the way his eyes move that he's intrigued by this little tidbit. His pupils do these abortive little orbits as he fits the pieces of my story together.

Me: "Tell me a little about you, Ed."

But Ed is not feeling communicative. After *a few more questions,* he gets up and goes back to wherever it is that he spends his coffee breaks, thumbing through copies of *Interrogator Monthly* or something.

Later comes dinner—I can tell it's dinner because two meals

ago it had been powdered eggs and these quadrilateral bacon strips that looked like they were snipped off a spool.

Something's different this time.

The sparrow's-egg-blue plastic plate is perched on a pedestal that turns out to be a book as thick as a brick. It's called *On Politics* by Alan Ryan. On the back it says that "As an accessible introduction to the nature of political thought, *On Politics* could scarcely be bettered."

An accessible introduction to the nature of political thought. Just what I always wanted.

I heft the book in my hand and riffle the pages, all eleven hundred or so. I inspect it for pictures. For exclamation points. For anything that might be considered vaguely interesting. I don't know, philosopher dish. Metaphysical dirty laundry. Who wore the toga best? Nothing.

Somebody has already taken a run at reading it, and judging by the wrinkles along the spine, he didn't get past this dude Machiavelli. I remember that he was the "ends justify the means" guy. Except he probably hadn't said that, because all the things people were supposed to have said turned out not to have been said by them, or it turned out they were being ironic. Pretty much no way of getting at the truth. Just like every time "they did a study" proving something, some other "they" did some other study that proved the opposite. That was why I hadn't been nuts about literature the way Jefferson had been. Not that it was so hard to get a handle on, but it turned out what you thought was a handle wasn't a handle after all, or somebody would just point out that there was a better handle. Plus, it was all just stories about imaginary people. What the hell could you get from stories about people who never actually existed? That's why I like the hard, gritty truths of *Cosmo* and *Teen Vogue*. Or hamsters eating miniature burritos.

And as far as intellectual pursuits, I preferred medicine. At least you knew you were doing something that was of some good to somebody. Maybe, just maybe, if everything hadn't gone to shit, I would have studied medicine. Mom, who was a nurse, would have pissed herself with joy at that. Of course, since I wasn't, like, a *genius,* I'd probably have had to take out huge loans and then have been stuck going into plastic surgery or something to pay them back. So, thanks to the Sickness, instead of a future in silicone boob installation and Botox, I'd had a crash course in combat medicine. Broken bones and lacerations and ballistic trauma, cavitation and hydrostatic shock.

I think about SeeThrough and how I managed to stop her sucking chest wound with a square cut out of a plastic bag before the internal bleeding got her. I decide to try to stop thinking about that.

So I nudge my mind back to Jefferson and how we didn't get enough time together. I mean, we had *loads* of time together. Since we were in first grade. But we didn't have Time Together until it was too late. Only one night on the *Annie* as she lolled in the swells off Plum Island, before the Islanders slipped over her sides and took us.

The impossibly lovely weirdness of lying next to someone, breathing his spent air, seeing your face in his eyes, and realizing that, after all, your purpose is happiness.

But this line of thought isn't any good, because I have no idea where he is, if he's even alive, if they're at this moment dissecting his body.

I pick up the book again. The front cover shows a picture of a bunch of beardy ancient dudes hanging out in togas.

I thumb my way to the first chapter. Apparently it has something to do with how the Greeks were all sort of chilling in their poleis, which were kind of like cities except also like countries. The Persians, who had a big-ass empire ruled by one guy, Xerxes, who was a major a-hole, wanted to take over all of Greece. They figured it'd be easy, because the Greeks were divided and squabbling over the remote and talking shit over and taking votes and everything, but it turned out that the Greeks actually got their act together and ended up kicking some Persian ass. There was a movie about that before What Happened, with all these buff dudes called the Spartans killing bajillions of Persians and saying badass catchphrases and wearing loincloths and generally being hot and awesome. I remember I appreciated all the glutes and biceps and abbage, but at the same time, I was just a little put off by the fact that all the bad guys had been sneering brown-skinned people with funny accents, while most of the Spartans looked like blond surfer dudes, which seemed kind of unlikely. Whatever.

Anyhow, in real life, as opposed to movie life, after the Greeks win, they all be beefing with one another, especially Athens and Sparta. The Athenians, who have a democracy, keep fucking up because they're arrogant and pissy and easy for politicians to fool. Plus, there's a plague (been there, done that) that weakens the Athenians to the point that public order totally breaks down (ditto). The Spartans win the war. Then they set up an oligarchy, which is Greek for a few dudes calling all the shots.

And you did not fuck with the oligarchy. This guy Plato, whose name means "fatty," writes about how Socrates, who was kind of his mentor, got brought up on charges that he was dissing the gods and "corrupting the youth." Despite the fact that this sounds like he was feeling kids up, it's actually because he was teaching them philosophy, which in this case meant, like, questioning the logic of everything.

Anyway, one of the big questions in *The Republic*, which was, like, Plato's bestseller or whatever, is *what is justice?* Socrates is at this sort of cocktail party, and he's all, "What is justice?" Everybody jumps right in, despite the fact that Socrates is famous for giving out intellectual pimp-slaps, so it's like Bruce Lee has just shown up and sort of innocently asked if anybody feels like sparring or whatever, like, no biggie.

So one after the other, Socrates pwns the different views of justice that the other dudes put forward. Like, helping your friends and hurting your enemies doesn't make for justice, because we don't really know who our friends and our enemies are. The strong forcing stuff on the weak doesn't mean justice, either, because it doesn't fit in with "virtue" and "wisdom."

After thinking about it a little, I start suspecting that Socrates is just playing word games. I mean, that's all you can say justice is for sure—a word. Everybody has their own private definition of that word, but it probably doesn't match up exactly with anybody else's. But these Greek dudes are acting like there is this thing called Justice that exists *out there*, outside of words, and if only you could see it clearly, you'd know how to act. Which, given everything I have seen and done, strikes me as pretty much bullshit.

Plato has Socrates lay out this plan for the perfect city, the Republic. Which is a nice idea, except Socrates comes up with all these totally shit-for-brains laws like shared property that you wouldn't follow unless somebody was watching you 24/7 making sure you didn't slip up. Not only that, some of the rules are downright evil. Like slavery is fine. And women should be owned communally by men. Which reminds me of the Uptowners. Those dudes got off on controlling women. And I don't mean controlling them, like, "don't talk to any other bros." I mean, like, *owning* them.

I think back to Evan, the Uptowner we called Cheekbones, lecturing me about how some people were better than others, his gun laid on the table pointing at my chest.

Well, fuck him, and Plato and Socrates and all of them.

The problem is, all of these totally ratched ideas, which were safe enough in a paperback, are *possible* in the new world. Or maybe

20

I should call it the young world. What Happened has cracked life into pieces, and you can put them back together in all sorts of weird ways. Nothing is true, and everything is permissible. Jefferson told me that, too, though I can't remember where he got it from.

I flip through the rest of the book, annoyed. And then I notice that even though the cracks in the spine leave off after a few hundred pages, somebody kept underlining words in the rest of the book, as if they've carefully marked stuff out beyond where they've actually read. The marks go all the way through the book.

The individual underlinings make no sense. They start in the middle of sentences and sometimes leave off halfway through a word.

But then—it's probably because I'm so bored—I try reading just the first word of each underlining, looking for a code. Very Encyclopedia Brown. And damn if they don't spell out a message:

your
friends
are
safe
do
not
cooperate
with
the
investigators

they

are

not

on

your

side

we

are

working

to

free

you

When my breath comes back, I pore over the book again. Could I be imagining this? Finding a pattern where there's none? I want to show it to Jefferson. I want to show it to Brainbox—he'd probably be able to prove statistically how likely it is for random words to form sentences that have meaning.

No. I don't need them to tell me this is for real. Somebody is talking to me. And telling me that Jefferson and Brainbox and Theo and Peter and Captain are alive.

I hadn't realized how afraid I was for them until now, and I cry grateful tears.

JEFFERSON

WE ARE SWALLOWED down into the gut of the ship; we are a virus in the works with our elbows grabbed by antibodies. A twisting rectilinear corridor opens to a vast hangar bay as full of weaponry as a child's toy box. I see helicopter gunships, brutal snub-nosed jets, elegant swallow-tailed fighters, cadres of marines. The whole lethal package hanging over the horizon like a little kid who's tucked himself behind the corner of a wall, waiting to pull some kind of mischief.

Underneath the plate with the ribbons of bacon, I find a copy of *Us Weekly* magazine.

I look at the hatch through which the guard came to deliver the meal, but it's already closed again. There's no note, nor any other indication of why it's arrived or who sent it.

Even though I never had time for celebrity gossip, or what Donna calls "pre-apocalyptic social structures," I smooth the paper down carefully. It's a luxury from the world outside, and I haven't read anything for weeks. It's all I have to put my mind to.

It's an old copy, from well before What Happened. Even I had been aware of the "Cheating Bombshell" on the cover. Still, information is a delicacy. The Ghosts, holed up in the public library, had been right about that, even if they had been horrifically wrong about so much else. So I ration it out, morsel by morsel, and shortly find myself, against my inclinations, getting attached to the people in the stories, who are alternately too fat or too thin, have made fashion blunders or have been seen kissing someone who isn't their girlfriend. Starved as I am for company, they become almost like real people to me, welcomed into the charmed circle of my empathy.

And, at the same time, removed for years from the society that produced these grotesques, I begin to see them through a different metaphorical filter than before.

People used to say that since Americans didn't have a royal family, we projected our urge for hierarchy onto entertainers. That does explain some of the fawning and fetishizing, shadow desires cast by the matter-of-fact glare of democracy. But now I wonder if the deficit being filled wasn't in fact deeper than the need to be subordinate. Celebrities, as described in Us Weekly, behaved more like Greek gods than aristocrats. Beautiful, fickle, arrogant, angry, slothful, jealous, occasionally taking a bride among the humans, spawning demigods and fabulous monsters. And what did that make the public? Not just commoners, but celebrants. Libation bearers, worshippers sacrificing to the holy mystery of Importance.

Reading it this way, translating the tack and folly to the sphere of mythology, I manage to enjoy myself and am genuinely sad when I reach the last page, having sucked the pith from every scandal and puff piece.

Only the crossword is left. But somebody has already done it, and not even correctly. The answers penciled into the boxes have nothing to do with the clues.

But after a while, they make a sort of sense of their own. If I ignore some random letters put there just to make it less obvious, I can read a message:

Your friends are safe. Do not cooperate with the investigators. They are not on your side. We are working to free you.

From somewhere out there, among a crew of thousands, someone is making contact.

My head buzzes, my veins run hot with adrenaline. And I worry that my feelings can be picked up by the surveillance equipment they must have trained on me. I make a show of obliviousness to the message, flipping the pages back and forth randomly.

We are working to free you. It brings home fully for the first time that I am imprisoned. I've been coddling myself with the thought that, like the interrogator said, I'm under a sort of quarantine rather than just locked up.

If they're not going to punish me, why am I stuck here? The initial pretext of protection against the virus has dropped away. The comical scenes of interviews with men in full hazmat suits have ended, and now my captors show no fear of transmission.

They want something from me, that much is clear. But amid all the questions, I can't figure out what the something is. Except that, again and again, their curiosity is directed at the lay of the land in Manhattan—what tribe is in control of what turf—and at events immediately before the Sickness took down the grid.

What on earth can they be afraid of?

Donna is safe. I haven't allowed myself to think I'd lost her, not after everything, but they haven't told me anything, and the news lets me lower my guard. I wallow for a while in the pangy sensation of wanting her here, now.

And the others...

And the kids back at the Square—what do the adults want with them?

There's a metallic rap on the door. I'm up and ready for whatever, a fight if they've discovered the message in the magazine. I roll it up tightly, slightly skewed so that the tensed and packed pages make a truncheon to jab into someone's eye.

When the hatch swings open, it's a new face, a balding man with a weary smile. He looks bemused at my tensed crouch and menacing magazine. He has a pair of marines with him who eyeball me as if I were a wild animal, but his body language is casual, a little slipshod, like his rumpled uniform.

"You want me to lay him out, Doc?" says one of the marines flanking him.

"No, thank you," he says. He holds out his hand to me.

"I'm Flight Surgeon Morris," he says. "I've come for your blood."

He has a sort of wry smile as he says it, as if we're both involved in some funny game of pretend.

I leave him with his hand outstretched, and he shrugs as if to say, *I get it*. Looks at the rolled magazine in my hand. "You can take that with you, if you like."

"Take it where?"

"Sick bay. Hardly the most exciting spot, but it beats being stuck in here all day." He smiles.

"You don't seem like the others," I say.

"These guys are lifers. I was a civilian until I turned thirty," says Morris. He clears his throat and, somewhat ceremoniously, motions me through the hatch.

It has been more sleepings and wakings than I can count since I have been out of my gray rectangle. If I run through the hatchway and close the door behind me—I try to remember if there is a latch on the other side or if it's opened by a key. Then what? Try to negotiate my way through the intestines of the ship, to get—where? Should I call for my mysterious pen pal?

No. It's a ridiculous idea. The chance of finding him or her in a crew of thousands is—well—one in thousands. And there's nowhere to escape *to*. Not yet at least. I've got to hang in and figure it out.

Flight Surgeon Morris takes my hesitation as fear.

27

"Don't worry," he says. "This won't hurt. Much." I follow him, with the marines following me, up and down a number of stairs and around turnings that very quickly become dizzyingly hard to hold onto in my memory. But my escorts know just where they're going, and at last we arrive at an expansion of the metal hollow. In a little cubby off one side of a row of thin beds stacked in bunks with miserly efficiency of space, a tech waits, her eyes wide with her first sight of the plague survivor.

She starts unpeeling a needle, looking past me to the flight surgeon for directions.

"You already took blood," I say. "When we got here."

"That was for testing. This is for manufacture."

"Manufacture of what?"

"I think I've already said too much. Go on, Ensign," he says to the spooked medical tech. "He won't bite. Will you?" He turns to me.

I don't respond—acknowledging a witticism seems like an act of collaboration. I just sit down on the metal stool and hold out my arm.

The ensign doesn't appear to know how to address me. "Can you—I need you to—"

I straighten the arm, offering her the soft hinge of my elbow. The ensign cinches a blue rubber tourniquet tight, then starts jabbing at me with the point of the needle, her hands shaking.

"Sorry," she says. She won't meet my eyes. I wait until she gets it right.

Squeamishness has kind of gone by the wayside since the days and nights at the lab on Plum Island. When you've strangled the life out of someone, the lesser violations of the human body—even your own—come more easily.

My blood leaks like tapped syrup into a test tube with a buttery dab of medium in the curve at the bottom. Sort of an elongated petri dish.

Morris nods. "I'll come back in a bit."

When one tube is full, the ensign pops it free of its plastic housing and pushes another one in. Two tubes and then three get filled this way.

A figure hovers in the doorway, at the edge of my vision. I turn to see a tall black marine who, unlike the others, appears to be seeking out contact, his face open.

"You with them?" he says. "From New York?"

I nod. Is this my pen pal?

The marine reaches into a pocket and withdraws a photograph printed on the corner of a creased sheet of paper. A girl, maybe fifteen, leggy, smiling in the time before the Sickness.

"Lanita Adams," says the marine. "You seen her? You know her?"

I look at the name tag on the marine's chest. "She's your sister?"

The marine nods. He seems about to say something but then he doesn't, or can't.

"I haven't seen her," I say. "I'm sorry."

The marine nods again, swallows. "What's it like there?"

Bad.

"It depends," I say. "Where did she live?"

"Manhattan, 134th Street."

"Things aren't so bad up there," I say. "They got things together. How old was she—is she?"

"She's seventeen," he says.

We both know what it means. The Sickness might not have killed her by now, but it will soon enough. And the world the Sickness made might have already done the job just as efficiently.

The marine's face relaxes just a little. "Listen," he says. "It's not like everybody's down with the program here." He looks at the ensign, whose face assumes a studiedly neutral expression—*I'm not hearing this*. "We're not down to just wait and let people die—"

"What do you mean?"

Something beyond the hatch makes Adams straighten up and move on.

Morris pokes his head back in. "Everything all right?"

By now four vials of blood are slotted into a little metal rack; a dozen empties wait to be filled.

"If you want to kill me," I say, "there are faster ways."

"Oh, no," says Morris. "We wouldn't want to do that. You're the goose that lays the golden eggs."

On the way back to my cell, I puzzle over this remark and what the marine said.

DONNA

WHEN I WAKE UP in the middle of the night, somebody is just standing in the room, all horror-movie-ish.

I don't scream, not exactly—more of a "whathafuh!" with a reflexive reach for a gun that isn't there. Homey is lucky that we're not back in New York, or I would have put a few holes in him.

Him: "Take it easy. I'm with the good guys."

Well, I've heard *that* before. I think the last time was in the lab on Plum Island. The Old Man, who turned out to be this freaky, evil scientist dude all jacked up on steroids, was telling us that we should see the bright side of getting injected with stuff that sped up the Sickness. His point was, he was trying to find a cure, which I guess was pretty cool of him? Except that he and his buddies were the ones who had let the Sickness out of the lab in the first place. Whoops!

Anyhow, Brainbox earned his trust, and then he spiked his steroids and poisoned his ass. Which was a pretty harsh thing to do, but, you know, the guy was going to kill us all. Just goes to show you—as if *Game of Thrones* and stuff wasn't enough to do it—there's no such thing as the good guys. Though, weirdly, unfairly, there *are* bad guys.

I suddenly remember that I had shucked off my camouflage before going to sleep and am now, as a neon sign I saw in front of a strip bar once put it, "strictly naked." Notwithstanding that, I resist the urge to cover up. There's no way I can figure to do it that wouldn't look weak and cringey. So there I am in the altogether, giving out as hostile a vibe as I can, totally mean-mugging him. I'm hoping he won't mistake it for a "come-hither" look, as Mom used to call it. It's definitely more of a *go-thither* look, but there's no accounting for taste.

Him: "Don't worry." He casts a what-do-you-call-it gimlet eye over yours truly's secondary sexual characteristics, such as they are. "Not my thing."

Figures, I think to myself. The kid is too good-looking to be straight. Fit and trim and smooth and easy on the eyes.

Me: "Okay. I am *super* not worried. To what do I owe the, like, pleasure of your visit, Mr.—"

Him: "Let's steer clear of names for now. Do you mind if I sit?"

Me: "Well, you've already let yourself in, watched me sleeping, and seen me naked, so I don't see how sitting down would be such a big step in our relationship."

As he turns to fetch the Ed chair, I take the opportunity to cover up my glorious form.

He must be in his twenties, but he has a face that hasn't quite lost the round softness of boyhood. A pleasant mug under carefully trimmed auburn hair. A self-contained air.

Him: "Did you get our message?"

Me: "I did. But I thought it was all hush-hush. How are you keeping this little visit a secret? I'm pretty sure this room is bugged."

Him: "Oh, it is. Normally. Everything you do or say in here is recorded. But right now it's gone dark. There are sporadic breakdowns in our systems, since we've been out of port for a long time and we're due for an overhaul. They're not worried, because usually you'd be asleep at this time."

Me: "What about the guards?"

Him: "This shift is on our side."

Me: "What side is that?"

Maybe I'm not being very friendly, but I'm all out of belief in mankind; my trust fund, as it were, has run kind of low.

Him: "That would take more explaining than I have time for."

Me: "Try. Gimme the tl;dr."

Him: "People don't say that anymore."

Me: "I do, and last time I checked, I was people."

Him: "It's better that you not know."

Me: "With respect, fuck you. It's better that I do know. If you want anything out of me, spill."

Him: "Okay. Well, you've probably worked out that the plague didn't kill every adult in the world."

Me: "Yeah, I figured you guys must have cracked it, since you're not wearing a big rubber suit."

33

Him: "More or less. In fact, there was no guarantee that we would survive exposure to you and your friends. We've been inoculating the crew against any transgenic shift that may have taken place in your version."

Me: "Trans who in the what, now? We have a different *version*? Like plague 2.0?"

Him: "The bug has been jumping around and mutating inside all of you. It happens."

Me: "That's why you haven't landed yet?"

Him: "Partly."

I can tell that there's something he doesn't *want* to say.

Me: "So...was it just all the ships at sea that made it through? Are you, like, all *Waterworld* up in this bitch?"

Him (smiles): "No, quite a few people made it."

Me: "How many?"

Him: "Six billion."

Six. Billion.

My mind turns upside down.

I'm used to the idea of everybody being dead. Well, almost everybody.

Me: "Grown-ups?"

He nods.

Me: "Little kids?"

My voice goes wobbly in a way that I hate his hearing.

Him: "Grown-ups, kids, the whole shebang. Well, it's not all good news. Unfortunately, all of the Americas went down. Except for the likes of you, of course. But, basically, a billion people gone. A total goatfuck from the Northwest Passage down to Tierra del Fuego. The rest of the world, however, made it."

Me: "But how? I mean—there must have been thousands of airplanes—ships—all kinds of things that could carry the disease..."

He's thinking of a way to phrase it.

Him: "Let's just say that extraordinary measures were taken."

Just now, I don't want to know what that means. Not yet. Just now, I want to think about a world with families, happiness, food, law and order, civilization, red velvet cupcakes.

Me: "But we never knew—nobody ever came to get us—"

Him: "Quarantine. Enforced by the death penalty. And believe me, there has been enough to occupy us in the rest of the world."

Me: "But—couldn't you have airlifted us some food—"

Him: "We were busy with the refugees back in the Old World. Besides, the rest of the world thinks you're all dead. The press is totally muzzled."

Me: "*Somebody* could have contacted us—told us—"

Him: "That'd get them locked up. The military won't allow it. They've got a stranglehold on information going either way."

Me: "But we'd have heard radio signals—"

Him: "Only shortwave would reach the US. And those frequencies were jammed."

Me: "Brainbox—that's my friend—"

Him: "Yes, I know."

Me: "He found a signal."

35

At the island, Brainbox had tracked down a creepy broadcast—a mechanical voice reciting numbers, followed by a crappy earworm of a ditty. Very found-footage-movie spooky.

Him: "Yeah, the numbers station? The Lincolnshire Poacher? That was us." He smiles.

Me: "Who is us?"

Him: "I told you. The good guys."

Yeah.

I take a deep breath and get ready for a truth slap.

Me: "So...I'm guessing that things are just hunky-dory?"

Him: "Well—it's not as simple as that."

Me: "Illuminate me."

Him: "For starters, you can probably imagine that things got a little messy when the continental US went down. What you call a power vacuum."

Me: "Nature abhors a vacuum." I remember Jefferson saying that once.

Him: "Totally." He smiles.

Me: "Hence the sides."

Him: "Hence the sides. Actually, *sides* implies that there are only two, or only a few. It might be more useful to look at them as *facets*. Of a very big diamond. Or...groupings. Fluid groupings. Sometimes they change, based on the circumstances."

Me: "So what are the circumstances? I mean...the circumstances that lead one *facet* to keep us here in the brig or whatever and the other facet to be you coming to visit me."

36

Him: "America is gone, but 'America' isn't." He makes the distinction clear with finger quotes. "For one thing, there are—were—over a hundred and fifty thousand American troops stationed abroad; that and one and a half million American civilians."

Me: "So this . . . the aircraft carrier . . ."

Him: "Still American. Still large and in charge."

Me: "And what about you?"

Him: "I think of myself as a patriot."

I decide to swim back to the shallow end. Only so much I can take at once. "Can I ask you a question? The rest of the world. Do they still have, like, television and computers and clothes and running water and toilets and stuff?"

Him: "All of that good stuff. And more."

Me: "And for me and my friends to get out of here and get to—*there*, what do you want from us?"

Him: "Who said I wanted something?"

Me: "Uh, puh-lease, Man with No Name." I take my eyes for a roll. "I might be young and semiferal, but I wasn't born yesterday."

Him: "Okay, simple. I want you to go back to New York."

JEFFERSON

THIS IS HOW the goose felt after it laid too many eggs.

I don't know how much blood I have left in me, but it's not enough to keep all systems running. For a while I feel too weak to get out of bed, and my spirit, sapped like my body, can't find a reason to try.

Then I think of Donna, and try to stand, and fall over.

They come in and help me back up, feed me some kind of protein drink, put me back to bed.

At length I feel stronger, and I devour a tray of food, and when the marine comes to get the tray back, I take a swing at him, thinking to escape, against all reason. The marine takes a half step back so my fist sails past his face, then he deftly catches me as I fall and gently puts me back in bed.

"Rest up, Hoss," says the marine.

Then one day Morris appears and tells me to get up.

"You won't want to miss this," he says.

I rise, my limbs unexpectedly light, and follow Morris and the marines through another unmemorizable sequence of doors and passages. Finally, we spill into a big chamber laid out in a semicircle.

It looks like a briefing room of some kind. A man and a woman in flight suits linger curiously at the opposite door. Then the round-headed interrogator appears behind them, with a gray-haired officer in tow who must be high-ranking since the pilots snap tight salutes at him and vanish.

I follow Morris to the dais with the electronic billboard that stands at the apex.

My interrogator smiles. "Jefferson! How are you feeling?"

This is uncharacteristically bright and friendly. I follow the bounce of the man's eyes and realize that he's at pains to impress or appease the officer at his shoulder.

"Anemic," I say.

The officer and the interrogator share a look, then Morris chips in. "This is Jefferson Hirayama. Mr. Hirayama has been kind enough to help us with our antibody production."

Mr. Hirayama? Kind?

"Are you Japanese, son?" The gray-haired officer makes a show of taking an interest. "I mean your family. I was stationed in Okinawa."

"Part," I say. "Mostly I was just American."

"Why the past tense?" The officer seems genuinely interested. I have nothing to say.

"This is Rear Admiral Rosen," says the interrogator.

"Your boss," I say.

"Yes," says the interrogator, but there's a moment's hesitation preceding it. He has another boss somewhere.

Rosen holds out his hand to shake, and I shake it. The admiral's hand is dry and firm and devoid of any macho finger crushing.

"I'm sorry for your loss," says the admiral.

"Which loss in particular?" I say. The admiral chooses to ignore this.

"We brought you a treat," says the interrogator, and a marine sets down a tray laden with cups and bags.

The insignia, a two-tailed green mermaid, is instantly recognizable. "Starbucks?"

"We have one onboard," says the admiral.

"Of course," I say.

The admiral makes an expansive knock-yourself-out gesture toward the tray, and I approach it cautiously. I take a sip of coffee and look into the bag. An assortment of pastries is jumbled together. I pick a cinnamon roll. The others watch me as if they have just given an Amazon tribesman a mirror.

I take a bite and feel the gorgeous engineered fat-and-carbohydrate rush of flour and sugar and palm oil. My eyes water, a Pavlovian emotional kick, and I turn away in embarrassment.

That's when the door in the other corner opens and Donna walks in.

To be exact, Peter, his head sprouting the stumpy beginnings of some dreadlocks he's been diligently tending, walks in, followed by

Theo, his big frame tensed and wary, then Brainbox, whippet-thin as ever, then Captain, his head shaved almost to the scalp, and finally Donna, peeking over the others' shoulders, her eyes bright.

But Donna is all I really notice at the moment.

I set down the food. I suddenly don't know what to do with my hands, what to do with my mouth. I want to go and kiss her, but I don't know if, under the eyes of the sailors and the marines, I should.

Donna bumps past the others and jumps into me, gluing her mouth to mine.

DONNA

KISSING JEFFERSON IS more than good; he tastes of sugar and cinnamon, which is even better than I remembered, and then I realize it's because he's been chowing down on snacks. He's acting a little shy, maybe because we're in the company of a military escort, but I just go full-on *The Notebook* on him, and the old guy in the uniform does a sort of kids-these-days chuckle, which is clearly out of embarrassment and meant to forestall further smooching, but I decide to ignore all that and let my feelings dart down inside of Jeff, where I know I'm always home.

There may be some tongue involved. I don't know.

Like he's catching PDAs from me, Jefferson takes my hand and doesn't let go, even as he dispenses high fives to the others. We'd already had our own little reunion in the mess hall, or as I called it, the "hot-mess hall," on account of things got kind of emotional.

After the high fives comes a lot of dude-ing and hugging and I'm-so-happy-to-see-you-ing, and then the sugarcoating of seeing one another again sort of dissolves and we find ourselves in this dinky screening room thing under the eyes of our captors. Only they're not acting like captors. They're all of a sudden acting like our *hosts*, like, can we get you anything to drink and so forth, which is kind of strange, since we'd been in lockup moments before. All deeply suspect, which is not to say that I don't scarf down three cake pops ASAP.

The old dude seems to be running the show, and Ed the Suddenly Friendly Interrogator is alternately kissing his superior's ass and trying to lock eyes with me and the others in a way I interpret to convey the message *don't fuck me over.*

Old Guy: "We hope you haven't been too inconvenienced." I laugh.

Then, before the old guy can ask why, Ed the Interrogator says: "These are hard times for all of us. We know you understand that the precautions we took were for everyone's protection."

Which, whatever. Only thing he's protecting right now is his ass.

Old Guy: "You are probably all wondering just what has been happening while you all have been..." He searches for the appropriate official term for *scrapping it out in a post-apocalyptic shitshow.* "Well, I don't even know what to call what you all have been through."

He kind of chokes up, and I suddenly think he must have had grandkids, and the whole feathery-silver-hair-and-crow's-feet thing starts getting to me, and then I remind myself that I've been stuck in the brig for God knows how long and Grandpa must have known.

Old Guy: "Your government"—and he smiles and nods like he's just told us that Santa Claus was real—"appreciates what you have...what happened. And wants to get you reintegrated into society as quickly as possible. To that end, we have a little informational film to fill in some of the gaps."

Then the lights dim, and a video projector bolted to the ceiling fires up. At first there's a blue screen, then an insignia for "Carrier Strike Group Nine," whatever that is, then an official-looking logo that reads "American Reconstruction Command—moving forward." They look like the snippets of film that used to go in front of movies, after the trailer but before the story actually starts, when production companies and studios and whatever announced themselves with little fanfares and anthems and animations meant to show you that they were important.

Fade to black, then up on the undulations of the flag, the old red and white nylon stripes with a blue rectangle in the corner. But instead of fifty stars, there's just one big star.

The urging of brass and the rumble of drums, a rousing, half-familiar tune that—to my embarrassment—strikes the anvil of my heart and sends painful sparks of tears to my eyes.

The star fades and faces ghost into focus—George Washington. Franklin Delano Roosevelt. Martin Luther King. Susan B. Anthony.

America, intones a smoky, raspy voice. Then: *Land of the free. Home of the brave. Light to the world. Beacon of freedom. Some thought that its light had been extinguished.*

The faces keep fading in and out—unknown ones now, children,

44

elders, careworn faces, laughing faces, faces set with determination, sorrow, joy, anger, faith, hope, love, despair, desire, humor.

A map of the United States in red, white, and blue. The rest of the continent is an unimportant gray. Black circles expand from the population centers, swamping the land. The music turns off-key and bleak.

Self-important tobacco addict: *But freedom is a fire that can't be put out.*

"Like white phosphorus," someone says, and I look up and see it was Brainbox.

Images now of refugees being rescued, food being distributed, children put back in their parents' arms by soldiers. I've seen these sorts of pictures before, but it was always, like—to be totally honest?—third-worldy people. Like, *here, brown people, have some leftover white-people stuff.* Now it's all kinds, but the camera seems to linger especially on the WASPy blond kids.

Slow motion as a mother and father—it has a sort of composed feel, like a scene made with actors, though the camera is kind of shaky the way they do it when they want things to feel "real"—turn their faces from the soldier who just handed them and their kids a box marked AID toward the sun, which, ooh ooh lemme guess, is meant to mean the Future.

We picked ourselves up. We found strength in one another. We showed the world that we were not defeated.

Gray ships plowing through the green sea, fighter jets wheeling in the sky, aligned to one another with spooky precision. Soldiers sliding down ropes from a helicopter. The big-star flag going up over a tropical island—Hawaii, I think, because next thing you know, people are, if you'll excuse the expression, getting lei'd. A handshake. Salutes. Then, the Union Jack, or at least I think that's what they call the British flag, a blue field with an asterisk of crosses in the center, flapping next to but ever so slightly below the big-star flag in a gray sky. A congregation bending their necks in prayer.

And now . . . faces again, white and brown and every shade in between and around, staring straight ahead in confidence and hope. A blurring series of individuality. *So many?* I ask myself. How could death have spared so many?

We will come home.

And back to the flag with the big star.

The crashing and banging of the orchestra round off and cinch shut like a garbage bag, and silence sits on us.

I'm confused. I'm crying—snot is, like, threatening to pour out of my nose and everything—I'm torn up inside by the grief and the hope of the faces, and I'm still high on the music. But, at the same time, I have a sense that my emotions are being pushed around, that there's something false to it all. It's been a long time since I've been advertised to, but that's the part of me that's being touched. Touched, like, in a creepy way.

Back at the Square we would watch anything on our movie nights, the lovingly maintained DVD player fed from puttering generators. Even ads, which reminded us of the world that was gone as much as anything else. This advertisement, if that's what it is, promised me something fresh.

Then again—it didn't actually *tell* me anything. There was practically no information in it. What I understand is that the government, or *a* government, of the country, or a country that is calling itself America, has survived. Something to do with Hawaii. Something to do with England. I also understand that there's some sort of plan to "come home." I assume this means people are ready to go back to America and defeat the Sickness. But I can't be sure. And I think about the message from the book: *Do not cooperate* . . .

Ed the Interrogator: "What do you think?"

Pause.

Me: "You guys changed the flag?"

A quick glance between the interrogator and the old dude.

Old Guy: "It's the same flag, but instead of the fifty separate stars, there is one single star, signifying unity."

Well, duh.

Me: "Oh. I thought that was Texas. The Lone Star thing."

Ed the Interrogator (a little annoyed, as if he doesn't know whether I'm being stupid or purposely provocative): "No, it means unity."

Old Guy: "*E Pluribus Unum.*"

Me: "Just a little more *unum* than *pluribus*."

The moment sits there.

Old Guy: "You must have something else to say."

A little more silence, then—

Theo: "It looks like bullshit."

The word *bullshit* was pronounced "buuull sheeeeeeiiit," to emphasize the bullshittiness of it all as much as possible, I guess. A way of saying it evolved to cope with thousands of hours and days of taking it from the Man.

The old dude and the interrogator don't seem to know how to respond to that.

Ed: "How do you mean, Theo?"

I think he uses Theo's name to put him on alert, like, *we can get personal about this if you want.*

Theo: "Look, don't take a genius to know you're selling us something. Question is what?"

Brainbox: "I'd say that, given the evidence, they want us to take it on faith that they know what's best for everyone. So we should do whatever they want us to, despite the fact that we have been kept in solitary confinement."

The old guy looks at Brainbox and the rest of us like we are the most heartless bastards that ever kicked a sack of puppies.

Old Guy: "I've seen this before. I don't want to hold it against you. Conflict can make a person cynical. I understand that you're not going to find it easy to adapt to new circumstances, son."

Theo: "I'm not your son. How could I be?"

Captain looks at Theo and lets him have it.

Captain: "Man, shut the fuck up. You know what he means."

I'm surprised that Captain just laid into Theo like that.

The old dude, disappointed, looks around at the rest of us.

Jefferson: "I think it's a little short on details." Then, after a moment's thought, he adds, "Sir."

Sir? I note his little tip of the hat to hierarchy and obedience. I look at him, and he blushes. I remember that his dad was some kind of ass-kicking Japanese-American war hero.

Old Guy: "What kind of details do you want?"

Then the questions come tumbling out, voices overlapping each other.

Me: "Who's left?"

Jefferson: "Is this a dictatorship, or what? Who's running the country? Is there a president?"

Brainbox: "You mean everybody's living in Hawaii? How is there enough food?"

Peter: "What the hell are you doing here off the coast? Why don't you try to save people?"

Me: "Have you cured the Sickness?"

Theo: "What about our allies? Are they still our allies?"

Peter: "What happened to the rest of the world?"

Old Guy holds his hands up and pushes down on an invisible mass, like the questions are coming out of a car trunk that he can't get closed. The interrogator looks at him, mouth twisted, as if to say, *I told you this wouldn't work.*

Finally, we quiet down and the admiral says, "We want to answer all your questions, in good time. But first we just need you to understand that we are all in this together. And that we need your..."

Peter: "Collaboration?"

Ed: "Your cooperation."

Jefferson: "If you want our cooperation, we need yours, too."

The old dude's neck straightens at that, and he's about to answer when the interrogator gets in first.

Ed: "Such as?"

Jefferson (looks at me, for strength maybe): "For starters, you could stop treating us like criminals. Instead of locking us up separately—"

Me: "Lock us up together."

Brainbox: "It's pretty evident that you're not worried about getting the Sickness from us. I'm gathering that we don't have the virus in our bodies anymore?" No response. "That's what I thought. So give us the run of the ship. Or at least the right to see one another and get some fresh air."

Jefferson: "And from now on, we talk to you, not to him."

He means the old dude and not Ed. Ed doesn't look too happy about this, needless to say. He's about to give Jefferson a grade-A can of verbal whup-ass when the old dude says, "Okay." Simple as that. *Okay.* I try to keep the thought, *Yeah, bitch!* out of my mind or at least out of my mouth as I look at Ed. Himself, he's swallowing whatever bile has just surfaced on his tongue. But I feel like we haven't heard the last of him.

It's like the mystery man said. There's lots of facets.

JEFFERSON

THE "COMMON AREA" that they give us a few days later looks
to be some sort of repurposed officers' mess. The place shows signs of
having been hurriedly cleared. There are drifts of paperbacks, comic
books, and magazines piled into the corners, and a dry-erase board on
one wall still carries an uninterpretable scrawl of symbols and acro-
nyms that I figure must be some sort of procedural recap.

The books are pre-Sickness, mostly dog-eared and broken-spined.
But the magazines are new.

At least—they're new to me. Most are weeklies covering the ram-
page of the Sickness. I have to deduce this from the pictures, since stories dealing with the disease have been redacted; swaths of text have
been blotted out with black ink. But whoever has been doing the job
has been unable to deal with nuance and ellipsis; in tangential refer-
ences from entertainment columns and sports reports and even from
the lacunae of the dark pen strokes, I start getting a sense of the recent

past, like feeling my way around a big, dangerous machine in a dark room.

As Donna has told me, the Americas are gone. Elsewhere, science and a pragmatic brutality (the details are sketchy, but I have the sense that a homicidal quarantine, like a firebreak of living people, was instituted) staved off the Sickness. Something terrible has happened in the Middle East. And everywhere there is mention of "the Shock." This is not the Sickness but some kind of knock-on effect, not physical but societal, that gets blamed for all kinds of political unrest around the globe.

I've been under a delusion all those days in the brig. Knowing that the Sickness hadn't eaten through the rest of the world, killing all the adults and the children the way it had in the States, I assumed that everything else remained as it had been before. As though a giant hand had plucked a continent from the face of the earth and left the rest of the world precisely the same.

Of course that made no sense. You couldn't have a seventh of the world disappear without pulling other things along in its wake. There's a sort of gravity to people and to societies. I don't understand it yet— most of the analysis that I can find is larded with terms I don't really understand—sovereign debt, exchange balance, currency crash. I was only halfway through AP econ when the Sickness hit, and we hadn't gotten to global trade yet. I do remember something around that word *shock,* though. In economics, a shock is a sudden change in supply or demand that threatens the economic equilibrium. Could that be what the stories are talking about?

All of the weeklies with pictures of demonstrations and riot police and firefights and car bombs actually don't even bother me as much as the "lifestyle" magazines, which balance lip service to the dead with a shrill acquisitiveness, as though the secret to maintaining sanity lies in fashioning a fictional self out of store-bought parts. We had it pre-Sickness: an obsession with weight, health, beauty, coolness, sexiness, hipness, stuff. But the tenor of it seems to have gone up an octave. And somehow this connects to the rest of it—the "Shock." As if consumption were the cure. Readers are exhorted to buy things to keep stores and factories open, and keep workers at work, and by implication, keep the world spinning.

In the occasional perverse and morbid flight of fancy in the rubble of New York, I had concluded that the silver lining of the extinction of humanity would be an end to global warming. But it doesn't look like that's on the table. They're cranking out shit even faster than before, as if to make up for the habits of the dead billion.

And I may be unused to it, since I've been away so long, but the preoccupation with youth seems to have hit a peak. All the fashions and gizmos and entertainments have veered toward an event horizon of the pubescent, as if the uncanny adolescent resistance to the Sickness has added another element to its usual fascination.

When I look at it cynically, everything is about hormones. That was what had kept us alive in the first place, the dip in binding proteins that made teens resistant to the Sickness. And, maybe, it's hormones that spur the youth fetish in the pages of the magazines, hormones that drive people to devise ingenious ways of killing one another, hormones that make them cling to the life the Sickness is trying to steal. We're puppets on chemical strings.

This train of thought is going nowhere I want to be. So I look at Donna. That's my favorite thing to do nowadays. Maybe it's only hormones that connect *us,* too. But I think it's more. Through all the chaos of the Sickness, and the hand-to-mouth scrabbling of the Square, and the blood-spattered road that led us here, what kept me alive was loving her.

I think about the *Annie,* the stout little tugboat we took to Plum Island. That was where my and Donna's parallel lines had, impossibly, converged. Something had warped the world's geometry in its gravity to allow it.

Was it love? That was just a word, like truth or justice. It was what it was, without saying it.

But we're on a different ship now, floating in its own saturated suspension of time. And I fall prey to the temptation to let go of my worries and take what happiness I can. Donna and I requisition one of the boxy cabins off the mess for our own and share the comically thin mattress, taking turns spooning each other through the night.

Maybe this is what living in a dorm would have been like. Donna even decorates with pictures of palm trees and flowers cut out of the magazines. She calls it "inferior design." But it turns out I'm easily the more domestic of the two of us, picking up Donna's cast-off clothes and making the bed. I mind her messiness, but I do not mind having the chance to mind, the grip she has on my awareness. The disparities and difficulties of sharing with someone only make me aware of the amazing fact that I'm not alone, after being trapped so long in the echo chamber of my own brain. I tell her things that I thought would never exit my head, and she tells me her things, and the feeling is like a great pressure being released and replaced with a kindling warmth. I suppose that this *is* love, or if it isn't, it will definitely do.

There are questions baying like dogs outside of this contentment, of course. What are we doing here? What will become of us? What do the people who sent the secret messages want, and when will they contact us again?

Brainbox and I discuss this under our breath as he beats me again and again at chess. We're all assuming that our new quarters are bugged.

"Did you get a—"

"Message from someone, yes." He answers before I can finish my thought. He repeats the message, and as his uncanny memory brings my vague recall into focus, I realize that he's remembered it verbatim.

"So?" I say.

"I'm not entirely convinced it isn't a trick to incriminate us in some way or open us up to betray one another."

"That's harsh, dude."

"So's solitary confinement," he says. "Look at it this way—what do they need us for?"

"A cure—"

"For who? For them? They've already figured it out on their side. You know what they would need our Cure for? To inoculate themselves against a transgenic shift in the virus in New York." He shifts a bishop behind his pawn defenses.

55

"There was a marine," I say, "who told me they were just letting people die in New York. So why would they—"

"They have plans for New York, just not yet," he says. "Your move."

I move my right-hand knight, forking his queen and bishop. A little hum of satisfaction in my gut as I feel myself getting the better of Brainbox. "Maybe they just want to make sure they know what they're doing before they go back and administer the Cure."

"Sure," says Brainbox. "Maybe they're our friends. Yes, maybe we should trust them. Maybe we should report the messages we received to ensure their trust." He drags his queen out of hiding, and before I can take my well-earned bishop, says, "Check."

He looks at me, blinking.

"I've lost, haven't I?" I say.

"In four more moves, yeah," he says.

"I don't think I'll report the messages."

"Me neither," he says. "Better to wait and see."

In the evening, Admiral Rosen appears again, this time without the interrogator. He says he's come to answer our questions—"to the best of my abilities."

"Do you mean," says Brainbox, "that you're going to tell us everything you know, or everything we're allowed to know?"

Admiral Rosen smiles at him, fixing him in his eyes. "Barracks-room lawyer," he says. "Well, they say you're smart. I could use people like you."

"Use me how?" says Brainbox.

"There's a lot of work to be done," the admiral says, "to rebuild."

And he starts to tell us, occasionally stopping and pondering what he should and shouldn't say, in the verbal equivalent of a redaction, about the way things are.

Yes, there is a president. He is elected by a direct plebiscite on the Internet. There's a House and Senate, though the states are gone; the overseas settlements are being redistricted. The government sits in Hawaii, which supports maybe half of the population. The rest of the population lives in the United Kingdom, where the Reconstruction Committee handles the almost impossible task of administering an entire country scattered within the borders of another country.

We ask what's in it for the British. What's in it, we gather, is the collected strength of the United States armed forces, especially the navy, which, as the most powerful maritime force in the history of the world, effectively has a choke hold on world trade. On the one hand, it sounds like the Americans have just bullied their way into some prime, if rainy, real estate. On the other hand, it seems like the affinity between the Yanks and the Brits makes for a sort of revived Anglo-American Empire.

The world has gotten a lot more dangerous. Seems like all the proxy wars and counterinsurgencies of the nineties and aughts were, in retrospect, a period of blissful calm. We've had full-blown wars in Korea and Ukraine. China's economy went down the tubes when there were no Americans to sell to, and they've oscillated between allying with the Russians to counterbalance the Anglo-Yanks and skirmishing over oil. Meanwhile, all the monarchies and dictatorships and oligarchies we'd been propping up in the Middle East have been rocked by armed revolt. A Sunni caliphate wanted to use oil as a cudgel. Then a Shia caliphate rose up to fight them. The essential disagreement seems to have been over who was going to succeed the Prophet Muhammad about fourteen hundred years ago. Anyway, war between the Shiites and the Sunnis gave us the opportunity to seize the Strait of Hormuz. Now if anybody wants to sell Middle East oil, they have to go through us. Sometimes the caliphates stop the flow and everybody holds their breath.

There are plans, Rosen says, to go back to the US. When? we ask. Soon, he says. But that's all he will say, and no amount of angling gets it out of him.

The day after they move us into our new dorm, some marines come to take us up to the flight deck, and we breathe fresh salty air and watch the gulls flocking. It becomes a daily routine. Twenty stories below is the ocean, stippled blue to the razor-sharp horizon. Smaller ships, the rest of the carrier strike group, lie off at a distance.

There doesn't seem to be any possibility of escape. I wonder whether I actually *want* to get away. Captivity aside, I'm warm and dry and fed. Nobody is trying to kill me that I can tell. I luxuriate in the idea of a life that won't be cut short at any moment. No, I don't mind being stuck here, with Donna's nimble mind and sleek body and soft mouth.

I notice the others putting weight back on, their scars fading, their postures unclenching. Even the kid we call Captain seems to be enjoying himself. He peppers the marines and sailors with questions, keen to absorb whatever he can of life on the ocean. I can practically see the bond with his tribe back in Harlem slackening, returning only now and then with an unexpectedly sharp tug that makes him surly and miserable.

At one point, we stand to the side of a crew drill, as different teams in color-coded uniforms hurry to unhook and replace the massive arresting cable that runs across the deck. In the clamor of the exercise, squads of men and women running to and fro, a marine's sidearm comes loose and skids across the deck to find a stop at Captain's feet.

It's the first time any of us has had a gun within easy reach since we were picked up. Only recently, a weapon had meant freedom or the chance of it, a chance to have some kind of say in life. All eyes turn to the gun and then to Captain as he ponders it.

He folds his hands behind his back and waits as the marine retrieves it.

Every time I meet someone's eye, I look for a blip of recognition, some kind of insinuating semaphore. But none comes. So I tell myself that the time has passed, and there's nothing I need to do other than play house with Donna, play chess with the others, look at the ocean, and feel my sinews knit back together.

Below the top deck, there's the hangar, a massive open space, big as a cathedral. Around the dormant jets is an informal running path where sailors exercise, and tucked into one corner by a bulkhead is a basketball hoop. Captain bullshits with the marine guards and arranges for us to play. Behind this, I can sense pressure from the admiral to humanize our living conditions.

Donna and Brainbox have no interest in playing and would rather wander the hangar deck with their watchdogs. To make up numbers, we play with whoever is on break at the moment.

I'm surprised to see that Peter can ball. He shrugs. "I'm stuck between two stereotypes. I want to defy them both, but they're contradictory. I'm supposed to be bad at basketball 'cause I'm gay, but good at it 'cause I'm black. But what can I do? To deny the world the pleasure of watching me play would be cruelty." He turns and sinks a jumper.

The serious business of half-court even overrides his constitutional good cheer and jokiness, turning him into a downright brutal trash-talker. Once off again, though, he's his usual pleasant self, "always down for some pickup," emphasis on the social meaning. In fact, he seems to have struck up a flirtation or two among the crew, which is impressive, given the lack of opportunity for fraternization.

So when a good-looking young crewman—he seems no older than eighteen—sits down next to me and strikes up a conversation, I wonder if I'm being cruised. "We should do this more often," the boy says, leaning in confidentially.

"Sure," I say. I'm not thrown by the idea of a gay guy hitting on me, but misunderstandings of any kind, especially those that could lead to hard feelings, cause me mental anguish. "But, um, I'm not sure you're barking up the right tree."

"I'm not barking at all, big boy. You like crosswords?" he asks, and I realize who he is. I cast my eyes around the vast, airy hangar, and see that no one is paying us any mind.

From his appearance, this must also be the guy Donna told me about—her late-night visitor for the Resistance. And in the moment, I don't know whether I'm glad or not.

"What do you want?" I say.

"Same thing you want," says the boy.

"Oh? What's that?"

The boy smiles. "They showed you the video? The—whatever—the ad?"

"Yeah."

"And?"

"And…" I think. "It felt like there was something wrong with it."

"You're right in thinking it's wrong." The boy looks at me as if he expects me to lead the conversation to the next place.

"Listen," I say. "I don't know what this is all about. I don't know what they want, and I don't know what you want. All I know is…"

I look away, see a ball in its lazy arc toward the basket, take in the satisfyingly chunky sound of the net blooming and recoiling.

I feel infinitely sad. "I just want to live. I just want to get free. And I want to rest, okay? I want to go…"

"Home?" says the boy.

I shake my head. "No. Home is gone. Home was the Village and school and Mom and Dad and Wash. They're all dead. Home was thinking about college, a job, the future, whatever. That's over forever. I don't know. Will they take me to England? Or Hawaii or whatever? If I do what they want and give them my blood and answer all their questions?" I'm only partly speaking to the boy next to me.

But he answers anyhow. "No."

61

I watch the ball squirt out of somebody's hands. Of course not.

"I'll tell you what they're going to do with you. They'll keep you like a specimen. You're the first kids to make it out of the plague zone alive, with whatever homebrew antidote your buddy and that freak back on Plum Island whipped up."

He appears to know as much as anyone.

"Anyhow," continues the boy, "they'll keep sucking blood out of you until they figure out it's safe to go in. But you know what they'll do first?"

I can guess, but I wait for him to say it.

"First, they let everyone who's left, in New York and everywhere else in the country, die."

"People wouldn't let that happen—if they knew—"

"They don't know. Only a few have any idea that there's anybody left. The ones at the top of the food chain. They've misreported the life cycle of the disease."

"But the kids there...they're American—"

"Oh, don't get me wrong, they won't feel *great* about it, and they have the *best intentions*"—he says this with a sneer—"but that doesn't beat *best practices*. The risk is too great, and the prize is too valuable. They'd rather let the Sickness burn itself out on what little human fuel is still left than sink precious resources into saving a load of semiferal, acne-ridden delinquents."

"What prize?" I watch Peter receive the ball in the post, dribble, drop-step, shoot. I feel a strong urge to get away from the whirlpool of this conversation, get on the court and forget myself in the soothing physical grammar of the game.

"What prize?" repeats the boy. "Did they ever tell you what the Sickness was?"

I nod. "A bioweapon. Destroy command and control."

"But leave the physical capital." The boy lists them off. "Factories. Mines. Oil fields."

I think about this for a minute. "They want to come back for the resources."

"In a while," says the boy. "First, let the Sickness burn itself out. Then scrape up the goo and get on with it." The boy looks out at the ocean, which can be seen out of a massive loading hatch. "Halliburton will be happy to do it. Hell of a cleanup contract, right?"

"But that's—"

"Evil? Not really. I mean, yeah. It's *sort of* evil. But I'm sure they could make a good argument for it. Spin it, reframe the issue."

"How?" I say. "How are they—I mean, the navy or the military or whatever—how can they keep all this going without, like, a home country, supplies..."

"Dude," says the boy. "Okay. I forget that you civilians never knew shit about how the world works. See, the US Navy is the most powerful force the world has ever known. *Ever.* By several orders of magnitude. Bigger than the next thirteen largest navies in the world *combined.* Ten aircraft carriers. That's ten mobile air bases to rain hell on whoever we want. Three thousand seven hundred airplanes. Seventy-two submarines. Thirty-three bases, not counting Pearl. You know what that means?"

"It means control."

"More or less," says the boy. "Actually, more or more. Nothing moves over the ocean without our say-so. We have a choke hold on world trade. And if you try to cut off our fuel and supplies? We send in the marines. Fuck, yeah." Though he's stated his opposition to the endeavor, he seems moved by the sheer power of it.

"Okay, so they're the evil empire. You're—what—the rebellion?"

"Is there no analogy that *Star Wars* can't serve?" he answers. "Well—not exactly. Things are more complicated than that, of course. But that'll do for now. I guess that makes me a Jedi."

"You want to go back," I say. I have a sick feeling in my stomach.

"I want you guys to *take* me back."

"Why?"

"Did I have you pegged wrong? I thought you were all about making the world better." The boy fixes me with his eyes. Butterfly and pin. "We need to go back to save your friends at the Square. And everybody else, for that matter. We need to go back to build something real, instead of *this*." He gestures around at the men in uniform, the dozing arsenal around him. "And *you* need to be free. It's the only freedom you'll ever know, Jefferson. Arguably, Washington Square was the only place you were *ever* free. You just didn't realize it."

I think of my tribe in Washington Square, two hundred souls in an armed camp scavenging and scrapping for survival every day.

"Who are you?" I say. "What are you doing here? If I'm going to trust you, if I'm going to make this decision, I need to know."

"I'll tell you who *we* are," he says. "We're the ignored. We're the used. We're the ninety-nine percenters. We're cannon fodder all over the Middle East. We're the sacrificed pawns. And we're *everywhere.* On this ship, in Hawaii, in England, all around the world. We're like you. Except we got left behind a long time ago. I don't think we should let millions of kids around the country die so that a bunch of immortal corporations can make a killing. Do you?" He says this fluently, angrily.

The idea hangs there.

"Three days," says the boy. "Be ready. We've got one shot at this. I've got all our people lined up, but getting the shifts right wasn't easy."

"I haven't said yes." I look down at the metal deck. "I don't even know if I trust you."

"So turn me in. You have the power of life and death over me. That enough trust for you? You decide for yourself. Turn me in, or help me out, or keep your mouth shut. Actually, if you don't mind, keep your mouth shut no matter what."

"The others—"

"We're reaching out to them separately. Don't discuss this stuff in your quarters. They're bugged."

"Tell me your name." It seems to matter.

"Chapel," says the boy. He gets up and takes some shots before the marines come to escort us back.

DONNA

AFTER THE GIRL midshipman—or should it be midship-woman? Midshipchick?—finds me in the head (which is what they call the toilet, which is a terrible name for it, it makes me feel like I'm peeing in someone's skull) and tells me about the plan to go back to New York, I keep looking at the others, trying to figure out whether they've been contacted, too. I'm not supposed to speak about it with them. *They,* the "they" who have us captive, who are the navy but not (I guess they're more like mercenaries now or maybe, like, military dictators, according to my night visitor), are watching and listening. So I go around just *looking* at my friends with slightly bugged-out eyes and hoping for a response that matches up, like, "Yeah, I *know.*"

Brainbox is unreadable as ever. He was unreadable back when he was double-crossing us at Plum Island, which was a good thing, because he was actually double-double-crossing the Old Man, which amounted to either triple-crossing or quadruple-crossing, depending on how you figured it. That saved us all. But I can't say I feel particularly like confiding in him.

Theo—who's great at affecting cool indifference—well, I don't know if he's been contacted. But Peter for sure has been told something's up, which might not have been the best idea, since his response to my *look* is to sing out, "Girrrrrrrrlll," as though he just heard the best gossip ever. Then he mimes locking his lips and putting the key in his back pocket. Not particularly discreet.

With Jefferson, it's easier to bring it up. We're lying in our tiny bunk in our cozy little battleship-gray love nest. And I put my lips to his ear and whisper, "What are we going to do?"

This starts a weird sort of conversation, like, one person whispers into the other's ear, then we look at each other—then the other person whispers back. Kind of like that game telephone without anybody in the middle.

Jefferson: "What we have to do."

This is typical. Jefferson is all, like, duty and responsibility and public service.

Me: "Please don't tell me that you want to go back."

He looks me in the eyes. Then—mouth to ear.

Jefferson: "I don't want to go back. But if we don't . . . everybody dies."

I don't have a good answer to that, not one I can speak out loud. The only answer I can think of is, *Yeah, but what about* us? But I don't say it.

I don't want to go back to the danger and the misery and the stink. Not now that I've gotten away. I don't want to fear for my life or for his. I want to just lie here with him forever, or for the next longest period of time available.

And also I want—is this wrong?—to *live*. To go somewhere. To see the world, or what is left of it. To sit in a quiet café and write self-indulgent crap in a journal. To go online and buy a song. Walk the dog. Tweet. Have kids. I can't see this happening in a big way back in the post-apocalyptic wasteland we just left.

What *should* happen is that the navy just whip up a bunch of antidote and save the day. Brainbox could show them how to do it—anyway, they already *know* how, otherwise they wouldn't be alive in the first place. Chapel said something about "transgenic shift," which sounds like a shitty post-punk band. Like maybe the Sickness has been mutating into something else, so they need to be sure they'll be immune to the new strain before they go back. Transgenic shift or no transgenic shift, they should just grow a pair of balls and cruise into New York harbor, or whatever, and start helping people. The kids in New York don't even have a notion that the rest of the world has made it.

Then a nasty little thought traipses into my brainpan, which is— tell Ed the Interrogator or Admiral Whatsisface what's going on. Rat out that guy Chapel and the Resistance. Then *nobody* would have to go back, and I'd have Jefferson and our friends safe and sound.

But I can't find it in myself to pull a dick move like that. So I say the only thing I can. This is what you get for falling in love.

Me: "Wherever you go, I'll go."

They come two nights later, not three the way they told us. It's past four in the morning—they've allowed us to have a clock, finally, which lets me know just how godforsaken the hour is. I'd been starting to catch up on my sleep after years of fretful waking and cold sweats. When Chapel shows up at the hatch and raps on the metal wall, for a moment I don't know who I am or what I'm here for.

Me: "It's too soon!"

But I know—the punch-in-the-heart feeling tells me—that we're going.

Chapel: "Sorry. Extra precaution in case any of you dropped a dime."

I don't even know what that means.

In the lounge, the others are already up and equally frazzled. By the exit hatch there's a guy in slouchy casual clothes and a beard, cradling a pimped-out carbine. He casts glances up and down the hall outside.

Captain is arguing with the midshiplady.

Midshiplady: "You've got to come. It's all or nothing."

Captain: "Then nobody's going. This is me. Right here."

Theo (glares at him): "What about home?"

Captain: "Man, I'm done. I served my time, a'ight? I'm not going back."

And I get it. The first time I met Captain was on his ship, the *Annie*. Since the Islanders took it and burned it, he's been grieving. But the carrier lifted his spirits—the sea and the machinery and the order. If he's got a chance at this life...well, I'm not gonna deny him that.

Captain turns and heads back to his bunk.

The lady midshipman points a pistol at him.

Me: "Don't!"

Theo grabs the gun, and the two of them wrestle, and the guy with the beard raises his carbine, and for an ugly moment, there's a scrap brewing, but Chapel hisses for them to stop.

Chapel: "We're not going to do that. That's not us."

By this point, Captain has turned to look at us.

Chapel: "You raise the alarm, and all of us are dead."

Captain: "Fuck you, man. Ain't raising no alarm."

Beard: "Whatever we do, we gotta go do it now."

So we leave Captain there. Theo glares at him like he hates him. Then, his fury snapping just like that, he goes and hugs him good-bye. Angry tears stream down his face when he turns back to us. Captain, face contorted with the pain of his decision, holds a hand up in farewell.

We hurry along through the metal halls. The lights are dim for once; nobody seems to be around. I keep banging my shins against the thresholds. An air of quiet, controlled panic.

Ladders, steps, hatches, Chapel navigates at speed. And suddenly, we're up on the flight deck.

Even in the queasy purple-black of the predawn, there is clamor and movement. A big fighter jet is idling nearby, and its engine sounds like an endless scream. The crews in color-coordinated jumpsuits seethe around it over the immense plateau of the runway, past the massive stays of the arresting cable.

At a signal from Chapel, somebody somewhere looses the cable, and it springs free from its moorings with a horrific *clang*, snaking across the deck, a lethal metal rope as wide as a man's leg.

A tumult of shouting and barked commands, and the crews are sucked in by the vortex of habit and the hurry to fix it, and Chapel motions us across the deck.

As I hurry, I can feel the sick lurching of the ocean underneath—I see the other ships that lie off the sides rise and fall, like buildings in the shock wave of an earthquake, and I stumble. Jefferson grabs me by the elbow and pulls me up.

We come into the blast zone of a big helicopter's chop, the wake of the rotors blowing my hair back and stunning my senses raw. It's gassing up, a snaking rubber line fastened like a limpet pumping fuel into its belly. I gag on the turpentine smell.

An argument is in progress—or in lack-of-progress. A sailor with a yellow helmet and yellow sleeves is pointing at a sheaf of papers on a clipboard. I make out the words "not cleared." Opposite him, a marine is barking back.

Barely pausing, Chapel takes an oblong object from his pocket and holds it to the yellow guy's neck. There's a crackling sound and a burst of purple spark, and he flops to the ground. Chapel motions us through the square hatch of the chopper.

We've barely squeezed in before we hear shots. Chapel scurries to a corner of the hold.

71

There, Admiral Whatsisface is secured to the hull by a ratchet strap. His mouth is covered with duct tape. His face is red.

The marine pulls himself up from the deck, then with the cracking sound of a shot, he falls backward. The guy with the beard fires over my shoulder, and the report of the gun deafens me.

So what happens now happens on mute.

First, I look out the hatch at the marine, and I see a pool of blood guttering out of him. And then I see that the blood is merging with a slick of some other liquid. And I realize that it's fuel. The hose is punctured and leaking.

Then I see the lick of flame not so far away, I see a crew of men in white running for a fire hose, I see the squad of marines with their guns trained on the helicopter.

I see the flame running up the fuel hose.

I see the fuel hose still stuck to the helicopter's gut as the flame climbs toward it.

So I jump out of the chopper. I scrabble along the deck toward the port where the fuel hose links up.

I grab the end of the hose and my hands slip. The flame gets closer and closer as I pull at the hose.

And I go with a lurch from hoping that I can fix it and get back to the helicopter to hoping that I can just get the thing loose and set the others free before I die.

I hear shouting behind me and look back, and I see Jefferson leaning out the door of the chopper, held back by the guy with the beard and Chapel. He's shouting my name.

THE NEW ORDER

And I twist the collar at the end of the hose, and the housing opens with a satisfying *clack,* and the hose falls to the ground as the flame catches and it gouts fire across the deck.

And Chapel shouts something to the pilot, and the chopper rises from the deck.

And I slip and fall and feel the metal deck smash me in the face, and I can barely roll over to see the chopper diminish and diminish as the blades pull it away into the sky.

I want to get up and catch it, but my legs won't move.

So I watch as it disappears into the low clouds, and inside I say good-bye.

JEFFERSON

I **SHOUT DOWN** to Donna until Chapel pulls me back from the door and the man with the beard slams it closed. Then he peels me off Chapel and smashes me against the metal insides of the craft. Chapel is coughing and rubbing the skin where my hands were around his neck.

"Take us back," says Peter, who has the female midshipman's pistol. He points it at Chapel, and Beard points his snub-nosed carbine at Peter.

"Too late," says Chapel, coughing. "We go back, and we're all finished."

"Put the gun down," says Beard.

Peter looks at him and doesn't put the gun down.

"She did good," says Beard. "She put it on the line, and she saved all of us. You can't ask for more than that."

Peter wipes his eyes, but he still holds up the gun, pointing death at Chapel.

"Now we gotta do what *we* can," says Beard. "Make what she did worth it. Put the gun down, dude. What's past is past."

Peter lowers the gun and hides his head in his arms.

I raise myself against the lurching gravity of the helicopter's ascent. I look out the little hatch next to the door just in time to see the *Ronald Reagan,* a toy on a dance floor of dark blue glass, vanish as we hit the clouds. Then we're in a big white nothing, no indication of where we're going except the buffets of the air and the urging momentum of the aircraft in my guts. And the thought *she's not here* dissolves into *I will never see her again.*

Nothing to see. I slide down the side of the hull and crouch in a corner. The walls are cold.

Across from me is Admiral Rosen, staring and astonished.

Chapel didn't mention anything about taking hostages. I wonder if something went wrong. But then a roar and a juddering shock to the craft make me realize why the admiral is with us.

A big Navy Hornet buzzes the chopper, streaking past like a shark sniffing out a swimmer. We're dead in the air, but the admiral onboard means they have to think twice about taking us out.

I take inventory. There's Peter and Brainbox, and the stone killer with the beard, and Chapel. There's a pile of gear secured to the inside of the fuselage, and from the markings, I can make out that it's ammunition, explosives, and medical supplies. A square box I take to be a radio. A rack of assault rifles—M16s, I think, not the semiautomatic AR-15s I'm used to.

75

I remember we're going back to New York and feel sick to my stomach. And my arms burn with adrenaline, and my head aches with the thought, which starts to cycle round like a laptop's waiting icon—she's gone, she's gone, she's gone.

But really I'm the one who's gone; it was my decision to leave. She is where she was. And she's alive.

Weeks ago, as we made our way from far downtown, the Square, to the charnel house at Plum Island, I was sure that I was committing one sin after another against self-preservation and common sense. But somehow I failed upward, and by and by, I came to think of the accumulation of poor choices as adding up for the good. Now I'm on the deficit side again, far in the red.

I contemplate the wreckage of my hopes, which lie invisible in my lap. *This is what you get for being happy.*

The helicopter swings into clear air, and I see the two forks of Long Island against a line of shimmer in the distance. And pacing us, the squadron of fighters, occasionally whipping into our space.

Chapel says, "They'll turn back now that we're in sight of land. We were under orders to stay out of visual."

The planes do peel away, and we lumber onward. The pilot keeps the razor-thin edge of land just in sight, but slides a ways west. When I ask Chapel where we're going, he pretends not to have heard.

Finally, we duck toward land, a controlled plummet that takes us screaming over the waves and, in a moment, across a thin spit of beach and over a highway. We skim over a chain-link fence and, with an abrupt backing and settling, land on an airfield lined with little prop planes under moth-eaten tarps. The pilot shuts the rotors off, and the quiet suddenly burrows into my ears.

Beard, unfazed by the sudden jerks of the landing, hops from the helicopter and scrambles to a nearby hangar. He shoots the lock off the little door to the side of the big gate, and after a while, the gate opens. Beard is driving a squat little vehicle like a tractor, using it to heave open the hangar. He signals to Chapel, and Chapel orders (or directs—or ushers—I'm not sure where we stand) everyone out of the chopper and into the hangar. The admiral is bundled in last; he resists at first, but a few raps on the head from the midshipwoman get him moving.

The inside of the hangar is a vast hollow edged with machinery and fuel drums. The little tractor has a twin sitting there unused, and other curious-looking vehicles of various sizes and obscure purposes perch here and there.

Beard fetches a long chain from the depths of the hangar, and he and Chapel struggle it out the door. I find myself helping them. We thread the chain through a steel eyelet at the tail of the chopper and attach it to the little tractor. Beard mounts and fires it up. It takes a bit of doing, since the chain threatens to break under the strain, but soon the helicopter is in and the hangar doors are closed. There were maybe five minutes when we might have been noticed—visitors from a world now beyond the imagination of anyone still surviving here in the kingdoms of the Sickness.

We spend the next couple of hours unloading. There's food, tents, guns, ammunition, and medicine, including cases of what appears to be the Cure.

The admiral sits against one of the corrugated iron walls, remote and impassive. It appears to be the midshipwoman's job to keep an eye on him, but after a while, she moves on to more productive things and helps the rest of us with the unloading.

Beard does some techy stuff with little gewgaws that look like baby monitors, except for being matte black (because, presumably, everything he uses has to be particularly badass-looking). He places one at the edge of each door—there's another gate at the back of the hangar—and wires them up to a battery in the chopper. Something tells me they're motion sensors, but to be honest, I have no idea if that's just a notion I got from watching *Aliens*. Anyway, they're pointed outward—the aliens in question being, I suppose, the natives, which is to say whatever kids might have survived up to this point in the suburban wilderness surrounding the airfield.

I wonder whether they've gone feral in these parts, like the tweens the Old Man had working for him on Plum Island, amped up on video games and some sort of homebrew meth. Even they wouldn't pose much of a threat, given the armament we're packing.

"What's all this about?" I ask. "Did we run out of gas or something? When do we go back to the city?"

Beard and Chapel exchange a look. "It's complicated," says Chapel.

"No, it isn't," says Theo. "We've got a cure, and people are sick."

"Who gets it first?" asks Chapel.

Theo says, "Harlem," and I say, "Washington Square," at the same time.

"That's my point," says Chapel. "We've got to think this through. This Cure is the power over life and death."

"That's right," says Theo. "*My* life and death. And my people. You don't have the right to keep it from us."

"I think we do," says Beard, and I note that he's the only guy currently carrying an assault rifle.

"Jefferson," says Chapel, "you were the guy who started this, right? Back in Washington Square?"

"Yeah…"

"Do you know for a fact you can trust the—whatever you call it, tribe in Harlem?"

"Fuck you, man," says Theo.

I think about how we ended up in Harlem at the mercy of Solon. He was ready to kill all of us until we promised him the Cure. He probably never expected us to find it, but he was pretty sure that if we didn't, we'd get killed before we could give away his secret—the cache of guns they were printing out of plastic. Enough to overwhelm the Uptowners.

I promised Solon that we would share the Cure with the Harlemites. In return, we got transport to Plum Island. And we were allowed to live.

"We made a deal," I say.

"At gunpoint, right?" Chapel knows everything. Looks like he had access to all the interrogation logs.

He looks to Theo. Theo doesn't have an answer.

"I'd say the situation has changed materially, wouldn't you?" says the midshipwoman. "The deal has got to change, too."

"They're just trying to get between us, man," says Theo.

Theo's right, of course. Now Chapel takes another tack.

"You need to think, really *think,* about what to do next. What's going to happen if we just show up and tell everybody not only that they can be cured of the Sickness but that they're not alone in the world?"

So I think about it. Ever since the Sickness hit, we had all been living like there were only so many tomorrows. And without any notion of order or law or government, we'd made our own tribes and our own rules, a patchwork of little fiefdoms. The Cure and the truth of what had happened in the rest of the world—call it the Knowledge—would change everything.

I wanted to believe that everyone would throw down their arms and embrace one another, drop the trappings of war and coercion and return to the way they'd been. But my heart tells me that it wouldn't be as pretty as that. It tells me that the new social contract would be written in blood. Once the light of survival started peeking through the door, people would trample one another to death in the race for the exit.

It would be a bloodbath. What the Cure would save, the Knowledge would destroy.

"Okay," I say, "talk."

DONNA

ALL THE SEATS face backward in this big-ass plane, which I guess is because it's safer in case the damn thing crashes. There's been, like, zero concession to luxury—forget having to return your seat to its upright position, because it doesn't move from its upright position in the first place. And there's, like, ten seats per row. Plus, they're made of crappy plastic and canvas and not pleather like in commercial airliners. And you can forget in-flight entertainment. I'm stuck without anything to watch or do, and Ed the Interrogator is not in the mood to loan me reading matter or anything.

I almost feel sorry for him, because presumably his ass is grass since my peeps escaped. He is definitely majoring in giving me the stink eye at the moment, with a minor in dropping dark hints about how Actions Have Consequences and the Kid Gloves Will Be Coming Off. I know a thing or two about metaphorical gloves of various kinds, all the way from Kid to Velvet-with-Iron-Fist-Therein, having knocked around post-apocalyptic Manhattan a fair bit, so I'm not exactly trembling in my boots.

Anyhow, it seems like they've decided to ship me off someplace, "kick me upstairs," as Ed put it. We've been flying around for a hella long time, which makes me think maybe Hawaii or England, like in the movie or advertisement or whatever they showed us.

Hope it's Hawaii. I'm not big on rain.

I'm a high-level prisoner now. I've got a couple of armed guards, would-be badasses with protruding Adam's apples. Plus, Ed is sporting a Beretta M9 in a sassy little side holster. Oh, and I have handcuffs on, linked up with chains to manacles on my ankles. All of which seems like a lot just for little old me. But I guess that overkill is the order of the day after our hijinks with the helicopter.

If there were any windows, I would be gazing dreamily out of them, but there aren't, so instead I gaze dreamily at the insides of my eyelids. Now, you might think that I'd be mooning about Jefferson, which would kind of make sense, given that for all I know, I'll never see him again. But for some reason, my mind just won't let me go there. Like, my heart—not the blood-pumping one but the metaphorical, lovey-dovey, pitter-pattering, breakable one—is an accessory that draws too much power, so the moment I start feeling, a fuse clicks over and the whole thing just goes dead.

To pass the time, I conjure up a music video in my head. It's set in Hawaii, of course, where I am welcomed with a big parade. There's a luau with all kinds of amazing food, not the navy crap from the *Ronald Reagan* or the scrapings and scavengings from the last two years in Manhattan. Coconuts and mangoes and fresh fish and pineapples and pork, and I even eat the pork, despite the fact that I know it smells like roast human, because I also know that here in Hawaii, there's no cannibalism. Cut to me learning to surf, and in no time, I'm riding monster waves and hanging ten and shredding. Then more food. Then—surprise!—Peter and Theo and Brainbox show up and—ta-da!—Jefferson emerges from the ocean like that clamshell lady. We go and eat some more, and then Jefferson and I retire to the honeymoon suite, with the DO NOT DISTURB sign swinging on the doorknob.

The cargo plane comes down with a *THUMP*, and I realize that I've been asleep. The massive buzz-saw engines jam into reverse, and we rattle thunderously to a stop.

One of the guards stands in front of me and motions me to stay in my chair, finger on the trigger of his carbine like I'm going to Hulk out and rip my chains to shreds. The big ramp at the back lowers. Outside it's dark and rainy, with big chunks of greenish light and mist-filled air standing out in the blackness.

I'm half expecting them to wheel me off in a handcart like Hannibal Lecter, but instead they just perp-walk me down to where a bunch of soldiers are waiting. Right as I leave the embrace of the cargo plane's stale funk, a damp chill gets at me, and I think, *Shit, I guess this isn't Hawaii.*

Now two things filter into my awareness. First, something about the soldiers waiting for us. They've got these cute little wine-colored berets on, which is different from the squared-off camo baseball numbers the marines are sporting. Second, and weirdly, there's a

83

guy standing there under a black umbrella, and unlike everybody else, myself included, he's not wearing a uniform. To be specific, he's in a tailored gray flannel chalk-stripe suit.

He approaches as I shuffle my way to the bottom of the ramp between my two goons. As the light from our hatch hits him, I get a quick read on his face—a pleasant, well-coiffed oval that just now appears to be registering some bemusement at my state of shackledness.

Chalk-stripe: "Welcome to RAF Duxford."

Ed snaps a salute and says his name, which I don't catch but, needless to say, isn't Ed.

Chalk-stripe: "Frank Welsh, Her Majesty's Foreign and Commonwealth Office."

He somehow manages to show that he knows it's a bit of a mouthful without making fun of it. He shakes hands with Ed, then turns to me. "And you must be Miss Zimmerman."

Me: "Yeah, I must." It comes out hoarse because I haven't spoken in a while. "But I'm called Donna. From Madonna. The singer, not the mother of God."

Welsh: "I'll keep that in mind."

Ed looks perturbed that Welsh is speaking to me at all and adopts this tone like he must not have gotten the memo about my being a traitorous bitch.

Ed: "I have orders to escort the...*her* to J2HQ."

Welsh: "Ye-es." He wears a *sorry about this* expression. "I'm afraid your orders have changed. Miss Zimmerman is to be put

84

under the charge of Her Majesty's government. Whose representative I am." Welsh holds out a sheaf of papers.

This appears to be a shockeroo to Ed, who stands there gaping
for a moment before he takes them. He goggles at the pages, and
Welsh points to a spot at the bottom of one. "You'll see your *J2* has
countersigned the order there."

Welsh (turns to me): "J2 is what in England we unimaginatively
call the Intelligence Office. Our term does have the benefit of being
clear, but then your military never met an acronym it didn't like."

I'm enjoying this new turn of events, and the humor that Welsh
seems to find in everything. Ed is not.

Ed: "I need to call this in."

Welsh: "Of course. There's a secure line in the wing command-
er's office. In the meanwhile, as it's a bit of a walk, I think we might
undo Miss Zimmerman—ah—Donna's chains."

Ed straightens. "Not on my watch."

Welsh: "That's just it. As those papers point out, it isn't your
watch anymore. It's *my* watch."

Welsh is all blithe and smiley as ever, but his meaning is clear—
he's in charge now.

So Ed decides to escalate, perhaps on account of how Welsh is
just a dude with an umbrella and a fancy suit, and Ed has a pistol. He
rests his hand sort of meaningfully on the heel of the Beretta, and
says, "I don't think so. We're going to do this my way."

"OI! FRANK SINATRA! GET YOUR HAND OFF THAT FUCKING
PISTOL BEFORE I SHOVE IT DOWN YOUR FUCKING THROAT!"

This is in a high-pitched shriek that somehow still manages to sound macho, coming from one of the dudes in the berets. All of a sudden, there are twenty submachine guns pointed at Ed and my two guards, and Ed does, in fact, takes his hand off the pistol.

I can't help but smile at the "My Way" Frank Sinatra joke and think to myself that it's pretty impressive to be funny while threatening someone. The British soldiers (genius deduction on my part) creep forward like they're ready for Ed and his guys to make a move any second. Which is not going to happen, because they're pissing themselves.

Welsh: "I'll take that pistol into safekeeping just for the moment so that you don't frighten Sergeant Major Rollitt anymore. You're frightened, aren't you, Sergeant Major?"

Shouty Guy: "I'M FUCKING PETRIFIED, BEGGING YOUR PARDON, *SAH!*" He doesn't look very frightened. But Ed does. He holds his hands way up high and practically sashays his hip forward so that Welsh can more easily take his gun. Meanwhile, Shouty and the other beret boys relieve the two marines of their M4s.

Welsh: "Sorry I don't have a receipt to hand, but I promise you'll get these back once you've made your call. Now—shall you undo her chains, or will I?"

Ed gives Welsh the keys, and lickety-split, I'm minus one set of manacles and handcuffs. "Thanks," I say.

Welsh: "My pleasure. I should reiterate that you are here at the pleasure of Her Majesty's government, so I must ask you to refrain from leaving under your own recognizance."

Me: "Say what?"

Welsh: "Please don't run away."

Me: "Where would I go?"

Welsh: "Well put. This way, please." He offers me the shelter of his umbrella, and then we turn and walk off, like he's my English uncle who just happens to have a squad of bodyguards.

Things may be looking up.

JEFFERSON

THE NOSE OF the trim little Zodiac bellies through the chop. We're close to shore, just past the impact zone of the waves. I've told Chapel that we're in range of potshots from land, but he's keen to stay as close as possible, in case the carrier group has dispatched boats to look for us.

The Zodiac is unremarkable, a tough shark-gray rubber inflatable with a little outboard. The high-tech stuff is all hidden: a bunch of medical equipment and self-heating MREs, H&K submachine guns, body armor, an Iridium satellite phone with hand-crank generator so that we can keep in touch with the others back at the airfield.

Shame keeps rising in me, like I've eaten something rotten, but there's no way to vomit it out. So I rehearse the justifications in my mind again.

Solon can't be trusted with the power of both life and death. That's no knock against him in particular—nobody can be trusted. So it's essential that we keep control of the Cure.

I shouldn't feel particularly beholden to Solon. He was ready to put a bullet in my head the day he met me, and he would have if it hadn't been for the outside chance that we'd return with the Cure.

But it doesn't feel right to violate the terms of our deal. I admire the little city-state the Harlemites have managed to establish in the north of Manhattan, and I understand why they're arming up. Personal attachment comes into it as well. Theo and Captain went through hell with us. Or maybe purgatory would be more accurate; we had our sins burned off. Our time on Plum Island had broken down us and them—although, when it came down to it, there were different overlapping kinds of "us." Just which "us" would come into play at any given time was the question.

If Solon finds out the truth of it all, there's no telling what he'll do. I expect he'd be true to his word with regard to my tribe. He promised that my people would get the Cure as well. But I don't believe he'd extend his sympathies any further. And I didn't go through what I did to let everybody else die.

That's why we've left Theo behind, guarded by Kroger—the midshipwoman—and the bearded guy, Dooley, who turns out to be a Navy SEAL. Chapel told Theo he's being kept "in reserve," and that he'll come into play if the plan changes, but on some level, we all know he's being held captive.

So instead, this is the plan—or, as I call it, the Big Lie.

We won't tell anybody about the *Ronald Reagan,* or all the survivors out there. Chapel says it's too much for people to handle. He talks about "social chaos," which I remind him is pretty much the constant state of affairs in New York, but he points out that it could actually be worse. Under the weight of the truth, he says, the fragile jerry-built constructs of tribe and allegiance and turf would collapse and it'd be everyone for themselves. He's probably right.

Chapel says that there's no rescue coming anyway, since the US has no intention of saving my fellow plague rats. The mainland is strictly no-go. The rest of the world is under the sway of a deliberate campaign of misinformation. If the folks back "home," that is to say, within the American Diasporic community, knew just what was going on, the push to save Teen America might be too much to resist, but the military is keeping a tight cap on the news. The official attitude is that there's too much risk of infection to justify an all-out rescue mission. Chapel candidly terms this "sheer bullshit" and says that the brass are just too cautious and too callous.

His idea is to create an environment in which the truth can eventually be released without causing too much harm. A society unified and strong enough to learn the truth without tearing itself to bits. Maybe Chapel's dossier on me is complete enough for him to know that this is the sort of thing that I'd find intoxicating. Because what he's got in mind is nothing less than building a new society. At least, that's what I make of it. Chapel's notion is entirely pragmatic—survival at all costs. My take on it is something more ambitious.

Either way, the plan still involves returning to Harlem. Given their imminent dominance of Manhattan, it makes sense to have the Harlemites on our side. But by no means can they know the truth. Instead, a diet of half truths. We'll maintain the story of our escape from the lab at Plum Island, along with the discovery of the Cure, but leave out the arrival of the navy and everything that followed. In the new version of events, Theo and Captain and Donna have been killed, and Chapel is a teenager from Plum Island who helped us escape. This last part shouldn't be too hard to pull off. He's barely twenty anyway, and his face is undeniably boyish. He can probably pass.

And maybe the story will work.

So long as we can lie fluently and consistently.

The top of Manhattan slips past, smoke visible and stench practically tangible. Notwithstanding the fires and the flies, it is a glorious summer day, and the sky is blue and insipid.

"The abomination of desolation," I hear Peter mutter; at least that's what I think he says.

"What?"

"Never mind, man. Just means we're back in the shit."

At the landing at the FDR Drive, where weeks ago we set off in the *Annie,* we turn the Zodiac's nose to shore. There's a squad of Harlem-ites waiting there for us with a pickup truck. They must have seen us coming, judging from the binoculars one of them is sporting and the general air of preparedness. Faces are hard. Guns are leveled. Not the welcoming committee I'd expected.

Somebody shoulders up to the front of the squad. It's Imani, the moon-faced girl who runs the tribe with Solon. If she's happy to see me, she doesn't let on.

"We figured you for dead," she says.

"We made it," I say.

"Not all of you," she says.

I nod. She doesn't add anything. Maybe shame looks like grief.

With this first scrap of dishonesty, it's begun, and there's no getting out. The spring of the Big Lie begins to unwind like a cheap toy, and we are clattering across the floor, not knowing where it'll stop.

The Harlemites are still in the vaguely menacing, untrusting mode that they were in when we left, which suits me just fine, since a hero's welcome would be even harder to take. The ride in the jerry-rigged pickup truck is silent except for one question from Imani:

"What happened to your girl?"

I'm surprised. I can't imagine her caring.

"Gone," I say.

That's it. No further questions until we are escorted up the stairs of Solon's, the snug little brownstone still in perfect trim. The grandfather clock whiles away the hours; there are apples still in the silver bowl in the waiting room.

In the moments we wait, a crowd gathers at the door. We see them through the lace curtains of the bow window. Ten, then twenty, then a hundred, a murmur of questions and a battery of eyes.

We are called on—the first time, forever ago, it was Theo who walked us up the creaking wooden stairway—and led into Solon's office.

Not an item out of place, but something new—a rack of the plastic guns they've been printing. Solon is working the safety of a piece-built plastic AR-15 with a barrel of freshly tooled pipe metal.

"Look who came back with his shield," he says.

Solon is as smooth as ever, his hair neatly buzzed, the white linen shirt crisp. But there is a laboring in his speech, a slackness in his usually alert face. His eyes are yellowish and shot through with red.

He's at the beginning of the end.

Maybe that'll make it easier, maybe not. Kids at the end have been known to make some fairly short-term decisions. I look at Imani, whose face shuts like a closed shop.

"Yeah, that," says Solon. "Been feeling my years."

A lot of kids in his position would dive into the conversation and look for the ring at the bottom—can you save my life?—but Solon is different. Gently he sets down the rifle and smiles. "Looks like you've been through some changes, too."

The story that Chapel and I have worked out is there in my head, ready to be spat out, but it doesn't come to my lips.

"Theo? Captain? Spider?"

Still nothing. I can only shake my head. And shame claws a tear from my eye. Shame that produces more shame—at the lie, at the tear itself.

Solon watches me, observes the passage of the teardrop like he's watching a train wind its way through a foggy landscape.

"Okay," he says. His face refracts a single ray of sorrow, then again assumes its angle of composure. "There were others—the two young ladies."

"Donna and Kath. They're—they didn't make it, either." Part of this is at least true—Kath is dead on a slab at Plum Island. And Spider, for that matter, is dead, too, by the hands of the Islanders who took the tugboat *Annie* by Orient Point. The sorrow now catches like a kick-started engine, and my hands come up to cover my face.

Solon waits me out like he has all the time in the world, then asks: "Who is this with you?"

"I'm Chapel," he says. "I saved their lives."

And then the cover story coalesces, pieces of a puzzle thrown on the floor that we shove into place, and at some point, I realize that it's the very jaggedness of the telling that makes it work. The tears and the grief—I can't tell if I'm mourning my friends or my self-respect or both—sell the lie. The capture by the Islanders. The experimentation. The rescue by Chapel, all salted with a handful of truth.

"Then I guess my question is," says Solon, "was it worth it? Did you find what you were looking for?"

He asks as though it doesn't matter to him more than any other question he might ask.

"Yes," I say.

A twitch of what—relief? Hope? Fear? Then the control is exerted again.

"A cure."

"The Cure," says Brainbox. "The only one."

"Hand it over," says Imani.

"Wait, Imani," says Solon. "Let me understand. Would it work on...if the symptoms are advanced." It's maybe the first time his diction has altered in midstride.

"Yes," I say. "It'll work on you."

"There are others...in the infirmary," he says.

"We have enough to get started. With the right materials and your assistance, we can make more. Much more." That's Chapel. Solon eyes him, trying to triangulate the gist of what's going on between all of us.

"Give it to him," says Imani.

"Not so fast," I say. It's a terrible phrase, something from a bad TV show, and I don't know why it sprang to my lips. I had imagined putting this forward calmly, rationally, sensibly.

"Oh," says Solon. "There's a catch." Again I'm amazed at his equanimity. "Well. Out with it."

"Everybody can live now," I say.

"I gathered as much," says Solon.

"Nobody has to die."

"Meaning?"

"Meaning, if we give this to you, we give this to everybody. Harlem, Washington Square, Midtown, the Moles...Uptown. Everybody."

"That wasn't the deal," says Imani.

"It wasn't the deal," says Peter. "It is now. It's a lot of people you're ready to let die. And we've seen enough death."

"You're asking us to keep from using our material advantage." Solon glances at the gun on his desk. *A gun for every girl and boy.*

"We're telling you this is how it has to be," says Chapel.

"*You* interest me," says Solon, looking at Chapel. "This is your idea?"

Chapel shrugs.

"This is my idea," I say. "And I would've made that clear if you weren't about to splatter my brains on the wall. Your people paid down

95

a lot. They gave up their lives. And for that, you get the Cure first. But I'm not here to set off a massacre."

Solon looks at Imani. Imani says, "Put it to the vote. Put it to the people."

Solon says, "I can say what goes right now." He coughs.

"No," says Imani. "This is too big. I say put it to the vote."

I had assumed, until now, that Solon and Imani were always in league; that she was his subaltern, with a voice of her own, but basically subservient. The advisor in the shadows. Now it looks like something else. Maybe a rival kept close by.

Solon nods. "All right," he says. "We put it to the vote. What?" he says, looking at me. "You think I'm the king here? Doesn't work like that."

Imani nods, like she's just won a point.

Solon says, "You're gonna have to decide, are you gonna risk it? If not, I guess things start going south pretty fast." He coughs again, but not before he grabs his gun.

I can't help but cast a look back at Chapel, who gives no indication of what he has in mind. It's up to me.

"Okay," I say, not knowing what's to come. "We put it to the vote."

"Fine," says Solon. "Now, just one thing."

He pulls back the sleeve of his shirt.

"Hook me the fuck up," he says.

DONNA

FLUFFY PILLOWS, smooth white cotton sheets, doughy-soft mattress. Above me, a worked pattern tapestry held up by wooden posts at the faraway corners of the bed.

I stay frozen in place for a little while, afraid that any move on my part will smash this dream into powder. Then, when I'm certain it all really exists, I sit up, slowly.

It persists. And there's more. I'm in a tall-ceilinged room with plank-wood floors that shine like they're wet. There are paintings of hills and dogs and birds and other classy stuff on cream-colored wood-paneled walls with shiny brass fittings. Above the tapestried four-poster, there's plasterwork that looks like sugar icing versions of those henna designs people used to get on their hands.

There's a door open, and beyond it I see a gleaming ceramic sink with silver faucets and racks of plump cotton towels. By my bed, a bottle of water the label says is from a spring in Wales, and a bowl of fruit, swollen and blushing and almost obscene they're so ripe. Pink and white lilies in a vase.

When I get out of bed, lowering my feet from the extra-high mattress, I find that I'm wearing a cotton nightgown. I vaguely recall fishing it from a delicate little box last night before I face-planted in the snowdrift of goose down.

This is all very *My Fair Lady* and stuff, but it makes me feel vulnerable, so I go to the chunky wooden chest of drawers in the corner to see if by any chance some other clothes have magically appeared. My current duds feel too much like I've stumbled into some rich, pervy English dude's harem.

Amazingly—but then, the whole thing is kind of amazing—there *are* more clothes. Wrapped in tissue and cellophane envelopes with some fancy logo, a whole month's worth of stuff, tops all the way down to socks and scarves and everything in between, all fresh and new and exhaling a breath of luxury like a sexy, throaty little whisper. I admit it, I shudder with pleasure, and I'm just a little ashamed of myself.

Doesn't stop me, though. I'm not saying I do a full-on pop-inflected-trying-on-clothes montage, but I take the opportunity to road test some of the great new crap before the first pang of hunger hits me and I bite into a plum. The juice slicks out of my mouth and drips onto the floor, and it makes me think of childhood summers, and then I remember my brother, Charlie, and I throw the plum away.

The windows are small paneled deals that swing outward on creaky old hinges. I can see along a slanted roof tiled with weathered gray stone slates edged here and there with moss. The roofline ends in a big clock tower, and just as I sight it, some bells go *Bing-BONG, Bing-BONG!* And a couple of pigeons take flight.

This is all reminding me of a movie I saw when I was little. Shirley Temple has been left in a fancy boarding school by her dad, who's a soldier and, frankly, given what transpires, not the sharpest tool in the shed. The moment he's split for whatever's the latest war they've got on, the headmistress turns into a total beyotch and starts treating Shirley like a good-for-nothing flunky. She's got to haul coal around, serve everybody else dinner, scrub various scrubbable things, and generally do all sorts of unpleasant shit. Worst of all, she's forced to live up in the cold and gloomy attic.

Turns out that across the way there's this totally hype guy in a turban who sees her through the attic window and takes pity on her; and one day he rigs it so that she wakes up surrounded by opulence and warmth and delectable goodies and whatnot.

Anyhow, I'm feeling a bit like Shirley T. in the movie. The window is big enough for me to squeeze out of, and the slope of the roof looks like I could walk it, but who am I kidding? Where would I escape to?

I mean, theoretically, I should be trying to find Jefferson and the others and get them over here, pronto. But how am I supposed to do that? Scramble out the window and down a drainpipe, ninja my way back to the air base, stow away or hijack a plane back to New York? That doesn't seem terribly realistic. I mean, I'm badass, but I'm not *that* badass.

99

The way I figure it, whoever got me here is the quickest way back. Like, there must be some reason I'm being given the Shirley Temple treatment, and probably my best move right now, until an angle makes itself known, is to play along.

Which, given the whole three-thousand-thread-count, kept-woman vibe of it all, isn't exactly bad. At least until the bill comes due.

I scarf down a few lavishly green pears and rosy apples, put on some incredibly comfortable yet stylish flats, and venture to the door. It's a heavy oak number, and I half expect it to be bolted shut from the outside. But it pulls back with a friendly meowing of the hinges.

Weirdly, there's another door about six inches past it. I hear a faint shuffling from the other side.

Not to be deterred or whatever, I open that one, too. It swings outward and stops on the metal leg of a chair that is struggling to contain the truly unlikely, almost imponderable size of a guy with a wicked buzz cut and a rugged face like a knuckled ham hock. He rises and almost bashes his head against the stone stairway leading up from the landing where he's roosting.

At full extension, the dude is six-ten if he's an inch. He wipes his mouth with a napkin—it would appear he's been scarfing some sort of gooey red-brown bean situation from a ceramic plate on a wooden tray—and yanks the lapels of his unfeasibly large suit to straighten it.

"Yes—Miss Zimmerman, is it?" he says, as if people had been

streaming in and out of this double-door arrangement all day and he's not entirely sure, despite having been set up here in his chair, if I am in fact who he's supposed to be waiting for. His voice is a barrel of honey and gravel.

Me: "Yeeees?"

He holds out a fleshy hand with knuckles like hillocks. "Titch."

Me: "Who in the what, now?"

Him (smiles): "Titch. It's what everyone calls me."

I shake his hand, or rather, his hand envelops mine like a boxing glove and he levers it up and down a couple of times.

Titch: "You'll be wanting some breakfast. A fry-up? Or something American? Frosted Flakes?"

Me: "What's a fry-up?"

Titch: "Ohhh, it's lovely."

Actually this sounds more like *laaavly*. He's not, like, *Downton Abbey* hoity-toity English; he sounds more like Johnny Depp in *Pirates of the Caribbean*.

Titch: "Sausages, beans"—he points at the pebbled goo he's been eating—"mushrooms, bacon"—bi-kun—"fried bread—"

Me: "You *fry* bread?"

Titch: "Oh, yes. Till it's nice and crispy."

Me: "Okay, let's do it."

Titch: "Coffee? Tea?" Suddenly I'm talking to a gargantuan flight attendant.

Me: "Uh…doesn't matter so long as it's strong."

Titch: "Builder's tea it is, then."

He holds up a metal square and starts poking at it.

I goggle at it. It's the first time I've seen a cell phone in years.

Let me revise that. It's the first time I've seen a *working* cell phone in years. With this stubby little box, he can, like, access all the world's knowledge and contact most of the surviving humans, friend or stranger, across the globe. Or, in this case, text somebody my breakfast order.

I feel a sudden and intense urge to go online. A little anticipatory jet of endorphins squirts in my brain. And I remember, in a flash, that I've lost my phone, the one with my past on it.

He sees me watching his sausagey fingers tap-dance across the little screen and shows it to me.

Titch: "New. Like it?"

Me: "They're square now?"

Titch: "Chocolate-box, they call 'em. You have been in the wars, haven't you?"

Me: "Yeah, the wars."

Titch: "I'm sure you'll be getting one soon. For now ... well, security, innit?"

Which I think means "right?"

Me: "Yes, innit."

He laughs.

Titch is friendly and expansive about his roots—he's from someplace called Clerkenwell, where he grew up as an assistant butcher before he joined the army. But he gets hazier when it comes to how he ended up here, in this suit, outside this set of doors, and beyond showing me his square cell phone, he won't tell me anything about what's going on in the world. So I tell him about where I'm from, the tribe and the Sickness and everything, and he's all "blimey...blimey...blimey!"—which is kind of funny and Dick-Van-Dyke-in-*Mary-Poppins*y.

Eventually a taut, dangerous-looking guy with buzzed hair and a suit that doesn't sit right on him—I'm guessing he's another military type in regular-people clothes—brings up my tray of food, and I invite Titch in for breakfast. Or rather, for looking at me eat breakfast. He watches me tackle the food in amazement.

Titch: "Didn't know there was that much room in there."

Me: "Dude, I've been hungry for years."

Titch: "Rough ride."

Me: "The roughest."

I crunch the last shard of fried bread—it's disgusting and delicious, sort of like toast soaked in oil—then lift the plate to my mouth and lick off the bacon grease and sausage juice and bean goo.

Titch: "Blimey."

There's a rap on the outside door—actually it's more like a genteel tip-tap. Titch rises and opens both doors, and there's Welsh, in a gray flannel number that's similar to but subtly different from yesterday's.

Welsh: "I see you've met Titch."

Me: "We're best buds."

Welsh: "I thought of taking a stroll."

He says this as if it had just occurred to him.

Welsh: "Perhaps you'd like to stretch your legs?"

It's dawned on me that these guys have everything pretty much planned out, and that this is just a less coercive approach to getting information out of me than what Ed was doing. But I decide to go along with the game of acting like I'm some kind of indulged house-guest or something.

Me: "I could promenade."

Titch nods to Taut Guy, who zips down the stairs double-time. It's like I've got my own entourage complete with bodyguards. Welsh sweeps his hand in an after-you gesture, and I squeak my way out on my new shoes.

The stairway is spiral, medievalish, and narrow, so we end up single file, with Welsh following and Titch kind of crabbing his way down half bent over.

At the bottom of the stairs, there's a glossy black square on the wall with a bunch of names painted on it, like a fancy-pants version of a buzzer panel. The names sit on painted-over lumps of all the names that have been there before—KENNY, R. J.; HAWKES, W. B.; RELLIE, E. N. C.; and at the top, OLD GUEST ROOM.

Me: "Uh, not to put too fine a point on it, Mr. Welsh, but where the fuck am I?"

He seems unfazed by my swearing.

Welsh: "Cambridge. Specifically, Trinity College, Cambridge, is exactly where the fuck you are."

He smiles like he's proud of the place.

Once, before It Happened, my class went on a field trip to the

104

Cloisters up on the Hudson River. It was a museum built by some rich dude who was crazy about the Middle Ages. It looked superold, with this cool arcaded courtyard and a garden in the middle. What I'm looking at is kind of like that but bigger—there's a perfect rectangle of new-mown grass in front of me, enclosed by a square of gorgeous two-story buildings of crumbly old stone. To our right is a big peak-roofed building; to the left, sunlight shoots straight through the windows that make up opposite walls of a library (that's what Welsh says it is) whose yellow sides are dotted here and there with rosy pink rectangles.

Kids about my age are wandering around dressed like normal people before the Sickness, some of them with books in their hands, a romantic couple carrying a bottle of wine and glasses. They look totally untroubled and unafraid. A couple of very, very old dudes in funny black robes are steaming across the lawn, chatting away. Birds are *tweet-tweet*ing, bees are buzzing in the flower beds, butterflies are butterflying around.

Mind officially blown. Like, this would have been a pretty idyllic scene even before my life was plunged into chaos, violence, and brutality. Now—it feels like heaven itself.

Me: "Please, stop. I'll talk."

Welsh: "Sorry?"

Me: "Never mind."

Welsh: "I thought you'd rather be here than in a sad, old ministerial building somewhere."

Me: "You thought right."

We take a right and head up some stairs into a little passageway that runs past the doorway to the Hall, which is what they call the college cafeteria. Except this doesn't look like a cafeteria—it looks like they based it on the dining hall at Hogwarts. A big oldy-worldy stone barn sort of thing with long wooden tables with benches on either side and a sort of low stage at the back where I guess the professors get their grub on. There's a big portrait of fatty bo-batty King Henry VIII looking down on the whole scene, deciding which of his wives to murder next.

Then down some more stairs, and we're in this gigantic court-yard with a big stone fountain that looks like a gazebo in the middle. Welsh gives me a whole travelogue, explaining that this is the big-gest enclosed court in Europe, and it's from three old colleges that Henry VIII turned into one big mash-up college, and Isaac Newton lived over there in that corner, etc., etc. We walk along the pathways, which are patrolled by dudes in bowler hats, and touristy-looking people stop to look at our strange group, especially Titch, who's lumbering after us like some kind of stalker grizzly bear.

Welsh points out a tower where Byron somebody lived.

Me: "This is great, but... why are we here?"

My bullshit detector is on high alert, since I can't figure out why I suddenly rate a tourist getaway instead of solitary.

Welsh: "We are working on a honey rather than vinegar footing."

Me: "As in, you get more flies with?"

Welsh: "Yes. We've received records of your—ah—stay with the navy, of course. I apologize, but it is necessary to do one's research."

Me: "Sure."

Like, *no big deal that you're looking through my interrogation recordings.*

Welsh: "It struck us—by 'us' I mean myself and my colleagues at the Foreign Office, the Home Office, and what people like to call MI6—that you might find yourself more willing to lend a hand in helping us through this interesting period in history if you were treated as an ally rather than an enemy."

Me: "Okay, sounds good..."

Welsh: "And I thought—I was inspired by certain answers you gave in the course of your questioning—that you might appreciate a chance to take up some studies."

Me: "College? Uh...I don't think I'm exactly Oxford material."

Welsh: "Cambridge. We're in Cambridge." (He says this with the littlest bit of huffiness.) "People often get that wrong. At any rate, the most difficult thing about Oxbridge—I mean Oxford and Cambridge—is *getting in*. After that...well, if you want, it can be a bit of a doss."

Me: "A doss is something easy?"

Welsh: "Yes. I should know."

Me: "So I'm here because you had a rockin' time at Cambridge?"

Welsh: "Well, I wouldn't exactly put it that way. The fact is that Trinity has always had affiliations with the intelligence services. Some of the most infamous traitors of the Cold War were educated here."

Me: "That doesn't sound like a good thing."

Welsh: "No, it's not. And as a result, Trinity shows a certain willingness to make up for the mistakes of her alumni."

Me: "So you're offering me—what—a Plague Survivor Scholarship?"

Welsh: "More or less, yes."

So it looks like the gub'mint has pulled some strings to get me into college. At first, I feel like that's kind of lame, but then I figure it's not much worse than some preppy dude getting into Yale because his dad donated a library or whatever. I mean, to make it this far I had to eat rats and perform field operations and fight cannibals, for starters, and I figure life experience counts for something. School of Hard Knocks, you know. I mean, I did, like, *AP* Hard Knocks.

This is all very fast, of course—one day I'm struggling for life in a post-apocalyptic hellhole, next I'm public enemy number one, next I'm Joe College. But I'm getting used to this kind of switcheroo; my brain is like, *bring it on, already.*

And, yeah, I'm thinking of taking up the offer because (a) what the hell else am I going to do, and (b) it beats the brig, and (c) it's a reasonable holding pattern until I can figure out how to help my friends.

Me: "What's the catch?"

Welsh: "The catch is that we would like to ask some questions of our own occasionally, regarding the situation in New York."

Me: "And the situation onboard the USS *Ronald Reagan*?"

Welsh seems a little thrown by this, or by my realizing that it might matter to him, then he smiles approvingly.

Welsh: "Maybe even that. Also I'm afraid the offer is contingent upon your remaining within the Liberties."

He says it like that—like Capital-Letter-L Liberties.

Me: "Within the what?"

Welsh: "Ah. Yes. Sorry. Due to the rather extraordinary events of the past few years, there are now different legal categories of urban space. 'The Liberties' in this case means, roughly, the city limits."

Me: "So no skipping town."

Welsh: "Not without prior approval, no."

Me: "Well...I suppose I had better have a look at the Liberties, then."

Welsh: "Why not?"

And he leads us through a teensy doorway set in the big castle gates of the college as Titch pokes away valiantly at his cell phone, informing whoever-it-is that the package is on the move.

Then I realize that if I'm going to do a good job of playing along, I should ask the question that'd be in the forefront of my mind if I were playing it straight. In fact, it *is* in the forefront of my mind.

Me: "Welsh, where are my friends? They didn't tell me back on the ship. Did they make it?"

Welsh smiles apologetically.

Welsh: "To be honest with you, I don't know. Your government is not being entirely transparent. I've put in requests for information. One can only hope for the best."

JEFFERSON

WE'RE PEERING DOWN at 125th Street from the greenroom above the marquee of the Apollo Theater, and it's time to discover our fate. The crowd keeps getting bigger, until the street is jammed, the way it must have looked when James Brown played.

It's like this: The Harlemites vote in a president every season—that's Solon. So far he's been reelected every time. In theory, Solon runs things the way he likes. In theory, he doesn't need to ask anybody's say-so to do anything, and people have to follow his orders. But he's not totally off the leash, since he won't get voted back in if he does stuff nobody likes, and a three-month turnaround is pretty quick. So when there's an especially gnarly issue in the offing, he can call a vote to take the temperature of his public.

In *theory,* this is only about the specific question to be decided. *Effectively,* this is what you call a vote of confidence, since if he gets defeated, there's a pretty decent chance that he's going to lose the next election.

So it'd be fair to say that Solon is putting his career on the line. And maybe his life as well, since I gather that the power of the office is what keeps him from paying the price for some of the more unpopular decisions he's made. To keep the peace, a little blood has been shed here and there.

"I'm what the ancient Greeks used to call a tyrant," he says with a touch of pride. "But the term didn't sound as bad back then. There were tyrants all over. A tyrant wasn't a king—he couldn't pass the crown down to his kid, and it was easy enough to just kill him and install a new dude. Elect a tyrant, and he knows if he doesn't bring the rain..." He doesn't finish the thought. "Shit got *real* back in ancient times. In Athens, when a general lost a battle, he got exiled for ten years. Had to leave his home country under pain of death. Called it ostracism. And that was them being *nice*."

Imani is nowhere to be seen. She's out rallying her supporters. Supposedly this is an up-and-down vote, but I gather it's not so simple. For one thing, the Apollo holds only about a thousand people, maybe one-tenth of the remaining population of Harlem. And only those inside the doors get to vote. So the electorate is a question of who gets there first and who's prepared to shove or fight their way in before the deadline. And those are usually what you would call the party faithful. Not the way I imagine the democratic process, exactly.

"Is that the best way to do it?" I ask.

"Oh, you were thinking more sunshine and light, every voice heard, that kind of thing? Well, that's not the way it worked out. We started our thing at the Apollo, and when we got bigger, it was hard to move, hard to change the way things get done, even if they haven't been done that way for long. Early on? I wanted to make sure everybody had a hand in everything, so we would vote every day. But nothing got done. Brothers arguing for hours over what we should vote about first. Fact is, most of the time, we only get a thousand or so people who want to vote. Everybody else could give a fuck so long as there's enough food and water. That's the way with politics, till the revolution comes. Maybe that's today." He smiles. "I don't know, maybe now I got a new lease on life, I'm ready to retire. Write my memoirs, see the world, know what I'm saying?"

Something about this makes me feel, for a heart-tripping moment, that Solon *knows* what's out there, knows that I'm lying. And this gathering is actually a surprise show trial, and I'm going to end up dead. *Lynched* is the word that pops into my head, and then I realize how inappropriate the thought is. In my mind, I see the frozen face of a blond child looking at the camera, at me, in the company of smiling picnicking townspeople, a twisted and abused body hanging from a tree in the background.

He sees my expression and laughs. "Man, don't worry so much. You'll get your chance to be heard."

He thinks I'm worried about the vote. And I am.

"Me?" I thought Solon was going to argue the case for peace.

"Nah, I can't do that." Solon is adamant. "I'm compromised. Took a hit of your wonder drug. *You're* the one shaking us down, flipping the script. So *you* argue your case. Don't worry, they always root for the underdog. That's an Apollo tradition. And ain't no underdog like a white boy."

"Actually, I'm half Japanese," I say.

"Even better, then."

Which is to say, even worse.

Whatever Solon says about voter apathy, it doesn't apply tonight. People are still trying to force their way into the auditorium by the time somebody powers up a sound system and a jaunty tune rings out with the lyrics—"Showtime! At the Apollo! It's Showtime! At the Apollo!" Which I guess is the sign for the session to convene.

Imani has reappeared, and she's glad-handing the crowd. Some people seem to know her well, some are friendly, some neutral, some outright hostile.

I suppose I was hoping for a blank slate of an audience if I have to plead my case. But in retrospect, that seems pretty naive. I mean, nobody comes to a decision with a completely open mind. And I can't expect people to forget everything they've felt and known and suffered through.

Soon I'm in the grips of a toxic mixture of stage fright, guilt, and sheer physical terror. I used to tell stories to my tribe, back in the Square. This shouldn't be any different—that's all a debate is, right? Two people tell stories, and the best story wins. But I *knew* my tribe, and they knew me. To the Harlemites, I'm just some white kid (okay, half-white kid) asking them to hold their punches. They're finally ready to take over. A gun for every girl and boy, and maybe nothing can stop them going to war.

I'm backstage steeping in flop sweat when Peter points out a curious wooden stump, sliced at an angle and worn shiny on top.

Peter says, "Rub it."

"For what?"

"For luck, fool," he says. So I do.

The murmur and seething of the people subside as we take the stage. The auditorium is done up in crimson velvet and steeply banked, so that the crowd appears ready to fall onto the stage at any moment. The staggered faces rise up like a cliff.

"What's the matter?" says Peter. "Never been alone in a room with a thousand black folks before?"

Alone with a thousand. Weirdly, that's the feeling. I realize I've always managed to blend in, thanks to the all-access pass of my Caucasian heritage, epicanthic fold or not. This is a little taste of what it must be like to be black in a white world.

Patched and jerry-rigged cables run up and down the walls and hang like vines over the deep chasm of air before me, powering the lights fitfully; they spike and dim to the pulse of the generators I can hear laboring outside.

There's Solon and me and Imani up front, like two boxers and a ref; the rest hang back. I'm terrified, just as scared as I was getting into the makeshift ring in Grand Central, where SeeThrough and I fought strangers for money a thousand lives ago.

Solon waits until the place falls silent. Maybe the crowd senses something big. The air between us is the womb of the future. The mood feels pregnant with hope and violence.

"You all know me," says Solon, his voice carrying to the upper reaches and bouncing back. "You know what I've done, you know what I've promised, you know what I've prepared you for."

There's a thunderous response from the audience, *hell yeah*s and *that's right*s and everything else besides. Solon lets it wash across us.

"But—I've got something better than that." The crowd quiets. "Maybe it's not time to kill—not yet, anyhow. It's time to think. To rethink. Because there is something new under the sun. There's news. There's hope."

The crowd makes a compound sound that adds up to confusion.

"This is Jefferson," he says. "Y'all want to hear what he has to say. Because Jefferson has the Cure."

Solon lets that sink in. It starts to.

"That's right. The Cure for the Sickness. We never thought we'd see it. But it's here. I'm gonna tell you I tried it myself. Just to make sure it didn't hurt. 'Cause I'm thoughtful like that."

Laughter from the crowd, cresting over astonishment.

"It works," says Solon. "Never felt better. And I intend to live a long, long life."

At this, all human noise drops away. A wave of silence purling up, ready to crash. And in that moment before it does, I see in the faces facing me a kaleidoscopic array of the same thought playing out in a thousand beings—*I'm going to live*. The force of a thousand reprieves. Instead of another year of life, fifty, sixty, seventy, a countless array of possibilities.

And then, the impact of that thought in a thousand shouts

threatening to carry us away. It's impossible at first to tell what people are saying—it's a buffeting, deafening cascade of joy and triumph and, down in the undercurrents, retroactive grief. Tears and shouts, hugs and high fives and faints. Then, poking through the clamor, questions—How? What? When do we get it?

Solon knows just when to seize the mood of the crowd on the fly, like a center fielder plucking the ball from the air in full stride.

"Easy. Easy. Be cool now. That's what we've got to do for just a little bit. Be cool. There's enough to treat us all."

The crowd settles, gentled by the stroking of Solon's voice. And I realize that, no matter what, they will love him forever for being the one who told them they'd live. There is no way they will turn against him now. If anyone is going to be thrown to the dogs, it's me, with the qualifications and requirements and conditions I'm about to put on the glorious news he's brought them.

He's not stupid.

"It's a lot of other things you need to know," he says. "And one big thing we need to decide. I want you to listen to Jefferson."

He gestures to me, a little showman's wave. I can't think of what to do as the crowd absorbs the sight of the pale alien visitor. So, stupidly, I bow.

A gust of laughter takes the crowd. Solon smiles and motions for quiet. "Jefferson is from the Washington Square tribe. Some of you may remember we sent Theo and Spider and Captain off with Jefferson and his people. Some of you maybe never heard of them. But I guarantee you they're gonna go down in history. These are the folks brought back the Cure." He includes Peter, Brainbox, and Chapel in another sweep of the arm. I look back and see their faces—guarded, cautious. When I turn back, I see Imani, tense with anger. She knows that Solon is working the crowd, building me up against whatever assault she has in mind.

"Jefferson has a proposal. Or maybe you'd call it a ... a *stipulation*." The word is well within the range of Solon's vocabulary, but he acts as if it's a curiosity that he's examining, turning it about in his mind's fingers. "He says call off the war. *Imani*—I *know* you know *her*—she's kept it all running here ..." I can't help but finish the thought—*under me*.

Solon nods at Imani. "Well, I think she's in favor of running up the score, if you know what I mean. We keep the Cure to ourselves and make our move like we planned *before*." He puts a touch of emphasis on *before*; the implication *before everything changed* rings out.

"We're going to put it to a vote. Do we get the Cure and live in peace, or do we *take* it"—Solon glances toward me, then away again quickly, as if suddenly ashamed—"and go to war. I'm gonna let Imani say what she has to say first. She's earned the right."

I can see, as Imani blinks, surprised, that Solon has used every lever of power he has. He's set things up to his design—unleashing the glory of the good news, bringing me out into the glow of it, framing the idea of seizing the Cure from us as a kind of dishonor, and, finally, throwing Imani into the fray first. From the look on her face, she was expecting to speak after me—which would make sense, since she's basically saying no to my plan. Now she has to present both her ideas *and* mine.

For a moment, seeing her standing there, round and ungainly, I almost feel sorry for her. But she gathers herself with a twitch of her brow and takes the bit in her teeth.

"Listen, y'all," she says, an acid expression on her face. "It's a lot of things Solon here didn't say."

Maybe Solon didn't expect Imani to go right at him instead of me, but he barely shows it. A twitch, like an invisible thread, plucks at his mouth for a nanosecond. I doubt anybody farther away than me sees it.

"Fact is, I was there when this boy came in. Him and *that* boy." She points at Brainbox. Brainbox looks like he wants to disappear. "Now, first of all, don't go thinking *he's* the one got the Cure." She points at me. "You didn't find nothing. That's right, isn't it? It's your *boy* figured it out."

I let a few seconds pass by before I say, "Yes." Which I can tell a moment later is a mistake. It makes me look suspect. Like I'm denying Brainbox his due.

"Second of all—*this* was the deal. I know because I was there. We let these trespassing fools live—and not only that, we sent Theo, and Spider, and Captain, on *our* boat, to go find the Cure. That's right, isn't it?" This time I acknowledge it right away.

"Then you remember what we agreed, don't you? If you find the Cure, it's for Harlem. Not for the Dominicans, not for the Puerto Ricans"—she pronounces it contemptuously—*portarickens*—"not for the motherfuckin' *Uptowners*." At this the crowd cheers and *uh-huh*s and *fuck them*s with a vigor that shakes the air and sends a thrill of fear down my back.

"You telling me you want to give *life* to the Uptowners? Hunted down every brother and sister below 110th Street? You want to let them *live*?"

*No*s and *hell no*s. A thunder of voices like a giant, slow machine starting up.

"What should we give them?"

The answer comes back: "Death!"

"What?" Imani puts her palm behind her ear and sticks her head out, leaning into the sound.

"Death!"

"What?"

"DEATH!" The crowd is up and shouting, pounding the seats.

Now, at this point she should probably drop the mic, as it were. There's no way in for me. But then she makes a mistake. Having provoked the crowd, she tries to reason out her point. And at this moment, reason is weakness.

"Look, man," she says. "I ain't saying this boy doesn't deserve our thanks. He and his gonna get the Cure, too. But we paid down too much. Theo. Captain. Spider. They died for *us*.

"We gotta make a lot of the Cure. Don't tell me anybody else has the *ability* to make enough. Don't tell me anybody else got the *organization*. The *equipment*."

True enough, I'm guessing, but her venture into practicalities takes the edge off the crowd's anger. People are sitting down. They're listening with their brains instead of their teeth.

"So that's what I'm gonna ask you. Vote that we keep this Cure. And we go to war."

There's another burst of applause and enthusiasm at *war,* but it's less rapturous than before; the anesthetic of rage has started to wear off.

Imani casts a glance at Solon—her eyes glide over me—and then, seeming not to know what to do with herself, she takes a seat with her legs dangling over the end of the stage. She looks like a child whose tantrum is spent.

The crowd and I size each other up. Their gazes are pinpricks, each drawing a bead of sweat. And then—and then I hear her voice, not inside, nothing spooky, but a memory of the timbre her voice shaped and fashioned for my purpose, from some location inside me: Donna says, "Tell them the story."

And so I do. I tell them how Brainbox found evidence of the lab. How we went to the library, and we contended with the cannibal Ghosts under the murals of heaven, how we were found by the Uptowners at Grand Central and were saved by the Moles who lived in the subway tunnels. How we unknowingly led the Uptowners to the Moles, and so the Moles to their deaths. How we found our way to the wildland of the park, how the bear sensed us and scented us and hunted us to the Metropolitan, where we fought him with sword and ax and spear, and killed him, and SeeThrough was lost, dying with her body broken. We mourned and went north, and passed into Harlem. We boarded the *Annie* and worked our way up the coast of the Island, until we were attacked by the Islanders and taken prisoner, to the lab. At Plum Island we were subjected to experiment. And some lived, and some died. And I lived, and my blood was rid of the Sickness, and from my blood was the Cure. And we left Kath dead, and found our way home.

The catcalls and the jokes and the insults trail off as I tell it. And they submit to the old thirst—to know what's next, to feel like others feel, to short-circuit the Self in the Other. Which is only the Self.

And at some point, I lose track of what is the truth and what is the lie, because after all, it is just a story, and I grieve for Theo, who is alive, as I grieve for SeeThrough, who is dead.

Quiet. And then—breaking through, a voice: "Go on, white boy!"

And I collect myself.

"There's not enough life," I say. "There's too much death. I can't give one person life and another death. I can't do it. I have to give as much life as I can. We were just kids..." On the faces of all the lost boys and girls, recognition.

"We'll never be that again. But we can become something more. Everybody can. If you go to war now, how many will die? How many of you who could have lived out the century?" They consider.

"I say...I *ask*...that we get another chance. We can make something better than tribes and war. We can make *life*."

There isn't a big cheer; there's nothing. A low murmur like loud heartbeats, perhaps. Or that's just me.

Solon nods. He looks at the crowd. "All right," he says. "What'll it be? War?"

A few hands shoot up—a few hands follow.

"Peace?" he asks.

Silently, they stand up. Hundreds, a thousand. The tears come.

DONNA

PEOPLE ARE WALKING the streets totally unarmed, totally disarmed, totally consciously unconscious of the danger that other people pose to them. They're all, like, "La la la, just chillin' here in the middle of the damn road, not worried that somebody's gonna steal my shit or drop a cinder block on my head or coldcock me." Which, I guess, is the root of civilization or something.

Actually, Jefferson used to say that sanitation was the root of civilization, and can I say something about the smell of this place? It doesn't. Smell, that is. Back in New York, the tentacles of organic corruption slithered into your nose the moment you woke up—in fact, the various stenches colored your dreams. Here, it's like everything has been scrubbed clean. There's no poop, no rot, no sweat. Nothing to remind you of change and death, which seems to be the point. Back home, everybody was young, sure, but they were also marked, like Death had sewn a big scarlet *D* on them. Here, there's old people and babies and toddlers and tweens and middle-aged and all, but they feel different. Like, they're all bending, in some invisible added dimension, toward life.

Except, not life like the natural kind—spring and wildflowers and whatnot—life like Life, some—what did Jefferson call it?—*simulacrum* of itself, some advertising thing, like a marketing version of it. The representation, not the thing. Anyhow, everybody is cruising around, smiling and laughing and bustling and getting on with things with a sort of shocking disregard for their peril. The only guns in evidence are the submachine guns on some of the cops. Welsh says that even those were rarely seen "until recently." But he isn't very clear about what happened recently to get them all armed up.

We stroll down the non-debris-strewn street, looking at the buildings. Welsh says that the university is made up of all these different smaller colleges and that each one has its own identity and traditions and affiliations. It's like tribes. I already feel a certain identification with Trinity, even though I've been there all of twelve hours.

The colleges mostly take their names from rich dudes who gave money to have them started, or sometimes the rich dudes would give them churchy names to suck up to God so that he would have second thoughts about sending them to hell for all the shitty things they probably did to make themselves rich and powerful in the first place. There's even a Jesus College and a Christ's, which sound kind of like evangelist schools, but Welsh says they're just like any of the others. Trinity is actually the College of the Holy and Undivided Trinity. It's just nobody calls it that because it's too much of a mouthful.

Eventually we get to a big one called King's, which has a gigantic chapel that looks like a science-fiction author came up with a giant medieval missile launcher. Welsh starts telling me something about the Duke of This or That.

Me: "That's great. But can we eat?"

We walk through the town market, which reminds me a little of the Bazaar back home, since there are all these stalls with people hawking their wares and whatnot. I tell Welsh, and he starts plying me with questions about the Bazaar: What did it look like, who ran the place, how did people buy things, what was available? I can see him filing away my answers neatly in his brain.

Meanwhile, I keep getting tripped up by little bits of behavior I'd forgotten existed. People dropping trash in trash cans (here they call them "rubbish bins"). People waiting in lines ("queues"). Holding open doors for each other. Like they expect to see the other person again, or even if they won't, they're *acting* like they'll see the other person again, or maybe even that they see themselves as the other person in the transaction in a sort of imaginary swap. This might sound kind of "duh," like these small acts are sort of obvious contributions to the general good that don't cost you anything or whatever, but you'd be surprised how quickly it goes out the window once you're in survival mode. The niceties get confined to the very limited circle of the few people you threw your lot in with. So I guess what I'm seeing is an expansion of the sense of the group or something. Which is maybe what a country is, or a "society." I'm watching somebody help lift a stroller over the curb when I catch the end of a sentence—

Welsh: "... which is why we've prepared a cover for you."

Me: "Huh?"

Welsh: "Is that an Anglicism? 'Cover story'?"

Me: "No, I know what a cover story is. You want me to do secret agent stuff? Like, take on a false identity?"

Welsh: "No and yes. No, in that we do not want or need you to do 'secret agent stuff'; yes, in that we think that your reentry into society will be easier if you are not lumbered with the distinction of being a survivor of the Sickness."

Me: "Oh."

Welsh: "You see, it is not generally known that there are so many survivors in the Americas. I'd go as far as to say that you are all presumed dead."

Me: "Why don't you tell people?"

Welsh: "A variety of reasons. Chiefly, that there is nothing that we can do about it at present, and the fragile state of affairs means that we are loath to inform the public."

Me: "You mean they can't handle the truth."

Welsh: "Mr. Nicholson rarely put it better. Yes. Besides, I'm afraid that if you were to proclaim yourself as the one survivor of the plague, no one would believe you."

Me: "Like, what are the chances?"

Welsh: "Yes. Besides, there have been a number of cases of

attention seekers doing precisely that in order to gain celebrity. And—I confess—some of my colleagues in the Office of Information have deliberately introduced rumors of survivors, in order to discredit them and inoculate the general public against the idea."

Me: "Jeez."

Welsh: "It is a dangerous world we live in. I think, in short, you might prefer to avoid the glare of attention you'd be under if you did, as it were, come out."

I hadn't thought about this before. And, yeah, now that I do, it would be kind of a hassle to be treated like a freak, and apart from Welsh and his MI-whatever boys, I'm not exactly keen on the idea of answering questions all day about what it's like back home.

Welsh: "You have qualms."

Me: "Qualms?"

Welsh: "Reservations."

Me: "Oh, I know what *qualms* means. And I don't. Have them, I mean. Not about lying. I've done worse than that. Besides, what does it mean to lie to somebody outside my tribe? Nothing."

Welsh doesn't seem to understand what I mean, but he doesn't follow up.

Me: "I'm just not sure I can get away with it."

Welsh smiles with what looks like a little bit of professional pride.

Welsh: "Oh, we'll help with that. You'd be surprised how incurious people actually are. The young especially. And especially in an atmosphere like this. Freshers at university ... everyone is, to some degree, reinventing themselves."

He holds open a door.

We order, and the waiter inputs our order into a little device. When the waiter goes, Welsh starts laying out the story. It'll be sort of like if I had been a real geek in high school, but I get transformed into a cool kid when I get to college because nobody from home knows me. Except in this case, I was a post-apocalyptic scavenger, and now I'm...

Well, I'm still Donna. We figure it's best that we keep my name. And, so that there's some credibility to my story, Welsh proposes that I'm a navy brat and that my folks got me on the *Ronald Reagan* when the shit hit the fan.

All this is, of course, exceedingly lame and bogus, but for now I see no advantage in coming out of the apocalypse-closet, no other angle that helps me help Jefferson and the rest. So, initiate Donna 2.0.

I feel kinda bad about sort of erasing my parents. Like, even though this cover story is obviously fake to *me*, it starts settling into the part of my brain where the real past is kept, and sort of ooches it out of the way. Like you can't pretend to be something without starting to believe it in some sense. Now, I don't have much of an issue dislodging my father. He was always, if I am being straight about it and not sugarcoating, a d-bag. Like, he hadn't planned on getting married or having kids in the first place. I was just a bummer that cropped up to harsh his mellow and, try as he might (and he didn't try that hard), there was always an air of making the best of it whenever he dealt with me.

Mom is another issue. I don't mean to hit the old single-mother cliché, but for sure she had a lot to deal with, and she always made me feel like she loved having me around, even if occasionally she did want to murder me. Anyhow, it feels bad replacing her with imaginary Officer's Wife Mom. I apologize to her internally.

Welsh: "We'll need to rehearse these specifics, of course. In the meanwhile, I've taken the liberty of informing your tutor of your situation. He is cooperating with us."

Me: "Tutor? Am I, like, that dumb?"

Welsh: "No, no. Tutor is an administrative position. The equivalent of a dean at American university. But a little more intimately involved. He doesn't actually teach you anything. You normally don't see him unless you've been...the expression is 'skiving.' "

Me: "Dicking around?"

Welsh: "More or less."

Me: "Okay. But how am I going to explain you? And Titch—"

He's sitting just down the way from us, a sort of human room divider keeping people from overhearing things, his mass overflowing the normal-sized design specs of the faux-rustic bench and table arrangement. Taut Guy is standing by the exit, buzzing with menace.

Me: "And Mr. Intensity over there."

Welsh: "The idea is that your father is a member of the Reconstruction Committee. That's the liaison branch between your government and mine. That makes you a high-value target."

Me: "For who?"

Welsh: "It's terribly complicated." He closes off the subject with a smile. "Besides," he says, changing one subject for another like Indiana Jones with the gold statue and the bag of sand, "it's not term yet. Most of the students haven't come up. When term starts, we'll keep our distance a bit more."

Food arrives—a number forty-two with rice noodles. Welsh and Titch watch me stuff the whole serving into my mouth before they've even separated their chopsticks. I ask for another and wipe my fingers off.

Me: "Sorry. It's been a while since I used cutlery. They didn't give us any on the *Ronald Reagan*. Thought we might use them as weapons."

Welsh: "I think you'll want to relearn the fork and knife if our plan is to work."

I nod. And I ask myself—the amazing thing is that it's for the first time—what's to become of me. Like, if I'm doing this whole con job, what'll happen to me in the end? Am I going full-on Witness Protection Program up in this bitch? Will I figure out a way to get back to Jefferson, or will I have to be this fake high-value-target chick for the rest of my life? And then I realize that, since I hadn't actually counted on having a rest of my life, or at least living past eighteen, I have no idea what I intend to do with all the years left in my body.

I'm sure that college students are facing all sorts of existential issues and whatever, of the "what do I want to do with my life?" variety. It just feels like my situation is a wee bit more complicated.

And I start thinking about the tribe, who are still dying off, that is unless Chapel and the rest really meant to save them. And I think of Jefferson and the others, and I wonder whether they've made it back home.

Me: "Welsh, if we're going to do this—if I'm going to cooperate and become this high-status chick—I need to know that my friends are okay."

Welsh: "I wish I knew. Your government is being very tight-lipped. Your escape, if I can call it that, was an embarrassment to them, and our intelligence services are not always working hand in hand, as you might have gleaned from our contretemps on the tarmac at RAF Duxford."

Me: "Yeah. Thanks for that. It was fun."

So there's no knowing how they are. For all I know, they were apprehended before they could get back to the Square.

Or worse.

So I play for time. I realize that underneath all of Welsh's smooth reassurances, this is the only way they'll let things roll. The con is my best option.

Then, out of the corner of my eye, I notice a guy in the far corner checking me out. He's copper-skinned, with swept-back black hair and gray-green eyes. And—this has nothing to do with anything, of course—he's totally beautiful, like, an eleven. A forkful of noodles is poised in his hand, but he's too busy looking at me to eat it. When I look back at him, he loses his composure, which is kind of charming, and takes a sudden deep interest in the noodles. Welsh follows my gaze and seems to kind of target-lock on the guy.

Welsh: "Not someone you know, I hope?"

Me: "Who? Oh. No. Never seen him before."

It's the truth, but despite that, Welsh seems to make a little mental note and file away the guy's face. I feel kind of bummed, like by looking at him I've managed to get him put on a terrorist watch list or something.

Titch: "I'm on it, boss."

Me: "Wait a second, Titch. Don't get on his case or anything."

Welsh: "Yes, Titch. I think we might file this one under *chercher la femme*, no?"

I don't really know what this means, but it seems to make Titch stand down.

Welsh: "Well. Shall we begin?"

JEFFERSON

BRAINBOX INSPECTS the heaping bags of pigeon shit we've gathered from our forays onto the local rooftops.

"So you're gonna make a bomb out of poop?" Peter is looking pretty skeptical. He got the easy job, gathering chalk from his old school. He sets down some cardboard cartons full of clinking little white cylinders and regards Box and his guano supply from a distance.

"Saltpeter," says Brainbox.

"Now you want salt?" Peter wipes his brow. The visit to the ghost-scape of Stonewall High School doesn't seem to have helped his mood.

"No," says Brainbox. "Not 'salt, Peter.' *Saltpeter.* I'm making it from the guano and chalk. And I'll add that to charcoal to make black powder. So, in fact"—he looks up at Peter—"I want charcoal."

"Charcoal got all used up," says Peter.

"Then we'll have to make some from scrap wood."

Peter's about to answer back when Chapel says, "I saw a Kmart on Astor Place. Maybe we can find some." Peter nods. He and Chapel seem to have some kind of rapport going. They head out, and a couple of minutes later, I observe them cautiously making their way south from our perch four floors up in a brownstone on Tenth, around the corner from Broadway. The windows are smeared to opacity, which suits our purposes. I've rubbed out a little circle of clarity in the glass to observe goings-on in the street below.

I go over our supplies. Some ammo, some packs of Meals Ready to Eat, assault rifles. We're not nearly as geared up as I'd like to be. Solon confiscated most of our hardware before we set off downtown, and left us just enough doses of the Cure to save my tribe. Theoretically. He kept the rest of our serum and equipment for himself, "against the chance of you blowing us off or dying, which amounts to the same thing." I have no choice but to trust him.

Actually, I'd trust him even if I *had* the choice not to. I can't say exactly why, other than having a sense that he's cast his lot in with us.

A Gathering of the Tribes, the first ever, is due to happen two weeks after we set off from Harlem, and the word has already gone out. That gives us ten days to free my people.

We've been observing Washington Square for three days now, ever since we came across Frank. We found him on Broadway, splayed across the curb, arms akimbo, back peppered with entry wounds. His body, once husky, was a testimony of scars and bruises.

Frank was a farmer's kid from upstate, staying with family down in the Village when the Sickness hit. His folks had wanted a good education for him, so he was shipped off to this Catholic school in the city, Holy Cross down by the Square.

Life hadn't been easy for him in the Village. The traffic and the crowds fazed him, and his classmates treated him like a rustic dumb-fuck. He was miserable and homesick, but his parents wouldn't let him give up. Frank didn't really come into his own until the apocalypse, when his way with growing things was finally appreciated by kids at the point of starvation. They toned down the attitude once they realized that food was running out and Frank was the only guy who knew how to tease more out of the ground. Under his supervision, we tore up the green spaces of Washington Square and raised corn, wheat, and beans. He stretched out the dwindling calories provided by scavenging the abandoned groceries and Korean delis of downtown. He kept us alive through two bitter winters.

When we headed out on that last reconnoiter, I left him in charge.

Anyway, now he's dead.

We've dragged him away from the ants and the rats eating his blood, and now his body is bundled up on a bed in the next room. We'll give him a proper burial once we've taken back the Square.

Through Chapel's Zeiss Victory viewfinder, I can see six of them on patrol, all male, skinheaded, in baggy camouflage. Uptowners for sure. Ten or so more are bunked up in Donna's old infirmary.

The workers they're supervising—my tribemates—are all boys. We haven't seen any of the girls. From what we know of the Uptowners, this is a bad sign.

"How big a boom is this thing going to make?" I say.

Brainbox looks over. "Pretty big."

Brainbox finishes pulverizing the dried pigeon shit and pours it into the strainer we found in the kitchen. He sets that over a ceramic bowl and turns to the chalk.

"Bring the propane and come with me," he says.

I follow Brainbox up the stairs, hefting the squat cylindrical metal tank we found in the basement. It's cool to the touch, much colder than the ambient temperature, and I can feel something sloshing around inside.

"Explain this to me, Brainbox," I say. "How can this stuff light on fire if it's *cold*?"

Brainbox looks back down at me. "Science," he says.

"Well, why don't we just use *this* as a bomb?"

"That's the whole *point*," says Brainbox. "You can't just set it off. You need to initiate the explosion. So first, we make black powder."

Brainbox finds what he's looking for. An ordinary gas barbecue grill, the kind you think you're going to use all the time when you buy it but never end up using because the neighbors complain about the smoke and you get tired of cleaning it anyway. We evict the family of sparrows living under the cover, then clear out the insides so there's nothing showing but the perforated tube that the flames come out of. Brainbox hooks up the propane tank to the gas hose on the side.

The matches from the kitchen still work, and we set the grill alight. Brainbox cranks it up to max and turns the tap on the propane tank, and the flames leap up two feet high.

"Is this safe?" I ask.

"No," says Brainbox. "Not at all."

Brainbox starts crushing the chalk to powder and motions for me

135

to do the same. Pretty soon we've got a big heap of pebbly chalk dust. We pour it into the empty bottom of the grill and close the cover. Brainbox watches the built-in thermostat as it rises and rises, eventually spiraling past the top mark on the dial.

"You might want to back up," he says. He twists open the white-hot vent with a stick. With a hiss, smoke starts escaping.

"Looks like dry ice," I say.

Brainbox almost smiles. "Very good. Yes, that's carbon dioxide."

"Bad for the environment," I say. Brainbox doesn't respond. Instead, he stares at the barbecue getting hotter and hotter. We wait for something.

I think about what happened before we left the Square that day, after the tribe voted me generalissimo. Donna said that I was running away. I told her the best way I knew to lead the tribe was to try to find a cure for the Sickness.

So now I have the Cure. And Donna is gone. And the Square has been taken over by our enemies. All in all, what could you say about my leadership?

After a while, Brainbox says, "You can spread limestone—that's what chalk is, basically—on the ground, and it reduces the acidity of the soil. Makes it better for growing things."

It takes me a second to catch his train of thought.

"You used to do that with Frank," I say.

Brainbox nods. "Yeah," he says. "We worked together sometimes."

I take in his angular, careworn face. For a little while, months ago, he was happy. At least, that's how it seemed. Then SeeThrough got killed, and I guess whatever sense he had of being just like the rest of us went out the window. He pulled his head back in and became unreadable again. Self-contained and lethal. At Plum Island, he entered into some sort of bargain with the Old Man, won his trust, and poisoned him. But before that, he had helped the Old Man experiment on us.

And thanks to that, we have the Cure. But Kath is dead. And Brainbox is...changed.

He's always been quiet. Now he's silent for hours, days on end. Back in the Square he'd been preoccupied; now he is obsessional. Like he's been boiled down to a more concentrated solution of himself.

It's things like this that absorb him now: intricate and painstaking manufacture. He has no time for the less controllable business of humankind. Watching him work, I have the strangest sense that he's grinding and sublimating his self and not the mute matter in front of him.

Brainbox opens the barbecue and lets the fire-treated chalk cool. I help him tip the grill over, and he carefully gathers the residue in a pan.

"Calcium oxide," he says. "Quicklime. Get upwind now." Brainbox holds his hands as far away from him as he can and dumps the powder into a deep baking tray of rainwater. It bubbles and hisses, as if it were suddenly boiling. He orders me to add more water as he scrapes a rake through the thickening slurry.

"Slaked lime," he says. "Use it for building mortar. Paint. All kinds of things. Now we take it downstairs."

He gingerly picks up the tray with its complement of grayish-white goo and carries it downstairs. I follow him, realizing again how much we owed to him in the early days after What Happened. Brainbox and his occult abilities. *Occult* meaning, as the dictionary will tell you, "hidden." The darkness that hid Box's skills wasn't supernatural; it was only our ignorance of the fabric of our own lives. We had all this magical technology but no idea of how it actually worked. That was for specialists and suppliers and corporations. Once the web of convenience was torn, we were helpless. Except for him.

Back in the apartment, I keep up the lab assistant routine. Brainbox has me hold another strainer to filter the liquid remnant of the quicklime slurry into a pitcher, then we pour this—Brainbox says it's "limewater"—through the strainer of pigeon crap. Brainbox tells me it has something to do with the nitrates in shit, which is why terrorists used fertilizer to make bombs back in the good old days.

Box boils away the gruesome sop of strained bird shit and limewater, and the apartment is suffused with a rank chemical tang. Finally, all that's left in the bottom of the pot is a handful of off-white crystals. He scrapes them together and spoons them into a jam jar from the cupboard.

"Very *Breaking Bad*," I say.

"What?" he says.

"TV. Never mind."

At this, he goes into conversational shutdown mode. After a few fruitless tries at chatting, I get bored and wander off to explore the little apartment.

Fortunately, whoever lived here was single, so I don't have to face any sad relics of children and family. My guess is he was a dude, since there isn't much in the way of photos at all. In fact, the décor is downright half-assed. I start poking around his bookshelf, trying to take his measure. It's a bit disappointing. College business textbooks and airport paperbacks.

Then I hear footsteps coming from the stairs outside the apartment. A ragged drumbeat—more than two people. I take the safety off my M4.

When I come back to the living room, Brainbox is still staring at the jar of saltpeter, shaking the crystals back and forth. I motion for him to hide, and he wakes from his reverie, but the door opens before we can do anything about it.

It's a familiar face, though the dirt obscures it. Carolyn, one of the girls from our tribe. With her, Holly, Elena, and Ayesha, also my people. They're raggedly dressed, sooty, and ripe, armed with baseball bats and a battered bolt-action rifle.

She precludes any question of mine with a hearty "Where the *fuck* have you been?"

"Long story," I say.

Peter and Chapel follow them in, each carrying a family-size bag of charcoal.

"We better feed these girls," says Peter. "They are *hangry*."

We decide to forgo the shitty flameless MRE heating pouches, since it's a reunion, and instead reinstate the barbecue to its former job. We open up our ration pouches—beef stew—and pour them into a big pot we set on the grill. I find some old dried pasta and boil it up in the last of the rainwater. And it turns out that business school bro had a taste for wine, so we open a few bottles of red.

"So," says Carolyn after the first few wolfed mouthfuls. "You first or me?"

I'm remembering the last exchange I had with Carolyn, back when the Uptowners first appeared at the Square, offering to trade a pig for two girls. In a non-gender-differentiated and totally unsexual way, I had been slapping the butts of a line of gunmen as I tried to rally them to the defense. Carolyn kind of took it wrong. Sitting with her now, I suddenly feel as if none of the things I've seen and done since have actually happened; I'm again Wash's insecure little brother.

"You first," I say.

"The Uptowners came back," says Carolyn. "And they were pissed. Something to do with you, Evan—the blond dude—and his sister?"

"Kath," I say. "Yeah."

"Well, he's not your number one fan, let's put it that way."

"Evan's *here*?"

"In the Square. Large and in charge. Yeah."

I think back to the moment at the Bazaar when, instead of sticking a knife in his heart, I mercifully pushed him down the stairs.

"He came back, with about fifty bros. They had a bunch of guns. This time, he wouldn't take no for an answer."

This time, he had a score to settle. This time they overwhelmed the defenders at the front gate. Then they gathered everybody together.

140

Then they searched the Square for weapons. Then they told them the new deal: They were officially a colony of Uptown. Their job was now to supply the Confederacy with food grown in the Square. In return, their lives and property would be protected. If they proved themselves useful in the new order of things, they would be allowed citizenship. This meant free movement within the borders of the Confederacy and the right to participate in the monetary system headquartered at the Bazaar.

The pitch would have gone over better with the tribe had it not been made literally over the dead bodies of their friends. And, it would have seemed a better offer had it not been restricted to the boys. The girls were to return Uptown under armed guard for a purpose that was never enunciated.

"We made a break for it that night," says Carolyn. "Most of us made it. A few got shot. A few got taken."

"So where did everybody go?"

"All over. Other tribes. Randoms. The five—the *four* of us stuck around the neighborhood. Laying low and watching. We're waiting for a chance to get back at them. They took Frank out about a week ago. Maybe he wasn't playing ball, or they figured they'd learned enough from him. Anyhow, we took some potshots at the execution squad, but it was a mistake. They fired back, and Chase got killed."

I remember Chase, bright eyes and a killer laugh. I'd call it infectious, but we don't use that term metaphorically anymore.

"However," says Carolyn, looking at our stock of semiautomatics, "looks like the balance of power could shift. So what happened to *you*?"

Chapel looks at me. The smallest shake of the head. So I tell them the lie, the one that nobody looks at twice because at the end comes the blinding light of the Cure.

Carolyn stares at the pack of serum doses. Holly and Elena hug. Ayesha says, "Well, that's upworthy." And rolls up her sleeve.

Brainbox and Chapel prepare the doses. "What the hell is this made of?" says Carolyn.

"Jefferson's blood," says Brainbox. "His antibodies from the Sickness. They were the most viable from all of ours."

"Who knew you'd ever amount to anything?" says Carolyn. "From nerd to savior."

"Yeah, man. You're, like, biblical," says Peter.

"Stop it," I say. I don't like the way they're looking at me. Like I'm a prodigy of nature. A precious monster.

Chapel injects Ayesha, then Holly and Elena. Carolyn shakes her head.

"It's safe," I say.

"Listen, I'm *dying* to get exposed to your blood, pal. Just…"

She goes quiet, struggling to find what to say.

"It's just…" She speaks through tears. "If I take it now, I know that I'll want to do whatever I can to stay alive. And I have to be willing to die."

"Why?" says Chapel.

"Because," I answer for her, "we have to take back the Square."

Carolyn nods. "We have to kill the Uptowners."

DONNA

WELSH HASN'T BROUGHT any pastries this morning, so
I wonder if I'm in trouble. I try to make eye contact with Titch, but he's
acting weirdly skittish, which is saying something for a guy his size.

Me: "Am I in trouble for switching subjects?"

News flash? I am now reading English. *Reading* means "majoring in." I started out reading medicine, which is sort of like premed,
which I thought I'd be good at because my mom was a nurse and
I've been treating scurvy and removing bullets from people for the
last couple of years, but fact is, it was a lot of chemistry and biology and not much combat medicine. Besides, I've missed a couple
of years of high school, what with the apocalypse happening when
I was a sophomore and all. Meanwhile, all the kids here have done
these tests called A levels, which are hella difficult, and they've all
arrived at college ready to concentrate on just one subject. In the
US you get to dick around, studying puppetry and experimental

dance for at least a year or two before you have to even *pretend* to get your ass in gear.

So, English it is. That's not to say that it's a *doss,* exactly, but I figure it'll feel a lot less like drowning. And in a weird way it makes me feel closer to Jefferson. The difficult part was convincing the fellows (that's Cambridge for professors) that I could hack it. I just pretended to be Jefferson and asked my tutor to put in a good word and got the go-ahead.

Welsh: "No. I'm glad you changed subjects, if it makes you more comfortable."

There's a crack of vulnerability in his demeanor. Back when he was facing down Ed the Interrogator, I had been surprised, like someone so polished and genteel and whatnot had no business being tough. Of course, that was all *Downton Abbey* stereotyping. In fact, everybody in this country has a thread of steel in their spine, which maybe explains how they survived having the shit bombed out of them by the Nazis.

Anyhow, Welsh is looking all down in the mouth and fatigued.

Me: "Then why the long face?"

Welsh: "I'm sorry to say—that is…certain facts have become known."

I pay a lot more attention to what people say, now that I'm read-ing English. That is, I always pay a lot of attention to what people say, I just find it easier to categorize, now that I'm studying practi-cal criticism and linguistics and whatnot. For instance, Welsh just shifted into the passive voice, which demonstrates an unwillingness to take responsibility for something.

Me: "Okay. What facts do you know?"

Welsh looks at his hands.

Welsh: "All right. I'm afraid that, in my job, I am occasionally required to be the bearer of bad news."

I wonder what bad news someone might possibly have for me. That the Sickness is back in my system? Nuh-uh. I get regular checkups. The bug is gone.

Welsh: "Some of my superiors would rather I kept you in the dark. But I feel that in our brief time together, we have become friends, of a sort."

Me: "Yes?"

Welsh: "At least, I have become rather fond of you. And I think that you deserve the truth."

I say nothing.

Welsh: "My office received a communiqué that was, for reasons too complicated to explain at present, delayed. An ongoing investigation of actions taken, proper channels, that sort of thing."

Me: "Okay?"

Welsh: "The substance of this communiqué is the events surrounding your actions on the deck of the *Ronald Reagan*."

He takes a folded piece of paper out of his sleek leather case. Sets it on the coffee table between us.

I let it sit there.

Me: "Tell me what happened."

146

Welsh: "It would be better if you read the communiqué. I don't want to get the details wrong."

I don't want to touch it. Maybe if I don't look at it, nothing it says will be true.

Of course not.

Me: "If you're my friend like you say, then tell me."

Welsh nods.

Welsh: "Fighters from the *Ronald Reagan* were launched to shadow the hijacked helicopter. It appears that at some point during the pursuit, it was mistakenly reported that the helicopter had opened fire upon the jets. They discontinued their pursuit, and a sea-to-air missile was launched from the USS *Higgins*."

Outside, birds are chittering at each other in the Master's Garden. Laughter from the river.

I rub the tears from my eyes.

Me: "Tell me the rest."

Welsh: "The missile hit its target. Air-sea rescue was sent to the site of the crash, several miles off the coast of Long Island."

He clears his throat, looks at his cup of tea, sets it down. He continues.

Welsh: "The bodies of all onboard the helicopter were recovered. There were no survivors."

Jefferson. Peter. Brainbox. Theo.

Welsh: "I'm very sorry."

Me: "You'd better go now."

Welsh: "Donna . . . if it is any comfort, it would have been quick."

Why is he still here?

Welsh: "If you had stayed with them... Well, you are alive. And you have so much to experience..."

But really, all I can think of experiencing is the loss of them. So long as they were alive, in some pocket of possibility in my mind, I was *from* somewhere.

So long as Jefferson was alive, I might live to see him again. I hadn't realized that I was thinking this, because I had told myself so many times that he was as good as dead—or I was as good as dead to him. But I had been wrong.

Me: "I would appreciate it if you would go now."

Welsh: "Of course. If there is anything I can do—"

Me: "There's nothing you can do."

He gets up, pauses as if contemplating some gesture of compassion. I pray that he doesn't think of one, and thankfully, he only nods and leaves.

I sit there for a long time. Then I stand up and look down at the communiqué sitting on the table, a slip of paper practically glowing with pain.

I can't touch it. I can't read it. I can't destroy it.

I leave it there and walk to my bedroom. I lie down and pull the covers over me.

JEFFERSON

I DO A LOT of thinking about Donna every day, like what she would do if she were here, what I would do if I were there, wherever there is, if there even is a there. She only has a there if she's still alive.

I think about whether it's worth keeping going, since I'll never see her again. Because I still haven't managed to slip the bonds of the pain that takes over every waking hour of her goneness. Like it's replaced the Sickness in my bones. Only there's no cure for it. Oh, I know they say that time cures everything. Maybe so. Not yet.

I try to shake it off and put my mind on the task at hand. I lay the barrel of the rifle on the cushion at the edge of the roof. I work out a good comfortable position on the mattress we dragged upstairs. I do a quick scan through the scope of the spots where the others are. The girls are slipping from Fifth Avenue onto Washington Mews, just parallel to Washington Square North. Chapel and Peter are waiting for Brainbox on West Eighth. My view of them jerks this way and that in the long lens of the scope.

I check the time on my Hello Kitty windup. Donna used to have the same kind. Now we have three of them, one with each team, synchronized to the second. Two minutes to go. I put my eye back to the scope and look in on the Square.

I can make out three or four Uptowners right away. The others must be obscured behind the buildings on Washington Square North. I dwell on their features, trying to distinguish one from the other so that we'll know how many are left if things go our way.

When I skip from one to the other for the third time, I see him—shaggy blond hair and high cheekbones. Evan. Brother of my dead occasional lover Kath. Murderer. Torturer.

I have him in my sights now. I can put a bullet in him if I just make a little beckoning gesture with my finger. I flick my eyes up to Hello Kitty. Still a minute and a half too soon. If I shoot him now, the others won't be in place.

I follow him around in the scope, hoping that he'll stay in view for a couple of minutes longer. But he slides under the cover of one of the townhouses. So I take hold of another Uptowner. He's on top of the school bus that serves as the north gate to the square, chilling in a puffy chair, his assault rifle across his lap. He seems to be sunning himself.

The hand of Hello Kitty is closing down on him. One more circuit, and I'm supposed to fire. I take in his slightly pudgy face, his dirty brown hair, his patchy growth of stubble. He's maybe sixteen. A kid like me. I think about who he was, his family, his friends, who he might have been if the Sickness hadn't happened. Maybe a life without harm, among loved ones, maybe even, with a little grace, a life with value and meaning.

Can I take the risk of sparing him? A half measure? A merciful blasting apart of his thigh? A generous symbolic maiming?

No. My people come first. When the second hand hits the twelve, I bear down on the scope and pull the trigger. Through the optics I see his head explode.

The kick of the shot shoves his body backward, and his chair tips over, spilling him down the side of the bus and onto the ground. The echo pulses around the Square, and everyone in the ten-acre expanse looks up, transformed suddenly into a passel of meerkats.

The Uptowners scurry to take cover in the school bus, where we want them. Ayesha, Holly, and Elena have made their way through the connecting back alleys of Washington Mews and Washington Square North, then through a basement hatch that only we know. Now they filter out into the Square, behind the defensive line of the gate. Ayesha and Holly cover the bus, while Carolyn and Elena drop to the ground about fifty feet from the door to Donna's old house. I hear the crack of gunfire; the first Uptowner must have tried to come out to help the guys in the bus. Carolyn and Elena keep plugging away at the unseen doorway while shouting for our people—any of them left in there—to get out.

I keep up my fire on the school bus, not certain if I'm hitting anything, but drawing a ragged return fire from the Uptowners inside. They don't realize they've been flanked until Ayesha starts yelling for our people to clear away from Donna's, and when they try to escape from the bus, Holly opens up on them.

A couple of our people stumble out from under the part of Donna's house blocked from my view; moments later, Carolyn sends up a flare that cuts the sky with a burning point of pink.

This is the signal for Brainbox, who has made his way to the back of Donna's building with Peter and Chapel from West Eighth Street.

A *smack* like two pieces of marble slapped together. A second later, a concussion wave blows my hair back. The black powder has lit up and ignited the propane through the carefully filed scoring on its tank, and the immolation of all the liquefied gas in the cylinder of metal tore it open and is spitting out a fearsome wave of pressure, pounding the air, smashing everything around it outward, heaving apart the tattered old supporting walls of the building on the other side.

The top of the building, loose of its support, sucks downward like sand through a funnel, and a titanic rumbling announces the floors beneath collapsing, collapsing, crushing.

After the rumbling, a hush.

I jump straight off the roof and take the fire escape down, the metal ladders clanging as they roll. As I reach the ground, I can hear shouting, the girls ordering the Uptowners still inside the bus to throw their guns out the windows.

"How do we know you won't kill us?" says a voice from inside. Broken and piteous.

"You don't," says Carolyn.

Nobody is looking north, so I make my way quickly to the bus. Peter, Brainbox, and Chapel are nowhere to be seen.

By the time I reach the bus, one of the kids inside is making a run for it, one leg already out a window. He sees me and in his panic gets stuck.

I take his gun, which is conveniently dangling out the window, and hit him in the face with the butt of the sniper rifle. He figures out a way to fall back into the bus.

Inside the Square, I find Brainbox, Peter, and Chapel entirely unscathed, accepting the congratulations of the rest of the tribe. The boys we left behind are gray and sallow-eyed, animated by the victory but lapsing occasionally into a glassy indifference.

From the front, Donna's old building looks like a movie façade, the sockets of the windows blank and staring, a frighteningly compact pile of rubble deposited in the middle. An autumn-like gust of paper and dust and scraps dances down through the air.

The three remaining Uptowners chunk down the steps of the bus, hands over their heads. "On your fucking knees!" says Carolyn, and they comply, their shinbones cracking into the ground. They look over at the collapsed building in astonishment. They're struck dumb, bovine. I don't see Evan among them. Maybe he's somewhere in that pile of stone.

A ring of boys from the tribe collects, staring at the Uptowners, gathering the courage for murder. For now, the compressed air of violence holds them back, but soon it will explode out, and nothing will save the prisoners. I'm not sure *I* want to save them.

Then Carolyn takes a knife from her belt and steps forward to loom over them. And I remember a picture of a man in orange, on his knees before a man in a salwar kameez, his beard poking from under a hood with two holes for eyes. The man in orange has a knife in his hand, not much bigger than a butter knife.

"Stop it," I say.

Carolyn turns to me. "Mind your own business."

"This *is* my business," I say. "I'm the head of this tribe."

"You *were* the head of the tribe!" Carolyn marches up to me, her voice breaking with anger. "You *left!*" Her knife hand is dancing with tension.

"I'm sorry," I say.

She spits on the ground in front of me.

"Carolyn, you're going to live a long time." I turn to the others. "You're all going to live a long time. What you do today lives inside of you."

Confusion. "Brainbox, show them."

He swings his backpack off his shoulders. "The Cure," he says.

The hatred starts to leak from their eyes. But Carolyn turns back to the Uptowners. I raise the rifle.

"Me?" she says. "You're pointing that at *me*?"

"You'll thank me," I say. "For keeping you from doing this. Someday you'll thank me."

She opens her fingers, and the knife drops to the ground.

"Get up," I say to the Uptowners. They don't move. I'm suddenly seized with rage. *"Get the fuck up!"* It seems they only understand abuse now. They find their way to standing.

"Go tell your tribe. Your 'Confederacy.' Tell them that the fighting is over. They send a representative to the UN. Ten days from today, at noon. If you want a chance to live past eighteen, you pass that message on."

DONNA

CHEERS," SAYS the beautiful guy from the noodle place, setting down his pint of beer.

They say "cheers" for pretty much everything here—it means "hi," and it also means "thanks," and it also means "good-bye."

And it also means "cheers." So—"Cheers," I say, for want of something better. I hold up my bottle of Bud. *Clink.*

True confession? I'm still only seventeen. So, back in the Old Country, this would have been against the law. Then again, the Old Country doesn't really exist anymore. It's the Young Country now. Anybody who would have taken away my fake ID is dead.

Anyhow, the drinking age is eighteen here, and since I look eighteenish, they don't bother to check. And the craziest thing? I am in the *college bar.* They actually have an official drinking establishment *inside the college* where you can get effed up.

All around, kids are doing just that, pounding pints of uncarbonated, hardly-more-than-room-temperature brown swill that they call "bitter," which tastes sort of like microbrew that somebody left open for days until it went flat. They love the stuff. When I ordered my Bud, the bartender said something about how American beer was "like having sex in a canoe—fucking close to water." But I don't drink it for the taste. I drink it to remind myself that the great American institution of Budweiser, shaggy advertising horses and all, has survived the apocalypse.

One gets the idea that Americans aren't too popular in these parts, probably on account of the huge influx of the Diaspora—which is what they call the Americans who were out of country when the Sickness hit. It's pronounced "die-ASS-poor-uh," and means a group of people who have been scattered. So basically I'm one of "the Dispersed." I'm a Disperson.

There's a whole undertow of feeling that I sense every time somebody finds out I'm part of the Diaspora. Like, there's some resentment, for sure. Like we're stretching the population too much, or taking people's jobs, or living off the government. Sort of the way people used to be dicks about undocumented immigrants back in the US. But *beneath* that, there's a sort of guilt. Like, sometimes people talk about *internment.* And even further beneath *that* is a sort of fear—like it's not just the Sickness that might be contagious, but also shitty luck, or a foul destiny. Like I'm some kind of monster.

With the result that I have not been able to Make New Friends that easily. It's not just the American Cooties, of course. I'm still trying to get my head around Jefferson being dead. All my friends. It feels like a betrayal to just go and make new ones. I'm a passenger in a fast car called grief, taking me who knows where. How could anyone get up to speed with me?

Plus, I'm not exactly geographically desirable. I'm the only student who lives in Nevile's Court. That's the library courtyard where I woke up the first time. My rooms—that's what they call it—and, in fact, I actually have a bedroom *and* a living room, it's mad luxurious—are up L staircase. That's just to the side of the workaday student library, as opposed to the razzmatazz version, the Wren Library, which has all the old stuff and manuscripts that would have given Jefferson a book boner. Anyhow, this must be handy to Welsh and Titch and everybody from a security point of view, but it sucks for social integration. Like, half the friends you make in college are supposed to be the fools who live in the same dorm as you.

Plus, the social life here is kind of lame. The college parties are these disgusting events called "sweaties," where you all jam into this basement room and the moment people start dancing, it gets superhot and all the vaporized sweat collects on the black stucco ceiling and drips down on everybody. This is considered a good time, but the one time I took a look, it gave me flashbacks to the Moles and the firefight in the subway tunnels by Grand Central, and I just couldn't deal.

Still, after weeks of lying in bed crying, then dry of tears, practically force-fed by Titch, I realize I can't just let myself die. Even though it seems like the easiest thing to do—the hunger is nothing I haven't known, and Death cozies up to me and licks my face like a Labrador puppy.

But I can't, even if it means walking around with my guts hanging out. Like, that would be a waste of everything we did, everything we sacrificed. I realize Jeff would tell me I am being stupid, that here is a chance at a real life. And I like the *idea* of being part of the whole campus (they don't call it that) community (that either) and whatnot. So of late I have been setting myself up in a snug little corner of the college bar and nursing (get it? nursing?) a couple of Buds through the evening, being generally lonely and miserable.

And now Beautiful Guy has come and spoiled everything.

Me: "I've seen you at Wagamama."

Beautiful Guy: "Yeah. Mine's the number forty-one. You?"

Me: "Forty-two with rice noodles."

Beautiful Guy: "Hmm."

He says it like it's an interesting reflection on my character. Then, "My name is Rob," he says. Which doesn't really seem right, since he doesn't look or sound like a Rob. More of a Vikram.

Me: "Rob?"

Rob: "No, Rab."

He says it with a slight *a* sound. Like with a Chicago accent.

Rab: "It's short for Rabindranath."

Me: "Whoa. Rabindranath."

Rab (of my pronunciation): "Not bad. Still, it's a little too much work for most people. So, Rab."

Me: "My name is Donna. It's actually short for Madonna, not the mother of Jesus but the pop star."

Rab: "That's even worse."

Me: "Yeah, tell me about it."

Rab: "So, not to sound cheesy or whatever..." There's a cute little nasal thing going on with the *r* sound at the end of his words—I mean, it's miles from Apu on *The Simpsons* and everything, but there's just the tiniest bit of a twist to the otherwise fancy-pants accent. "But I've noticed you hanging around. By yourself."

Me: "Yeah."

I want to explain myself, since I guess it's sort of nice for him to notice and say hi and whatnot, and besides he is gorgeous, not like I want to get with him or anything, but you sort of can't help wanting beautiful people to like you sometimes. But I don't. Explain myself, that is.

Rab: "Okay. So then I'll tell you a little about myself."

He doesn't say this in a snarky way, just as though he is indicating, *I'll do the heavy lifting for now, to make you feel more comfortable.* It's very unselfconscious and disarming.

He tells me about how his fam is from Kolkata, which is the city they used to call Calcutta, which is famous for being incredibly poor and miserable except it's not all that way. In fact, it is the literary hub of West Bengal, which is the most artistic state in India, and his family is old and wealthy. He doesn't make a big deal out of this, doesn't act like it should make me like him or as though he wants to throw them under a bus so that he can seem more normal or whatever. Just telling things like they are. So for centuries his family has sent kids to England to get educated, and Rab went to this brainiac school called St. Paul's, where at first he was sad and homesick and then he started to like it. So now he's at Trinity reading history, which he loves.

At Trinity it's kind of Not Cool to say you love what you're studying. At least, that's what I've gleaned from my various broken bits of conversation and eavesdropping. Like, everybody has probably busted their ass to get here, and they're always conscious, what with living in these incredibly beautiful medieval-castle-like places, that they're superlucky and privileged, even if they *have* busted their asses, so they cop this attitude where they could give two shits about it and they don't study and all they want to do is watch Australian soap operas and get wasted. So it's a little refreshing to hear from somebody who actually appreciates being here.

So I tell him the whole lie, the stuff about how I'm a navy brat and my dad's on the Reconstruction Committee.

Rab: "But you don't hang out with the other Americans."

That's true. I have, like, zero interest in hanging with the Other Americans, who kind of strut around like rich cousins.

Me: "Oh, them. They can blow me."

Rab: "Yeah, they can blow me, too, mostly. Except I've met some really nice people from the Diaspora, too."

He's got this honest, open thing going that reminds me loads of Jefferson, like, an innocent sort of embrace of the world and people and what they have to offer. Like being nice counts for something.

Me: "There's a friend of mine you'd have liked."

Rab: "We'll get everybody together."

Me: "Yeah, sure."

Then—I'm not proud of this—I look at my new phone. Because there has been the tiniest lapse in the conversation, like, a millisecond, and I'm embarrassed, and my attention wants to flee to someplace more comfortable. Frankly, it's been my only companion through all the cold days of mourning.

This sort of flight from the present moment used to go down all the time back before What Happened; so much that it had been sort of agreed upon by everybody that it was okay—like, you could just be in the middle of a conversation with a friend and it was perfectly acceptable to bail for a bit and check Twitter or e-mail or your texts or whatever. People got used to being kind of half in and half out of conversations. It was sort of like being there and being someplace else at the same time, but the other place was this weird mental realm of quasi-communication, a kind of magic zone where you were receiving pulses of attention and interest from far away.

Except here, it's become cool to *ignore* your phone, like, to triumph over the seduction and remain In the Moment, and people take it badly if you just wander off to Internetville. Which is a problem for me because I have been away from working phones for *so* long and they've gotten *so* good at distracting you, like, miles better than what we had.

Nothing interesting has occurred in the five minutes since I last checked it, though. I look up and see Rab watching me.

Me: "I'm really sorry."

I blush, because this is the first person I've had an actual conversation with in the past week besides Titch, and I don't want to accidentally tear the little thread suddenly tying me to the rest of humanity.

Rab (shrugs it off): "Who's your buddy?"

This is not as strange a question as it sounds. Apparently, while I was scavenging for out-of-date canned tuna and exchanging gunfire with assorted psychos in the streets of Manhattan, Apple and Samsung and whatnot were amping up the performance of their phone software agents, like Siri and Cortana and whatever. They've gotten *really* good, like, they don't sound like freaky robots anymore, and they're all wired up to the Internet, and they're learning as they go along, so there are times when you could almost think you were really talking to a living person. It's not like that Scarlett Johansson movie where they can have phone sex with you, or anything, but they're superhelpful, and what's even cooler is that you can buy these personalities to lay over them. Like, you can have regular Siri, or you can buy a sort of bro version who is especially tweaked to talk about sports and tell you when soccer matches are on and stuff, or a hot-chick version (if you happen to be a total loser) who is always making you feel awesome and is down with porn and whatever. You can buy celebrity versions, too, like, all these musicians and actors have hired out their voices, so you can get a flirty Brad Pitt version. (Yeah, he made it out before the Sickness. Vital cultural asset.)

The problem with the believability of these "buddies," or "peeps," or "personae," as some people call them, is that they all kind of share the same basic wiring, which is that they want to sell you shit. Like, Brad Pitt will be all "may I say that you look especially fetching today?" but then suddenly he'll be all "hey, I just found out that they've got the new fall outfits in at French Connection." Which doesn't *really* seem like Brad. But if you go deep, you can start tweaking the settings, so that you can opt out of certain ads. You can even up the personality features so that, instead of being on it all the time, buddies can exhibit more normal personality features, like spacing out every once in a while, and then apologizing when you call them on it. Like, there's a stoner buddy who isn't 100 percent reliable but who is really great at just hanging out and suggesting cool shit to search for.

As you can imagine, buddies like Kine Budz Brah (that's the stoner buddy) are not exactly what Apple and Microsoft had in mind, so technically they're not allowed, but if you jailbreak your phone, you can use them. It's just too big a business to stamp out.

So who's my buddy?

I don't really feel like talking about it.

Me: "Who's yours?"

Rab: "Naanii."

He starts up his buddy app and a picture of a really cute, plump gray-haired lady in a sari appears. You can add plug-ins where the buddy moves on-screen and whatever, but most people prefer to just talk to theirs.

"What can I do for you, darling?" A comforting elderly voice with a slightly lilting Indian accent. Rab smiles sheepishly.

Rab: "She reminds me of my grandmother in Kolkata."

The "Naanii" buddy hears his tone of voice and chips in with a loving little chuckle.

I can't help but smile. A grandma's boy.

Rab: "I know, it's lame. I spend way too much time tweaking her. You'd be amazed at what sort of character features you can get on the open-source sites."

Me: "I love it. Hello, Naanii!"

Naanii analyzes the tone of my voice and responds, "Hello, dear!" then remarks, as if confidentially, to Rab, "She seems a very nice girl."

Rab: "All right, Naanii. Good-bye for now."

Naanii: "Good-bye, darling," as Rab closes her app.

Me: "Your buddy is very friendly."

Rab: "Yes. It can be a bit of a pain sometimes. She doesn't always appreciate being closed. And she can be quite nosy. But—life wasn't meant to be easy all the time. May I—"

He reaches out for my iPhone. I nod, and he picks it up and expertly starts gesturing through my settings.

Me: "What are you doing?"

Rab: "I'm shutting off your microphone's passive receiver. Don't worry, I do this for everybody. It's just that nobody thinks to do it. Now your phone won't hear what you're saying unless you want it to."

Me: "You mean . . . it's always listening?"

Rab: "The government snuck it into the latest telecom bill. It's on page one-seventeen of the end-user license agreement you agree to."

Me: "I never read those."

Rab: "Nobody does." (He hands the phone back to me.) "Now they can't listen to your conversations."

Me: "They do that?"

Rab: "Oh, yeah. They run everything through speech analysis algorithms. Say the wrong combination of words, and you'll get a visit from the Met or your dad's pals in the Reconstruction Joint Security Scheme."

I take a while to absorb this idea. Rab takes it as my feeling attacked.

Rab: "I'm sorry. I didn't mean to offend you."

Me: "You didn't. Thanks for letting me know."

He downs the rest of his bitter, then does the usual gathering-yourself motions that mean *I'm about to leave,* and I suddenly feel sad that he's about to go, but then he says—

Rab: "Shall we?"

Me: "Shall we what?" Is he propositioning me?

Rab: "I'm going to show you the town. Well, what I know of the town. It won't do for you to just sit in the corner of the bar drinking Budweiser and talking to your top secret buddy."

At "top secret," a jet of anxiety shoots through me, like he knows all about the deal with Welsh and the Foreign Office and MI this and MI that, and he knows that I've been lying to him, and suddenly I feel downright naked. But then I see from his face that he's just teasing me because I wouldn't show it to him (introduce him, I guess?).

Me: "Okay. Shall we? We shall."

Only problem is, usually whenever I leave college, Titch or Taut

Guy (actually his name is Vince) either accompany me or keep an eye on me from a distance. This makes me feel a lot like the president's daughter in a lame rom-com or something, like I always kind of want to ditch them so that I can have adventures and whatnot. To be honest, I've mostly enjoyed the company, but I don't want to spook my new friend by having us followed around by my own personal Chewbacca.

Me: "Listen. Not to be all *First Kid* about this, but it might be an idea to give my bodyguard the slip."

Rab: "Ah. *First Kid.* Sinbad, Brock Pierce, Disney, 1996. Not to be confused with *First Daughter,* starring Katie Holmes and Marc Blucas."

Me: "Wow. Impressive."

Rab: "Depressing, actually. Brain space I would rather have for something else. You want to do a runner on your gigantic minder?"

Me: "Yeah, Titch. He minds me. And he minds me going too far out in the world, I think, which is totally ridiculous because everything here is so goddamn safe."

Rab: "Well... there's the fire exit in the men's bog. The alarm is broken. Gives out onto Trinity Lane."

Trinity Lane, aka Pisspot Lane, according to Rab, is an echoey, spooky alley between Trinity and Caius (which, in another example of their desire to make everything harder than it has to be, British people pronounce "Keys"). It's one of the spots in town where you can convince yourself you're not in the present at all. We clop along the cobbles toward Trinity Street, the main drag.

Me: "Where to?"

Rab: "A random walk. Coin toss."

We get to the bottom of the lane and, the coin coming down tails, take a right past King's.

I feel kind of like a dick cutting out on Titch. I mean, we're homeys and all, but I figure since he usually just chills outside the bar anyway, I can be back before he knows I'm gone. It's still a couple of hours to last orders. Besides, it feels amazing to be out in the cool air, scuffing over damp paving stones.

Somebody calls from across the street—a girl and a dude wearing purple college scarves that show they're from King's. "Hey! Rab!"

Rab: "Hey, yourselves!"

Me: "You know somebody from *another college*?"

I overemphasize it like I'm joking, but in fact I'm a little impressed.

High fives and greetings that wouldn't have been out of place in Detroit before It Happened. The girl is called Soph; the boy is Michael. He's from Northern Ireland, which apparently is different from Southern Ireland; she's from "London," which she says in a sort of embarrassed, unspecific way, which I take to mean she's rich.

Rab: "This is Donna. Not for the mother of Jesus, but the pop star."

Me: "I'm American."

Which is kind of stupid, but I want to get it out of the way.

Michael: "Oh, we love fallen empires, don't we, Soph?"

Michael is small and sprightly. He seems to be giving Soph a good-natured hard time.

Sophie (affectionately, to Michael): "Piss off." (Then to Rab and me.) "We were just considering how we could find Oliver Cromwell's skull in Sydney Sussex and steal it."

Michael: "If I took it back to Ireland, I'd be a fecking hero. Free drinks for life."

I do know sort of that Oliver Cromwell was some kind of English Civil War dude, but I have no idea why his skull is kept in one of the colleges, or why it would be such a big deal to Irish people.

Michael explains the deal to me while we head to a party they've invited us to. (Basic deal: Oliver Cromwell invaded Ireland and killed and enslaved shitloads of people.) He even illustrates it with a croony rendition of a song by some guy called Morrissey. Rab and Soph and Michael and I chat away, and they don't treat me like a freak, and I start to *feel* like I'm not a freak, and somehow, with just this little bit of human contact in the right place in my brain, I start to get a sense of a future that isn't just to the end of the day, and feel something besides grief.

The party is at somebody's digs (i.e., crib) in Portugal Place, which is sort of like off-campus housing but in these cute little

169

townhouses. Your usual, music and cigarettes and beer and vodka, kids testing themselves out conversationally on one another, trying to get laid or make friends or just let go of themselves for a bit. It's utterly ordinary. And utterly fun. For a few hours, I'm not even thinking about Jeff, much. Soph and I hang out, and I learn a bit about her, like she's from this upper-crusty family, but she's totally not down with her parents and their attitudes about the government and economics and whatnot. At one point, she's talking about politics or whatever, and she's telling me about how the US Navy bombed the shit out of Iran so that they could keep control of the Shatt al Arab, which is this choke hold that ships have to pass through for oil to get from the Middle East to the rest of the world. There's still a carrier strike group hanging out there. Seems that the thing about the home country going down is that the military took it as a free pass to throw its weight around without anybody being able to strike back, so they basically sell their services to the highest bidder, at least that's how Soph sees it. Needless to say, this is not how Welsh or anybody else put it to me. Soph is talking about the likelihood of a war with China and then stops and looks at me.

Soph: "Shit, you're not going to grass me out to the Reconstruction Committee, are you?"

Me: "Grass you out?"

Soph: "Oh." (She laughs. Then, in a run of American-accent-inflected synonyms, she goes—) "Bust me. Turn me in. Shop me. Drop a dime. Turn stool pigeon."

It's amazing how many American idioms these people know,

but then, they've kind of been studying the infection of their culture by ours for decades.

Me: "Hell, no!"

I mean it, but then I feel terrible about my bullshit cover story, and I decide, then and there, that whatever I tell Welsh about, I am not saying *shit* about my new friends. There's something good and real happening, and I'm not going to eff it up.

After a while, Michael reappears, and he's plastered. He says he made out with some dude but then the dude's girlfriend showed up so it's time for him to leave. Rab peels himself away from a group of crunchy-granola-looking kids he's been holding forth to—he seems to be quite the Big Man on What They Don't Call Campus—and he and Soph and I help Michael out the door.

It's been a long time since I was hanging out. Like, yeah, I've been around people, and, yeah, even my friends when we were on the *Ronald Reagan,* but that was all so *fraught.* I had forgotten what it was like to spend time with people just spending time, without there being something heavy going down. So just helping this dude home, making sure he doesn't hurl on us, is a great, totally life-affirming experience.

The streets are very quiet this late, and it's surprising that I don't see the bunch of guys until we're almost on top of them. They're probably not much older than us, but I can instantly tell that there's a *difference,* mostly because of the hostility that's radiating off them.

They're hanging around on the corner, drinking from tallboy cans and smoking. Jean jackets and sneakers, shitty normcore

171

haircuts. They're eyeing the purple scarves that Michael and Soph are wearing.

I'm getting a clear "townie" vibe here, like for sure they have done a scan of us and determined that we are students and they don't like us. I guess you could say that we have scanned one another, like, superquickly and with 100 percent accuracy, because one of the guys throws away his cigarette butt in a sort of practiced tough-guy gesture and says, half to himself, kind of just putting it out there, "Fuckin' poof."

Now, I'm not certain, but I'm pretty sure that "poof" is a mean name for a gay guy. Tough Guy must have, like, an amazing gaydar, which would make perfect sense, given that homophobes are often latent homosexuals trying to keep their feelings at bay; anyhow, it doesn't really matter. It's a little trial balloon, a pebble thrown into the pond of our awareness so that they can watch the fear ripple out. And sure enough, Soph and Rab just lower their heads and keep maneuvering Michael along.

A squirt of adrenaline runs along my bones.

I don't really feel like pretending that I didn't hear anything, so I keep on looking at them, which earns a "what you lookin' at?" from the guy standing next to the guy who said "poof."

And, I know I probably shouldn't do this. Like, I ought to have just done whatever would have gotten us home fastest and safest. But I suddenly feel that I've gone through just *far* too much in *far* scarier situations than this, and eff it. So I say—

"A piece of shit in denim."

Pretty good, right? I'm not usually much at comebacks. And just processing this takes them a second, enough for us to pass through them, and who knows, maybe that would have been that, had the guy only laughed it off, but, unfortunately, it's his *buddy* that laughs first, which means that instead of being a bro who's cool enough to laugh off an insult from a chick, he's a bro who's been shown up in front of his other bros.

So now he can't let it lie or let it pass. And he opts for the go-to, the baseline insult for a bro to call a girl.

"The fuck you say, c——nt?"

So, as indicated, there's a kind of logic and geometry to all this, and, theoretically, if I were able to just swallow the c-word and move on without a response, we could get away with no more than a bit of mocking laughter at our backs. But, hey.

I turn around. "Did I *stutter,* bitch? Let me repeat myself. A dick-less piece of shit in an ugly jacket his mama patches for him when she's not blowing truckers."

So there's a frozen moment here when it could go either way. Basically there's a does-not-compute kind of situation going on with the dudes, because, in theory, they're not allowed to fight girls. No, for them, presumably, it's only okay to hit their *girlfriends*. So we *still* might get away unscathed, except—

Rab seems to think that he has to play the chivalry card and defend my honor, which is sweet and everything, but it's not like I'm defenseless. It's nice of him, I guess, to say, "Don't call her that," over Soph's urgent, "Don't."

Which doesn't really make any sense, since they've already called me "that," so what does he want, an official retraction? I can tell that Rab doesn't exactly know what he's doing; he's nervous as hell, probably knowing that he's going to get his ass handed to him any moment now. Which makes me appreciate his gesture even more, since his mouth is writing checks his body can't cash.

Everything starts proceeding along predictable lines. The townie dudes do some throwing away of beer cans—throwing stuff away seems to be the really macho thing to do these days—and an as-yet-unheard-from genius says, "What did you say, Paki?"

Not exactly eloquent, that reuse of the old "what did you say?" trope. And I think *Paki* is kind of like saying the n-word except directed at Indian people. Let's leave aside for the moment the fact that Pakistan is an entirely different country last time I checked.

They're coming toward us now, and probably the best thing to do in this situation would be to run, but for one thing, I'm not sure Michael is exactly in shape for running, so leave no man behind and all that jazz, and for another thing, fuck that noise.

So I walk up to the guys, saying, hands up and palms empty, in as soothing a voice as I can, "Hey, guys, look. I'm sorry about what I said. We don't want to fight. Let me buy you a drink."

This sort of scrambles their brains for a moment, because (a) since these guys have a totally Neanderthal mind-set, they don't realize that girls can fight, too, so they're not even concentrating on me, and (b) somewhere in even the angriest dude's mind is the thought that they might maybe just maybe get laid.

So one of them, presumably the group's theoretical Romeo, takes his beady eyes off Rab and turns to me, with a sort of amorous look. "'Smore like it, love," he says, cocking his head back.

Which suits me just fine, since it makes it easy to punch him as hard as I can in the neck. The Adam's apple, to be precise. Hit somebody hard enough there, they won't be doing or saying much anytime soon. It's kind of tough to pull off in a world where people are walking around with guns, even in a situation where somebody *expects* that you'll be fighting them. Fortunately for me, this moron was thinking he might get some action. So there's a ripe sort of *crunch*, and he staggers back, holding his throat, spitting up blood and wheezing.

A sudden storm of expletives from both sides as everybody realizes what just went down. Then the guy's buddy, at least one of the ones who isn't helping him to the ground, takes a swing at me. Now, this isn't an action movie or anything, so I don't dodge it, but I am at least a little ready, so it sort of bounces off my shoulder.

The guy's now right on me, which would be a problem except for the knife I bought in the market square the other day. I've already unsheathed it from its spot on my hip, and now I jam it as hard as I can into his knee.

He screams in pain—I can't really blame him—and stumbles backward, almost taking the knife with him, but I yank it out, ready for the next guy. Except, the two unscathed dudes have made a very

175

quick estimate of their prospects and have decided to pursue the path of nonviolence. One of them takes off down the street like a little bitch, and the other, to his credit, drags Mr. Adam's Apple away as the dude with the now-bisected kneecap staggers after them. There's no "you'll pay for this!" or anything like that. These guys are, after all, just some drunk shitheads, not the feral tribesmen I'm used to.

Me, I'm going to have a nasty contusion on my ear and a sore shoulder, but right now I'm too juiced with adrenaline and endorphins and whatnot to notice. I daresay I'm downright ecstatic, albeit also on the edge of tears, because it isn't very nice to punch and stab people, and at heart I'm a nice girl.

If this were a Wachowski movie or something, I'd probably be all coiled up in a balletically badass pose, but, in fact, I'm on my knees, having fallen forward when I pulled my knife out of the guy's cartilage. So I pick myself up and turn to the others, pretty sure that they're going to be gaping at me in sheer horror and disgust.

I've had a kind of epiphany in the short moment of turning around, which is about fighting and violence. I used to think that the reason I was scared of fighting was that I was scared of getting hurt. Which I was. But beyond that, the reason I was scared of getting hurt was that I knew I was less willing to inflict hurt than the other person. Like, part of winning a fight, beyond the obvious fact of being better at it than someone else, is getting over all the societal conditioning that tells you it's wrong to hurt people. That, and the fact that it's kind of intensely *intimate* as well, an extremely emotional sort of *connection* with the person whose ass you're kicking.

As far as violence is concerned, I lost my innocence and my fear long ago. And those fools currently dragging their bleeding asses along the street had thought they were dealing with a virgin.

So when I turn back to the others, I feel like they're going to see the, like, pox-addled face of someone so debauched with violence that she's barely even human anymore. And I'm already mourning the friendships that might have been.

But instead, they erupt into applause. Like, somehow they've been anesthetized with the same drug that made it possible for me to do the things I just did. Maybe it's just surprise. Maybe it's a hitherto unrecognized sadism. They're all "whoaaaa!" and "wick-eeeed!" and "I don't believe it!" and "that was so badass!" They come up and hug me and slap me on the back and shake their heads in amazement, and the only sign that it's incredibly weird is that Michael leans over and vomits.

Alone back in L6 Nevile's Court, I ride the swell of adrenaline down to where it bottoms out in exhaustion and shame. I think of the guy with a reorganized windpipe and the guy with a permanently fucked knee and wonder if the moral equation wouldn't have balanced out better with them intact and me humiliated instead. I try to breathe through it. This isn't me—this is more like Jeff, like he's always watching me from somewhere and I'm influenced by him as an audience, even though he's gone. Or is he, really? I feel like I feel him. Jefferson was a Buddhist, and he was always all, like, *we're just bits of the universe who mistakenly think we're separate entities*. Maybe some of his atoms are floating around me, or he's looking for a baby to incarnate.

Enough of that. I'm getting sick of my own company, so I give my phone a little rub.

Charlie: "Hi!"

It's a childish little voice, the voice of a five-year-old boy. As close to my little brother Charlie's voice as I could manage.

Me: "Hi, monkey."

Charlie: "What time is it?"

The little boy voice sounds sleepy. Some programmer worked hard on this.

Me: "Dude, you know that. You're a cell phone."

A tiny delay.

Charlie: "No, I'm not. I'm software."

He—it—pronounces it "softwayew," with a lisp just like Charlie's. A deep hit of nostalgia and love and pain.

Me: "That's right, you're softwayew."

Charlie: "Wow—it's after midnight! What did you do tonight, Donna?"

The seams between its coded bursts of manufactured speech are almost impossible to hear.

Me: "I met some people."

Charlie: "You met some people?"

He often operates by paraphrasing language cues or parroting them back.

Me: "Yeah. Nice people."

Charlie: "That's good."

Me: "Yeah. But I'm glad to be back here alone. With you."

Charlie: "Me too."

Then, after a silence—

Charlie: "Donna, I love you."

Me: "I love you, too, Charlie."

And I cry some and fall asleep.

PETER

IT'S LIKE THIS. I'M NOT A SIDEKICK, I just play one in life.

People want to categorize other people, they want to label, they want to simplify so that they can deal with them more efficiently. Appreciating nuance is not a big priority, and bandwidth is limited. So to most folks, I'm the gay best friend, or the gay black guy, or just the gay dude. Safely marginalized.

And truth to tell? I've been content to play the part. I mean, just that little pocket of air in the drowning pool that is society has been enough at times. For the boy who grew up different, knocked down, beat up, at times it was enough just to have any place at all. I had my thing. I knew the job description.

Yeah, you could call it a niche position. I mean, do you know how rare it is for a brother like me to see himself represented on TV or in the movies or whatnot? Like, probably, when you read these words and hear this voice in your head, which is your voice but not your voice, both me and you in that weird way that you do when you're reading?

Probably you think to yourself, as I/you describe my life, *That's not me.* Maybe you're even put off, like, concerned whether my voice is going to say something that your voice doesn't want to say, anything super-*gay*, that will refer to doing or feeling things that you're not comfortable doing or feeling. It's the same way with me every time I read the story where the guy gets the girl. Or even the girl gets the guy. Still not me. I want to be the guy who gets the guy.

But don't worry. That voice in your head can't change you, not for real. All it can do is help you see what it's like to be another person. Maybe.

For a while, down at Stonewall High School, life was better. Stonewall was founded for the gay kids, the trans kids, the non-cisgendered kids. Everybody thought they were a special snowflake. I had a life out of the shadows and the closet, I had friends, I had boyfriends, I had room to breathe, the whole nine.

Of course, there *was* one relationship people weren't exactly copacetic with, which was me and my homeboy Jesus. They said the Bible says homosexuality's a sin. I said Leviticus says eating crustaceans is a sin, too, and ending your marriage is a sin, which makes any divorced guy eating a lobster *exponentially* worse than me. Besides, JC came to change all that anyways. Call that cafeteria Christianity? Picking and choosing what I like? Well, *I* call bullshit. Cafeteria Christianity is what the Evangelicals went in for. They chose the God-Jesus of the Book of John, not the person-Jesus of Matthew, Mark, and Luke. *I* say the majority wins.

Anyhow, it was okay, me and the other queers and Jesus. We were cool. Then the Sickness comes and tears everything up. Lot of the kids head home to their dying folks. Some of us don't have much of a home to head back to, so we hang out. Most of us get knocked off in the ensuing land grab/ethnic cleanse/tribal Harry-Potter-sorting-hat massacre that follows.

Me, I end up inside the walls of Washington Square along with some other Stonewall survivors and the Catholic kids from Holy Cross and Wash's bunch from the Learning Outpost or whatever they called that crunchy granola school they were from. Me and Wash and his little brother, Jefferson, we were cool, though Wash was tough enough about any other kids joining up after he figured out the carrying capacity of the land and the local scavenging grounds. Hence the whole gated medieval fortress thing.

It was there I met Donna. I can't say that I was in the market for a fag hag or anything—it was never my thing—but I liked her right away. That's not how it was anyhow. I mean, living off the fat of the land before It Happened, sure, a girl had all sorts of leisure for things like Accessory Friends. *After*, friendship was for real, not some style thing. I had that bitch's *back*, which is why I made the damn fool decision to go with her that day she and Jefferson were heading up to the public library. It was only supposed to take an hour or two. Worst time estimate since Gilligan's motherfucking Island.

Anyhoo.

I miss her. I do. I think about her lying out on a beach in Hawaii, a tan, buff waiter bringing her a mai tai or whatnot. I *hope* she's out there enjoying herself for the rest of us. Because me, I have returned from the fire to the original frying pan.

Except it's all okay. 'Cause I'm mainlining a drug called Love.

Okay, maybe a drug cocktail of love and lust.

I know what you're thinking—wasn't I in love with Theo? Well, okay, maybe I did find the whole Strong Silent Brother thing kind of intriguing. But Theo turned out to be 100 Percent Grade-A Straight and, contrary to stereotype, not every gay man is trying to seduce straight boys like they were some kind of video game achievement to unlock or whatever. Never wanted to go to a party where I wasn't invited. It was enough to make me want to take my gaydar into the shop for repairs, but it didn't break my heart or anything.

Now, Chapel—that's a different matter. Homey is going in on stealth mode and shit. I don't know if the Very Large Array telescope of gaydar would register him as so much as a blip. So when I catch him a few times eyeballing me like I'm some piece of modern art he's trying to figure out the meaning of, I figure he's just doing some fifth-column, French Resistance, special-forces threat-assessment thing. Trust no one and all.

Well, turns out he has taken a shine to yours truly. And I shine right back at him. And damn if it isn't a lot like being alive.

Consider if you will how difficult it is to be a little gay black kid. Consider not having the choice to be a little *straight* black kid. Consider that the life you want to have, which is so much like the life everybody else wants to have except for this one tiny difference, is, because of this difference, seen as an abomination or a joke or a tragedy. And then, just when things start to look up, like, we can get married and hold hands in the street and all kinds of stuff that boring people do, the apocalypse hits.

Definitely thins out the dating pool.

But here's Chapel, all purpose and commitment and sacrifice and *hot*.

And all mine. Maybe.

Oh, it's not like he's got a boyfriend or anything. I think I'm pretty much his only option at the moment, which is kind of encouraging. And he seems to like me. Like, lots. It's just that he's all mission. Setting up this thing at the UN, getting the Cure out, is all he thinks about. Well, *almost* all. Honestly, I never thought I'd meet anybody more idealistic than Jefferson. But Chapel actually chose to risk his life to save people he doesn't even *know*. I don't get it.

But I'm not complaining.

We're still maintaining the bullshit story that he's some random we met on Plum Island. And I have to sit on the biggest piece of gossip in human history. But I get it. Shit would get real pretty quick if everybody knew they were missing out on the Lush Life out there beyond the ocean. Chapel says the truth will be told eventually. I'm not looking forward to the lynch mob when they find out we've been neglecting to mention a few teeny, tiny little things like the survival of human civilization, but for now, everybody's buying it.

Apart from Carolyn, there's not a whole lot of guilt-tripping about our disappearance. Actually, most everybody thought we were dead, so we're kind of instant celebrities. Which is funny. Donna always said I just wanted to be famous. Now I am.

And *Jefferson* is a superstar. It's not just that he was the leader of the expedition that led to the Cure. It's something more, because the serum or whatever is made from his blood.

We use the big Moroccan tent to administer the doses, since Donna's infirmary is nothing but a pile of bricks now. And damned if it doesn't look a little familiar to me, the crowd of waiting supplicants, the solemn administering of the precious gift. You Catholic kids will know what I mean. It's a religious happening, a medical Mass. Brainbox may as well be saying, "The blood of Jefferson," as he drops the Cure onto their tongues. As each of the kids walks away, savoring the nothing-taste in his mouth, he makes sure to find Jefferson and embrace him. Tears of gratitude. Worship. Some serious first-commandment-breaking in the offing: *I am a jealous God. Thou shalt put no other gods above me.*

In a dark corner of the tent, Chapel looks on, smiling. "That's my boy."

"I thought I was your boy," I say.

"Oh, you are," he says, and flashes the blinding beam of his smile into my eyes. "But I think I just realized. We've got our new king."

"Jefferson?" I say. "I think you've got the wrong guy. Jefferson's all Occupy Apocalypse. Like truth, justice, and the democratic way."

"We'll see," says Chapel, and gives me a don't-worry-your-pretty-little-head kind of wink.

Jefferson does have a Big Plan, of course. It's typically pie-in-the-sky.

The idea is to call a Gathering of the Tribes at the UN. Unite all the survivors in Manhattan and form a sort of supertribe. Stop fighting over limited resources and help one another.

Leaving aside the possibility that the UN may first have to be cleared of spree-killing cannibals for all we know, the idea is cockamamie for a bunch of reasons. Not the least is that everybody hates one another. And with good reason. There's not a grocery store on the whole island where you won't find the skeleton of some kid murdered by some other kid over the last bag of Kibbles 'n Bits. And the Uptowners? Man, how am I supposed to make peace with those fascist, misogynist, homophobic crackers? And by the way, what did they do to the girls?

Brainbox says it'll come down to rational decisions about how we want to live. But I know that most decisions *aren't* rational. Especially political ones.

But when I tell that to Jefferson, he has a snappy response.

"So? Politics is just the organization of hatreds," he says. I know he got that from somewhere, but I'm not going to give him the pleasure of telling me. "We don't have to love one another. We just have to understand that it's in our interests to *act* that way."

There's barely time to settle into the old crib before we head back on the road. Chapel follows me up the dark stairwell, down the dark hallway, into my dark apartment. I throw open the blinds I closed months ago, and my giant Facebook wall is struck by the sun.

Chapel says, "You know nobody uses Facebook anymore, right?"

"You trying to make me feel old?"

Chapel has a look in his eye, and if it's not pity, it's definitely pity-adjacent. Like, you poor, poor boy, all you've been through.

"What?" I say. "Don't feel so bad for me. I would *never* have been able to afford this place if it weren't for the apocalypse."

He laughs—I appreciate that.

The last time I was here, I was gearing up for my little jaunt with Donna. It was a blue spring day, pleasant but for the smell of decay, and our whole lives were behind us. Now who knows?

I walk over to the Facebook wall. Wipe out the status **Out kicking ass**. Pick up a piece of chalk and write **in love**.

He doesn't laugh.

JEFFERSON

CHIQUITA, OUR BELOVED armored pickup truck, was put to the torch by the Uptowners outside of the public library long ago, so we've got to proceed by foot to the UN, which occupies a big complex of buildings by the East River in the Forties. There's about twenty of us, sporting rifles and as much food as the camp can spare. Given our latest run-in with the Uptowners, we figure it's best to head east first, outside their turf, before heading north.

It's a no-man's-land most of the way to the river, except for a little enclave at Tompkins Square Park in the East Village. Before What Happened, this used to be a hot spot for heroin, then it was a sort of homeless campground for a bit, then yuppies started buying up the buildings around the square and the cops booted all the transients out. Now it's back to a pregentrification feel, nylon tents by the basketball courts and mangy dogs prowling the perimeter. The local tribe calls themselves the Dead Rabbits, which they got from some movie or other, and they're working a sort of hipster, murderer vibe with a lot of old hats and wooden clubs.

We exchange a few trade goods (cigarettes, bullets) and spread the gospel of the Gathering of the Tribes. I promise them they won't regret it.

On we go up the East River, with a flock of kids following now. People hover close, as if, because the Cure came from my blood, there's something magic about me. When a sailboat full of Fishermen—river pirates—slips up the water toward us, my people safety-tackle me the way the Secret Service used to do to the president in movies. But the Fishermen don't want to fight; for one thing, we're too many and too well armed, and for another, they're curious about seeing two tribes together strolling up the FDR Drive. Chapel evangelizes, and soon enough, they've been recruited to spread the word up and down the island.

The United Nations Secretariat is a big concrete slab shadowing the river up around Fortieth. We cut in from the water, over the shell that makes a tunnel of the FDR, to the front of the UN.

We come to a statue that looks like a giant revolver whose barrel has been twisted and tied off.

A body hangs from it. The statue isn't actually big enough to have served as a gallows; this was just a convenient or symbolic place from which to suspend a corpse. There's a piece of paper pinned to the body. I recognize the writing as Cyrillic, but can't translate. Presumably it's the name of the crime he committed.

We arrived in a state of optimism, and this lowers our spirits just a bit. It also makes me realize that for some reason we had presumed the UN complex would be uninhabited. Now the buildings seem anything but hollow and inert. I think about the halls of the public library and the cannibals living there. If they get the message about the Gathering, will they come? Can they ever be turned back to sanity and civilization? Should they be? Or should they be put down, sacrifices to the new order?

Ahead of us are the main buildings—a long white chevron of marble abutting a black-and-gray shoe box. Half the windows are smoked out and broken from the fires that followed the Sickness. A row of tattered flags snap fitfully in an uneasy wind.

There's about a hundred of us by now, an enthusiastic rabble from all over. Word has filtered out about the Gathering, and people just attach themselves, pulled by hope and pushed by a sort of epic desperate boredom. Our procession has a weird noisy holiday feel, as if the danger of walking openly in the street were somehow held in check by our numbers and spirits. It all reminds me of the First Crusade chapter from *Extraordinary Popular Delusions and the Madness of Crowds*, which we read for AP history. But I tell myself not to be so cynical.

Now the wave of enthusiasm has broken against all the evidence of chaos and violence left over from What Happened. The skeleton of a moving van juts over the huge metal wedge of a safety barrier; whatever exploded from inside it smashed the guard kiosk to bits. Another car bomb twisted back the bars of the fence; they look like the exploded space jockey's ribs from *Alien*.

Bodies—really just skeletons with a light frosting of rotting flesh and torn uniforms—are scattered all over the forecourt. Some kind of battle went down here, right around the time the Sickness was hitting.

But why? What happened here? I cast my mind back to the days before all the power went and the news as we knew it shrank from the vast scope of the global news to the isolated domestic tragedy of our apartment.

We tried to triangulate the truth in those days, as if surfing between Fox, CNN, and MSNBC—right, middle, left—might give us some more accurate picture of where reality might be hovering somewhere in between.

In the last days there was a conference on the Sickness, convened at the UN. The president was there—I remember Donna told me that she had seen him when she was on a field trip to the Security Council. Other world leaders attended, but some took a pass. They were concerned that nobody could guarantee attendees' safety from the Sickness or an opportunistic attack by terrorists. The concern was not unfounded. The situation in New York at the time was often described as "pandemonium."

Trivia? The word *pandemonium* means "all of the demons." It was invented by Milton for *Paradise Lost,* referring to the congress of defeated angels that Satan addresses when he's planning the fall of man. This more or less fit the right-wing view of the UN, actually; to them, it was the headquarters of a secret cabal that aimed to take down the United States. You'd hear a lot of that kind of thing on Fox in those final days. To them, the meeting on the Sickness was a sort of Black Mass to celebrate the ultimate downfall of America. This idea, that the spread of the Sickness was due to some sort of conspiracy, was really attractive to a lot of people; it had a contagion of its own. And, though it signaled the end of our way of life, there was a certain satisfaction for the Cassandras—you could detect the glee concealed in the faces of some pundits, even as they bemoaned the tragedy.

I know that the release of the Sickness from Plum Island was an accident, albeit one that couldn't have happened had we not been developing it in the first place. But in the stew of paranoia, legitimate fear, and contempt that came with What Happened, there was no way to get at this truth. The irony of holding a conference in New York being roughly equivalent to holding a conference in Freetown, Sierra Leone, during the Ebola epidemic was lost on most Americans. Nonattendance by heads of member states was viewed as a betrayal of our trust, and long-standing alliances frayed as America finally lost its grip on centrality and influence.

The jihadists invoked God's wrath as the explanation for the disease, an opinion shared (again with little appreciation of the irony) by Evangelical Christians.

So what we see in the forecourt may be the evidence of some kind of terrorist incident, or riot, or militia attack, or all three. One way or another, it's hard to avoid the stink of history here, the smell of decayed hopes and fears.

"You still sure this is the place for it?" I ask Chapel.

"Yes," he says, his face set. "This is the place for it. If you're going to rebuild the government—*your* government—do it in the right environment. You do it in a high school gym, people are gonna think they're running for student council. You do it in the UN Security Council..."

He may be right. Or it may end up as pandemonium.

Politics is the systematic organization of hatreds. That's Henry Adams. On the one hand, it's a pretty cynical remark: There is no political harmony, no Utopia, only the pragmatic and momentary balance of opposed groups. On the other hand, it is a sort of comfort: As ugly as the emotions at play may seem, a sort of order can emerge from it. I remind myself that I'm not looking for agreement. I'm looking for cooperation. My aim is to get kids who have been killing one another and competing for food to help one another. Maybe I'm starting on an impossible venture. Or maybe I can manage to organize all our hatreds.

I survey the littered paving stones, the addled façades of the buildings. I can feel the past buzzing up from the ground, buzzing out of the buildings, louder than hope.

We have a week to get ready for the Gathering. Security, sanitation, food, power. Chapel, who knows a surprising amount about the complex, borrows Peter and Brainbox to locate an emergency generator and get it cranking. We send some of the Dead Rabbits out to siphon fuel and start scavenging for food. Others head to the Bazaar to spread the word. With any luck, the Uptowners won't kill them.

I'm still not sure how the Uptowners will respond to the call. Both they and the Harlemites aimed at nothing less than owning Manhattan; but I never could see much point in the ambition. At the current rate of the Sickness, there can't be more than two years left to most of the kids alive today. I can offer them something better. If I can bring them to heel.

Inside, the air is thick, choked with dust as Carolyn, Ayesha, and I crab our way through the darkness, flashlights taped to the ends of our rifles. We're looking for the Security Council chamber, where the emergencies of history were debated, bold statements decided upon and issued and then ignored by the powers that won the Second World War.

The designers hadn't seen fit to provide sufficient illumination from the outside, a strange casino-like rejection of the world and its time frame that slows our progress through the obstacle course of office chairs, drifts of paper, and temporary barricades.

There was a battle here, or more than one. We walk over a ground mulch of uniformed security guards and a higher stratum of more recent casualties, their makeshift clothing no more than rags. In the sickly glare of the flashlights, it takes on a nightmarish quality, like the engravings in an edition of *Inferno* I used to have back at the Square—naked, twisting bodies, suffering flesh everywhere.

I remember the Ghosts at the public library on Forty-Second. When this began, Peter and Donna and SeeThrough and Brainbox and I went to the main branch to find the scientific journal that Brainbox thought might give a clue to the source of the Sickness. We found it; we also found a cult of murderous cannibals welcoming the End Times, and barely escaped. Now, inching our way through another benighted Cyclopean maze, I start at every scurrying rat and rustling paper.

Bad things have happened here. There are bodies that fell still stabbing each other, and decay has blended their flesh together; heads bludgeoned with laptops, bodies garroted with headphone cords. Clubs fashioned from table legs. Flags turned into spears.

Plowshares into swords, I think.

"You believe this shit?" asks Carolyn, prodding at a half-naked body, a broken sword sticking up from the rib cage.

"Yeah, I do," I say.

We make our way up a staircase clotted with the dead. As we strike deeper into the heart of the building, closer to the Council chamber, the crowd of bodies becomes thicker, as if we are getting to the epicenter of a gyre of violence.

"Do you remember *Aliens*?" asks Ayesha.

"The part where they're going through the atmospheric processing plant and nobody's there and suddenly the aliens start coming from everywhere?"

"Yeah, that part."

"Yeah."

At last, behind a wrecked safety cordon, X-ray machines, and security scanners toppled to make a barrier caked with dried blood, we find the entrance to the Security Council chamber. The windows set in the door have been smashed to opacity; through the cracks between them, nothing but blackness.

In the seconds we count down before kicking open the door, I reflect, in the vast relativity of the tiny moment, on what it's like to be afraid of dying now that I know I might live another half century or more. And I realize that I have become more frightened. It was much easier to risk death when I thought it was coming soon anyway. Death and I had a nodding familiarity. Now that He has retreated into the shadows of the future, He feels vast and strange and unknowable, a terrorist in a distant country who might contrive some outlandish scheme to snuff me out at any moment or just let me stagger on in the dark tunnel of the present.

I used to think of myself as a Buddhist; that was my background, anyhow, and we are told to take life lightly. Not to give it *no* value, but to realize that, like anything of value, it can be snatched from you, so it's best not to become too attached to it. It served me pretty well, through one attempted robbery after another. But to be given *more* of life—an unexpected lavishing of riches—that's the challenge. How not to become attached, a miser with a windfall, a traumatized lottery winner?

I take a breath, signal to the others, and kick the door open, looking over the barrel of my gun.

The flashlights glance over the backs of a dozen rows of leather chairs raked and oriented toward a horseshoe-shaped table at the bottom of an incline. Perhaps twenty people could sit at the far desk, eyeing one another across the empty keyhole of space that the curve makes.

There's a gloomy circle of light above, a thick window of opaque glass mediating the glow of the sun. We turn off our flashlights.

There are people in all the chairs, sitting dead still.

To my right, a line of bodies in various stages of decay, flyblown and swarming with maggots. A line of clasped hands, like a massive Thanksgiving grace, stretches down the row. At the end, a skeleton reaches its hand forward to the body in front, and the handholding snakes its way up the next row, down again in a chain to the front of the auditorium.

"Damn," says Ayesha. Other than that, the only sound is the buzz of a million flies.

We make our way down to the horseshoe-shaped table, where the corpses face one another, appearing to smile as decay pulls their lips and gums back.

Above it all, there's a mural stretching across the back of the room. Idealized mannequin-like figures in uncomfortable attitudes and slashing strokes of gilt and tempera, contained within lozenge-like panels: At the center, a phoenix rises from its own ashes. A man and woman, a sort of dressed-up Adam and Eve, hold a bouquet between them. Dark, silhouetted soldiers strive upward. Children dance.

I wonder if the diplomats who met here ever thought about these stout-limbed symbols, who look as if they have been flash-frozen in their incoherent motions.

"Only the dead have seen the end of war," I hear—a cracked, reedy voice.

It isn't one of us.

I turn to look at the array of corpses lined up, staring back at us with hollow sockets. The voice came from somewhere among them.

But none of the tattered, gnawed relics seems like it could be a living person.

"Show yourself," says Carolyn, "or I start shooting."

There's no response. Carolyn fires into the chest of one of the corpses. The report rings through the chamber, and a spent shell casing tinkles down the aisle.

Then one of the bodies stands up.

"Welcome!" he says. "My name is Hafiz."

DONNA

SOPH: "DRINK?"

Me: "Why not?"

Soph hands me a big tumbler of champagne, then asks for it back, then drops a couple of mushed raspberries into it. All's quiet but for the occasional *PLUNK* of the pole as it hits the gravel bottom of the river.

Rab is pushing the flat-bottomed punt along the water, expertly changing its direction with little tweaks of the pole during each after-stroke. Between pushes, he heaves the pole up and lets it slide down again through his fingers. Water slicks off the pole and trickles down his arms, matting his white shirt to his body and showing the tan skin underneath.

Soph: "Go on, Donna. We've got a half case to get through."

Soph, Michael, Rab, and I spend most of our free time hanging out, drinking. At some point, we realized that my account at the Buttery—which is where we get our meal vouchers and other supplies—is being paid, automatically, by the government, no questions asked. (Actually, Rab had a few questions, like how I managed to get this sort of special treatment, but I put him off.) That—combined with the fact that the Buttery stocks this yummy champagne called Veuve Clicquot, which means "the widow Clicquot" (she doesn't seem to have minded being single; in fact, she looks fat and sassy)—has made for a pretty bubbly term.

My grief is dissolving in a solution of wine and poetry. I'm reading Byron as I lie in the punt, slipping downstream and sipping champagne. I read:

> There lies the thing we love, with all its errors
> And all its charms, like death without its terrors.

And the sense and music of it work through my brain, two lines like a spring-loaded machine of meaning, and I think of a night long, long ago when I looked at a sleeping Jefferson and wanted to tell him everything. And for a moment, the pain is almost too much, but then knowing that somebody had felt just that way, hundreds of years ago, makes it better, and then a duck quacks at its family from the bank, and I trail my fingers in the cool water, and the white limestone underbelly of Clare Bridge is passing overhead as Rab kneels down and threads the punt through the gap with the pole trailing tail-like behind. In the gloom under the bridge, he looks at me, and I feel or fear that he can read my face, so I look away, start joking around with Michael and Soph.

THE NEW ORDER

Am I disappointed that it's not just him and me? Of course not. Why would I think that? We come to the lock between the upper river and the lower river, under the windows of an old pub called The Mill. We get out of the punt and push it up the rollers to the upper river—a tough effort after all the champagne, but passersby help us— and then Michael punts us another half mile or so, to a field that rolls down from Grantchester. We tie up the punt to a tree by the water and hike up a field of cows to a pub called The Green Man. They get me to try warm beer. I like it. We eat fries and mackerel pâté and Scotch eggs and then visit the little old church, cool and quiet and dreamy, and then we head back to the punt and find crows eating our bread and cheese, and then we set off again. A little tougher now, since our heads are lighter, and I give punting a try, and I'm absolutely terrible at it, zigzagging the punt from one side of the river to the other, and Soph takes over, and she's great at it, and Rab and Michael try bridge-jumping, which is when you stand at the front of the punt as it's moving and lift yourself onto a bridge as the boat passes under it and then run across the road and jump back in before the punt is gone past, and Michael manages it and Rab falls into the river, which is hilarious, except that people say the Cam is infected with rat syphilis, whatever that is.

Laughing, we pull Rab back into the boat. He takes off his shirt to dry, and I watch the water drip from his hair down the rounded sluice of his collarbone, down the muscles of his stomach. Rab sees me seeing him, and I stop. Frankly, I don't know why I'm doing it. I mean, I guess I'm a little tipsy. My brain is just taking everything in randomly—nice sunshine, nice leaves, nice water, nice muscles. Anyhow.

By the time we're back at the boathouse, the buzz is wearing off and turning into a dull headache. We scrabble together all our stuff and return the punt and the pole to the boatman, and I head back to my rooms, dazed.

Past Titch, sullen and resentful from being left behind. Welsh is waiting in my living room for tea. That's what he prefers to call what, back on the *Ronald Reagan,* they would have called a "debriefing" (which always made me feel like I was supposed to take off my underwear) and I would have called an "interrogation session."

Welsh always brings something from a French patisserie in London, carefully tied up in a powder-blue box, to break the ice.

He knows that I love almond croissants and pistachio macaroons; he has even gifted me an espresso machine with climate sensor. Such is the intimacy of "handler" and "agent," which is how he defines our relationship.

It always begins very easy breezy, glancing off the surface of things, like an awkward parental visit. How am I settling in? Making friends? Anything I need? I point out to him that, since I appear to have an open line of credit, if there's anything I need, I can just get it.

Me: "Which I meant to ask about. I really appreciate the, uh, bottomless allowance and everything, but given as how I am not likely to be a big earner anytime soon, what am I going to do when the bill comes due?"

Welsh: "In fact, you're already paying your way. Her Majesty's government is very happy to employ you as a consultant. You're quite a rare commodity."

Me: "Commodity?"

Welsh: "I thought I wouldn't sugarcoat it."

Which is funny, given that he's bribing me with pastries, but...

Something occurs to me.

Me: "Why did the US give me up so easily?"

Welsh: "Who said it was easy?"

Me: "What did you pay for me?"

Welsh: "Oh, nothing like money. That would be unseemly. Besides, you're invaluable. You were part of an accommodation with the Reconstruction Committee."

I don't like the sound of that. Makes me feel like an object.

Welsh: "And, your higher-ups had determined that they had reached the end of their workable relationship with you."

Me: "Whereas you felt like you could still get me to put out?"

Welsh shifts uncomfortably.

Welsh: "I am continually impressed with the...pungency of your turn of phrase. But...yes, I suppose we felt that there might be information that had been overlooked, or forgotten, or seen from the wrong angle."

Me: "You think I'm holding out."

Welsh: "We think you may have forgotten something that might be useful."

Me: "So what about hypnotism?"

Welsh: "Fanciful."

Me: "Truth serum?"

Welsh: "Overrated."

Me: "Torture?"

Welsh: "Counterproductive."

I look at him. The way he answered makes me think that, if it actually *were* productive to him, he might be just fine with torture.

Welsh: "And not something that allies engage in, of course."

Me: "If I have all this useful information, wouldn't other people want it, too? How about, like, China? Or Russia?"

Welsh: "Oh, I don't see how you'd want to assist them. Everything I know about you tells me that you are devoted to the idea of individual liberty."

I think of the Uptowners; I think of my people at the Square. Yeah.

Welsh: "But—yes, you would be a subject of great interest to foreign powers and enemies of our governments. That is why we take such pains to protect you. And why your...spree the other night was of such concern to us."

He means the townie ass-kicking evening. They're still mad at me about that. I change the subject.

Me: "So—on the individual liberty thing. I've noticed that, like, not everybody has the liberty to enter and exit the city limits."

I've been wandering, kind of ruminating. That's a word Jefferson told me about once. It has to do with cows. People associate it with walking around, which is what cows do, except really, it refers to the biggest stomach that a cow has, the rumen, which is where food goes first before it's vomited back into the mouth as cud for chewing. A person wandering and chewing over thoughts again and again is like a cow chewing grass, except he's belching ideas back and forth in the different parts of his brain. Sometimes I find myself at the city limits after a long session of brain-cud-chewing; and there I see cops and soldiers, standing by unobtrusive laser-light-and-sensor barriers. Lots of people can pass back and forth without any to-do, but sometimes an alarm goes off, and the cops and soldiers cluster around the offending passerby like white blood corpuscles around a virus, and they go over a bunch of authorizations on their iPhones. I've never seen anybody let through after that. There are always a few people lurking at the end of the road, checking out the back and forth, but the vast majority just go about their business and don't try their luck, like dogs that have been trained by those Invisible Fences they used to sell in SkyMall.

I might ask anybody about this, Rab or Soph or whatever, but I don't want to seem like I don't know something I should. Besides, I'd prefer to get an answer from the horse's mouth, presuming the government is the horse and Welsh is the mouth.

Welsh: "Yes. That's a result of the Safe Cities Act."

He appears ready to leave it at that.

Me: "Safe Cities Act?"

Welsh: "Back in the old days, before the…considerable increase of the already considerable influence of your country's politics on mine, it would have been known under a more—shall we say—honest name. Something like the 'Restriction Act,' say. But 'Safe Cities' has a certain ring to it."

Me: "And?"

Welsh: "And, in brief, every citizen—you'll be amused to know that for my countrymen, the official term is *subject*, by the way—has a freedom of movement corresponding to his individual security profile and residency status. Of course, most law-abiding and economically participatory citizens can go most places, and the Home Office's system handles automatically any requests for travel outside personal boundaries, through their app. Most people have very few issues with it."

He takes a bite of macaroon.

Me: "Economically participatory?"

Welsh: "Those who have not opted out of the system or been encouraged, indirectly or directly, to opt out. What in your country you would have called good citizens, or 'fully functioning members of society.'"

Me: "So...some people are not allowed to come to Cambridge? Like, actually enter the city? Ever?"

Welsh (shrugs): "Is everyone allowed into the college? No and no. Only fellows and students. Even visiting the college is restricted to members."

Me: "But..."

Welsh: "Is everyone allowed onto military bases? Government buildings?"

Me: "Yeah, but that's because of security, right? Like, official secrets and whatnot."

Welsh: "You've hit the nail on the head, Donna. Our conception of what is secure and what isn't has changed."

Me: "Why?"

Welsh: "The tragic effects of what you call 'What Happened' are not limited to America. A panoply of indirect effects has caused great turmoil throughout the world. In prehistory, if an entire continent had its population obliterated, there might be no effect whatsoever on the rest of the globe. But by the beginning of this century, the economic, social, and political fabric of the world was a rather tight weave—everything was connected. Consider the damage the loss of the American market did to European industry. The reorganization of global markets toward China, Russia, and India. Massive unemployment. Social unrest. Riots. Cultural strife—as you can imagine, the apocalyptic destruction of the United States was viewed by some religious groups as a validation of their particularly extreme form of fundamentalism. Then came the US Navy's seizure of the Strait of Hormuz and the war with Iran. You'll hear people referring to all of these factors generally as 'the Shock.' A pretty apt term, if one wants to boil down a very complex state of affairs. Anyway, to make a long story medium-length, the Shock demanded what they call, euphemistically and optimistically, 'a robust response.' The Unity government felt it had to take steps to ensure calm at home as well as abroad."

Welsh eyes me over the rim of his cup.

Me: "Well, I guess I better remember to keep my phone with me, in case I ever want to get a beer in the wrong place."

Welsh: "You can always get the chip."

He means a subdermal implant. Like the precleared status the TSA used to have. I've seen it on a lot of the students, a button-sized lump under the nape of your neck.

Me: "No thanks. In my time, they only did that to dogs."

And that's the thing: I'm years behind here. For starters, back in New York, we'd been plagued back to the Stone Age. And while we were slugging it away back home, the rest of the world was on fast-forward.

My mind is kind of sorting through all this when Welsh pulls the old quid-pro-quo deal. This happens after the macaroons and the answers; as though these kinds of piddling offerings substituted for an invitation to start fiddling around in my memory.

Welsh: "Now. The last time we spoke, you were telling me about the Uptowners. Forgive me if I'm getting this wrong—they were a fairly aggressive bunch?"

Me: "Uh, if by 'aggressive' you mean homicidal, yes."

One part of my mind plays a video of Cheekbones, sitting opposite me in the Campbell Apartment at Grand Central, telling me that if God meant women to speak for themselves, he would have made them stronger. I tell him to try me; he threatens to torture me and the others to death.

Welsh: "And...socially backward?"

Me: "Like, caveman backward."

Welsh: "But they controlled the Bazaar, which was the central marketplace?"

Me: "They had more guns than anybody else, so, yeah. And they wanted to run things by way of a bank. Like, reintroduce money and control the money, so they could control who got what. Brainbox called it Ferrari currency."

Welsh: "Ferrari currency? Extraordinary."

Me: "Wait. A different car. Fiat currency. That's it. And a 'state monopoly on violence.' Which I guess means that it's okay for you and your friends to kill people, but nobody else can."

Welsh: "I see. And this 'state'—or rather, city-state, since we're dealing with a relatively small geographical area—how far did it extend?"

I think about that.

Me: "Well, on the west, it stopped at Central Park, which is Fifth Avenue."

Welsh: "Someone else owned Central Park?"

Me: "The escaped polar bear owned Central Park. Until we killed it."

After it killed SeeThrough.

Welsh: "You astound me."

Me: "I astound myself. On the south side, I'd say they controlled as far down as the mid-Forties."

Welsh straightens in his chair a little bit at this. It's like he's a hunting dog that suddenly got a whiff of fox or whatever, except he's trying to act cool. I might not have noticed if he hadn't done this before; like, I can tell what he's after by the questions he's asking. He tries to hide the ones he really cares about by asking all sorts of other questions, but I can tell which ones he thinks are trivial by his body language and how I feel while answering them. Sometimes it seems like no big deal, and other times it feels like I'm on the spot, even though, on the surface, there's nothing special about the way he's asking. As though, beneath the business of the two of us sitting there and talking, there were two other selves having a different sort of dialogue.

Anyhow, I know that he is really interested in the UN for some reason. And sure enough—

Welsh: "I see. Did the territory extend all the way to the East River?"

And I really want to say, "You mean did their territory include the UN?" because I know that's what he's really asking and I want him to know that I'm smart enough to know it; but sometimes it's handy not to seem as smart as you actually are.

Me: "Uh...not sure."

I can see that he's disappointed, even though he's acting unfussed. "Up on the north end, they had a border with Harlem. Bad blood up there."

Welsh: "Between the Uptowners and the—ahhh—"

Me: "The black kids? Yeah. They be beefin'."

Welsh: "Why?"

Welsh doesn't care about that, I can tell, but he's trying not to show it.

Me: "Oh, I don't know. Because the Uptowners are racist thugs? Because there were no cops left to keep the Harlem kids down? Because why not?"

Welsh takes this in with an owlish look. Then he makes his stab back at what really concerns him.

Welsh: "To jump around just a bit, I wonder if you might tell me a bit more about the final days of the Sickness, before your 'tribe' formed, before..."

Me: "Before the whole *Lord of the Flies* deal?"

Welsh: "Yes. As it were, before the age of city-states. I'm wondering what it must have been like, as the structure of society began to collapse. For instance—what sort of picture do you have of the Crisis Meeting at the United Nations?"

Me: "The What Meeting?"

Welsh: "It was known as the Crisis Meeting at the time. The president called upon the heads of state of the UN member nations to attend a summit convened at the General Assembly Building. Some came. Others refused."

Me: "Oh, yeah. I remember that. It was on TV. Some people were pissed that people were blowing off the president. Some people sort of got it, like, who would want to fly into a crisis, even though the CDC was saying that the UN would be safe and everything? That was just before the power went."

Welsh: "What was the last thing you remember? About the UN meeting?"

Welsh is acting all casual.

Me: "It's a little hazy. Everybody in my building was dying. Including, you know, my family and whatnot."

Welsh (nods): "Yes. I apologize."

Me: "For what?"

Welsh: "It can't be a very happy time to revisit."

Me: "Not so much."

He sits there a moment, perhaps pondering the awfulness of the situation, then, perhaps, considering whether he can afford, in the overall economy of cooperation, to press me further.

Welsh: "Leaving that aside for a moment, I wonder if we might go over the list of known tribes in New York..."

When Welsh and I are done, I go out for a little shopahol, which is what I call what you consume when you're doing retail therapy. *Consume* is a strange word when you apply it to shopping, actually. I mean, it's not the same as actually swallowing something. You still have the thing right there. Maybe the consuming refers to what's being eaten up far away, the burning off of coal somewhere in China where the plastic is being molded, or the eking out of spindles in Bangladesh where the fabric is woven by giant machines and little children. On this end, it feels a lot more like creation—I walk in with empty hands and leave with a pair of shoes or a bag or a book. Something from nothing. In theology, this is called creation *ex nihilo,* which is Latin for "from nothing." (I am loving English; it's so much more than I thought it would be.) So maybe that's the reason it makes me feel good—at least, it makes me feel good for a little bit. It soothes the anxiety that a visit from Welsh tends to bring. It feels like being a creator. Especially with my magical line of credit from Her Majesty.

Of course, I know that none of this is ex nihilo. In fact, as Brainbox once told me, nothing is either created or destroyed. All of this stuff came from someplace—that's where the factories in China and the little kids in Bangladesh come in. Trace this dress back—the cotton of the fabric from plants in Egypt, the plastic of the buttons from petroleum by-products from the ground of Iraq and shipped to Shanghai—and you start to see this web of causes, this wonder of raw stuff becoming finished stuff, raw resources becoming fine things as they travel around the world to find their way to a shelf in a shop in Cambridge. That's the altar I'm worshipping at, the altar of the transubstantiation (not bad, huh, Jefferson?) of stuff. That's my faith, and the blessing of that faith is the squirt of pleasure I get as I donate my tithe and carry away the miraculous product.

But wait, you're saying—that's all very well, but what about the kids in Bangladesh? What about the workers in China? What about the factory smoke that paints the insides of their lungs and the foremen who whip them and the factories that fall on top of them? The standard answer is that it's all very sad but the money that they get improves their lives; they are upwardly mobile in the magical economic hierarchy of being.

But I know the real answer—the answer is this: *Fuck the kids in*

213

Bangladesh. Fuck the Chinese workers committing suicide. I like this phone. I like this dress. This phone is here. This dress is here. Those kids aren't here. So fuck 'em.

And fuck the kids back in New York, the system says, because we don't have a use for them. According to Chapel, anyway. My tribe back home is fighting and dying, and here I am loaded down with shopping.

The thought kind of puts a sour endnote to my shopping expedition. I'm glad when my phone buzzes at me to tell me somebody texted.

Me: "What is it, babe?"

Charlie: "Uh . . . somebody sent you a message."

If the buddy was set for standard efficiency, he would tell me, but as I have my jailbroken, five-year-old-boy plug-in, it doesn't get to the point.

Me: "Uh-huh. Who, honey?"

Charlie: "Um . . . what was his name?"

The phone pauses. Then—"RAB!" It practically shouts at me.

Me: "You like Rab, huh?"

Stupid question to ask a phone, but I enjoy feeling out the AI.

"*YEAHHH!*" shouts the phone.

I take all my crap back to my rooms. Truth? I don't actually wear it or use it. I just put the beautiful bags and boxes on shelves or in closets. Like, it was enough to keep the lifeblood of capitalism flowing or whatever. The point of it was that magical endorphin rush of getting, not having.

Wordsworth says:

> The world is too much with us; late and soon,
> Getting and spending, we lay waste our powers.

Which, if I am honest about it, I don't totally understand, but I think is 100 percent right. Anyhow, I hide the evidence of my private little ecstasy of consumption before I join Rab in the library.

Michael and Soph are there, too, as usual. Like me, they look hungover and mopey. I sit down at their table and, in a sudden flip of feeling, go from appreciating how wonderful it is to be able to just sit and read books and think, to feeling resentful of the books, the quiet, the privilege, angry at myself and angry most of all at the government. From punting to pouting in less than a day.

I slap my book shut.

Me: "This is bullshit."

Michael: "What exactly is bullshit?"

Me: "All this. This library. This college. This country. Us. The Safe Cities Act. The Shock. The government."

Rab and Sophie and Michael all look at one another with a sort of confiding air, as if there's something they know that I don't.

Rab: "Interesting you should say that."

KATH

IT'S OUR DAMAGE THAT MAKES US INTERESTING, I figure. Which means, if I'm right, I'm pretty damn fascinating. Back from the dead and all.

Actually, ipso facto, I wasn't dead—only *left for* dead. Which I intend to address, down the line.

Anyway, I've seen a few things, I've done a few things, I have a certain tolerance for extremes of behavior.

Still, I draw the line at Abel peeing on dead kids, which for some reason he likes to do. Some reason? Well, if I'm to stretch my mind around it, I guess it would have to do with a sense of dominance, a defiance of mortality, and a canine habit of marking covered ground.

But he needs to learn how to behave. So I slap him upside his head. He zips up and says sorry.

"Can't find good help these days," I say to him and the others, and as usual they look at me with doggish incomprehension.

There's the blond twins, Abel and his sister, Anna, angelic and sky-blue-eyed and dangerous. And Curtis, latte-skinned and wiry and probably not the most emotionally grounded kid even before the apocalypse.

The rest of the kids from Plum Island are either dead or fled. Probably some of them have filtered back to that Extreme Haunted House of a lab and are, without the command-and-control presence of the Old Man, busily rotting away when I emerge from my coma, slowly starving to death.

These three were the ones I found after I woke up, or recovered, or whatever you want to call it, with tears of blood streaking laterally across my face like some kind of couture runway makeup look and a raging pharmaceutical hangover.

Out in front of the lab, the concrete was churned up by machine-gun fire and splattered with human roadkill, a few of the Islander kids having gotten on the wrong end of a firefight.

I thought to myself, not for the first time, *What is the point of it all in this butcher's shop of a universe?* And my mind came back with the usual answers, to wit, *Why not stick around to see what happens? You must have survived for a reason,* and *Get some.*

Get some. Action, that is. Revenge.

But there was nobody to take it out on.

And then I noticed Abel and Anna and Curtis—I didn't know their names yet, of course; at that point, they were just some of the kids who had imprisoned and tortured us—hiding out in the bushes like the proverbial shy woodland creatures. This was a change from their demeanor during my stay as a mandatory guest of the lab, when they had acted like smirking tween sadists.

217

They didn't seem to be up to much in terms of hostilities—if anything, they looked like they had had the bejeebers scared out of them—so I wasn't overly fussed. I looked around for something to kill them with, and shortly found a near-mint AR-15 with an almost-full mag.

Get some.

So I raised the gun and sighted them, but, unexpectedly, they didn't scatter. They just sat there like the headlight-dazed rabbits we used to see on the drive home from East Hampton at night.

Reader, I did not kill them.

Maybe I'm getting soft in my old age. Or maybe my cured condition—which is what I realized, I was cured—gives me a love for all life, like that hot android dude at the end of *Blade Runner* when he spares Harrison Ford.

Anyhow, I tell them to shoo. Except they don't. They sort of lurk while I go about finding something to eat, and, finally, I just throw them my leftovers and they have at it. It's like having a dog follow me home, except instead of a dog, it's three murderous and probably insane thirteen-year-olds.

What's that? You thought *I* was crazy? That's soooo unfair. Sure, I've killed a few people, but nobody who didn't have it coming. If that dude Keith had done to you what he did to me, you would have shanked him, too.

Anyhow, you can't blame me, because I never knew love.

Which is my second priority after food, which is to say, where the hell is Jefferson? I was pretty damn sure that we had a moment there, that, in fact, he told me he loved me. Okay, so I *asked* him to, and okay, I was dying at the time, so it wasn't like he felt he'd have to marry me or anything, but still. I think maybe he does. Love me. And just doesn't know it. He was ready to move on from Donna to the harder stuff.

He must have thought I was dead. I mean, *I* thought I was dead, and I'm me, so you can't blame him for that one. Can you?

Or can you.

I mean, he didn't even bother to bury me. Which, if I *had* been dead, would have been kind of lame of him not to. What was he thinking?

I want some answers. Which I guess is an answer in itself, the answer to "why bother to stick around when you could put a bullet in your head?" How's that for a Hamlet reboot? The answer is: because answers.

I'm sure there's a reasonable explanation for why Jefferson left me on a slab, comatose and alone. And if it's a good explanation, I definitely won't kill him.

That's the word of the day: *mercy*. Which is why I spared the three pathetic little psychopaths who are currently my entourage.

As time passes, I get the feeling that, once you've gone through a certain identity-annihilating level of trauma, your allegiance quickly attaches to anyone you encounter who has a stronger will than yours. Which explains why these three kids, formerly my captors, are suddenly my followers and I am their new Mama Bear. It's actually kind of amusing how devoted they are, how quickly they skip to it when I tell them what to do. Ransack that house! Get into the car! Kill that guy! Take his food! *Yes, ma'am! Right away, ma'am!* I could get used to this.

I aim to get off Plum Island and then go west on Route 27. I intend to get out of the sticks just as soon as possible and make my way back to the big city. Way I see it, the world is my oyster. The world is my gift card.

The world is my bitch.

I send Abel and Anna and Curtis on a scavenging expedition, then have them load into one of the boats they used to take the ship, back—weeks ago? Months? Days? Who knows. Feels like I've been out of it for a while. My cute poochy stomach is all gone, and my tits aren't as *pow!* as they used to be.

I'm all George Washington crossing the Delaware on the way back to Long Island, looking for signs of life. Here and there, a bonfire, a silhouette flitting on the edge of the water.

I think about maybe diverting to Shelter Island to hang out at the Sunset Beach like in the good old days, but I just don't feel like the company is right. These three aren't much fun.

"What do you think?" I ask Abel. "Should we down a few mojitos?"

"What's a mojito?" says Abel.

"Never mind." Honestly. Nobody is any fun anymore. Back in the day, we could take a seaplane out to East Hampton, then it was maybe fifteen minutes by taxi to the ferry. Cocktails and a few bumps on arrival, lay out, party, a few zannies to round things off, sleep in.

If everything and everybody fell with the Sickness, consider that some people fell further, and pity me. I had it *made*. Sure, other people lost more *emotionally* speaking—that is to say, it wasn't like I *loved* Mom and Dad, so I guess there's that, but I mean I had been kind of expecting to benefit from their finally kicking it, not to be turned into an extra in some shitty video game.

One thing I know is, I was not made to be an extra.

I am above the motherfucking title.

We make landfall, if that's what you call it, in Sag Harbor, by the long wharf. Main Street is all jacked up. Honestly, people just go too far. Broken storefront windows, moldering skeletons, crows, rats, whatever. The American Hotel is burned out. Pity.

We manage to start a fashion-statement pickup truck and begin making our way east, my minions sliding around in the truck bed like doggies.

Twenty-seven is jammed, except everybody's dead and there are no cops to arrest you for driving on the shoulder. I use the truck to bash through whatever's blocking the way, and we're making decent progress, the old familiar names slipping by, Bridgehampton, Water Mill, when I hear something impossible—I look up—

And a helicopter makes its way west, stuttering through the sky.

What. The. Actual. Fuck.

Here's where I get the sense that I've been missing out during my little vacation from reality. Because last time I checked, there *were* no more helicopters. That is, sure, there were helicopters, but there were no helicopter *pilots,* on account of they were dead.

My curiosity is aroused.

I determine to track down the helicopter, which is a bit of a challenge, given, you know, it's flying and I'm on the ground. But, fortunately, the South Fork is only, like, five miles wide, and the helicopter is making a line for the city. I keep on 27 and, when the helicopter ducks left in the distance, cut down to Old Country Road. Eventually I come to the fenced border of an airfield. I stop the car and listen, and I can't hear the chopping of the blades anymore. Either it's passed west, out of sight and hearing, or they've landed somewhere nearby.

Anna pokes her angelic little face through the window to the truck bed. "What are we doing, Mommy?"

"We're getting some answers," I say. "And I'm not your mommy."

She giggles, like I'm just joking.

Down from the bed of the truck, they stretch their legs, rub their bruises, and look to me for orders.

"We're going to find that helicopter," I say. "But we're going to do this stealthily."

No response.

"Like ninjas," I say.

Now they get it. So we start along the fence, then cut over to a parallel street when the outbuildings give way to a clear runway.

Nothing indicates life. Impotent old fighter jets, rusting Cessnas. Wind-whipped tarps.

I'm not too keen on ambushes, having walked into some, most notably when my three teen zombies and their friends took us in the water off Plum Island, so I decide that watch and wait is the best strategy for the moment.

Outside the southeast corner of the airstrip, there's an old Mexican restaurant. In the kitchen we find, amid the festering chaos of years-old guacamole and sour cream, some cans of pinto beans and salsa. They're only a few months past expiration, so we dig in.

Just picture me, the paleo girl, the Dr. Junger's *Clean* girl, the juice faster, hoping against hope to find a can opener. Finally, Curtis comes up with the goods, and the look of pride on his face is downright pathetic. He hands it to me and waits for a pat on the head or something.

We class it up with bowls and flatware, and I fish some lukewarm Coronas from behind the bar. As I hand them out to my peons, I feel like the old dude kids used to waylay in the parking lot of the 7-Eleven. "Can you buy us some beer?" I wonder if I should feel guilty, then remind myself that these kids have murdered people, so my being concerned about their ethical development and long-term life prospects is probably beside the point. Cheers.

In the decaying, exquisite light just after the sun sets, the tacky cantina deco looks strangely cozy, at least for half an hour or so. I take up a spot near the door and see if my hunch is going to pan out.

The lineup of hangars and sheds on the edge of the strip is, needless to say, not particularly riveting, and I find my gaze straying to the sky, which is going all yellow and pink and purple as the rays of the sun take their last gasp from past the horizon. I guess it's beautiful, but I have no time for it. Getting hung up on that kind of thing is dangerous, like any form of luxury. I could miss something important.

But a voice—actually, it's *my* voice, just coming from an unasked

223

me inside my head—tells me that there's no point living without beautiful things. Why else am I preoccupied with seeing Jefferson? Isn't it because I experienced something that was bigger than pleasure?

I shake the voice silent. We are just animals stuck with unnecessary organs of sentiment. We squeeze what we can in and out of ourselves, sustenance and sensation, but at the end we are just flesh puppets jerked by the strings of our DNA.

And at that moment, as if conjured by the idea of a double helix, I see a curving brushstroke of smoke easing out of a vent in the side of a hangar about a hundred yards away.

I yank the kids down below the window ledge, though by now it's so dark in the restaurant that most likely we can't be seen from outside.

"What's happening?" asks Anna.

"I don't know. Yet."

So we wait. Anna and Abel and Curtis mooch around and nap like dogs while I keep my eyes glued on the hangar. I'm convinced, now, that the helicopter must be inside it, though I can't say why.

After a couple of hours, a silhouetted figure comes out of the hangar. He pulls someone else after him. There's something wrong with the second guy—his hands are tied behind his back, but that's not it—

It's the gray hair. And then I see the other guy—

A beard.

Suffice it to say that I haven't seen many beards lately, since everybody dies from the Sickness around age eighteen. So this can't be right. Except it is. The dude has a full-on Al-Qaeda, not some fuzzy undergrowth.

The fuh.

I've only actually *seen* one person who survived the Sickness other than me. That was the Old Man, who was some kind of genetic anomaly patching himself together with epic doses of steroids. His face was crawling with blotches, and his body was racked with twitches. Not these two. They appear to be in full health.

One guy who shouldn't be alive pushes the other guy who shouldn't be alive into a shed near the hangar. The way I read it, an outhouse visit.

I rouse the kids and tell them to get moving.

"What is it?" says Anna.

"Answers."

DONNA

SOMETHING HAS TO GIVE. The police have to charge us or we have to charge them or *something*—we've been staring at each other too long. I'm tired of seething back and forth against the bodies of the rest of the crowd as they push us tighter and tighter together.

It's called kettling, for some reason, and it works like this: The cops gradually block off all the streets around the route of a protest march until the crowd, like a rat slithering through a pipe, is finally bottled up from behind. Then the cops just hang out, with tea and sandwiches piped in to them from outside, while the demonstrators are stuck without food, water, or a place to pee. It's kind of a sad testament to human frailty that this method works. Like, people can say they're willing to *die* for their beliefs, but when they're denied access to a bathroom for long enough, all they want to do is go home and take a pee.

To their credit, or discredit, some of the hippier students and ballsier of the outsiders have just been relieving themselves right here in the market square, which solves one problem but creates several more, which is to say it kind of smells. Plus, it's hard to win over the populace when you piss on their town.

It all started so well. Rab and Michael and Soph had welcomed me into their world of covert action, or rather, a bunch of students and political organizers getting together and drinking beer and complaining about the government. Up with the 99 percent, down with the Reconstruction Committee, etc., etc. To be honest, I was more excited by the fact that they trusted me than by the plans for the demonstration, which seemed to me kind of wimpy. Like, let's give the cops an excuse to beat the shit out of us. But to them, it was a big step, what with my being, as far as they knew, a daughter of the Reconstruction and all that entailed.

Standing in the square, happy to be risking my comfort and convenience and maybe neck in defense of individual liberty, especially to bond closer with my new friends, I'm aware that I have been badly influenced by my environment, which is to say the chronic guerrilla warfare of Manhattan. Once you've traded gunfire with rival gangs, it's kind of hard to get jazzed about shouting "Hey, hey! Ho, ho! Restrictions on movement have got to go!" over and over again for hours on end. If the aim is to bore the authorities to death, I kind of get it. But basically it seems to be a lot of parading by news cameras and waiting to get clubbed on the head.

Anyhow, it makes me love Rab and Michael and Soph, who care so much about the World and the People and Politics, so I go along with all of it. Plus, they're right—that has to count for something.

And the beginning of the demonstration really had its inspiring moments. Maybe a thousand of us students, who had a higher freedom of movement than lots of other people since we were basically monitored 24/7, trooped down to the edge of the Liberties. There, we looked across the invisible barrier that kept out the hoi polloi (*hoi polloi* means "the mob," which basically means that when you're saying "the hoi polloi," you're saying "the the mob," but whatevs). A couple thousand people who didn't have the right to enter the town center without permission were waiting there. We crossed over the line, and then, which was the cool part, we escorted everybody else back over to our side. All sorts of sirens started going off, and you could tell that it was messing with the cops' data systems, because phones were ringing all over the place, a cacophony like a crazy dawn chorus of birdcalls and pinging and bleeping. By now, of course, the cops were onto us, but they didn't do anything, just hung back and watched us break the law en masse.

The difficulty started when we tried to head down Trumpington Street from Trumpington Road, aiming to process past the colleges where the news vans were waiting. The cops blocked our way but left us the option of heading down Lensfield Road and then jigging back toward the market square. The crowd took the way that was offered. Along Tennis Court Road, the ways to the side were closed down, and we found ourselves shunted along, away from the cameras and the colleges. Finally, we spilled into the market, like a liquid composed of people, stopped up by a particularly unfriendly looking contingent of paramilitary types who we hadn't realized were shadowing our route.

So here we are in the square, trying to keep up our spirits while the average-Joe-looking police are gradually being replaced by hard-faced mofos with riot shields and long batons.

If these guys are scared by our well-rhymed chants, they are not showing it.

Me: "Rab, I don't like the looks of these guys."

Rab: "What guys?"

Me: "Look at him, over there. And that guy."

Rab takes this in.

Rab: "He's got a shield, okay. So they're riot cops."

Me: "Yeah, so where's the riot? And besides. They're not like the other cops. Look at the haircut. And the cauliflower ear. He's military. And the scars on his knuckles. The guy's a bruiser. He's here for a fight."

Rab: "They won't start anything with all the cameras."

And it's true, some cameras have managed to worm their way into the buildings above the square, despite the police blockade. But when I look farther up the buildings, I can see heads peeking over the roof edges—and here and there, the blunt end of a rifle. Snipers taking aim.

Me: "Rab, get Michael and Soph. We've got to figure a way out of here."

Rab: "What? We can't just go."

Me: "We're going one way or another, on our feet or on a stretcher."

Rab: "But they can't just do that in front of everybody—people will see..."

He looks like he's trying to convince himself. The idea was to embolden the populace by violating the Safe Cities Act in the full light of day, in front of God and everybody, but it seems to me like neither God nor everybody cares, particularly. To the shoppers and shop owners around the market, all we're doing is fucking up their day. The few members of the People I've seen who aren't us seem to be annoyed rather than inspired. They'd rather go back to their daydream about everything being okay.

Me: "Let's get out of here, kid."

I take out my phone.

Rab: "What are you doing?"

Me: "I'm turning myself in. Titch'll come and get us. They've got pull with the authorities."

Rab looks at me like I'm canceling Christmas. Why am I drawn to these idealist types?

Rab reins in his emotions, puts his hand on my elbow.

Rab: "Donna. I'm not going to judge you. I understand you're in a bad position because your parents are Reconstruction. It's easier for me. Get yourself out. I'll be okay."

Honestly. *He's* worried about *me*.

Me: "You're not coming with me?"

Rab: "I can't."

Me: "Shit. Fine. I'm staying."

I put away the phone.

And at that moment, somebody from our side, a guy with a bandanna over his face, takes something out of his bag. It's a bottle with a bit of rag sticking out of the neck.

Me: "Rab, step back."

Rab: "What's happening?"

Me: "Molotov cocktail."

The last time I saw one of those, I was firing a rifle out of the front doorway of the main branch of the New York Public Library on Forty-Second Street. Jefferson had gone out to the forecourt to help SeeThrough get back in. One of the Uptowners heaved a bottle with a flaming spout at the truck, and in a few moments it exploded.

Rab: "No—no way—"

Everybody had been crystal clear at the organizational meetings. No weapons. No violence.

Me: "Something's wrong. Come on."

I pull Rab deeper into the crowd as the bottle soars into the air and crashes in front of the police, a puddle of liquid flame spilling out and onto the boots of the first rank.

Rab keeps saying, "An agent provocateur—he's an agent provocateur—" and I wonder why he's talking about lingerie, but then I realize that he means the guy who threw the cocktail has to be working for the cops. Well, stranger things have happened. And it definitely seems like the cops were ready, since fire extinguishers put the blaze out within moments. But the first blow has been recorded by the cameras above the square. And now the cops are slipping gas masks over their heads, and tear gas launchers are poking through their ranks—

POOM! POOM! The canisters are launched, and suddenly they're coming from all sides. The crowd wrenches and contracts, everyone trying to take off at once, nobody knowing where to go.

"Donna!" I hear, and I see Michael and Soph making their way to us, faces pale. I realize that for most of the kids in the crowd, this was a fun day out with friends and a way to feel good about themselves. They didn't have a cop riot in mind. Maybe the worst they imagined was being escorted to jail for a night of camaraderie and protest songs.

Now the paramilitaries are setting out, wading into the crowd with batons swinging. Some of the protesters are fighting back, but most of them are reeling backward, with no backward to reel to. Soph falls to her knees and for a moment looks to be churned up under the feet of a wave of retreating protesters, but Rab shoulders people out of the way and picks her up.

I'm a pretty experienced runner-awayer, having been chased in my time by cannibals, fascists, and bears, so I figure it's time to take charge.

We have been well and truly kettled. Columns of paramilitaries and police are plugging every street out of the market square. It's time for some lateral thinking.

Me: "This way."

I lead Rab, Michael, and Soph to a sporting goods store on the edge of the square.

Rab: "It's locked."

I pay that no mind, of course, and kick the door in. Practice makes perfect—the aluminum housing of the dead bolt gives way with one blow, and we're in. An alarm goes off, which would be a problem if the entire square behind us weren't a riot of activity. Like, literally a riot. There's even a helicopter hovering above, though whether it's for the news or for surveillance or both, it's hard to say. Clouds of tear gas are lowering visibility in the square, so nobody has noticed our maneuver, and we're able to slink through the store and out the back to Rose Crescent just ahead of the fumes.

Here, shopping continues unabated, the sound of the market a curious distraction.

We walk along the street with a careless saunter, practically whistling our innocence.

We needn't have tried. By some form of social geography, once we're out of the market, we seem to be of no interest to the police, who are pushing toward the square as if there were an invisible piston behind them urging them forward. Now we're no different from early-evening shoppers, but for a few cuts and bruises from the jostling of the crowd.

At King's Street, Michael and Sophie split off toward their college, and Rab offers to walk me back to Trinity, but I wonder if I'm actually the one walking him back. He's jittery, sweating, and gaunt, adrenaline spent. At first, we can hear shouts and screams and orders and the explosive pops of tear gas launchers, but a minute down Trinity Street, there's no sign of any disturbance.

Rab: "They didn't have to do that. The gas and the clubs."

Me: "No, they didn't. They wanted to say something, though. It's a kind of language."

Rab: "How do you know so much? About violence and all."

Me: "It's...I guess it's the military background."

I feel sick of myself. I want to tell him who I am. Because I'm used to fighting, and he's not, but he's willing to put himself in harm's way anyhow. And that takes more courage than my doing it.

Rab: "And what did we say? By running away?"

Me: "We live to fight another day. Right?"

Rab treads along unhappily.

Rab: "Are you on our side, Donna?"

Me: "I'm on your side, Rab."

And I mean *you* singular, but it's ambiguous. Language is funny that way.

When we get back, Rab sort of lingers by my stairway. I don't really know what post-riot etiquette demands. I think of asking him up for tea, which is what you do at various moments, but the air is charged with emotion, and it might head the wrong way. It feels like it might sound too much like *hey, come upstairs, and let's make out.* And yet I linger, too. Rab has recovered his usual calm demeanor, and after all the shouting and running and shared danger, there's a sort of woozy, bonded feeling.

Rab: "Are you okay?"

Me: "What? Yeah. Sure. What do you mean?"

Rab: "Just..." He doesn't seem to know what to say, which is rare. "I just feel, occasionally, that there's a whole lot of stuff you're not telling me. Us."

A stone of guilt in my throat. I think of the millions of things I'm hiding.

Me: "No."

Rab smiles and nods. "Okay. But... I want you to know that if you ever needed to talk about anything... you could trust me. I mean... I could just listen. Not judge you or anything."

I feel suddenly like crying, though with relief or shame I can't tell.

Me: "Thanks, Rab. If I ever...have something to talk about. I mean, other than what we talk about. I mean we talk all the time, don't we? We're buds, right?" I wonder if I'm going to lose the sustenance of his and Soph and Michael's friendship.

Rab: "Buds, yeah."

I turn to go up the stairs, but he says, "Have you ever considered—"

I'm a couple of stairs up, practically level with him.

Rab: "Have you ever considered, right, that we could be something much better than friends?"

He's looking right into my eyes, honest and forthright as ever.

"Because..." he continues, when I don't say anything back, "I have. And past a certain point, it's dishonest for me to hide it."

I guess he means past *this* point. And what's my honest response? Am I not attracted to him? Am I not alone in the world? I am.

Me: "Rab."

Rab: "That doesn't sound good."

Me: "I'm scared. Know why? Because you and Michael and Soph are... all that connect me to the world."

Rab: "But how is that possible—"

Me: "And I don't want to lose you."

Rab: "But."

Me: "But... there was somebody. He died. I loved—I love him."

Rab: "Oh."

Rab takes a deep breath, like he's inhaling the poison gas of this news. He's beautiful. I want to kiss him to make it better. I could. I can't.

Rab: "What was his name?"

Me: "Why?"

Rab: "I want to deal with this. I want to deal with reality, not a mystery."

Me: "Jefferson."

Rab: "He was back on the ship you lived on?"

Me: "Yes." That much at least is true.

Rab nods.

Rab: "I'm sorry. I am. I'm also sorry for myself. But... I think you can't... make people feel the way you want them to. So."

He smiles sadly at me, then turns around and leaves.

KATH

THE FENCE IS JACKED, so it's easy enough to figure a way in. And the moon is only a little gouge in the sky, so we slip close to the hangar pretty easily. There's a dull glow smearing through the windows. Somebody is keeping a fire going in there.

Anna, Abel, Curtis, and I crawl on our bellies until we reach the metallic walls of the hangar. From inside, a low murmur of talk. I hear a man's—not a boy's—voice—and a woman's. Something, something "make contact." Then another voice, different from the first two, lower in tone but younger, strangely familiar. The male voice cuts off the low-timbred one with a sharp "shut up!" Then the man and the woman keep talking, at a lower volume.

"Curtis!" I hiss. "Take a look through the window—*carefully*. Tell me what you see."

Curtis nods, and slowly peeks his eyes over the edge of the window. I'm hoping it's too dark for anybody to see him.

"Three people," he whispers. "Wait. Four. Two old guys like you said and an old lady and a kid. The oldest guy is tied up. So is the kid."

"Good work," I say to him, and he smiles at me. Then there's a *POP* and his head jerks back. He collapses onto the tarmac, and blood starts pooling around his head.

I'm not overly emotional about these things. Curtis is dead. I am not, and I intend to keep it that way. I'm half expecting Abel and Anna to lose their shit and run for it, but, in fact, they're just crouching there, utterly unfussed. Anna hikes her smock out of the way of Curtis's blood, but that's about the extent of their reaction.

"Take off!" I say. "Go!"

They look at me, confused, and finally shift when I wave my hands at them. Myself, I scurry over Curtis's body and around the back corner of the hangar. I hear the door on the other side rasp open.

"What is it?" says a woman's voice from inside. No response from the guy with the beard, who shortly appears around the far edge of the hangar. He has on a pair of night-vision goggles, metallic cylinders projecting from his sockets. If he was wearing them inside, looking out, it means that he could see Curtis as plain as day, which also means I got him killed. Whoops.

The guy with the beard scans the horizon with his goggles, sees something—presumably Anna and Abel trying to hide. He raises a snub little machine gun with a chunky silencer on the end.

He still hasn't seen me. It's either let the rest of the kids get shot or take him out. All in all, given the fluidity of the situation, there's not much that I can do other than perforate him with a burst from my AR-15.

He rag-dolls onto the ground, wheezing. From inside, the woman's voice again. "Dooley? Dooley, what's going on? Report!"

Yeah, what's going on, Dooley? I crab over to him and pry his knife out of his hands. He's still alive, but not much, blinking up glassily at me.

I barely know where to begin, given that there's not much time before he bleeds out.

"Dooley? You don't know me, but I need some answers. Where are you from? Were you at the lab?"

Dooley looks up at me, blinks tears from his eyes.

"You can still make it," I lie. "Just give me some answers."

He fixes me in his gaze, and I can see that he can see I'm lying. He takes a deep breath—as deep a breath as he can manage, that is—and rasps, "Fuck you."

Well, that's just rude.

"Get your hands up where I can see them!" says somebody behind me. And it appears that I have allowed myself to be blindsided just the way Dooley was. I do as the lady says and stretch my fingers up to the empty sky.

"Turn around," she says. I find myself looking at a powerfully built chick in some sort of uniform. Like Dooley, she's impossibly old, maybe late twenties, but her face has a sort of well-fed roundness that is maybe the most alien thing about her. She's got a snub-nosed pistol pointed at me.

"I think your friend needs help," I say. "Somebody shot him."

"Step back," she says. "Slowly. Keep facing me. Don't move your hands down or I'll shoot you."

Fair enough. I do as she says. I am reminded of when I met Jefferson. I had him dead to rights, he went for my gun, and then we started making out. Heck of a meet cute. I don't see things going that way this time.

"It was two blond kids," I say. "They had me captive. They killed him." Not the best story, but I'm vamping. At least it seems to confuse the woman, which may give me a few extra nanoseconds.

She kneels down by Dooley and fumbles about with her hand, trying to find the pulse in his neck while still looking up at me.

"Just let me go, lady," I say, with my best Sad Orphan tone. "I didn't do anything!"

She looks down for a moment at Dooley, realizes he's dead, and decides to kill me. At least, that's what I figure.

"Turn around," she says.

I'm not sure what the point of that is. I mean, presumably it's to make her feel better about shooting me, since she won't have to look me in the eyes. It's odd, because if you think about it, the back of a person's head is every bit as personal to her as the front of her head. At least, I can't do very well without either of them. And from *my* point of view, I'd rather know the moment I'm going to die than have to spend the next ten seconds guessing when the light is going to go out.

Of all the answers I want, the one I want *least* is to the question *what happens when you die?* I figure I'm getting to that no matter what; in fact, it's the only big question you're guaranteed to get the answer to, no matter how stupid or uninquisitive you are.

"No," I say.

"Turn around," she repeats.

"Hell, no," I say. "If you're gonna do it, go ahead and do it."

She looks like she has a momentary crisis of confidence—what I'm hoping for. Then she gets some steel in her spine and closes one of her eyes to aim.

I look into the barrel.

The next sound is not a single shot but a volley that takes chunks out of her. Abel and Anna saving my bacon. She slumps against the hangar and slowly slides downward.

One answer postponed, I guess.

We look through the bullet holes in the side of the hangar. The tortured metal radiates heat.

Inside, a little campfire beats back the gloom.

"Anyone left?" I shout. "Make yourself known!"

"Yeah," says a thick young voice from the darkness. "Don't shoot, man!"

We kick in the side door, guns up.

At the circumference of the firelight there's a lump that turns out to be a body. An ancient guy with white hair, hands tied behind his back. A little hole above his right temple. Presumably killed by the twins' blasting.

And behind a pile of equipment, a tall, solidly built black kid, maybe seventeen years old. Also zip-tied up.

Abel says, "You want me to let him go?"

Anna says, "You want me to kill him?"

"No," I say. "Neither. Yet."

The kid, squinting against the dust, looks at me.

"I know you," he says.

"Now, that's a nice whip," says Theo, looking at the metallic-purple Ferrari.

"Little showy, isn't it?" I say.

"Man, fuck you." He looks at me with distaste. Distaste? Disdain. Distrust. General dissing.

I don't take it personally. Here's what I know he took me to mean: *You're black, so you want a flashy car. I'm white, and I have some taste.* And, frankly…who am I to say I didn't mean that when I said it, though I didn't know that I meant it. That is to say, everybody likes to think that they're not racist. But saying "I'm not racist" is like saying "I'm good-looking." It isn't really up to us. I know for a fact that I have prejudices. Like, for instance, I didn't even recognize him at first. He had been filed away with all the black people who didn't matter to me. He's prejudiced, too. He looks at me and thinks, *Spoiled white bitch.* I mean, he hasn't *said* it, but he's *thought* it pretty loud.

I try again. "There's no room for the Hitler Youth." That's what we call Anna and Abel. Actually, Theo called them that, and it stuck. I don't like the guy, but he has a pretty good turn of phrase.

"Man, there's plenty of room. Look how skinny they are." He looks at them. "This is a nice whip, right?"

The Hitler Youth turn from Theo to me, asking with their eyes what they should say. I flutter my hands, a gesture that means *this is up to you.*

"It's a nice whip," says Abel.

"Badass," says Anna.

"That's my dogs," says Theo, and he gives out some fist pounds.

We're on our third car. Each time our car runs out of gas, we just leave it on the side of the road and bust into another one. If we're lucky, the key is still in it.

Anyhow, I chose last time, so I guess Theo gets his way. And, as it happens, the keys are tucked above the window shade, and the gas tank is full. It comes to life growling like a pit bull with bronchitis.

"Tight," says Theo. The Hitler Youth squeeze into the cramped excuse for a backseat, and I lower myself into the passenger side. Actually, the car *is* pretty fly.

Theo lets out the clutch, and we lurch forward and stall. He fires it up again, and we judder to another quick stop.

"You're gonna fry the clutch," I say. "This is a Ferrari, not a Honda."

Theo is annoyed. He starts it again, then moves forward, gently. A little progress, as the tone of the engine changes to a different order of anger, then another stall.

"You've never driven one of these before, have you?" I say.

"Like *you* have," he says. Then he looks over and sees from my face that I have.

I say it for him. "Rich white bitch, I know. Switch."

He doesn't like the idea, but he also doesn't want to face the humiliation of stalling out again, so he gets out and we swap places.

"Car's just out of tune, that's all," says Theo.

I start it, press the clutch down, shift into first, let up the clutch gently, then more as the throttle engages, and pull out, the honey-throated engine roaring happily. I smile.

"Whatever," he says, and looks out his window.

"So let's imagine," I say to Theo, "that the plan works. They get to Harlem, sell them a line of bullshit, and Solon swallows it. What next?"

"They wanted to go to the UN, start, like, some sort of government or some shit. So that they could stand up to the army and navy and shit when they come back in."

I'm still trying to get my head around this new state of affairs. In fact, I wouldn't have believed Theo if I hadn't seen the oldies at the hangar. I would just think he was spinning some bullshit story with the eventual goal of getting laid, which is the reason for about half of the bullshit that dudes say, if not more. Anyhow, it would appear he's telling the truth. Which would mean that while I was working my way west and off the island, Jefferson and his crew were on an aircraft carrier. Which I guess explains why he didn't call or write or text or smoke signal.

I have to go off-road to get around a pileup, and the Ferrari's undercarriage scrapes on the shoulder. I awake from my reverie.

"So," I say, "you have a better idea?"

"I don't know if I have a better idea. But my people have to know the truth. Then we can all think of a better idea, or agree to go ahead and make up a country or whatever, except not because we didn't know what the hell was going on."

"The truth will set you free?" I say.

"Maybe. Maybe not. Lies sure will fuck you up, though."

I confess he is rising in my estimation. First time I met him, when we were thrown against some police cars by a bunch of Harlemites, I just figured I was gonna get used for fun and disposed of. That's probably what the Uptowners would have done to one of them had they wandered into Uptown territory.

"I don't know," I say.

"You don't know what?" he says.

"Just what to do," I say.

"Well, you best not try to stop *me*," he says.

So—do I help Theo, who I don't know at all, or help Jefferson, my…my ex, I guess. That is to say, he *did* break up with me. For that tomboy pip-squeak Donna. Whatever. Donna and I…we're cool.

Imprisonment will do that to you, change your attitude. All we had in that cell was each other. Frenemyship was taking root.

But Donna's not here.

So what place do I have with Jefferson? If he's off forming a nation? Can I be first lady? Hell with that. I should be queen. He can be my royal consort.

What gives him the right to move on? To just forget about me and my killer brain and my hot bod? Sometimes I don't know whether to put a bullet in his head or try to get back together. The eternal quandary.

"I don't think I'll try to stop you," I say, "but I don't know. Maybe I will."

Theo looks over at me, bemused.

"At least you're honest," he says.

The corridor of trees on either side of the highway widens in the overture to a town. I make out a Rite Aid sign and pull over.

"The hell we stopping?" asks Theo.

"I'll be back in a minute," I say.

"We shouldn't stop," says Theo. "Too dangerous."

"I need something, okay?"

"The hell you need?"

"You wouldn't understand."

"Bullshit, I wouldn't understand." Theo is insistent. Like I've called him stupid.

"Lady stuff, okay?"

"You're risking our lives for makeup?"

"*Tampons,* all right? I'm stopping for tampons because, against all reason, my period is starting! Jesus."

Theo sits there. "Oh," he says.

Yeah, I started feeling the crampy, fidgety working of my lady lab on the ride. It had been so long since the Sickness hit and neutered us that at first I thought it was a reaction to some of the truly crappy comestibles we'd been prying out of cans lately. But then, yeah, sure enough.

All you bros who are reading and can't handle the idea of menstruation, just—deal with it. Can we move on? Okay.

I figure it's a quick in and out at the Rite Aid. I mean, there wasn't any demand for tampons after What Happened, on account of everybody went sterile. Or so we thought. It appears that the factory has reopened. Personally? Except for the obvious mess and bother, I'm overjoyed. I think I would be a great mom.

I hear you laughing. But laugh at your peril. See, I regard my whole life as a tutorial on how *not* to raise kids. From creepy, distant dad to drunky, shrieky mom to feckless and preyed-upon au pairs and distracted and berated nannies. Emotional repression, hysterical outbursts, infidelity, contempt. I am an encyclopedia of what not to do. So all I have to do is the opposite, right?

Okay, so I killed a few people here and there. Maybe I have a little

247

teensy bit of an impulse-control issue to work through. But we all make mistakes, don't we? Besides, some of them weren't mistakes. Trust me.

Anyhow, I'm wending my way through the usual accumulated patina of years of social unrest—rotted-out bodies, lots of crap on the floor, spent shells, dead flies—when I realize that I forgot my bag of stuff in the car. Most everything I have is in there. First and foremost, the sweet AR-15 I snagged at the lab. This is a major blunder, since Theo could just drive off with the car and all my crap, or, worse, kill me, then drive off with the car and all my crap. Would Anna and Abel stand up for me? I can tell that their loyalties are already shifting; their tissue-thin excuses for personalities are bending to the gravitational pull of another alpha.

I guess I was, for a moment, back in a world of quick shopping stops and errands. Maybe it was because of a little iron deficiency. Whatever. The long and the short of it is that I suddenly feel quite alone and vulnerable.

What if I was to go out the back door, circle round quietly, attack Theo from where he isn't expecting me? I do still have a knife I lifted off Dooley, a nasty, aggressively sharp flat green metal-composite called a Gerber De Facto. Maybe I could get the gun back before he could defend himself. No. No time. No chance. Idiot.

I hear a shuffling sound and a hushed whisper. I scan the false twilight of the cavernous unlit store. Nothing. Then I see, in the gap between some denuded shelves, a figure pass by. And from the other side of me, down another alley of shelves, more forms slithering along through the undergrowth of garbage.

This really won't do, to have somebody get the drop on me for the second time in a row. I pretend, as best I can, that I haven't seen anything. I make to find something off the shelves, meanwhile palming the De Facto from its pressure sheath. The feel of the handle raises my spirits a bit.

I take some lipstick from a sales rack and look into the cheap mirror mounted under a chintzy glamour shot. I apply the lipstick, checking the reflection over my shoulder. I see the wicked little point of an arrow notched to a hunting bow. A hand pulls the arrow back—

And I spin and throw the knife as hard as I can, threading the gap between shelves and boxes. There's a squelch followed by an awful gasp, and the arrow looses, caroming off the floor and into the shelf by my shin.

So far so good, but I'm short one knife. I look down the aisle, to see that some kind of monster has rounded the corner.

It's green and scrofulous, with bits of thick braid-like hair hanging from its slack flesh. No neck or face but a shaggy head that slopes down over its shoulders.

In a moment, it's clear the monster is a kid in some kind of over-the-top head-to-toe camouflage. He has a crossbow with a rifle stock. When I turn the other way, I see another one down at the other end, a shotgun in his shaggy paws.

The kid with the crossbow aims and fires, but I manage to juke out of the way, and the bolt whips past me, striking home in the shoulder of the kid with the shotgun. Blood and swearing. I take the straight route to my knife, climbing one side of the shelves like a ladder and jumping down to the kid who's leaning slack-legged against the opposite shelf, bleeding out. I pick up his bow and slide an arrow out of the bracket mount—pull the string back until the compound's cocking mechanism takes over—turn to face the aisle between me and the door—and hear laughter.

"Look," says a voice. "It's Katniss!"

More laughter. A group. Six or seven of them, maybe.

They step into the gap on either side of me, with the courage of the already dead. Crossbows, guns, bows. They laugh. They laugh over the groans of their wounded friends.

I try to work out who the leader is. I look back and forth. All of them just shaggy forms. They look back. There is no leader. They're led by their hungers.

"She's hot," says one.

"Has anyone ever told you you're beautiful?" says another.

I have nothing to say. I have nothing to do, except take my shot, get the knife, die.

"'Samatter, bitch?" says one of them. I can't tell which. I can't see faces. It's like it's coming from all of them and none. "Don't you like us?"

And they start to move in.

Then I hear Theo. "Kath, get down," he says, his deep voice seeming to shake the rafters.

I drop.

With a sound like rocks falling on steel, bullets shred the kids in front of me. Some of the ones behind get hit by the tail-end of the burst.

The ones left standing are killed by Anna and Abel, coming up from behind them. In a moment, there's only one left, who makes a run for me, some kind of sword in his hand, but Theo sprints and catches him before he reaches me, taking him in a tackle that leaves them both gasping.

The kid still has his sword. He raises it up to stab Theo, who's too winded to move.

But I get him first. With one hand, I capture his arm at the top of its recoil, with the other, I jam the De Facto into his neck. Blood billows out, and he slumps sideways.

I crawl over to Theo, awkward as a puppet with a string cut, the adrenaline spent and burning my muscles.

I lean down and hug him.

"Thank you," I say.

He catches his breath.

"You forgot your bag," he says.

DONNA

CAMBRIDGE NEVER REALLY gets that cold, it just becomes more and more damp. The water comes from the sky, and it seeps from the walls, and it kind of gasses from the ground in the rare moment of sun. Mostly the sky and the buildings and the people are gray. We loiter around our ancient space heaters, coiled springs that glow orange when electricity is run through them; we cup our hands prayerfully around mugs of hot tea; our eyes linger about the trees and lawns and their green promises.

The drinking goes on, the drinking goes up. We tell ourselves it is fun, but really it is because we are bored and cold, and it helps us stay interested in the tight circle of people and the formulaic days of lectures and tutorials and essays and classes.

Then one night, deep into a session, I break the rules. I start telling Rab the truth. *In vino veritas,* they say, which means "in wine, truth." But the truth isn't in the wine, it's in me; the wine only makes the more fearful me go away for a bit. We stay up through the night, me talking and Rab listening.

As I let him in on my secret, I feel almost as if I am a different person. Telling Rab should make me feel more like myself, but it doesn't work that way; I feel less and less like the person whose story I'm unraveling to him. Maybe because it's only Rab I'm telling, and he is the perfect listener. He doesn't interrupt, and he doesn't judge, and he doesn't tire. I should be paying him by the hour.

He's a fire on which I'm burning my memories like unneeded possessions.

And then, one night, he kisses me. And I kiss him back.

I know that it's not supposed to be this way. Like, I'm supposed to mourn forever, I'm supposed to die of sorrow, or become a nun at least. That's what a heroine in a book would do. Maybe she'd go around in black and adopt fetching mournful poses. She'd resist to the end of the movie. She'd resist past the end of the movie and into the flashbacks of somebody else's movie, and she'd be the old lady who ain't nobody thought had an interesting life but who actually has a tale of tragic love to tell.

Maybe I should tell you that this is the way Jefferson would have wanted it. Like, he wouldn't want me to grieve too long; he wouldn't want me to stop living. Honestly? I think he'd be really jealous. But he can't be jealous, because he's dead.

He's gone, and with it first love is gone, and everything that attached to it, my soul, whatever. I'm stuck here with what's left.

This is what I would want for me if I weren't me, and I was telling me what I wanted for me if I were me. That I not be alone in this world. That I fight my way clear to a life.

And maybe this would seem better if I had a really romantic scene to report, like it would be more forgivable if it were more dramatic, with clenched jaws and running after trains and tears and feverish embraces.

Instead: It's late at Rab's place. Michael and Soph have headed home. A pot of spag bol sits on the carpet, plates piled on the tea table. Two empty bottles of plonk, one with the cork stuck inside. A saucer with Soph's spent rollies. Old music coming from the speakers.

I curl up with my head on Rab's lap. It's been that way awhile—the slippery slope of touch—at first it was like putting your head in the lion's mouth—ta-da! We did it without any sexual tension!—and it became the new standard—maybe it's possible for boys and girls just to be friends and to touch and be close and there's no harm done.

And then Rab strokes my cheek, and it feels good. But I put my hand on his to stop the feeling good but then it becomes us holding hands. And he leans down and kisses me. And it feels good, better than anything has felt in a long time, and everything after feels good and keeps on feeling good.

This is life.

And it feels healthy, if my saying everything that's on my mind and finally being able to speak the truth to someone is healthy, which it's supposed to be, right? He doesn't have that thing where he's jealous of somebody who came before him. Which makes sense, of course, only not making sense has never stopped anybody. Rab says everything I've seen and everyone I've known and loved is part of me, and it's me, all of me, that he wants to know.

Rab asks me about Welsh and the whole soft-sell, free-pastry interrogation thing we've got going on.

Rab: "What do you think they want to know?"

Me: "Everything. But Welsh seems to get especially interested when we talk about current events, or then-current events, like what happened right around when What Happened was happening. Like not just what was on the news but what I *saw* happening."

Rab: "Why you? I mean, no offense, but you weren't exactly at the center of things. Why are you the one they set up at Cambridge? Why not that kid Captain? Or one of the others?"

Me: "The others escaped before..."

Rab: "Donna—these people don't do things by accident. If the Reconstruction and the government thought the others were of use, they would be here."

Me: "Because I'm the only one left. Well, me and Captain. They liquidated everybody in quarantine a couple of years ago, right?"

He looks ashamed and angry. Nobody wants to talk about that.

Rab: "Yes. They had to. Well. They said they had to. It was agreed on in Brussels."

He means the European Union. They had a protocol for everything, including, it turns out, what to do with a global pandemic.

Me: "Well, there you go. I'm special."

I smile.

Rab: "Yes, you are special, you are a special, special, most won-derful creature. But in addition to that . . . there must be something. Tell me what you were up to that they might be interested in."

So I tell Rab what I haven't told Welsh.

Me: "Well . . . there's this thing I haven't said. Right? You may not know this, but I was South Korea."

Rab: "Excuse me?"

Me: "Yeah, South Korea, Model UN. Do you guys have that here?"

Rab: "No."

So I tell him what it is.

Rab: "I'm imagining you in one of those dresses that looks like a tulip."

Me: "It's not like that. You don't wear national dress. You study up the issues, like the US military presence and the standoff with North Korea and whatnot. You make speeches. So, anyway, our teacher was very rah-rah and used to take us to visit the actual UN. She had connections there, some functionary or other. So we got to see the General Assembly and hear them talk and stuff."

Rab: "Interesting."

Me: "Not really. You're thinking it's all Cuban Missile Crisis and that general dude holding up a fake vial of anthrax, but actually it's more like one schmo after another making a speech about the same boring commemoration of this or that. But there was one time where it was really interesting, which is when Mrs. Geleitner got us in to see the opening remarks that the president was going to make at the big meeting on the Sickness."

Rab: "Wow."

Me: "Yeah, it was pretty intense. Everybody was up in arms about how the Russians and the Chinese were blowing it off, and security was nuts. The president had, like, a zillion Secret Service guys with him, and this was when they started open carrying—like, they obviously had guns and stuff besides their cool suits. And there was this whole entourage of, like, power-suit ladies and an army officer and stuff—and a general-type guy, and he had this kind of puffy briefcase. Very dowdy. Anyhow, the president was about to give a speech when we heard these big booms from outside. It was some kind of terrorist attack, only it was sort of half-assed, thank God. Everybody was freaking, and the Secret Service was all human-shielding the president, and UN security told us we had to leave in an orderly manner. So pretty much that was that."

Rab: "Where did the president—"

Me: "Oh! Except I was within, like, twenty feet of the president, which is as close as I ever got to a president. His entourage was heading out, and I heard something about a secure room."

Rab: "And then what?"

Me: "Then I headed back home and switched on the TV, except the TV was gone. Blank screen. That was how it was those days. No Internet, the TV gone, no news, only rumor."

Rab: "What happened to the president?"

Me: "Look, I know this sounds nuts, but everybody and their uncle was getting sick. I really didn't have time to think about it. It was the least of my worries. I had been thinking about quitting school anyhow, but my mom insisted I go, like it was going to make things normal or whatever. So I go on a field trip, and somebody tries to blow the building up. I know that sounds pretty extraordinary, but shit like that was going down all the time."

For a moment, Rab's eyes look glazed over, like he's cogitating deeply, chewing over a bone. Then he comes back.

Rab: "I'm sorry. I didn't mean to …"

Me: "It's okay. I feel okay telling you. Anyhow, I never told Welsh that."

Rab: "Why?"

Me: "Because he wanted to know. Like, really wanted to know. And I don't trust him."

Rab: "But you trust me."

Me: "Of course I do."

Actually, I don't.

Call it cynicism. Call it an inability to take life as it comes. I don't know. But lately, I've been getting the feeling that this is all too good to be true.

That is to say, everything that happened from the moment I woke up in the bed in the Old Guest Room. The Shirley Temple moment. Seeing Rab staring at me in the noodle restaurant. His approaching me at the college bar. His patience. His goodness. His ability to listen.

What, I've begun to think, if he's just another kind of listening device?

Maybe it is a sign of low self-esteem. Like, maybe I can't believe that I rate this sort of attention from him. That would be damn embarrassing, if I turn out to be wrong. Still, I hope I am. Wrong.

I wake up alone, which is odd. Rab usually stays, or at least says good-bye.

He's not in the sitting room, so that covers the entirety of my domain. Maybe he's down in the bathroom. That's one of the charming eccentricities—read: incredible pains in the ass—about the rooms at Trinity. Most of the bathrooms and showers are at the bottom of a stairwell if they are in your stairwell at all; in fact, I have to go all the way down and walk through the colonnade to the next staircase along to find a shower. It's kind of a drag having to cruise through a fifteenth-century courtyard in a bathrobe with wet hair.

When I get to the bottom of the staircase, barefoot for better sneaking, Titch is not at his usual post on his tortured metal chair, nor is Taut Guy. That's strange.

The air is chill and clear, Nevile's Court is a flitting hologram caught in the silver-blue gaze of the moon. My feet catch the chill of the stones. I marvel for a moment at the beauty of it, the hushed secrecy. All the drunk students are in bed and the libraries are in hibernation and there is no one but me and the nightingales.

But then—I hear a serpentine whispering and a vague thrumming as the deep pocket of the arcade beneath the Wren catches the low notes.

Three figures are silhouetted against the green-gray of the Backs of the Cam at nighttime. One is gigantic, unmistakably Titch.

I slink along the wall, out of sight of the silhouettes, who haven't noticed me and continue their hissing. I creep slowly past M staircase, closer and closer.

I take in another face—it's Welsh.

He's talking to Rab.

Rab: "There isn't much time before she notices I'm gone."

My legs give out, and I slide down the wall to sit on the pocked marble. I so wanted to be wrong about this. My heart makes one last stab at an explanation—maybe Welsh ambushed Rab at the bottom of the stairs and is giving him the third degree, or trying to talk him out of something, or trying to talk him into something.

But it doesn't sound that way.

Welsh: "Get her to repeat the story. Verify the details."

Rab: "It's taken long enough to get to this. She's very closed. If I push on this—"

Welsh: "There isn't much time."

Rab: "Is it necessary to—"

Welsh: "Yes."

Rab: "Fine. But I think you've got what you need. We should wrap it up or—"

Welsh: "Or what? Ah. You've gone native."

Rab: "She's not a native. Nor is she the enemy."

Welsh: "That's where you're mistaken. She is a native. She's a tribeswoman from a savage land. We are explorers in that strange country. And there's a ways yet to go."

Rab: "I should get back."

I make my way quickly and quietly along the colonnade and then up the stairs and, my skin still prickling with the sense of betrayal and anger, I slip into bed and wait.

JEFFERSON

THIS IS WHAT HAPPENED to Hafiz, the last survivor of the
United Nations School.

When the shit hit the fan, Hafiz, son of an Indonesian delegate, and
his classmates retreated uptown from Cooper Plaza to the UN complex
itself. Special security arrangements had been made for the families,
and it was reassuring to the diplomats to have their children nearby
with chaos erupting through the rest of New York.

Things went the way of all flesh in the compound, as elsewhere, and
before too long, there was nothing but teens left—a sort of supertribe
of kids from all around the world.

Unfortunately, they found it difficult to live up to the high purpose
of the UN; factions formed, often around linguistic, religious, or ethnic
lines. They fought over the control of the food supplies that had been
laid in at the complex, and when there was nothing tangible to fight
over, they fought over old or new grudges. What made it different from
the way things were Before was that the old balance of power (if it was

actually balanced at all) didn't matter. It came down to the size of the teenage population of each delegation. Africa was the continent with the most countries, so for a while, they all faced the unaccustomed situation of being in charge, until the Europeans and Asians teamed up to fight them. Then the Oceanians came in on the Africans' side, and for a time, there was parity as each side whittled away at the population of the other. The few Americans had either fled to their homes or been summarily dispatched by all and sundry for one historical crime or another. For a while, the North and South Americans had maintained an alliance, but they fell to squabbling and liquidated one another. And then the rest fought over their meager treasures. By the time we found Hafiz, everyone was dead or gone, and he alone was left to tell the tale.

This he did, pointing out the heroes and villains of the story, whom he had installed in the seats formerly occupied by their delegations. They sat in total agreement and amity, slowly decaying as Hafiz endlessly reworked the diorama.

Hafiz took some convincing when it came to removing all the bodies, but once we began, he took to it with a sort of creative fervor, constantly tweaking the pile that grew and grew behind the Secretariat building. I've begun to think that he is just looking for something to manifest a little control over, so we let him rearrange the corpses as he will. At first, he wanted to organize them by geographical origin; then he rethought it and, in a burst of energy, shifted them around according to political alignment. Since we are going to light them on fire anyway, it seems beside the point. In fact, it seems deranged.

In fact, it *is* deranged. But it is preferable to his dogged attempts to keep us from dismantling his "work of art" in the Security Council chamber.

We need the space. The Gathering of the Tribes is coming, and I think it best to clean the Security Council of murdered kids.

Whatever it took for Hafiz to survive the massacres and melees, he seems pretty harmless himself, soft-handed and doe-eyed, a willing and able guide through the darkened labyrinth of the complex.

As we set the torch to the pile of dead, I find Hafiz at my right shoulder. "Beautiful," he says. When I look at him, he explains, "The end of the old world order. The ashes that are needed for the phoenix to rise. Right?"

"Maybe," I say.

"Always," he says. "The hope of a new world smells like the burning flesh of the old."

I remember the platter of roasted human meat—shank, in retrospect—that the Ghosts tried to feed us in the library. If they're still alive, no doubt it is because they are still preying on the rest of us. What will we do if they appear at the Gathering? What sort of crimes can be forgiven?

Can mine?

By the next day, the Council chamber is ready and people have started arriving. My tribe and the Dead Rabbits keep order and give the lay of the land.

Security is lax. There's no question of getting people to give up their weapons—everyone's too keyed up and paranoid. May as well ask them to give up their clothes. Instead, we let it be known that we're operating on a strict eye-for-an-eye policy. Each tribe can nominate a security chief who's responsible for their tribe's behavior. Really, they're glorified human collateral, but people are so nuts about titles and distinctions that they take the job willingly.

The Harlemites, led by Solon, arrive. The Fishermen from South Street. The Hop Sing Boys. Chelsea and Clinton. Gansevoorts, Meats, Fourteens, Thuggees, Baseball Furies, Lady Killers, Buckley Bums, West Siders, True West Siders, One and Only West Siders, Heads, Knicks, Flatirons, and a hundred tribes I don't know. There are even delegates from the Drummers, looking about as stoned as I remember. But no sign yet of the Uptowners.

Finally they arrive, a jarring combination of gray suits and camo. Fifty strong, the delegation barges its way into the hall, ripples of anger and fear spreading out from their vanguard.

I'm at the front, by the vast horseshoe-shaped table, trying to figure out some sort of seating plan with Hafiz, Chapel, Brainbox, and Peter. I head up the aisle toward the Uptowners, my heart drumming against my rib cage.

I've known they would come, hoped they would come, feared they would come, and now that they are here, I don't know what to do. Grudges are easy to come by in this assembly, but the Uptowners have collected more than anyone else. They run the middle of the island, netting everyone they can in the market that's run out of the Bazaar at

Grand Central; those they can't co-opt or dominate, they kill. And only they can tell me where the rest of my tribe is to be found.

I hear a familiar voice. "We can start now." And Evan steps to the front of his delegation.

I'd counted on his having been crushed in the collapse of Donna's old house.

But I never was particularly lucky.

Carolyn and her posse have filtered up from the round table. She steps right up to Evan, eyeballs him as his soldiers tense up.

"You remember me?" she says.

"Sorry, babe, I got a lot of bitches."

Evan was born to be punched. But we can't have a fight break out before the Gathering even begins.

"Stop it, Carolyn," I say.

"He knows where our friends are," she says.

"I know," I say. "We'll get to that. But not this way." Carolyn looks at me, her fury transferring. "Please," I say.

She steps back. Evan smiles. "I see you still need to muzzle your females," he says.

"When this all blows up," says Carolyn, "I'm coming for you first."

"Let's go now," says Evan. He reaches for the nine millimeter where it sits in a chest holster.

"Easy." I hear Solon and turn to see him and his soldiers standing behind me. A slick, 3-D-printed AR-15 emphasizes his point. "Let's all relax. See how this goes before we start to fussing and fighting."

Harlemites and Uptowners face one another, guns out and up, me in the middle. An overblown scene from a bad action movie. The moment balances on a pinpoint.

"Go on, Jefferson," says Solon. "Like the boy said. Now you can get started."

Again a seething sea of faces. A hundred different groupings, a thousand, a menagerie of aspects and types. The only thing they have in common right now is that they are looking at me and wondering why the hell they are here.

"I want to thank you for coming," I say. It seems an oddly formal statement to make to a crowd of kids who, in other circumstances, would just as soon be killing one another on sight. Still, you have to start somewhere, somehow.

"I—we, my friends, my tribe, and I—called you here because we have an amazing opportunity. I'm going to tell you about that in a little while, but first I want to tell you about...a dream I have for all of us."

I feel the falling sensation that I feel whenever I step out of the fortifications of my detachment and reserve. Out here is where a lot of people live. Myself, I only venture out every once in a long while. The last time was in the public library, when I told Donna for the first time that I was in love with her.

Why is speaking to a crowd like telling a girl you love her? No time to work that out now. The crowd is alert and skeptical—it's the word *dream* that's done it; a word that's the tool of politicians, reformers, and performers. They're wondering if I'm any of these things, or just an idiot.

"For years now," I go on, "we have been living in a state of anarchy. Actually, the way we live gives anarchy a bad name. We've been living in hell.

"Part of it is just the cards we were dealt. We lost our families. We lost our country. We lost our technology. Food is running out. Medicine is running out. Even time is running out. We all know this. The Sickness is waiting, not someplace far away, but inside of us.

"But part of this hell is ourselves. Our actions. Our decisions. Part of this hell is our own doing.

"We have killed, not to defend ourselves, but to enrich ourselves. To please ourselves. We have betrayed our friends. We have stolen. We have abandoned the sick and abused, the weak."

At this, there is catcalling and cries of "Hell, yeah!" from the Uptowners, and from others. But, surprisingly, they are shouted down by the rest of the crowd.

"Some of these things we did, we did because people want more than what they can get. More food, more life, more love. There never was enough. All of these things were always scarce. That is what it is to be alive and to be human. To have less than we think we need.

"But we don't have to be this way. We don't have to hurt each other, or dominate each other, or steal from each other."

"Fag!" comes a catcall from the Uptowners. But that, too, is shouted down.

"We don't want to be against one another. Not really. We all want the same thing. We want to be happy in the time we have left, don't we?"

Silence. Whether it's the silence of complete bafflement, or of everyone pondering, I don't know.

"There is no place in the world where nobody dies. There is no place where nobody is hungry, or nobody hurts. That place is only in our imagination. But if we only get our heads around it, we can go a little way toward making this real place more like that imaginary place. They call that place Utopia.

"So what kind of people live in Utopia? People like us. We are all different," I say. "And we are all the same. They used to say, 'All men are created equal.' Myself, I don't know if I was created. I don't know if I'm here by design or by accident. My parents taught me some crazy shit. They taught me I was God, only I had forgotten. You believe that?" Laughter from the crowd.

"Anyway, *if* you believe that, the good news is, so are you. That's it, in a nutshell. We're not just similar. We're the *same*. If I help you out, I'm helping myself out. If you help me out, you're helping yourself out. No matter what you believe, that's the way it was supposed to work, right? That's the golden rule. Treat others the way you'd want them to treat you. How do we get there?

"Well, some people think that the only way that ever happens is if there's someone bigger and stronger forcing you to do it. After all, that's the way our folks did it, didn't they? They're the ones who kept us in line; they're the ones who kept us from abusing our brothers and sisters.

"But Mom and Dad are gone. And I don't want to replace them. I don't want to replace Mom and Dad with a king or a queen or a president or a dictator." I can't help but look at Evan, then at Solon, as I say this.

"In ancient Athens," I say, "they had the *Ecclesia*. It meant 'Assembly.' Like in school, I guess. The *Ecclesia* was composed of every Athenian citizen. They were the ones who ran the country, according to the laws. Not senators or representatives. People spoke for themselves. Direct democracy. One person, one vote.

"That's what I'm here to say. One person, one vote. One tribe, one constitution. All of us. Working together. We could start something here that, if we all die, which we all will, someday...then someone will know...in the last moment, with our last breath, we didn't act like animals. We acted like people. We acted like human beings."

The place is quiet.

"I want us to make something new here. And I hope you'll help."

I don't have anything more to say, for the moment. Then, a little at first, more and more, until it is the sound of rain on a tin roof, clapping.

I realize that I have been expecting the worst. Is it possible that all anyone was waiting for was someone to say it?

The applause turns into foot stomping, a surprisingly aggressive reaction to a proposal for peace. Solon rises out of the Harlem delegation and heads to the front. He has, incongruously, a football tucked under his arm.

"Wise words from brother Jefferson," he says. "Speaking for all of us up in Harlem, I can say that we could all use a little peace. That's why I'm here. But—before we get all...*churchy* about democracy, I want us to think about a few things."

Solon eyes the crowd. "You ever heard the expression 'Democracy is two wolves and a lamb deciding what's for dinner'?" Laughter. "Now, most of the people I see here are wolves. If you weren't, you wouldn't have made it. It has not been a great time for lambs."

I think of the Mole people, hiding underground in their gussied-up subway stop, until we led the Uptowners to them.

"There are wolves and *wolves*, though. Once you take all the tribes and make one big tribe out of them, yesterday's wolves are tomorrow's lambs. Always somebody bigger and meaner than you are, am I right?

"Maybe you're thinking, we'd all be citizens, we'd all be the same. We'd all have the same rights. My brothers and sisters are here to tell you it ain't necessarily so.

"Brother Jefferson talked about Athens and about the Assembly, and I'm named after the dude who gave Athens its laws, so you *know* that sounds good to me. But—you all have to know *this*. You know how many citizens there were in Athens? Round about forty thousand."

He shrugs, building up the pause for rhetorical effect.

"Now. You know how many slaves there were in Athens?" Another pause.

"One. Hundred. Thousand." He thumps on the table for effect. "One hundred thousand. Each person who had a vote owned, on average, more than two other human beings who not only didn't have a vote but didn't have any rights at all. And let's talk about the girls. You want to know how many women could vote in the Assembly?"

Another moment of quiet before it drops. "None. Women didn't have the vote. Kind of like when things got started here in America, right? No vote for women. People bought and sold.

"If we're gonna start afresh," he says, "then we've gotta start on the right foot. We've got to know that we are doing this for the lambs as well as the wolves."

There's shouts and wolf howls from the Uptowners, who lean back in their seats, feet up.

"Hey!" shouts Solon, and—such is his native authority—they quiet to listen. He holds up the football. "See this? Personally signed by Mr. Jerry Rice, wide receiver for the San Francisco 49ers, greatest football player that ever lived. Needless to say, it is worth something, even in this benighted time when fools can boost Bentleys for free. You heard of a talking stick? Native American thing where only the person holding it gets to talk? Well, this is the talking *ball*. I'm willing to pass it— even to you." He looks at Evan, who looks back with reptilian scorn. "But right now, I'm the motherfucker has the football. Understand?"

At the word *football*, I notice Hafiz twitch with recognition. He stares at Solon, perturbed. "That's not the football," he says to himself.

"What do you mean?" I ask him.

"That's not the football. The football is underground."

I really have no idea what he's saying, and I figure it to be a little glitch of his system, an artifact of his crazy.

"As I was saying," Solon continues, "democracy is a fine thing. The law is a fine thing. But none of it matters if it's wolves and lambs. Know why? Justice. Everybody has a different idea of what that is. Lambs think that justice is everybody eating grass and leaving everybody else to eat grass. Wolves think that justice is eating lambs.

"So the question is, what is justice? That's all 'the law' is, an answer to that question. So we're here to make a city-state. All well and good. We're here to make the laws. All well and good. But let's not lose sight of what we're really here for. To answer the question: What is justice?"

There's a long silence, and then Evan stands up. He and Solon look at each other.

"I'm open," he says.

Solon looks down at the ball. Hefts it. Throws it in a long, perfect spiral to Evan.

Evan catches it clean and climbs his way over the chairs in front of him and down a row of contorting tribesmen. He makes his way down the aisle to the front of the room.

"My name's Evan," he says, "and I'm a wolf."

A little laughter from the crowd, a little whooping from his tribe.

"A lot of you know me or know about me. I definitely recognize some of the faces here. For what it's worth, I come here to represent the Uptown Confederacy. We have a thousand soldiers under arms. We run the Bazaar. We rule the center of the island. We kick ass, and we take names. I came here to talk about the terms under which all of you would surrender. I figured when else would I have a chance to get all of you motherfuckers in the same room? Now that I'm here, I can see that all you want to do is talk about truth and justice and the American way or some shit. Like the way the world works is up for discussion.

"But it's not. You want to know what justice is? Justice is the guy with the gun telling the guy without the gun what to do. Anything else is just opinions. And I don't have time for the opinions of a bunch of sheep. Why should I listen to all this bullshit?" He looks at Solon. "Okay, you got shiny plastic guns. Good for you. You want to change things, use them. We'll see who ends up getting served for dinner. Until then? We're out."

Evan takes the ball and spikes it. It bounces high, up and back, finally ricocheting off the mural at the back of the room. Having done his microphone drop bit, he heads toward the exit. His delegation gets up and follows. Some of them actually seem to have doubts, but not enough to keep them here.

"Evan," I say. He turns.

"We can't do this without the Uptowners. You're too important."

"I know," he says. He turns to go again.

"If you don't stay, you're going to lose everything."

He turns and laughs. "Bring it."

"You're gonna want to stay," I say.

"Give me one good reason."

"I've got one," I say.

He waits, expressionless.

"The Cure."

A long moment.

"Bullshit."

"He's for real," says Solon.

"That's the reward for citizenship," I say. "Life."

They're listening.

DONNA

I LEAVE THE LIGHTS OFF and wait for Rab. The little college-issue clock on the wall does its job pedantically, filling up the moments. Pedantic, pedantock. Maybe it's a sort of Geiger counter measuring my illusions as I shed them. Gone—the future. Gone—love. Gone—peace. Gone—trust.

In truth, I knew it in my bones, I felt it in the quiet places. But I took what I could anyway. I wanted the love, even if it was poisoned. I could use the attention. I did. And it's not so easy to subtract emotion from pleasure. So, for all my cold assessment, there's something else, affection turning into anger.

In the cold hollow air, it is easy to hear footsteps hissing on the stone stairs and easy to hate myself for recognizing them as Rab's and not anyone else's. What a useless talent to have.

Rab enters in a perfect impression of normality, clearly expecting me to be asleep, to be stupid, to be clueless. When he sees me in the chair, and sees the gun, he is genuinely surprised.

Rab: "Where did you get that?"

Me: "I made it." I kept this from him, my trip to the university FabLabs to commission the gun from one of the boffins in the university 3-D Printing Club. If I was wrong, I thought, it might scare him away, another sign that I hadn't shaken off old habits of violent thought and violent action.

Rab: "Why?"

Me: "Because it's fucking impossible to buy a gun in this country."

Rab: "No, why are you pointing it at me?"

Me: "Rab—I assume that's your actual name, right?—sit down with your hands where I can see them and stop fucking with me. Okay?"

Rab sits. His eyes look away briefly, an involuntary motion as he thinks up something to say.

Me: "Let me guess. You can explain. You can explain why I saw you snitching on me to Welsh, who you are supposed to distrust, because you're such a lefty and ninety-niner and free spirit, right? You can explain how you got into my knickers under false premises." (Nice deployment of local idiom, that.) "You can explain what you're doing here."

He takes a deep breath.

Rab: "Not really. That is, I can explain what I'm doing. I just can't explain it in a way that . . . keeps things the way they were."

Me: "You mean with you and me having sex and being boyfriend and girlfriend and whatnot, and me not knowing that you were a total fucking liar?"

277

Rab: "Yes. But I want to say that ... I meant the sex."

Me: "Lucky me."

Rab: "And I care for you."

Me: "Stop, before I use this."

Rab: "And how about how you lied to me? You told me you were the daughter of someone high up in the Restoration. You're not. You're a ..."

Me: "A what? Tell me."

Rab: "You're a survivor. I admire that. And part of that surviving was telling lies. When you were with me, were you lying about that, too?"

Me: "Yes, lying. I just needed you to survive. You were a soft landing."

A squall of anger casts a shadow on his face.

Rab: "Okay. Well, you've got questions, I've got answers."

He says it in a sort of mordantly humorous way, as if we've both found ourselves in a difficult position, as opposed to my finding him out. I don't like his tone.

Me: "Fine, question one. Who the fuck are you?"

Rab: "I am who I say I am. 'Rab' isn't a cover or anything. It's me."

Me: "But you're a spy, not a history student."

Rab: "I am a student. I was. I was also caught up in some stuff that would have earned me some serious jail time."

Me: "So you flipped. You're an agent ... agent whatever? Are Soph and Michael in on it?"

Rab: "No."

Me: "So you're gonna get them busted, like some shitty police informant?"

Rab: "No. They really have nothing to do with this. College idealists, that's all. If they weren't protesting government policies, they'd be into music. Same difference. This is about something much bigger."

Me: "You work for Welsh?"

Rab: "I'm under him, yes. He's my handler. He 'runs' me."

Me: "Like you're an app."

Rab: "I guess I am, in a way."

Me: "Can he hear all of this?"

Rab: "Probably."

Me: "Then he'll hear me when I say that I'm going to put a hole in him if he comes through that door. *And* Titch."

Rab: "Okay."

Me: "And I'm seriously thinking of airing you out, too."

Rab: "I can understand that."

Me: "So why shouldn't I?"

Rab: "The same reason I agreed to do this."

Me: "Not because you're into me, obviously."

Rab: "Don't sell yourself short."

He smiles. That smile.

Me: "Don't go thinking I give a shit about you."

Rab: "You're going to want to help. The way I wanted to help. This is important. Look, it was only a matter of time before I told you. I didn't like hiding what was going on."

Me: "Seemed like you enjoyed it at the time."

He looks ashamed. Why do I care?

Rab: "It's about what happened at the UN."

Me: "The field trip?"

Rab: "What you saw on the field trip. Your interrogation logs from the *Ronald Reagan* pointed to the possibility that you might know something about the president's entourage that day. That would make you the only eyewitness we have access to. We've been working out the significance of that. Thanks to you, we think we know."

Me: "I had some kind of evidence? Did you ever think of just asking me?"

Rab: "We did ask. You weren't telling. Welsh couldn't get to it, no matter how he tried."

Me: "So he thought that if he used some kind of, what, gigolo, I'd be so loved up I'd spill everything?"

Rab: "Technically they call it a honeypot. And yes. And you did tell me. You opened up."

Me: "Because I needed you."

Rab: "And I'm grateful for that, Donna. You don't know how much you've come to mean—I don't care if the others are listening—"

Me: "Stop it before I put a fucking bullet in your brain."

Rab looks at me with his beautiful face that I'm ready to destroy, his pretty lie of a face.

Rab: "Listen. I wouldn't have done any of this if it weren't really, really important."

Me: "Why?"

Rab: "Because your president died at the UN, in a terrorist attack during the conference."

Me: "Bullshit."

Rab: "It's true. We didn't know for sure until recently."

Me: "Okay, boo-hoo. Lots of people died."

Rab: "Yes, but he had the football."

Me: "What football?"

Rab: "The football is the name of the briefcase that contains the launch codes for America's nuclear arsenal."

Cold sweat starts.

Me: "I remember I saw that in a movie. But that was just so that he could give the order, right? It was just a bunch of codes so the president could prove he was who he said he was."

Rab shakes his head.

Rab: "That's what it was from the fifties until relatively recently. A list of instructions for the Emergency Alert System, a folder with a list of secure locations, a notebook containing the various strike options, and the biscuit, which was a laminated card with the codes you're thinking of. But they changed it after the outbreak of the Sickness. They wanted to be able to override the system remotely. In case the civil and military infrastructure went down."

Me: "Which means what?"

Rab: "Which means that, in theory, whoever has the nuclear football can bring the US nuclear arsenal out of hibernation and launch it whenever they want."

I take a while to absorb this.

Me: "So...doomsday?"

Rab: "Possibly. In the wrong hands."

Me: "Whose are the right hands?"

Rab: "Look. I'm not going to pretend that I always agree with what the government and the Reconstruction Committee do. But they are doing what they're doing so that the world as we know it can continue."

Me: "What if the world as we know it shouldn't continue?"

Rab: "You want to get rid of this? For what? Utopia? That's Jefferson, not you. Utopia isn't coming."

My face flushes. He has no right to say his name. He continues—

Rab: "You were always more practical than that, Donna. I don't think you want a nuclear war, do you?"

Me: "Well, that's kind of a loaded question, Rab. Who's going to start this war?"

Rab: "When you met them, they called themselves the Resistance."

Chapel and the rest. The enemies of the new order.

Me: "So—what—these are just some sort of mustache-twirling baddies you're up against? Why the hell would they want to start a war?"

Rab: "They don't want to start a war. They want to start a revolution. They want to bring down the system. You've seen that kind of thing, right? The system crumbling? No authority? No laws?"

I nod.

Rab: "How did that work out for you?"

Me: "So what do you want from me? You were going to come to me sooner or later, right? What do you want?"

He smiles.

Rab: "We want a man—we want a woman—on the inside."

Me: "You want me to go back?"

Rab: "We do."

Me: "Fuck you."

Rab: "Think about it."

Me: "I thought about it. No way. I'm not going back. Throw me in jail. I'm not going back to New York. There's nothing for me there."

Rab: "You're wrong. There is something for you there. Or rather, there's someone."

I can't speak. There is no more bandwidth. Too many feelings.

Rab: "Yes."

Is it possible that he doesn't look too happy about it?

Me: "Jefferson."

Rab: "Yes. Jefferson's alive."

Me: "No. Welsh told me he was dead."

Rab: "He was lying."

Me: "Fuck you. Fuck him. I'm going to kill him."

Rab: "I understand."

Me: "No, you don't."

Rab: "For all we know, he may be dead. He was alive when he left the ship. There was no shootdown. I didn't want them to tell you that, but . . . they wanted to make you more . . ."

Me: "Emotionally available?"

Rab: "Open. To me. Yes. They play for keeps, Donna. I don't like it, but they think they have to do it that way. If it were up to me . . . well, I always felt like you and I belonged together no matter what. Without any lies."

I look at him and balance the hatred I feel for him and all of them with what I feel for Jefferson.

Me: "I'm going back for him."

I'm going back to him.

PETER

THEY DO THE CURE-AS-SACRAMENT THING AGAIN, a long line of kids waiting in hushed anticipation for new life in the form of Jefferson's reengineered plasma.

The old Moroccan tent at the Square felt like a little parish church; this is more like a cathedral. The big old mural with its handsome stereotyped figures and millions of crazy-pants, indiscernible meanings looms over us. The crates of serum that Solon brought down with him are heaped within the magic circle of the Security Council desk; we block the way in with our bodies and administer to the throng one by one.

Given that we know we are giving new life to all of them, it's hard not to cop a certain messianic attitude. Don't get me wrong, I don't think I'm the Second Coming. More like we're evangelists. Hold the dropper over their tongues and let half a century of future drip down their throats. It's hard for the kids we're saving not to get rewired by the experience. They look up at us like we're more than rescuers, more than benefactors. Word has gotten round about us, and especially Jefferson, and he walks in a radiation cloud of worshipful gratitude, a supercelebrity. Maybe people need that sort of thing. Not so much that they want to see people as greater than so much as that they want to be lesser than. That way they don't have to make their minds up for themselves.

That's the problem I see in this whole democracy thingamajig we've got going. Ain't no way that Jefferson counts as just one vote, given that he's suddenly Florence Nightingale meets George Washington meets Jesus. People *listen* to him, like everything he says is in boldface. And since he was the one who got this whole thing started (at my guy Chapel's urging, I hasten to add), it seems like he gets to set the agenda. Everybody around him who has been part of getting the Cure to the people has a kind of special status, too.

Right beneath that in the political pecking order is Cheekbones, aka Evan, who seems to derive his special status from the fact that he's opposed to Jefferson and Solon on pretty much everything, which means he attracts all the people who are in his ideological vicinity, the thugs and meatheads and wing nuts.

Below that, you've got the people with a rap, who can talk up a storm and convince people of things, whether or not the content of what they're saying is actually worthwhile or even sensible. Sometimes it doesn't matter how good your idea is if you can't express it right, and you can get all sorts of wrong-ass ideas across if you put them the right way.

Anyhow, motherfuckers be *talking*.

They talk about justice and they talk about rights and they talk about laws, and they keep going on and on, the football flying around here and there like nobody's business. It's Jefferson's wet dream, DIY Utopia.

Which is great, I guess, except that it feels to me like a too-many-cooks-spoil-the-broth type sitch? Every time Jefferson proposes sweeping legislation or whatever, it gets barnacled with ideas by what I'll call special-interest groups. People look out for their tribes. They all want to be considered as legal entities or whatnot, as nobody can really get their heads entirely around the idea that we're just one big tribe. Or they think the idea sounds like it'll be hunky-dory until the shit hits the fan. So right away we get to a sort of two-for-one deal where there's an assembly of tribes that decides what the full Assembly is gonna vote on. Of course, this means that the littlest tribe has as much say as the biggest in what's on the docket. Which seems to me like it's gonna lead to a lot of fracturing, like big tribes turning into confederations of smaller tribes, as the Uptowners claim to be.

The Uptowners are the biggest problem. For now they go along with everything, but it's pretty clear to everybody that they can choose to blow the whole thing up whenever they want. They're hanging with the process so long as they're guaranteed the Cure. Meantime, they're holding their own carrot and stick, which is they've got half our tribe hostage.

Jefferson and Solon and the Assembly are, as far as I can tell, cutting and pasting off whatever constitution they can lay their hands on, from the US one to the UN charter to something some dude called Hammurabi wrote, whoever the hell he was. Freaky Hafiz keeps arriving with new books from some diplomatic library on the compound, suggesting laws like he's a waiter pointing out good items on the menu.

Anyhow, you know how it is. It's great to be high-minded and stuff, but the moment-to-moment is kind of a bore. The first bunch of laws are pretty big and simple to decide on, your basic "ape no kill ape" type of common sense.

Then we get into some more involved arguments about what private property is when you're living a scavenging post-apocalyptic lifestyle. Of course, most of the stuff we actually have nowadays used to belong to somebody else, except they're unlikely to claim it back, since they're dead. Up until now, the rule has been that your private property is whatever you can keep somebody else from grabbing first. Of course, that doesn't work in the perfect city-state-of-grace that we're whipping up. Can't have everybody jacking everybody else all the time.

But when you try to define what property is, things get kind of twisty. Turns out the only thing you really own is your body. I mean, theoretically, that's the only thing you can't be separated from and remain you, right? So that's where we start. And it means more than you think. Like, nobody else has a right to your body. Somebody using it without your permission, or damaging or destroying it, otherwise known as slavery, rape, and violence, that's against the law.

Of course, we're used to owning other stuff, too. But what does it mean to *own* something? We spend about an hour or so on this. We decide that owning something means you can keep somebody else from having it. You can also give it to somebody, but they can't take it from you.

See where I'm going here? I'm finding all this a little bit conceptual and tedious. Why don't we just go back to the way it was before What Happened? Needless to say, Jefferson isn't down for this. Nothing but a complete reboot will do. From time to time, I ask myself whether it's worth it. Like, was it just less of a headache living in armed compounds instead of having to work it all out in a massively multiplayer group therapy sesh? But then I remember that we're trying to lay down some ground rules for the long term. Like, I plan to end up being one old-ass queen. And for that to happen, I gotta make sure nobody steals my snacks, know what I'm saying?

Days pass. At noon and six, we break to eat, and when the sun goes down, we break to sleep. The constitution of Utopia, known colloquially as the Doc, takes shape—laws, principles, medical corps, constabulary, sanitation.

One day Chapel and Jeff and I are eating sandwiches in a garden overlooking the East River. Sautéed Spam in fresh-baked rolls from a pizza oven they've fired up down the street. That's what the future tastes like, I guess. Spam calzone.

"Well," I say, "we're practically there."

"Where?" says Jefferson.

"The future."

Jefferson smiles.

"We should commemorate it," I say. "Like, when all of us sign the Doc. We should dress up. This is big, man."

Jefferson thinks. "Frock coats and tricorn hats?"

I shrug. "Whatever you want, man. You're the president."

That's what people have started calling him, and I bet if they actually held a vote, that's what he'd be. But Jefferson isn't comfortable when you call him that. He was the same way about being generalissimo of Washington Square. People thought he was humble and diffident. Myself, I wasn't so sure. I figured he was just scared.

"I'm not the president," he says. "Presidents *make* history. I'm just a tool of history."

I chew that one over. That's kind of a weird thing to say, I figure. As if he thinks he's fated in some way.

True confession? I used to be just a little teensy eensy bit obsessed with celebrity. Not individual celebrities—I could take them or leave them—but the whole ecology of celebrity: how people became famous, what kept them famous, what brought them down to disgrace or obscurity. It was like sports for me. Except the rules weren't written down, and they were bafflingly complex and subject to change without notice. The best players could even change the rules themselves.

I always figured I'd be one of those players down the line. Which is odd, because I didn't actually *do* anything, like the way Taylor Swift sang or Brad Pitt acted. I just figured my magnetic personality would assure me money and adoration. Anyhow, the apocalypse wrecked all that.

So I once read this thing on the Web—a psychologist made up this diagnosis? Acquired Situational Narcissism. The idea is that becoming famous leads to a warped sense of self because everyone around you starts treating you as if everything you do is great. You become frozen in the mind-set you had when you first became famous and can't move past that point because you don't have the same growing experiences as everyone else. Instead, your life becomes a bizarre series of outsized rewards in a social milieu that gives you an utterly inflated idea of self. Which sounded great.

But I wonder, as I hear Jeff call himself a "tool of history," if he isn't suffering from a bit of ASN, given the general adulation he's been experiencing, being Patient Zero of the Cure and whatnot. Which is a bit worrisome, since this city-state is built on some pretty shaky ground.

"We have to let them know the truth soon," Jefferson says to Chapel, as though he's picking up my train of thought.

Chapel nods. "Soon enough. But we have to be careful about it."

Jefferson says, "How is Theo? When can we let him go?"

"I've lost contact with Dooley and the others," says Chapel. He tries to keep worry out of his voice. "It's no big deal. Comms get messed up all the time.

"After the signing," he says, "we tell this story: We've picked up signals from the *Ronald Reagan*. Then we let them know that they're hostiles. Which they are, of course. If we're careful, it all dovetails in without a hitch."

Jefferson doesn't look happy about this.

"The truth needs a soft landing," says Chapel, "or they're gonna burn us at the stake."

I've forgotten all about that in the flow of good feelings and kumbaya. But he's right, of course. I'm not saying that just because we're in love. I think that life is an even bigger game than fame. And sometimes you've got to deceive people. For their own good. That's right, right?

"What about Theo? What if he still doesn't want to play ball?"

Chapel shrugs. "I don't know." But I feel like he does.

We get back to the session. A last push before victory is declared and the Doc signed. They start hashing out whether the city-state is going to take over the Uptowners' bank at the Bazaar or they're going to start a federal reserve, and I sorta kinda lose interest again. I notice Chapel looks a little antsy himself. He's been watching the proceedings, taking a note here and there, mostly staying out of it. His cover story is holding. Nobody figures he's any older than them, since he's all cute and twinky.

Anyhow, round about the time the scintillating banking discussion rolls into its second hour, the lights that have been running off the complex's emergency generators flicker and die. We're left in the blue darkness. There's a universal *awwwwww*. Chapel jumps up and says he'll go check it out; Brainbox says he'll go, too, but Chapel says he's got it handled. Brainbox insists. They head off.

After a while, I decide to follow them. I'm more interested in Chapel than fiat currency anyhow.

BRAINBOX

NEVER STOPPING THINKING FROM THE MOMENT I wake that's me and welcome to it we keep going down down I did not know there were so many levels but of course there must have been so many countries peoples ideologies in contact so much hatred influence and pressure brought to bear does Jefferson have any idea how difficult this will be they couldn't organize themselves and make peace or stop the earth boiling or feed the potbellied children or stop the plague and he thinks he can get a hundred thousand juveniles to stop killing and raping and stealing oh well that is why I like him I suppose the way you like a dog chasing birds good boy what a dreamer she was a dreamer too Chu Hua her flower-petal hands and exquisite face and matchless courage and now she's dead and her flesh is feeding the bugs and rodents and the corruption of her beauty is aloft in the air and maybe drafts of air carry her past all the paintings in the Metropolitan that's enough of that I grab my attention and rope it back like I do all day like I do all my life the aim now is one foot in front of the other down the raw concrete stairs we have taken 1,217 steps since we left Jefferson up at ground level and have descended 72 stairs what use is that to me now I remember when I recited that whole page back to Mom when I was only six it was just as clear as a PDF scan in my mind's eye and she looked proud amazed scared and this is a blessing and a curse I remember every moment with her every slice of the extruding spheroid of my witnessing of space-time like I notice that Chapel and Peter tend to brush against each other more than is statistically likely and especially more than would be invoked by the rules of society curious perhaps an impulse toward the continuation of the species but then the action of evolution is on the level of the gene not the species I believe Dawkins not Wilson it's all the same to me I mean it's all the same smiling breathing touching pleasure attachment plus what I have realized since she is gone and part of me with her there is not enough love in the world anyhow why would I find it wrong we are as we are made by nature which is the only God and love really is only a spandrel in the architecture of biology but the accidental beauty of the world is the only reason to live now the stairs level out and we are in the underbelly of the complex vast and dark and damp I suppose if I were poetic I would compare it to something like a living organ but things are what they are exactly and precisely if we had the equipment to see things truly instead of these five weak and lopsided senses we would know that and Washington said people are the sensory organs the universe uses to apprehend itself and maybe that's why I'm stuck here in this little machine of a body I'm just a taste bud on the tongue of God ha-ha how's that for a metaphor there

CHRIS WEITZ

is a central corridor rooms to the side at first the corridor is blank
but then we find evidence of a fight not kids but adults of long ago
something went wrong here even in the larger going wrong of it all
skeletons in dark suits earphones umbilicaling up to their skeleton
nonears their guns fired empty and others with submachine guns
clubs knives a wall blown out and collapsed from an explosion Peter is
registering shock and gooseflesh fear but Chapel looks excited why is
that we stop at a metal door where someone died jammed in the door-
frame beyond that a round room comfortable but utilitarian a panic
room maybe here everyone is in a gas mask guns in hand we look at all
of them and I see a face through the pane of a mask I have seen this
man many times he was the president of the United States when there
was one Peter says is that I say yes it is holy shit says Peter and Chapel
says nothing he is not even looking at the president he is looking at
the bodies nearby and he finds what he is looking for a fat soft black
leather briefcase or suitcase it is attached to someone by a stout gray
wire Chapel is staring at it I say what is it nothing he says just some
papers but he has not even looked inside so why would he say that I say
we should look inside he says no time we need to get the generators
going so we keep going and down at the end of the corridor we find
the works department a big genny there are stores of fuel to get her
going a simple business for me I tell Chapel I need to go back for more
fuel though and Chapel looks like he does not believe me but he says
go I go back to the room with the president and his men and I open
the bag a kind of satellite phone a fat binder full of plastic-coated sheets
of protocols a card with codes now I know what this is I look over all

of it and take pictures with my mind and I thought so says Chapel he
is standing in the doorway I understand I say the whole reason this
makes sense the Resistance what do you really want and he says justice
and I say this can't give justice and he says it is the only thing that can
give justice his gun FLASHES

JEFFERSON

WE WAIT FOR THE LIGHTS to come on again. As ever lately, I feel the thousand pinpricks of eyes on me, the way people look at me as if I were different. As if I had a grotesque deformity, only in reverse.

I tell Solon I'm heading out for a walk.

It's true that my blood and DNA run in their veins now, and that's why they will live past the next spring. Who can blame them? But I didn't ask for this. It was Wash who was supposed to be the leader, not me. I just wanted to hang around with Donna forever if possible.

These days I have had the oddest sense that I am in a movie she is watching, and assessing myself through her eyes, my words and actions shaped by her imaginary gaze. She would tell me that I had finally got what I wanted, a new society, Utopia, and I had made my bed, and now I had to sleep in it.

And what if we do pull it off, and the Doc is signed? How long do we have to set up the city-state of Newest York before they send in the marines?

One thing at a time. One lie woven into the fabric of the truth and then another, and I'll be clean.

What about Theo? What if I can't convince him to toe the line? I have a brief sickly feeling that Chapel will silence him permanently. Then my mind rejects it. The Resistance can't save us with one hand and kill us with the other, can it?

Once, I started a journal. The problem was that it was impossible for me to figure out to whom or for whom I was writing it. So everything came out wrong. I would find myself writing in some high-flown style, like people whose diaries have been published, historically and culturally relevant people. Important people, or rather, "important" people. It didn't really suit trips to Starbucks and pickup basketball. And I found myself hiding things. Stupid things I did and said, masturbation, rejections, whatever. Which was odd, because I never expected anyone to read it except me. I thought maybe I was crafting a persona for my future self to take at face value. But eventually I realized that I actually *did* see other people reading the journal in the future, as though I were going to be important, or "important," or famous down the line. I was burnishing my credentials for those imaginary people, making a résumé for eternity. The idea was ridiculous, of course, since I knew that people who end up being famous or important don't write adolescent journals with an eye toward posterity. And as a Buddhist, I saw the whole thing was preposterous, a hanging-on to a past that manifestly didn't exist for display to a future that didn't exist. It got me twisted in my head in a neurotically recursive way that Donna would point out was very me.

But now I think maybe what I am doing here will be important. It will be something for the history books. It is history. And that makes me a historical figure, I guess. What does that mean to me? Does it make me happy? I will need to figure that out.

Night has risen, and I can see an almost-round silvery moon above the blocky patchwork of building silhouettes. I hear a commotion from the Security Council chamber. Maybe the lights have come on. But no, the corridor is still dark. Then, angry shouts, screams, a sharp report of gunfire.

Something's wrong.

It can't fall to pieces now—not when we are so close—

I head back inside and toward the Council chamber, jogging and then running as the level of noise rises, the sound of a hornets' nest.

I round a corner, and suddenly I am falling, sprawling to the floor, tasting a cocktail of worn institutional carpet and blood. The orbit of my eye sings out in pain. I gather myself and look up and—

A vulpine tween face looks down at me from behind the business end of a machine gun.

It's one of the feral kids from Plum Island. But it can't be. He must be dead; he must be far away.

For a moment, I wonder if I am in a cell somewhere in the lab and I have hallucinated everything since, and then the reality of the corridor and the sounds beyond anchor me in the here and the now.

"Hi, Jeff!" says a girl, willowy and blond like the boy. "Remember us?"

So they've come to kill me.

But the boy lifts his gun. "You better come with," he says.

"For your own safety," the girl says, and giggles.

I push myself to my knees, spit the blood out of my mouth. "Why?"

"Because the poo-poo just hit the fan," says the girl. "You're in big trouble, Jefferson. Don't you know it's wrong to lie?"

Down, around, down, down, into the guts of the building, as deep as it is tall. Out of the clad interiors of bureaucracy to the raw concrete and grit of the organs that used to keep the place going. And still, from above, I can hear a hornets' nest buzz.

The boy sees me listening. "Know what that is? They're looking for you. Gonna tear you apart if they find you."

The girl switches on a headlamp, and we feel our way farther in the dark until we come to a metal door. She pushes it open. Some Coleman lanterns and flashlights point out spare things in the blackness.

Peter is cradling Brainbox's head on his lap, his pants leg soaked with blood. His shirt pressed to a bloody wound in Brainbox's side.

"I found him like this," he says.

"Who did it?" I ask.

"Your friend Chapel," says a familiar voice.

I turn and squint. And there is Kath. Every bit as real and beautiful as the day she died.

"Surprised to see me?" she says. I can't muster up an answer. "Of course you are. You thought I was dead, right? That's why you left me alone on a fucking slab, right?"

"Yes, I thought you were dead," I say.

"Well, I'm not." She smiles. "Good news for you, I guess, since I'm gonna get you out of this shitstorm you created. Somebody busted you, pal. And people aren't too happy with you up there." She gestures up toward the hornets' nest.

"You know," I say.

"Yeah, I know," she says. "Looking forward to a nice vacation in Saint-Tropez. But first we better go. Sounds like Theo has done his job up there."

"Theo told them."

"Yep."

"You helped him?"

She shrugs. "I guess. I dunno. Was that wrong? I think your buddies in the Resistance—nice name by the way, good marketing—were going to kill him."

My mind is tumbling on the details, a lock not quite opening. And as ever, unbidden, the consciousness of Kath's beauty, undoing sense.

"Chapel," says Brainbox from the floor. "He has the football."

Peter looks up at me, distraught. "He keeps saying that. He's delirious."

"I'm not delirious, you idiot," he says. "The codes. He's got the codes for the nukes."

"What nukes?"

"*All* of them."

"I don't believe it," says Peter. "He wouldn't...he wouldn't..."

"So I guess that explains why the Resistance gave a shit about us, right?" Kath smiles an impish smile, the look of the always-let-down.

The enormity of it hits me. Chapel's recruiting of likely pawns—like me—planned from the beginning. A convenient posse of dupes to get him where he needed to go. His insistence on hiding the truth from the Harlemites. The use of the UN and the Gathering as a distraction.

Playing to my idealism and my vanity.

I feel a thousand feet deep in the truth, crushed by the pressure. Worst of all—my conceit, my need to dream up a future. Above, all of that is falling to ruin. One part of Chapel's story wasn't a lie—they will crush one another stampeding to the exit for the old world.

But first, they'll kill me. And my friends.

Was there a Resistance at all? Or had that been a little drama arranged to get us back to the city and maneuver us to the prize? The answer has gone wherever Chapel has gone.

I lean over to catch my breath. Collapse to my knees.

From Brainbox, the most unlikely of sounds. A laugh.

I wonder if, finally, the membrane of his sanity has parted.

"Don't worry," he says.

"What's not to worry about?" says Kath.

"Chapel can't fire the nukes," he says. "Not without this."

He holds up a device that looks like an overlong cell phone or a slender satellite phone. Glossy black numbers.

"The biscuit," says Brainbox. "Wired to the dead-man's switches at NORAD."

"Sneaky, Brainbox," says Kath.

Brainbox musters a shrug, even in his blasted state.

"But the briefcase is gone. He's got the codes," adds Peter.

"So do I," says Brainbox.

"How?" I ask.

"Helps to have a good memory."

"Brainbox, are you saying you can stop a nuclear war?"

He smiles again. "Or start one. That is...if I make it. I'm afraid Chapel shot me in the guts."

Silence.

"Well, this is fun," says Kath. "Now, if you don't mind, I think we better leg it out of here ahead of the lynch mob. Sooner or later, they're going to find us. There has to be a security exit to the FDR Drive, right?"

"Chapel—"

"Will have to wait," says Kath. "First we survive."

She's right. Peter and I help Brainbox up, and we stumble through the darkness, looking for a way out.

BRAINBOX

JEFFERSON LOOKS AT ME with concern he thinks I am slipping out of consciousness but I am looking at the numbers scroll through my mind and over the black black sky I can put them away and summon them up when I choose and with them I can end the earth they wanted to let us die and the others lied and now it is me with the power me and my friends if I can call them friends what would they do if they knew what I know knew the numbers that can kill the world we slip along the river silently and dark and quiet afraid to make a sound and we hear the riot take over the compound they are looking for us what next the others must listen they all must listen and even you Jefferson if you do not listen you are no better than the others and I will join you my love in the dark and this human trial of the world will be done and some less passionate and foolish animals will take over and they will not even know there was a boy they said was a freak and they didn't listen and they laughed ha-ha-ha and one day he said you are not worth the troublesome coherence of atoms and you do not deserve life and they will say no they will say no please no no no

JEFFERSON

BRAINBOX FLOATS at the edge of consciousness. The wound in his side has stopped leaking blood, but the bullet will have to come out...I wish that Donna were here.

No. I hope that Donna is far away, in a happier place. I wish that I were with her. But I am here, slipping along the black water, hunted.

Panic is reaching its claws under the door. Change the focal length. Wide to tight. First survive. Then decide what to do with the magic numbers in Brainbox's head.

The biggest stick in history.

They had the chance to make a new world. One where they made the decisions.

Now we will have to tell them what to do.

DONNA

WE SWEEP LOW OVER THE ROOFTOPS, kids waving at us as we pass. A holiday air below, verging on abandon and panic. I don't think they'd be waving if they knew who was inside.

I glance back at the squad of Special Air Service commandos behind me. Silent-faced killers. They're using Brits; they speak the language but have no particular attachment to anybody in the US. That way they can murder with the fewest prickings of conscience.

Rab: "I've never been to New York." He's trying to be funny and winning. It doesn't work. I look at my other false friend—Titch, back in more suitable fatigues but deeply uncomfortable crammed into the space-efficient fuselage.

Somewhere down there, if he's still alive, is Jefferson. I'm sorry I failed you, my love. I'm coming back.

I've brought a box of scorpions with me. But I promise I'll save you from them. I'll save us all.

And I'll make them pay.

ACKNOWLEDGMENTS

Thanks to Nikki Garcia and Alvina Ling at Little, Brown for their patience and support; and to Suzanne Gluck at WME every bit as much.

Thanks also to Chantal Nong and Rachel Benveniste.

And my wife and children. To put it as a somewhat grammatically confused friend once did, "For whom it has all been for."

Apologies where necessary to my alma mater, Trinity College Cambridge, and my soul mother, the Ashram Galactica.

A couple of books were especially inspiring in the writing: *The Evolution of Cooperation* by Richard Axelrod; *Noble Savages* by Napoleon Chagnon.

Higher
Biology

2003 Exam
_____

2004 Exam
_____

2005 Exam
_____

2006 Exam
_____

2007 Exam
_____

Leckie ✕ Leckie

© Scottish Qualifications Authority

All rights reserved. Copying prohibited. No part of this publication may be reproduced, stored in a retrieval system, or transmitted in any form or by any means, electronic, mechanical, photocopying, recording or otherwise.

First exam published in 2003.
Published by Leckie & Leckie Ltd, 3rd Floor, 4 Queen Street, Edinburgh EH2 1JE
tel: 0131 220 6831 fax: 0131 225 9987 enquiries@leckieandleckie.co.uk www.leckieandleckie.co.uk

ISBN 978-1-84372-548-0

A CIP Catalogue record for this book is available from the British Library.

Printed in Scotland by Scotprint.

Leckie & Leckie is a division of Huveaux plc.

Leckie & Leckie is grateful to the copyright holders, as credited at the back of the book, for permission to use their material. Every effort has been made to trace the copyright holders and to obtain their permission for the use of copyright material. Leckie & Leckie will gladly receive information enabling them to rectify any error or omission in subsequent editions.

2003 | Higher

[BLANK PAGE]

FOR OFFICIAL USE

Total for
Sections
B and C

X007/301

NATIONAL
QUALIFICATIONS
2003

MONDAY, 26 MAY
1.00 PM – 3.30 PM

BIOLOGY
HIGHER

Fill in these boxes and read what is printed below.

Full name of centre

Town

Forename(s)

Surname

Date of birth
Day Month Year

Scottish candidate number

Number of seat

SECTION A—Questions 1–30 (30 marks)
Instructions for completion of Section A are given on page two.

SECTIONS B AND C (100 marks)

1   (a)   All questions should be attempted.

    (b)   It should be noted that in **Section C** questions 1 and 2 each contain a choice.

2   The questions may be answered in any order but all answers are to be written in the spaces provided in this answer book, and must be written clearly and legibly in ink.

3   Additional space for answers and rough work will be found at the end of the book. If further space is required, supplementary sheets may be obtained from the invigilator and should be inserted inside the **front** cover of this book.

4   The numbers of questions must be clearly inserted with any answers written in the additional space.

5   Rough work, if any should be necessary, should be written in this book and then scored through when the fair copy has been written.

6   Before leaving the examination room you must give this book to the invigilator. If you do not, you may lose all the marks for this paper.

SCOTTISH
QUALIFICATIONS
AUTHORITY

©

SECTION A

Read carefully

1 Check that the answer sheet provided is for Biology Higher (Section A).

2 Fill in the details required on the answer sheet.

3 In this section a question is answered by indicating the choice A, B, C or D by a stroke made in **ink** in the appropriate place in the answer sheet—see the sample question below.

4 For each question there is only **one** correct answer.

5 Rough working, if required, should be done only on this question paper—or on the rough working sheet provided—**not** on the answer sheet.

6 At the end of the examination the answer sheet for Section A **must** be placed inside the front cover of this answer book.

Sample Question

The apparatus used to determine the energy stored in a foodstuff is a

A   respirometer

B   calorimeter

C   klinostat

D   gas burette.

The correct answer is **B**—calorimeter. A **heavy** vertical line should be drawn joining the two dots in the appropriate box in the column headed **B** as shown in the example on the answer sheet.

If, after you have recorded your answer, you decide that you have made an error and wish to make a change, you should cancel the original answer and put a vertical stroke in the box you now consider to be correct. Thus, if you want to change an answer D to an answer B, your answer sheet would look like this:

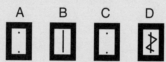

If you want to change back to an answer which has already been scored out, you should enter a tick (✓) to the **right** of the box of your choice, thus:

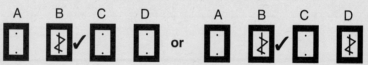

SECTION A

All questions in this section should be attempted.

Answers should be given on the separate answer sheet provided.

1. The table below shows the concentrations of three ions found in sea water and in the sap of the cells of a seaweed.

	Ion concentrations (mg l^{-1})		
	potassium	*sodium*	*chloride*
sea water	0·01	0·55	0·61
cell sap	0·57	0·04	0·60

Which of the following statements is supported by the data in the table?

A Potassium and sodium ions are taken into the cell by active transport.

B Potassium and chloride ions are removed from the cell by diffusion.

C Sodium ions are removed from the cell by active transport.

D Chloride and sodium ions are removed from the cell by diffusion.

2. A piece of muscle was cut into three strips, X, Y and Z, and treated as described in the table.

Their final lengths were then measured.

Muscle strip	Solution added to muscle	Muscle length (mm)	
		Start	*After 10 minutes*
X	1% glucose	50	50
Y	1% ATP	50	45
Z	1% ATP boiled and cooled	50	46

From the data it may be deduced that

A ATP is not an enzyme

B muscles contain many mitochondria

C muscles synthesise ATP in the absence of glucose

D muscles do not use glucose as a source of energy.

3. DNA controls the activities of a cell by coding for the production of

A proteins

B carbohydrates

C amino acids

D bases.

4. The diagram below shows part of a DNA molecule during replication. Bases are represented by numbers and letters.

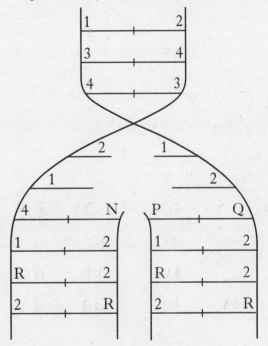

If 1 represents adenine and 3 represents cytosine, which line in the table identifies correctly the bases represented by the letters N, P, Q and R?

	N	*P*	*Q*	*R*
A	guanine	cytosine	guanine	thymine
B	cytosine	guanine	cytosine	adenine
C	guanine	cytosine	cytosine	adenine
D	cytosine	guanine	guanine	adenine

[Turn over

5. The table below contains statements which may be TRUE or FALSE concerning DNA replication and mRNA synthesis.

Which line in the table is correct?

	Statement	DNA replication	mRNA synthesis
A	Occurs in the nucleus	TRUE	FALSE
B	Involved in protein synthesis	TRUE	TRUE
C	Requires free nucleotides	TRUE	FALSE
D	Involves complementary base pairing	TRUE	TRUE

6. A fragment of DNA was found to have 60 guanine bases and 30 adenine bases. What is the total number of deoxyribose sugar molecules in this fragment?

    A   30

    B   45

    C   90

    D 180

7. The diagram represents part of a molecule of DNA on which a molecule of RNA is being synthesised.

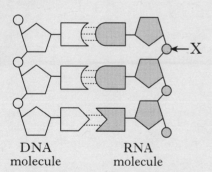

DNA molecule   RNA molecule

What does component X represent?

    A Ribose sugar

    B Deoxyribose sugar

    C Phosphate

    D Ribose phosphate

8. The sequence of triplets on a strand of DNA is shown below.

ATTACACCGTACCAATAG

During translation of mRNA made from the above sequence, how many of the tRNA anticodons will have at least one uracil base?

    A 3

    B 4

    C 5

    D 7

9. The function of tRNA in cell metabolism is to

    A transport amino acids to be used in synthesis

    B carry codons to the ribosomes

    C synthesise proteins

    D transcribe the DNA code.

10. Which of the following identifies correctly the sequence in which organelles become involved in the production of an enzyme for secretion?

    A Nucleus → Ribosomes → Golgi Apparatus → Rough ER

    B Ribosomes → Vesicles → Rough ER → Golgi Apparatus

    C Nucleus → Rough ER → Vesicles → Ribosomes

    D Ribosomes → Rough ER → Golgi Apparatus → Vesicles

11. In a pea plant, the alleles for plant height and petal colour are located on separate chromosomes. The dominant alleles are for tallness and pink petals; the corresponding recessive alleles are for dwarfness and white petals. A heterozygous plant was crossed with a plant recessive for both characteristics. If 320 progeny resulted, what would be the predicted number of tall, white plants?

    A 20

    B 60

    C 80

    D 180

12. The relative positions of the genes M, N, O and P on a chromosome were determined by the analysis of percentage recombination. The results are shown in the table.

Genes	Percentage recombination
M and O	5
N and O	16
N and P	8
M and P	19

The correct order of genes on the chromosomes is

A O M P N

B O M N P

C M O N P

D M N O P.

13. The base sequence of a short piece of DNA is shown below.

A G C T T A C G

During replication, an inversion mutation occurred on the complementary strand synthesised on this piece of DNA.

Which of the following is the mutated complementary strand?

A   T C G A A T G A

B   A G C T T A G C

C   T C G A A T C G

D   T C G A A T G C

14. In a diploid organism with the genotype HhMmNNKK, how many genetically distinct types of gamete would be produced?

A   2

B   4

C   8

D   16

15. Scientists visiting a group of four islands, P, Q, R and S, found similar spiders on each island. They carried out tests to see if the spiders from different islands would interbreed.

The results are summarised in the table below.

(✓ indicates successful interbreeding. ✗ indicates that fertile young were not produced.)

Spiders from

		P	Q	R	S
Spiders from	P	✓	✓	✗	✗
	Q	✓	✓	✗	✗
	R	✗	✗	✓	✗
	S	✗	✗	✗	✓

How many species of spider were present on the four islands?

A One

B Two

C Three

D Four

16. In sexual reproduction, which of the following is **not** a source of genetic variation?

A Non-disjunction

B Linkage

C Mutation

D Crossing over

17. Which of the following statements regarding polyploidy is correct?

A It is more common in animals than in plants.

B It is the term used to describe the four haploid cells formed at the end of meiosis.

C It can produce individuals with increased vigour.

D It always results from non-disjunction of chromosomes.

[Turn over

18. In genetic engineering, endonucleases are used to

A join fragments of DNA together

B cut DNA molecules into fragments

C close plasmid rings

D remove cell walls for somatic fusion.

19. Which of the following is a plant response to invasion by a foreign organism?

A Increased production of tannin

B Engulfing of invaders by specialised cells

C Production of antibodies

D Closing of stomata

20. Which of the following adaptations allows a plant to tolerate grazing by herbivores?

A Thick waxy cuticle

B Leaves reduced to spines

C Low meristems

D Thorny stems

Question 21 is at the top of the next column

21. In which of the following do **both** adaptations reduce the rate of water loss from a plant?

A Thin cuticle and rolled leaf

B Rolled leaf and sunken stomata

C Sunken stomata and large surface area

D Thin cuticle and needle-shaped leaves

22. The diagram below shows a transverse section through a plant stem.

In which region would cambium cells be found?

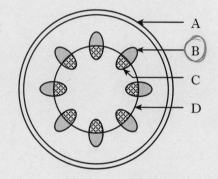

23. The graph below shows the blood glucose concentrations of two women before and after each swallowed 50 g of glucose.

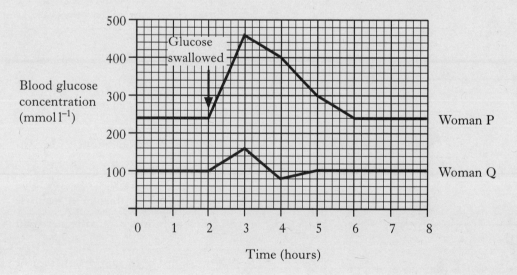

When did the rate of change of blood glucose concentration of the two women differ most?

A Between hours 2 and 3

B Between hours 3 and 4

C Between hours 4 and 5

D Between hours 5 and 6

24. During the germination of barley grains, the plant growth substance GA (Gibberellic Acid) promotes the synthesis of the enzyme α-amylase in the

   A aleurone layer

   B endosperm

   C embryo

   D cotyledon.

25. Which of the following statements about the plant growth substances IAA (Indole Acetic Acid) and GA (Gibberellic Acid) is correct?

   A An increase in IAA content of a leaf promotes leaf abscission.

   B A decrease in IAA content of a leaf promotes leaf abscission.

   C An increase in GA content of a leaf promotes leaf abscission.

   D A decrease in GA content of a leaf promotes leaf abscission.

26. Which line in the table below identifies correctly the sites of production of the hormones ADH and glucagon?

	ADH	Glucagon
A	Pituitary gland	Liver
B	Kidney	Liver
C	Kidney	Pancreas
D	Pituitary gland	Pancreas

27. Which one of the following factors that can limit rabbit population size is density independent?

   A Viral disease

   B The population of foxes

   C The biomass of the grass

   D High rainfall

28. Which of the following best defines "population density"?

   A The number of individuals present per unit area of a habitat

   B The number of individual organisms present in a habitat

   C A group of individuals of the same species which make up part of an ecosystem

   D The maximum number of individuals which the resources of the environment can support

29. Which of the following does **not** occur during succession from a pioneer community of plants to a climax community?

   A Soil fertility increases.

   B Larger plants replace smaller plants.

   C An increasing intensity of light reaches ground-dwelling plants.

   D Each successive community makes the habitat less favourable for itself.

30. Dietary deficiency of vitamin D causes rickets.

   This effect is due to

   A poor uptake of phosphate into growing bones

   B poor calcium absorption from the intestine

   C low vitamin D content in the bones

   D loss of calcium from the bones.

Candidates are reminded that the answer sheet MUST be returned INSIDE the front cover of this answer book.

[Turn over

DO N
WRIT
TH
MAR

SECTION B

Marks

All questions in this section should be attempted.

1. (*a*) The diagram below represents cells in the lining of the small intestine of a mammal.

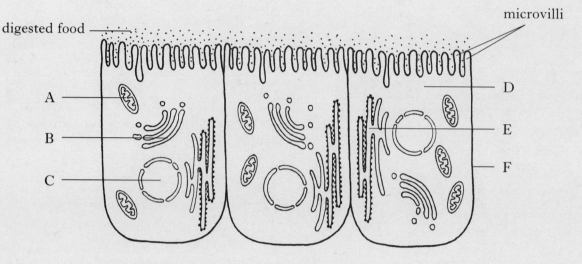

(i) The table below gives information about organelles shown in the diagram.

Complete the table by inserting the appropriate letters, names and functions.

Letter	Name of organelle	Function
E	Rough endoplasmic reticulum	transport proteins
A	mitochondria	Site of aerobic respiration
B	Golgi apparatus	packages and secretes
C	cytoplasm	Site of mRNA synthesis

3

(ii) Suggest a reason for the presence of microvilli in this type of cell.

increase surface area for

absorption

2

Marks

1. (continued)

(b) The diagram below summarises the process of photosynthesis in a chloroplast.

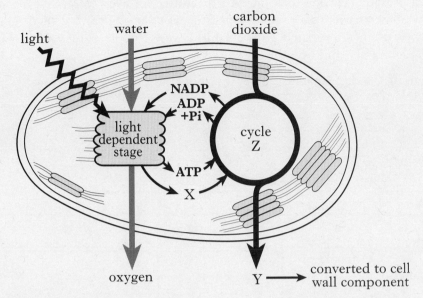

(i) Name molecules X and Y.

X _____

Y _____   1

(ii) State the exact location of the light dependent stage within a chloroplast.

_____ 1

(iii) Name cycle Z.

_____ 1

(iv) Name the cell wall component referred to in the diagram.

_____ 1

[Turn over

DO N
WRIT
TH
MAR

Marks

2. An investigation was carried out to compare photosynthesis in oak and nettle leaves.

Six discs were cut from each type of leaf and placed in syringes containing a solution that provided carbon dioxide. A procedure was used to remove air from the leaf discs to make them sink. The apparatus was placed in a darkened room. The discs were then illuminated with a lamp covered with a green filter. Leaf discs which carried out photosynthesis floated.

The positions of the discs one hour later are shown in the diagram below.

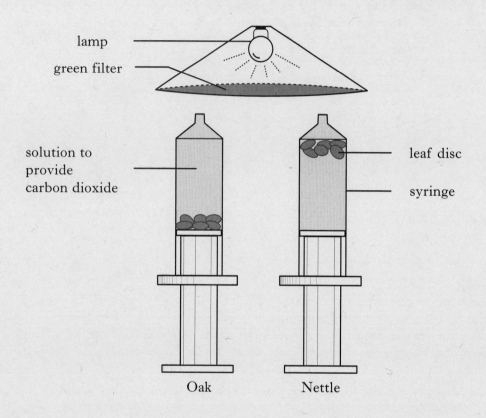

(*a*) Suggest a reason why the investigation was carried out in a darkened room.

_____light intensity kept constant_____

_____ 1

(*b*) Explain why it was good experimental procedure to use six discs from each plant.

_____average_____

_____ 1

Marks

2. (continued)

(c) In setting up the investigation, precautions were taken to ensure that the results obtained would be valid.

Give **one** precaution relating to the preparation of the leaf discs and **one** precaution relating to the solution that provided carbon dioxide.

Leaf discs _____

_____ 1

Solution that provided carbon dioxide _____

_____ 1

(d) Suggest a reason why the leaf discs which carried out photosynthesis floated.

_____ 1

(e) Nettles are shade plants which grow beneath sun plants such as oak trees.

Explain how the results show that nettles are well adapted as shade plants.

_____

_____

_____ 2

(f) What name is given to the light intensity at which the carbon dioxide uptake for photosynthesis is equal to the carbon dioxide output from respiration?

_____ 1

[Turn over

DO N
WRIT
TH
MAR

Marks

2. **(continued)**

(g) In another investigation, the rate of photosynthesis by nettle leaf discs was measured at different light intensities. The results are shown in the table.

Light intensity (kilolux)	Rate of photosynthesis by nettle leaf discs (units)
10	2
20	26
30	58
40	89
50	92
60	92

Plot a line graph to show the rate of photosynthesis by nettle leaf discs at different light intensities. Use appropriate scales to fill most of the graph paper.

(Additional graph paper, if required, can be found on page 32.)

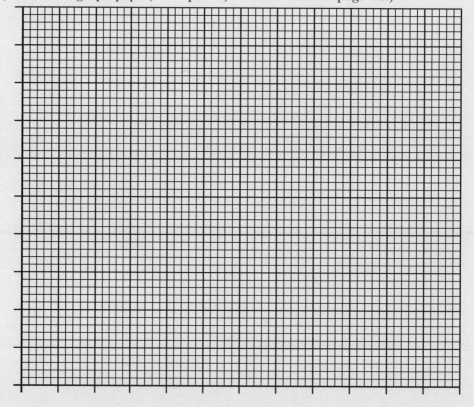

2

(h) From the table, predict how the rate of photosynthesis at a light intensity of 50 kilolux could be affected by an increase in carbon dioxide concentration. Justify your answer.

Effect on the rate of photosynthesis _____

Justification _____

2

1

Marks

3. The stages shown below take place when a human cell is invaded by an influenza virus.

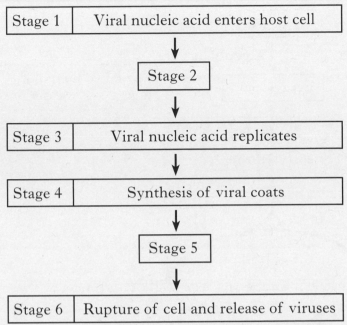

Stage 1	Viral nucleic acid enters host cell

	Stage 2	

Stage 3	Viral nucleic acid replicates

Stage 4	Synthesis of viral coats

	Stage 5	

Stage 6	Rupture of cell and release of viruses

(a) Describe the processes that occur during Stages 2 and 5.

Stage 2 _____

_____ 1

Stage 5 _____

_____ 1

(b) Name the cell organelle at which the viral coats are synthesised during Stage 4.

_____ 1

(c) During a viral infection, a type of white blood cell is stimulated to make antibodies which inactivate the viruses.

  (i) Name this type of white blood cell.

_____ 1

  (ii) What feature of viruses stimulates these cells to make antibodies?

_____ 1

  (iii) New strains of influenza virus appear regularly. Suggest why antibodies produced against one strain of virus are not effective against another strain.

_____

_____ 1

DO N
WRIT
TH
MAR(

Marks

4. An outline of the process of respiration is shown in the diagram below.

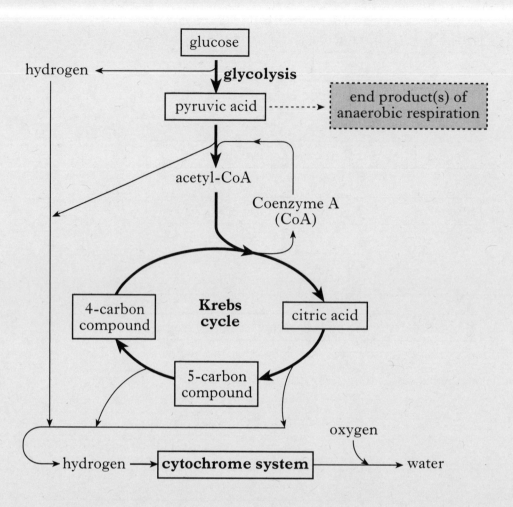

(a) Apart from glucose and enzymes, what chemical substance is essential for glycolysis to occur?

_____ 1

(b) Name the end-product(s) of anaerobic respiration in an animal cell and a plant cell.

   (i) Animal cell _____ 1

   (ii) Plant cell _____ 1

(c) Name the carrier that transfers hydrogen to the cytochrome system.

_____ 1

Marks

4. **(continued)**

    (*d*) Explain why the cytochrome system cannot function in anaerobic conditions.

    _As _ _needs oxygen_

    _____

    _____ 1

    (*e*) The energy content of glucose is 2900 kJ mol^{-1} and during aerobic respiration 1178 kJ mol^{-1} of this energy is stored in ATP.

    Calculate the percentage of the energy content of glucose that is stored in ATP.

    Space for calculation

    _____ % 1

    (*f*) Which stage of respiration releases **most** energy for use by the cell?

    cytochrome _system_   1

    [Turn over

    LEARNING RESOURCE CENTRE

DO N
WRIT
TH
MAR

Marks

5. The diagram below represents a stage of meiosis in a cell from a female fruit fly, *Drosophila*.

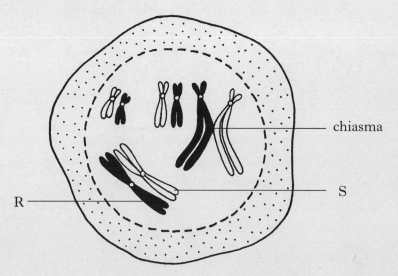

chiasma

S

R

(a) Name the tissue from which this cell was taken.

_____   1

(b) What is the haploid number of this species?

_____   1

(c) Chromosomes R and S are homologous. Apart from their appearance, state **one** similarity between homologous chromosomes.

_____

_____   1

(d) Explain the importance of chiasmata formation.

_____

_____   1

Marks

6. In humans, the allele for red-green colour deficiency (b) is sex-linked and recessive to the normal allele (B).

   The family tree diagram below shows how the condition was inherited.

   ☐ Male without the condition
   ■ Male with the condition
   ○ Female without the condition
   ● Female with the condition

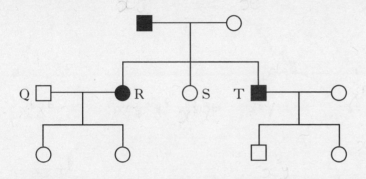

   (a) Give the genotypes of individuals S and T.

       (i) S _____   1

       (ii) T _____   1

   (b) If individuals Q and R have a son, what is the chance that he will inherit the condition?

       Space for calculation

                                    Chance _____   1

   (c) Explain why individual R has the condition although her mother was unaffected.

       _____

       _____   1

[Turn over

Marks

7. Hawaii is a group of islands isolated in the Pacific Ocean.

    Different species of Honeycreeper birds live on these islands.

    The heads of four species of Honeycreeper are shown below.

   (a)   (i) Explain how the information given about Honeycreeper species supports the statement that they occupy different niches.

        _____

        _____ 1

       (ii) What further information would be needed about the four species of Honeycreeper to conclude that they had evolved by adaptive radiation?

        _____

        _____ 1

   (b) The Honeycreeper species have evolved in geographical isolation.

      Name **one** other type of isolating barrier involved in the evolution of new species.

      _____ 1

Marks

8. The marine worm *Sabella* lives in a tube made out of sand grains from which it projects a fan of tentacles for feeding.

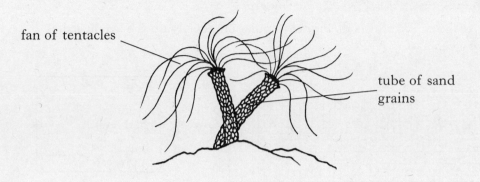

fan of tentacles

tube of sand grains

(a) If the worm is disturbed, the fan is immediately withdrawn into the tube. The fan re-emerges a few minutes later.

   (i) Name the type of behaviour illustrated by the withdrawal response.

   _____ 1

   (ii) What is the advantage to the worm of withdrawing its tentacles in response to a disturbance?

   _____

   _____ 1

(b) If a harmless stimulus occurs repeatedly, the withdrawal response eventually ceases.

   (i) Name the type of behaviour illustrated by this modified response.

   _____ 1

   (ii) What is the advantage to the worm of this modified response?

   _____

   _____ 1

[Turn over

9. Limpets (*Patella*) feed by grazing on algae growing on rocks at the seashore.

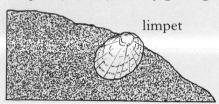
limpet

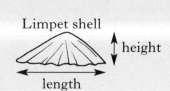
Limpet shell
height
length

Graph 1 below shows the effects of limpet population density on the average shell length and total biomass.

Graph 1

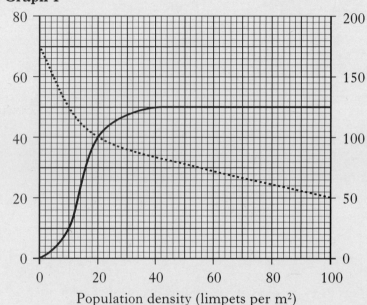

Average shell length (mm)

Total biomass (g per m²)

Key

Average shell length ....

Total biomass ———

Population density (limpets per m²)

(a) What is the total biomass at a population density of 10 limpets per m²?

_____ g per m²   **1**

(b) Identify the population density range (limpets per m²) in which the total biomass increases most rapidly.

Tick the correct box.

0–10 ☐   10–20 ☐   20–30 ☐   30–40 ☐   40–50 ☐   **1**

(c) Calculate the average mass of one limpet when the population density is 20 per m².

Space for calculation

Average mass _____ g   **1**

(d) Use values from Graph 1 to describe the effect of increasing population density on the total biomass of limpets.

_____

_____

_____   **2**

Marks

DO
WRIT
TH
MAI

9. (continued)

Marks

(e) Explain how intraspecific competition causes the trend in average shell length shown in Graph 1.

_____

_____ 1

(f) The table below shows information about limpets on shore A which is sheltered and on shore B which is exposed to strong wave action.

Graph 2 below shows the effect of wave action on limpet shell index.

Limpet shell index = $\dfrac{\text{shell height}}{\text{shell length}}$

Shore A (sheltered)		Shore B (exposed)	
Shell height (mm)	Shell length (mm)	Shell height (mm)	Shell length (mm)
16	52	9	21
19	54	11	26
20	55	14	31
21	56	16	34
22	57	17	35
23	58	17	36
26	60	–	–
Average = 21	Average =	Average = 14	Average =

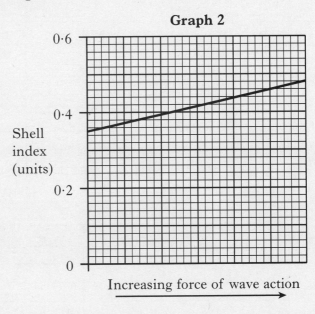

Graph 2

Shell index (units)

Increasing force of wave action

(i) **Complete the table** by calculating the average shell length of limpets on both shores.
Space for calculation

1

(ii) Express as the **simplest whole number ratio** the average shell height for shore A and shore B.
Space for calculation

Ratio _____ : _____ 1

(iii) A limpet shell collected on one of the shores had a length of 43 mm and a height of 20 mm. Use Graph 2 to identify which shore it came from and justify your choice.

Tick (✓) the correct box   Shore A ☐   Shore B ☐

Justification _____

_____

_____ 1

Marks

10. (a) The grid below shows adaptations of bony fish for osmoregulation.

A	few, small glomeruli	B	active secretion of salts by gills	C	high filtration rate in kidney
D	active uptake of salts by gills	E	low filtration rate in kidney	F	many, large glomeruli

Use letters from the grid to answer the following questions.

(i) Which **three** adaptations would be found in freshwater fish?

Letters _____ , _____ and _____ .

1

(ii) Which **two** adaptations would result in the production of a small volume of urine?

Letters _____ and _____ .

1

(b) The table shows some adaptations of a desert mammal which help to conserve water.

For each adaptation, tick (✓) the correct box to show whether it is behavioural **or** physiological.

Adaptation	Behavioural	Physiological
High level of blood ADH		
Lives in underground burrow		
Nocturnal foraging		
Absence of sweating		

2

Marks

11. (*a*) The diagram below shows a section through part of a root.

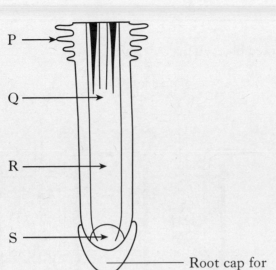

P

Q

R

S

Root cap for
protection

(i) Which letter shows the position of a meristem?

Letter _____   1

(ii) Name a cell process responsible for increase in length of a root.

_____   1

(*b*) The diagram below shows the growth pattern of a locust.

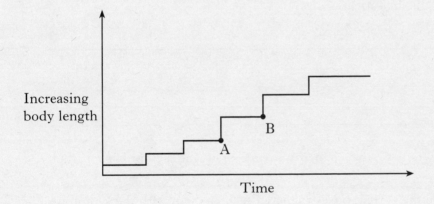

Increasing
body length

B

A

Time

Explain the reason for the shape of the growth pattern between A and B.

_____

_____

_____   2

[Turn over

DC
WR
T
MA

12. The diagram below shows the apparatus used to investigate the growth of oat *Marks*
seedlings in water culture solutions. Each solution lacks one element required for
normal growth.

The containers were painted black to prevent algal growth.

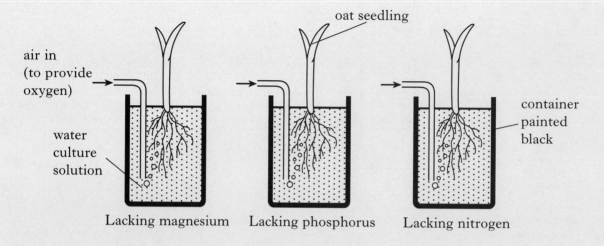

air in
(to provide
oxygen)

oat seedling

container
painted
black

water
culture
solution

Lacking magnesium   Lacking phosphorus   Lacking nitrogen

(a) Describe a suitable control for this experiment.

_____

_____

_____   1

(b) Suggest a reason why algal growth should be prevented in the culture
solutions during the investigation.

_____

_____

_____   1

(c) The table below shows the elements investigated and symptoms of their
deficiency.

Place ticks (✓) in the correct boxes to match each element with the symptoms
of its deficiency.

Element	Symptoms of deficiency	
	Leaf bases red	*Chlorotic leaves*
Magnesium		
Phosphorus		
Nitrogen		

2

Marks

12. **(continued)**

(*d*) Name a magnesium containing molecule found in oat seedlings.

_____

1

(*e*) Explain why the uptake of elements by oat seedling roots is dependent on the availability of oxygen.

_____

_____

_____

2

[Turn over

D
W
M

Marks

13. The production of thyroxine in mammals is controlled by the hormone TSH. Thyroxine controls metabolic rate in body cells and has a negative feedback effect on gland X.

The diagram below shows the relationship between TSH and thyroxine production.

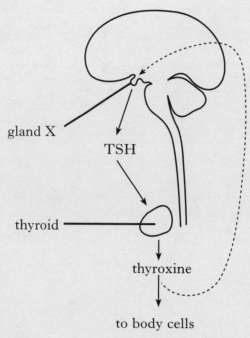

gland X

TSH

thyroid

thyroxine

to body cells

(*a*) Name gland X.

_____

1

(*b*) In an investigation into the effect of thyroxine, groups of rats of similar mass were treated as follows.

    Group A were fed a normal diet.

    Group B were fed a normal diet plus thyroxine.

    Group C were fed a normal diet plus an inhibitor of thyroxine production.

The table below shows the average hourly oxygen consumption in cm^3 per gram of body mass in rats from each group.

Group	*Average hourly oxygen consumption* (cm^3g^{-1})
A	1·6
B	2·8
C	1·2

(i) Explain how the results in the table support the statement that an increase in metabolic rate leads to an increase in oxygen consumption.

_____

_____

_____

2

Marks

13. **(b)** **(continued)**

(ii) What evidence suggests that rats fed a normal diet make thyroxine?

_____

_____ 1

(iii) How would the level of TSH production in group A compare with group C?

_____

_____ 1

(iv) Calculate the percentage decrease in oxygen consumption which results from feeding the thyroxine inhibitor to rats.

Space for calculation

_____ % decrease   1

(v) The table below relates to aspects of the appearance and behaviour of rats in groups B and C.

Group	Appearance of ears and feet	Behaviour
B	Pink	Lie stretched out
C	Pale	Lie curled up with feet tucked in

Complete the following sentences by underlining **one** of the alternatives in each pair.

1 Compared with rats in group B, the rats in group C have a $\left\{ \begin{array}{c} \text{lower} \\ \text{higher} \end{array} \right\}$

metabolic rate and show $\left\{ \begin{array}{c} \text{dilation} \\ \text{constriction} \end{array} \right\}$ of skin blood vessels.   1

2 The behaviour of rats in group C allows them to $\left\{ \begin{array}{c} \text{lose} \\ \text{conserve} \end{array} \right\}$ body

heat.   1

[Turn over

DC
WR
T
MA

Marks

SECTION C

Both questions in this section should be attempted.

Note that each question contains a choice.

Questions 1 and 2 should be attempted on the blank pages which follow.

Supplementary sheets, if required, may be obtained from the invigilator.

Labelled diagrams may be used where appropriate.

1. Answer **either** A **or** B.

    A. Give an account of gene mutation under the following headings:

        (i)   the occurrence of mutant alleles and the effect of mutagenic agents;   **3**

        (ii) types of gene mutation and how they alter amino acid sequences.   **7**

    OR   **(10)**

    B. Give an account of water movement through plants under the following headings:

        (i)   the transpiration stream;   **8**

        (ii) importance of the transpiration stream.   **2**

                                                                            (10)

In question 2, ONE mark is available for coherence and ONE mark is available for relevance.

2. Answer **either** A **or** B.

    A. Give an account of the mechanisms and importance of temperature regulation in endotherms.   **(10)**

    OR

    B. Give an account of the effect of light on shoot growth and development, and on the timing of flowering in plants and breeding in animals.   **(10)**

[END OF QUESTION PAPER]

DO NOT
WRITE IN
THIS
MARGIN

SPACE FOR ANSWERS

[Turn over

SPACE FOR ANSWERS

SPACE FOR ANSWERS

Page thirty-one **[Turn over**

DO
WRI
TH
MAR

SPACE FOR ANSWERS

ADDITIONAL GRAPH PAPER FOR QUESTION 2(*g*)

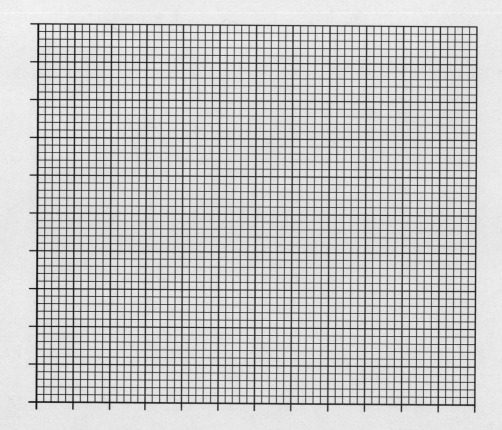

[BLANK PAGE]

FOR OFFICIAL USE

Total for
Sections
B and C

X007/301

NATIONAL
QUALIFICATIONS
2004

WEDNESDAY, 19 MAY
1.00 PM – 3.30 PM

BIOLOGY
HIGHER

Fill in these boxes and read what is printed below.

Full name of centre

Town

Forename(s)

Surname

Date of birth
Day Month Year

Scottish candidate number

Number of seat

SECTION A—Questions 1–30 (30 marks)

Instructions for completion of Section A are given on page two.

SECTIONS B AND C (100 marks)

1   (a)   All questions should be attempted.

      (b)   It should be noted that in **Section C** questions 1 and 2 each contain a choice.

2   The questions may be answered in any order but all answers are to be written in the spaces provided in this answer book, and must be written clearly and legibly in ink.

3   Additional space for answers and rough work will be found at the end of the book. If further space is required, supplementary sheets may be obtained from the invigilator and should be inserted inside the **front** cover of this book.

4   The numbers of questions must be clearly inserted with any answers written in the additional space.

5   Rough work, if any should be necessary, should be written in this book and then scored through when the fair copy has been written.

6   Before leaving the examination room you must give this book to the invigilator. If you do not, you may lose all the marks for this paper.

SCOTTISH
QUALIFICATIONS
AUTHORITY

©

SECTION A

Read carefully

1   Check that the answer sheet provided is for Biology Higher (Section A).

2   Fill in the details required on the answer sheet.

3   In this section a question is answered by indicating the choice A, B, C or D by a stroke made in **ink** in the appropriate place in the answer sheet—see the sample question below.

4   For each question there is only **one** correct answer.

5   Rough working, if required, should be done only on this question paper—or on the rough working sheet provided— **not** on the answer sheet.

6   At the end of the examination the answer sheet for Section A **must** be placed inside the front cover of this answer book.

Sample Question

The apparatus used to determine the energy stored in a foodstuff is a

A   respirometer

B   calorimeter

C   klinostat

D   gas burette.

The correct answer is **B**—calorimeter. A **heavy** vertical line should be drawn joining the two dots in the appropriate box in the column headed **B** as shown in the example on the answer sheet.

If, after you have recorded your answer, you decide that you have made an error and wish to make a change, you should cancel the original answer and put a vertical stroke in the box you now consider to be correct. Thus, if you want to change an answer D to an answer B, your answer sheet would look like this:

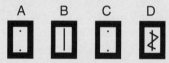

If you want to change back to an answer which has already been scored out, you should enter a tick (✓) to the **right** of the box of your choice, thus:

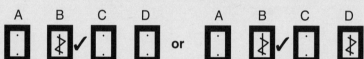

SECTION A

All questions in this section should be attempted.

Answers should be given on the separate answer sheet provided.

1. Which of the following processes requires infolding of the cell membrane?

   A   Diffusion

   B   Phagocytosis

   C   Active transport

   D   Osmosis

2. The diagram shows the fate of sunlight landing on a leaf.

   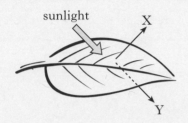

   Which line in the table below identifies correctly the fate of sunlight represented by X and Y?

	X	Y
A	transmission	reflection
B	absorption	transmission
C	reflection	transmission
D	reflection	absorption

3. Which of the following colours of light are mainly absorbed by chlorophyll a?

   A   Orange and violet

   B   Blue and red

   C   Blue and green

   D   Green and orange

4. The graph shows the effect of temperature on the rate of reactions in the light dependent stage in photosynthesis.

   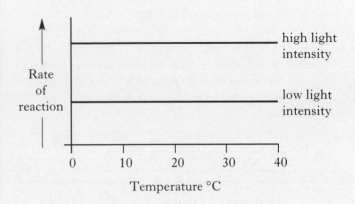

   From the graph, it may be deduced that

   A   enzymes are not involved in controlling these reactions

   B   enzymes act most effectively at high intensities of light

   C   at the high intensity of light, carbon dioxide is the limiting factor

   D   the rate of the reaction increases with increase in temperature.

5. The graph shows the effect of increasing light intensity on the rate of photosynthesis.

   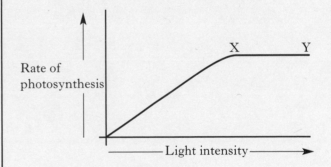

   Two environmental factors which could limit the rate of photosynthesis between points X and Y are

   A   light intensity and oxygen concentration

   B   temperature and light intensity

   C   temperature and carbon dioxide concentration

   D   carbon dioxide concentration and light intensity.

6. In respiration, the sequence of reactions resulting in the conversion of glucose to pyruvic acid is called

A the Krebs cycle

B the citric acid cycle

C glycolysis

D the cytochrome chain.

7. Which line in the table describes correctly both aerobic respiration and anaerobic respiration in human muscle tissue?

	Aerobic Respiration	Anaerobic Respiration
A	There is a net gain of ATP	Carbon dioxide is not produced
B	There is a net gain of ATP	Oxygen is required
C	Carbon dioxide is produced	There is a net loss of ATP
D	Lactic acid is formed	Ethanol is formed

8. Cyanogenesis in *Trifolium repens* is a defence mechanism against

A water loss

B fungal infection

C bacterial invasion

D grazing.

9. A sex-linked gene carried on the X-chromosome of a man will be transmitted to

A 50% of his male children

B 50% of his female children

C 100% of his male children

D 100% of his female children.

10. The inheritance of eye colour in *Drosophila* is sex-linked and the allele for red eyes (R) is dominant to the allele for white eyes (r).

The progeny of a cross were all red-eyed females and white-eyed males.

What were the genotypes of their parents?

A $X^r X^r$ $X^R Y$

B $X^R X^r$ $X^R Y$

C $X^R X^r$ $X^r Y$

D $X^R X^R$ $X^r Y$

11. Black coat colour in cocker spaniels is determined by a dominant gene (B) and red coat colour by its recessive allele (b). Uniform coat colour is determined by a dominant gene (F) and spotted coat colour by its recessive allele (f).

A male with a uniform black coat was mated to a female with a uniform red coat. A litter of six pups was produced, two of which had uniform black coat colour, two had uniform red coat colour, one had spotted black coat colour and one had spotted red coat colour.

The genotypes of the parents were

A BBFf × bbFf

B BbFf × bbFF

C BbFf × BbFf

D BbFf × bbFf.

12. A tall plant with purple petals was crossed with a dwarf plant with white petals. The F_1 generation were all tall plants with purple petals.

The F_1 generation was self pollinated and produced 1600 plants.

Which line in the table identifies correctly the most likely phenotypic ratio in the F_2 generation?

	Tall purple	Tall white	Dwarf purple	Dwarf white
A	870	325	305	100
B	870	0	0	730
C	400	400	400	400
D	530	260	270	540

13. The table below shows the percentage recombination frequencies for four genes present on the same chromosome.

Gene pair	% recombination frequency
P and Q	33
R and Q	40
R and S	32
P and R	7
Q and S	8

Which of the following represents the correct order of genes on the chromosome?

A   Q   P   S   R

B   P   Q   S   R

C   Q   S   P   R

D   P   Q   R   S

14. Which of the following describes the term non-disjunction?

A   The failure of chromosomes to separate at meiosis.

B   The independent assortment of chromosomes at meiosis.

C   The exchange of genetic information at chiasmata.

D   An error in the replication of DNA before cell division.

15. Which of the following is true of polyploid plants?

A   They have reduced vigour and the diploid chromosome number.

B   They have increased vigour and the diploid chromosome number.

C   They have reduced vigour and sets of chromosomes greater than the diploid chromosome number.

D   They have increased vigour and sets of chromosomes greater than the diploid chromosome number.

16. Somatic fusion is a technique which is used to

A   fuse cells from different species of animal

B   fuse cells from different species of plant

C   transfer genetic information into a bacterium

D   alter the genes carried on a plasmid.

[Turn over

17. The graph shows the carbon dioxide gain or loss in a shade plant and in a sun plant during part of a day in summer.

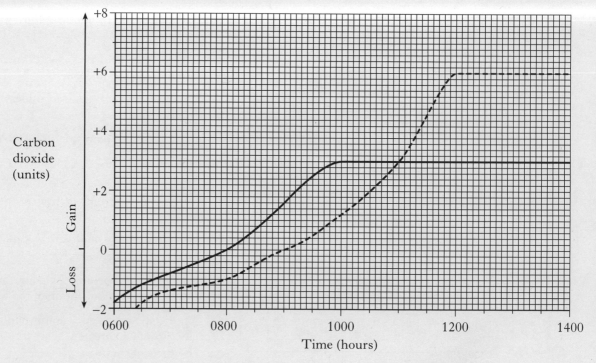

At what time does the shade plant reach compensation point?

A   0800 hours

B   0900 hours

C   1000 hours

D   1200 hours

18. The table shows water gain and loss in a plant on two consecutive days.

	Water gain (cm^3)	Water loss (cm^3)
First day	100	120
Second day	95	90

Conditions on the second day may have differed from conditions on the first day in some of the following ways.

1   Higher temperature

2   Lower windspeed

3   Lower humidity

4   Lower temperature

Which two conditions could account for the differences in water gain and loss from the first day to the second day?

A   1 and 2

B   1 and 3

C   2 and 4

D   3 and 4

19. Grass can survive despite being grazed by herbivores such as sheep and cattle. It is able to tolerate grazing because it

A   is a wind-pollinated plant

B   grows constantly throughout the year

C   possesses poisons which protect it from being eaten entirely

D   has very low growing points which send up new leaves when older ones are eaten.

20. When the intensity of grazing by herbivores increases in a grassland ecosystem, diversity of plant species may increase as a result.

Which statement explains this observation?

A Few herbivores are able to graze on every plant species present.

B Grazing stimulates growth in some plant species.

C Vigorous plant species are grazed so weaker competitors can also thrive.

D Plant species with defences against grazing are selected.

21. Which of the following describes an advantage of habituation to an animal?

A The animal becomes very good at an action which is performed repeatedly.

B An animal shows the same behaviour patterns as all those of the same species.

C A particular response is learned very quickly.

D Energy is not wasted in responding to harmless stimuli.

22. Which of the following examples of bird behaviour would result in reduced interspecific competition?

A Great Tits with the widest stripe on their breast feed first when food is scarce.

B Sooty Terns feed on larger fish than other species of tern which live in the same area.

C Pelicans searching for food form a large circle round a shoal of fish, then dip their beaks into the water simultaneously.

D Predatory gulls have difficulty picking out an individual puffin from a large flock.

23. The table shows the relative percentages by mass of the major chemical groups in a sample of human tissue.

The remaining percentage is made up of water.

Chemical group	%
Carbohydrate	5
Protein	18
Lipid	10
Other organic material	2
Inorganic material	1

What mass of water is present in a 250 g sample of this tissue?

A   64 g

B   36 g

C   90 g

D   160 g

[Turn over

24. The diagram below shows the human body's responses to temperature change.

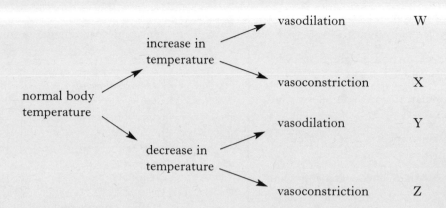

Which letters indicate negative feedback control of body temperature?

A W and Y

B W and Z

C X and Y

D X and Z

---

25. Muscle cells differ from nerve cells because

A they contain different genes

B different genes are switched on during development

C the genetic code is different in each cell

D they have different chromosomes.

26. A deficiency of Vitamin D in humans leads to rickets as a result of poor absorption of

A nitrate

B calcium

C iron

D phosphate.

27. Which line of the table identifies correctly the hormones which stimulate the inter-conversion of glucose and glycogen?

	glucose → glycogen	glycogen → glucose
A	insulin	glucagon and adrenaline
B	glucagon and insulin	adrenaline
C	adrenaline and glucagon	insulin
D	adrenaline	glucagon and insulin

28. Which line in the table describes body temperature in endotherms and ectotherms?

	Regulated by metabolism	Regulated by behaviour	Varies with the environmental temperature
A	ectotherm	endotherm	ectotherm
B	endotherm	ectotherm	endotherm
C	endotherm	ectotherm	ectotherm
D	ectotherm	endotherm	endotherm

29. Chlorophyll contains the metal ion

A iron

B copper

C magnesium

D calcium.

30. A species of plant was exposed to various periods of light and dark, after which the flowering response was observed.

The results are shown below.

Light period (hours)	Dark period (hours)	Response of plant
4	20	Maximum flowering
4	10	Flowering
6	18	Maximum flowering
14	10	Flowering
18	9	No flowering
18	6	No flowering
18	10	Flowering

What appears to be the critical factor which stimulates flowering?

A   A minimum dark period of 10 hours

B   A light and dark cycle of at least 14 hours

C   A maximum dark period of 10 hours

D   A dark period of at least 20 hours

Candidates are reminded that the answer sheet MUST be returned INSIDE the front cover of this answer book.

[Turn over

DO
WRI
T
MA

Marks

SECTION B

All questions in this section should be attempted.

1. Two magnified unicellular organisms are shown in the diagrams.

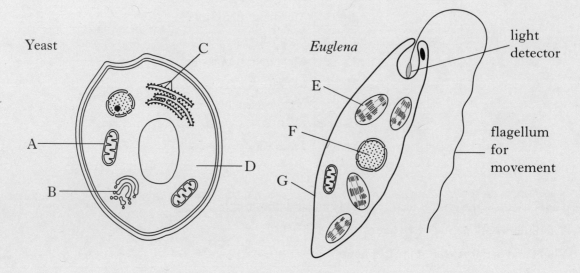

(a) (i) Name the **two** chemical components of structure G.

1 _____

2 _____   1

(ii) Complete the table by inserting letters from the diagrams to show where each process takes place.

Process	Letter
Glycolysis	
Transcription	

2

DO NOT WRITE IN THIS MARGIN

Marks

1. (continued)

(*b*) What evidence from the diagram supports the statement that yeast cells secrete enzymes?

____ **1**

(*c*) *Euglena* lives in pond water. Explain how the structure of *Euglena* shown in the diagram allows it to photosynthesise efficiently.

____

____

____ **2**

[Turn over

DO
WRI'
TI
MAI

Marks

2. An investigation was carried out into the effects of osmosis on beetroot tissue.

Pieces of beetroot were immersed in salt solutions of different concentration for one hour.

The results are shown in the table.

Concentration of salt solution (M)	Mass of beetroot at start (g)	Mass of beetroot after 1 hour (g)	Percentage change in mass (%)
0·05	4·0	4·8	+20
0·10	3·5	4·2	+20
0·20	4·4	4·7	+7
0·25	3·7	3·7	0
0·35	3·9	3·4	−13
0·40	3·5	2·8	−20

(*a*) On the grid, plot a line graph to show the percentage change in mass of the beetroot pieces against concentration of salt solution.

(Additional graph paper, if required, may be found on page 36.)

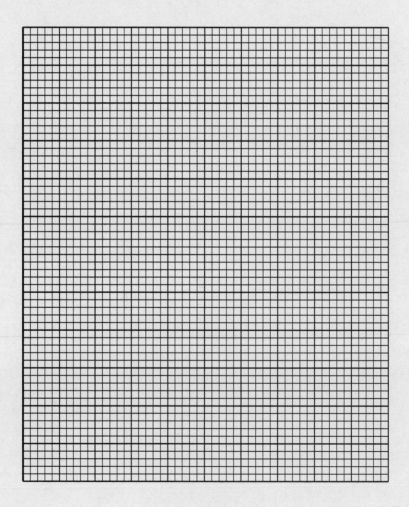

2

Marks

2. **(continued)**

(b)   (i)   Identify a concentration of salt solution used in the investigation that is hypertonic to the beetroot cell sap.

Explain your choice.

_____ M

Explanation _____

_____

_____   1

(ii)   What term describes the condition of a plant cell after immersion for one hour in a 1·0 M salt solution?

_____   1

(c)   From the information given, why was it good experimental practice to use percentage change in mass when comparing results?

_____

_____   1

(d)   Predict the percentage change in mass of a piece of beetroot immersed in 0·45 M salt solution for one hour.

_____ %   1

(e)   In setting up this investigation, variables were controlled to ensure that the results obtained would be valid.

Identify **one** variable related to the salt solutions and **one** variable related to the beetroot tissue which must be controlled.

Salt solutions   _____   1

Beetroot tissue   _____   1

[Turn over

DO N
WRIT
TH
MAR

3. (*a*) The diagram shows the role of the cytochrome system in aerobic respiration.

Marks

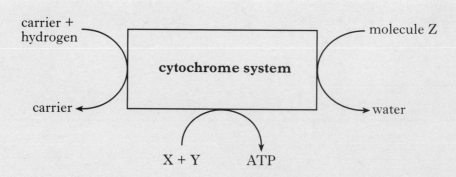

(i) State the exact location of the cytochrome system in a cell.

_____ 1

(ii) Name the carrier that brings the hydrogen to the cytochrome system.

_____ 1

(iii) Name molecules X, Y and Z.

X _____ Y _____ 1

Z _____ 1

(*b*) The graph shows the effect of different conditions on the uptake of nitrate ions by barley roots.

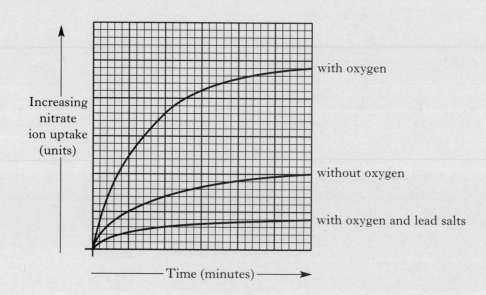

(i) State the importance of nitrate for the growth of barley plants.

_____

_____ 1

DO NOT WRITE IN THIS MARGIN

Marks

3. (*b*) (continued)

(ii) Explain why the uptake of nitrate ions is greater when oxygen is present.

____

____

____ **2**

(iii) Explain the effect of lead salts on nitrate ion uptake.

____

____

____ **2**

[Turn over

DO N
WRIT
TH
MAR

Marks

4. (*a*) The replication of part of a DNA molecule is represented in the diagram.

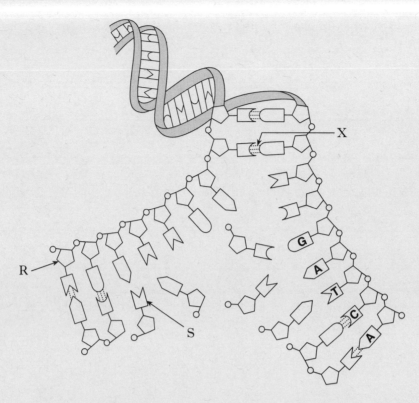

    (i) Name the nucleotide component R and the base S.

       R _____   1

       S _____   1

    (ii) Name the type of bond labelled X.

       X _____   1

(*b*) Explain why DNA replication must take place before a cell divides.

    _____

    _____

    _____   1

Marks

4. **(continued)**

(c) Part of one strand of a DNA molecule used to make mRNA contains the following base sequence.

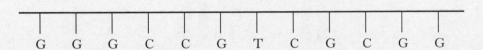

G G G C C G T C G C G G

The table shows the names of six amino acids together with some of their mRNA codons.

Amino acid	mRNA codon (s)	
Glycine	GGG	GGC
Serine	UCG	AGC
Proline	CCG	CCC
Arginine	CGG	
Alanine	GCC	
Threonine	ACG	

(i) Use the information to give the order of amino acids coded for by the DNA base sequence.

_____ 1

(ii) What name is given to a part of a DNA molecule which carries the code for making **one** protein?

_____ 1

(d) Name the molecules that transport amino acids to the site of protein synthesis.

_____ 1

(e) Complete the diagram below which shows information about protein classification.

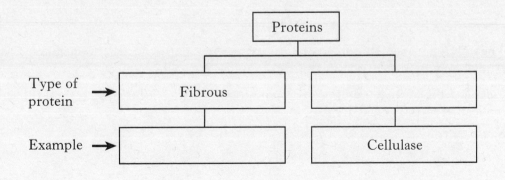

Proteins

Type of protein → Fibrous

Example →

Cellulase

1

[Turn over

DO
WRIT
TH
MAF

Marks

5. (a) The diagram shows two chromosomes and their appearance after a mutation has occurred.

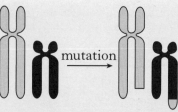

mutation

(i) Name this type of chromosome mutation.

_____   1

(ii) Name a mutagenic agent which could have caused this mutation.

_____   1

(b) Individuals with Down's Syndrome have 47 chromosomes in each cell instead of 46.

How does this change in chromosome number arise?

_____   1

(c) The diagram shows part of the normal amino acid sequence of an enzyme involved in a metabolic pathway. It also shows the altered sequence obtained after a gene mutation had occurred.

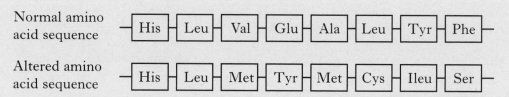

Normal amino acid sequence — His — Leu — Val — Glu — Ala — Leu — Tyr — Phe —

Altered amino acid sequence — His — Leu — Met — Tyr — Met — Cys — Ileu — Ser —

(i) Name a type of gene mutation which could have produced this altered amino acid sequence.

_____   1

(ii) Explain the effect this gene mutation would have on the metabolic pathway in which this enzyme is involved.

_____

_____   1

(d) The DNA in one cell consists of 40 000 genes. During DNA replication, random mutations occur at the rate of one altered gene in every 625.

Calculate the average number of mutations which will occur during the full replication of this cell's DNA.

Space for working

_____   1

Marks

6. (*a*) A gene from a jellyfish can be inserted into a bacterial plasmid using a genetic engineering procedure.

Some of the stages involved are shown in the diagram.

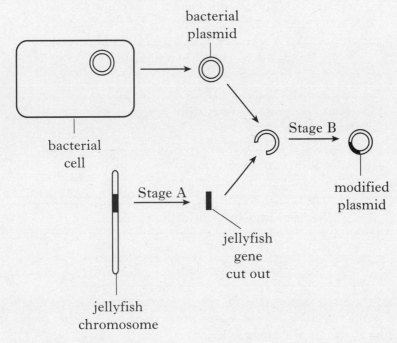

(i) Give **one** method which could be used for locating the gene in the jellyfish chromosome.

_____ 1

(ii) Name the enzymes involved in the following stages of the genetic engineering procedure.

1 Cutting the jellyfish gene out of its chromosome (Stage A).

_____ 1

2 Sealing the jellyfish gene into the bacterial plasmid (Stage B).

_____ 1

(*b*) Name **one** human hormone that is manufactured by genetically engineered bacteria.

_____ 1

[Turn over

DO N
WRIT
TH
MAR(

Marks

7. (*a*) The flow diagram shows some stages in the regulation of water concentration of blood in mammals.

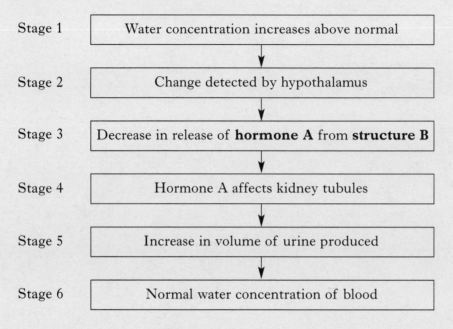

Stage 1 — Water concentration increases above normal

Stage 2 — Change detected by hypothalamus

Stage 3 — Decrease in release of **hormone A** from **structure B**

Stage 4 — Hormone A affects kidney tubules

Stage 5 — Increase in volume of urine produced

Stage 6 — Normal water concentration of blood

(i) Give **one** reason why the water concentration of the blood could increase above normal at stage 1.

_____ 1

(ii) 1 Name hormone A _____ 1

2 Name structure B _____ 1

(iii) Describe how hormone A is transported to the kidney tubules.

_____ 1

(iv) Describe the effect of hormone A on the kidney tubules.

_____

_____ 1

(v) What would be the effect of a decrease in hormone A on the concentration of salts in the urine?

_____ 1

Marks

7. **(continued)**

(b) Salmon migrate between sea water and fresh water.

The table contains statements about osmoregulation in salmon.

For each statement, tick (✓) **one** box to show whether the statement is true for a salmon living in sea water or in fresh water.

Statement	Sea water	Fresh water
Salmon drinks a large volume of water		
Salmon produces a large volume of urine		
Chloride secretory cells pump out ions		
Salmon gains water by osmosis		

2

[Turn over

Marks

8. An experiment was carried out to investigate the growth of pea plants kept in a high light intensity following germination.

The graph shows the average dry mass and average shoot length of the pea plants.

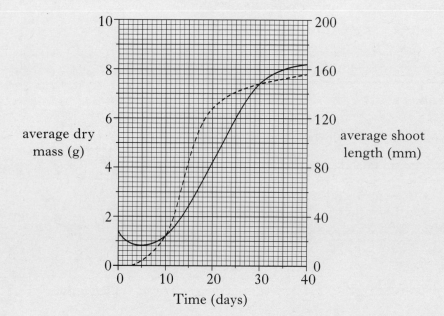

(a) (i) From the graph, how many days does it take for the shoot to emerge from the seed?

_____ days   **1**

(ii) During which 5 day period is there the greatest increase in average shoot length? Tick (✓) one box.

Day 5–10	Day 10–15	Day 15–20	Day 20–25	Day 25–30

1

(iii) Explain the changes in average dry mass of the plants during the first fifteen days.

_____

_____

_____   **2**

(iv) Explain why measurement of average shoot length alone may not provide a reliable estimate of plant growth.

_____

_____

_____   **1**

8. **(a)** **(continued)**

(v) On day 30 the shoots made up 50% of the average dry mass of the plants. Calculate the average dry mass of the shoots per millimetre.

Space for calculation

_____ g per mm   1

(b) The experiment was repeated with pea plants kept in the dark.

Complete the following to show how the results on day 15 would compare with the results obtained from plants grown in the light.

In each case, underline **one** alternative and give a reason to justify your choice.

(i) Average dry mass would be $\left\{\begin{array}{l}\text{greater.}\\\text{less.}\\\text{the same.}\end{array}\right\}$

Reason _____   1

(ii) Average shoot length would be $\left\{\begin{array}{l}\text{greater.}\\\text{less.}\\\text{the same.}\end{array}\right\}$

Reason _____   1

(c) The grid shows some of the effects of the plant growth substances Indole Acetic Acid (IAA) and Gibberellic Acid (GA) on the growth and development of plants.

A	stimulates α-amylase production in barley grains	B	promotes the formation of fruit	C	inhibits leaf abscission
D	causes apical dominance	E	involved in phototropism	F	breaks dormancy of buds

(i) Use **all** the letters from the grid to complete the table to show which effects are caused by IAA and which are caused by GA.

Effects caused by IAA	Effects caused by GA

3

(ii) Give **one** practical application of plant growth substances.

_____

_____   1

Marks

9. The diagram represents a section through a woody twig with an area enlarged to show the xylem vessels present.

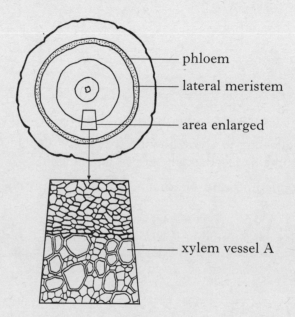

          — phloem

          — lateral meristem

          — area enlarged

          — xylem vessel A

(a) Name the lateral meristem shown in the diagram.

_____ 1

(b) Explain how the appearance of xylem vessel A indicates that it was formed in the spring.

_____

_____

_____ 1

(c) What name is given to the area of the woody twig section that represents the xylem tissue growth occurring in one year?

_____ 1

Marks

10. Duckweed (*Lemna*) is a hydrophyte that has leaf-like structures which float on the surface of pondwater.

    Some *Lemna* plants are shown in the diagram together with a magnified vertical section through one of the floating leaf-like structures.

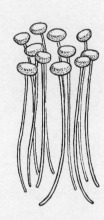

Lemna plants

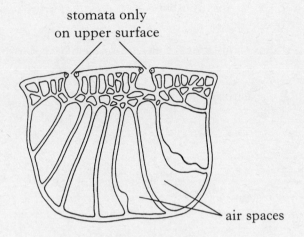

magnified vertical section

(*a*) Complete the table to describe the effect of each adaptation in *Lemna*.

Adaptation	Effect
Many large air spaces	
Stomata on upper surface	

1

1

(*b*) What term describes a plant that is adapted to live in a hot, dry habitat?

_____ 1

[Turn over

Marks

11. An investigation was carried out into the effects of competition when two species of flour beetle, *Tribolium confusum* and *Tribolium castaneum*, were kept together in a container with a limited food supply.

    Tribolium beetles can be infected by a parasite which causes disease.

    Graph 1 shows the numbers of the two species over the period of time in the absence of the parasite.

    Graph 2 shows the effect of the presence of the parasite on the beetle numbers.

    Graph 1 Parasite absent

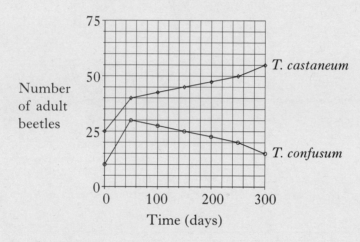

    Graph 2 Parasite present

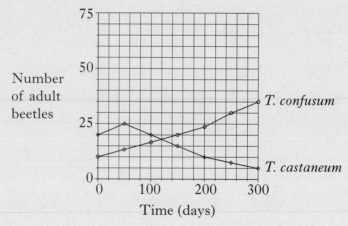

    (a) Use values from **Graph 1** to describe how the numbers of *T. confusum* change over the period of the investigation.

    _____

    _____

    _____

2

Marks

11. (continued)

(b) From **Graph 1**, express as the simplest whole number ratio the population size of *T. confusum* to *T. castaneum* at 250 days.

Space for calculation

T. confusum : *T. castaneum* _____ : _____   **1**

(c) From **Graph 2**, calculate the percentage increase in the *T. confusum* population over the 300 days of the investigation.

Space for calculation

_____ % increase   **1**

(d) Suggest an explanation for the improved growth of the *T. confusum* population in the presence of the parasite.

_____

_____

_____   **2**

(e) From the information in the graphs, suggest an improvement to the design of the investigation.

_____

_____   **1**

(f) Certain factors may affect the numbers of beetles in this investigation.

Place ticks in the table to show whether each factor would have a density-dependent effect or a density-independent effect.

Factors	Density-dependent	Density-independent
Presence of disease causing parasites		
Availability of food		
Extreme temperature		

2

DC
WR
T
MA

Marks

12. The diagram shows parts of the chromosome in the bacterium *E. coli*. The list has three molecules involved in the genetic control of lactose metabolism.

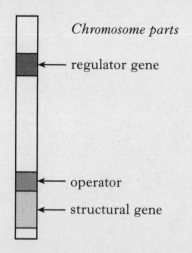

Chromosome parts

← regulator gene

← operator

← structural gene

List of molecules

lactose-digesting enzyme
repressor
inducer

(a) Complete the table by writing **True** or **False** in each of the spaces provided.

Statement	True/False
The repressor can bind to the operator.	
The structural gene codes for the repressor.	
The inducer can bind to the repressor.	
The regulator gene codes for the lactose-digesting enzyme.	

2

(b) Name the inducer molecule.

_____

1

(c) Give **one** advantage to *E. coli* of having this type of genetic control system.

_____

_____

1

SECTION C

Both questions in this section should be attempted.

Note that each question contains a choice.

Questions 1 and 2 should be attempted on the blank pages which follow.

Supplementary sheets, if required, may be obtained from the invigilator.

Labelled diagrams may be used where appropriate.

Marks

1. Answer **either** A **or** B.

    A. Give an account of meiosis under the following headings:

    (i) first meiotic division; **6**

    (ii) second meiotic division; **2**

    (iii) importance of meiosis. **2**

    (10)

    OR

    B. Give an account of the evolution of new species under the following headings:

    (i) isolating mechanisms; **4**

    (ii) effects of mutations and natural selection. **6**

    (10)

In question 2, ONE mark is available for coherence and ONE mark is available for relevance.

2. Answer **either** A **or** B.

    A. Give an account of chloroplast structure in relation to the location of the stages of photosynthesis and describe the separation of photosynthetic pigments by chromatography. **(10)**

    OR

    B. Give an account of the nature of viruses and the production of more viruses. **(10)**

[END OF QUESTION PAPER]

SPACE FOR ANSWERS

[BLANK PAGE]

FOR OFFICIAL USE

Total for
Sections
B and C

X007/301

NATIONAL
QUALIFICATIONS
2005

WEDNESDAY, 18 MAY
1.00 PM – 3.30 PM

BIOLOGY

HIGHER

Fill in these boxes and read what is printed below.

Full name of centre

Town

Forename(s)

Surname

Date of birth
Day Month Year

Scottish candidate number

Number of seat

SECTION A—Questions 1–30 (30 marks)

Instructions for completion of Section A are given on page two.

SECTIONS B AND C (100 marks)

1   (a)   All questions should be attempted.

     (b)   It should be noted that in **Section C** questions 1 and 2 each contain a choice.

2   The questions may be answered in any order but all answers are to be written in the spaces provided in this answer book, and must be written clearly and legibly in ink.

3   Additional space for answers and rough work will be found at the end of the book. If further space is required, supplementary sheets may be obtained from the invigilator and should be inserted inside the **front** cover of this book.

4   The numbers of questions must be clearly inserted with any answers written in the additional space.

5   Rough work, if any should be necessary, should be written in this book and then scored through when the fair copy has been written. If further space is required a supplementary sheet for rough work may be obtained from the invigilator.

6   Before leaving the examination room you must give this book to the invigilator. If you do not, you may lose all the marks for this paper.

SCOTTISH
QUALIFICATIONS
AUTHORITY

©

Read carefully

1   Check that the answer sheet provided is for **Biology Higher (Section A)**.

2   Check that the answer sheet you have been given has **your name**, **date of birth**, **SCN** (Scottish Candidate Number) and **Centre Name** printed on it.

    Do not change any of these details.

3   If any of this information is wrong, tell the Invigilator immediately.

4   If this information is correct, **print** your name and seat number in the boxes provided.

5   Use **black** or **blue ink** for your answers. **Do not use red ink**.

6   The answer to each question is **either** A, B, C or D. Decide what your answer is, then put a horizontal line in the space provided (see sample question below).

7   There is **only one correct** answer to each question.

8   Any rough working should be done on the question paper or the rough working sheet, **not** on your answer sheet.

9   At the end of the exam, put the **answer sheet for Section A inside the front cover of this answer book**.

Sample Question

The apparatus used to determine the energy stored in a foodstuff is a

A   respirometer

B   calorimeter

C   klinostat

D   gas burette

The correct answer is **B**—calorimeter. The answer **B** has been clearly marked with a horizontal line (see below).

Changing an answer

If you decide to change your answer, cancel your first answer by putting a cross through it (see below) and fill in the answer you want. The answer below has been changed to **B**.

If you then decide to change back to an answer you have already scored out, put a tick (✓) to the **right** of the answer you want, as shown below:

SECTION A

All questions in this section should be attempted.

Answers should be given on the separate answer sheet provided.

1. When a red blood cell is immersed in a hypertonic solution it will

   A   shrink

   B   become flaccid

   C   burst

   D   become turgid.

2. The diagram below represents some of the structures present in a plant cell.

   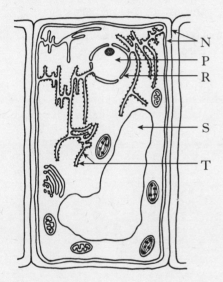

   Which line in the table matches the structures with the materials of which they are mainly composed?

	Materials	
	protein and phospholipid	nucleic acid and protein
A	R	P
B	R	S
C	T	R
D	R	N

3. Which of the following is a structural carbohydrate?

   A   Glucose

   B   Starch

   C   Glycogen

   D   Cellulose

4. The graph illustrates the effects of light intensity, temperature and carbon dioxide (CO_2) concentration on the rate of photosynthesis.

   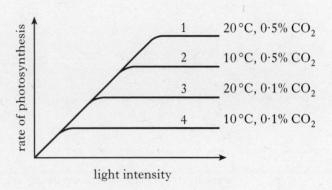

   Which of the following pairs of lines in the graph suggest that carbon dioxide is acting as a limiting factor?

   A   2 and 4

   B   2 and 3

   C   1 and 4

   D   1 and 2

5. Which of the following elements is essential to the formation of chlorophyll?

   A   Potassium

   B   Magnesium

   C   Copper

   D   Calcium

6. Which of the following is composed of protein?

   A   Nucleotide

   B   Glycogen

   C   Antibody

   D   Polysaccharide

[Turn over

7. How many adenine molecules are present in a DNA molecule of 2000 bases, if 20% of the base molecules are cytosine?

   A   200

   B   300

   C   400

   D   600

8. Which of the following statements is true of all viruses?

   A   They have a protein-lipid coat and contain DNA.

   B   They have a protein-lipid coat and contain RNA.

   C   They have a protein coat and a nucleus.

   D   They have a protein coat and contain nucleic acid.

9. The genes of viruses are composed of

   A   either DNA or RNA

   B   DNA only

   C   RNA only

   D   enzymes and nucleic acids.

10. In infertility clinics, samples of semen are collected for testing.

    The table below refers to the analysis of semen samples taken from five men.

Semen sample	1	2	3	4	5
Number of sperm in sample (millions/cm^3)	40	19	25	45	90
Active sperm (percent)	65	60	75	10	70
Abnormal sperm (percent)	30	20	90	30	10

   A man is fertile if his semen contains at least 20 million sperm cells/cm^3 and at least 60% of the sperm cells are active and at least 60% of the sperm cells are normal.

   The semen samples that were taken from infertile men are

   A   samples 3 and 4 only

   B   samples 2 and 4 only

   C   samples 2, 3 and 4 only

   D   samples 1, 2, 4 and 5 only.

11. Alleles can be described as

    A   opposite types of gamete

    B   different versions of a gene

    C   identical chromatids

    D   non-homologous chromosomes.

12. Which of the following defines linkage?

    A   Genes which are transferred from one chromosome pair to another

    B   Genes which are present on the same chromosome

    C   Genes which are transferred from one chromosome to its partner

    D   Genes which are present on different chromosomes

13. The table below shows the recombination frequency between genes on a chromosome.

Crossing over between genes	Recombination frequency
F and G	4%
F and J	6%
G and H	6%
H and J	4%

   Use the information in the table to work out the order of genes on the chromosome.

   The order of the genes is

   A   H   G   F   J

   B   F   G   H   J

   C   F   G   J   H

   D   G   H   F   J.

14. In *Drosophila*, white eye colour is a sex-linked recessive character. If a homozygous white-eyed female is crossed with a red-eyed male, what will be the phenotype of the first generation?

    A All females will be white-eyed and all males red-eyed.

    B All females will be red-eyed and all males white-eyed.

    C All females will be red-eyed and 1 in 2 males will be white-eyed.

    D 1 in 4 will be white-eyed irrespective of sex.

15. Which of the following may result in the presence of an extra chromosome in the cells of a human being?

    A Non-disjunction

    B Crossing over

    C Segregation

    D Inversion

16. Which of the following is an example of the result of natural selection?

    A Modern varieties of potato have been produced from wild varieties.

    B Ayrshire cows have been selected through breeding for milk production.

    C Bacterial species have developed resistance to antibiotics.

    D Varieties of tomato plants have resistance to fungal diseases through somatic fusion.

17. The dark variety of the peppered moth became common in industrial areas of Britain following the increase in the production of soot during the Industrial Revolution.

    The increase in the dark form was due to

    A dark moths migrating to areas which gave the best camouflage

    B a change in the prey species taken by birds

    C an increase in the mutation rate

    D a change in selection pressure.

18. Which of the following is true of the kidneys of a salt-water bony fish?

    A They have few large glomeruli.

    B They have few small glomeruli.

    C They have many large glomeruli.

    D They have many small glomeruli.

19. The Soft Brome Grass and Long Beaked Storksbill are species of plant which grow on the grasslands of California. The Storksbill is a low-growing plant with a more extensive root system than the Soft Brome, but does not grow as tall as the Soft Brome.

    Under which of the following conditions would the Storksbill become the more abundant species?

    A Drought

    B High soil moisture levels

    C High light intensity

    D Shade

20. Which of the following best describes habituation?

    A The same escape response is performed repeatedly.

    B The same response is always given to the same stimulus.

    C A harmless stimulus ceases to produce a response.

    D Behaviour is reinforced by regular repetition.

[Turn over

21. Hawks are predators which attack flocks of pigeons. The graph below shows how attack success by a hawk varies with the number of pigeons in a flock.

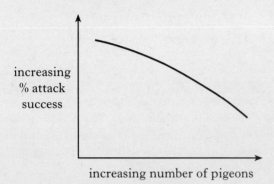

Which of the following statements could explain the observations shown in the graph?

A   A hawk only needs to eat a small percentage of a large flock of prey.

B   Co-operative hunting is more effective with small numbers of prey.

C   A predator can be more selective when prey numbers increase.

D   A hawk has difficulty focussing on one pigeon in a large flock.

22. Root tips are widely used for the study of mitosis because

A   the cells are larger than other cells

B   they contain many meristematic cells

C   their nuclei have large chromosomes

D   their nuclei stain easily.

23. The graphs below show the average yearly increase in height of girls and boys.

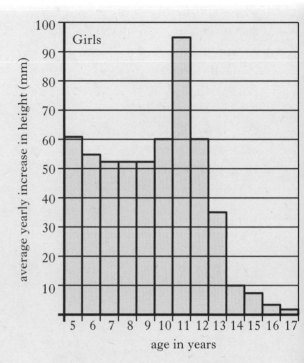

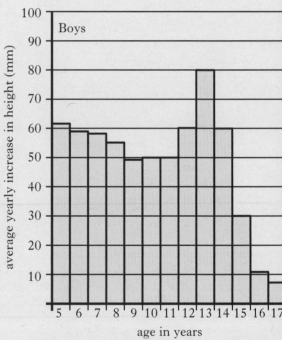

Which of the following statements is correct?

A   The greatest average yearly increase for boys occurs one year later than the greatest average yearly increase for girls.

B   Boys are still growing at seventeen but girls have stopped growing by this age.

C   Between the ages of five and eight boys grow more than girls.

D   There is no age when boys and girls show the same average yearly increase in height.

24. The following diagram shows an enzyme-controlled metabolic pathway.

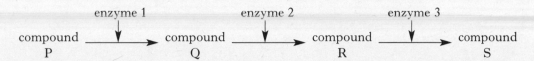

If enzyme 2 is inactivated (eg by adding an inhibitor) at time X shown in the graphs below, which graph predicts correctly the final concentration of compounds Q and R?

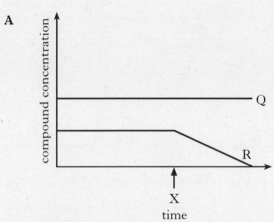

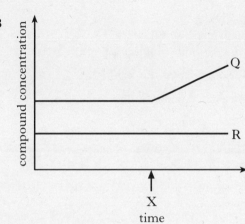

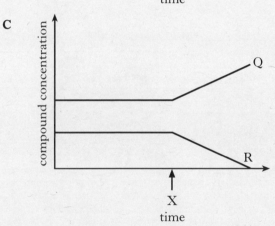

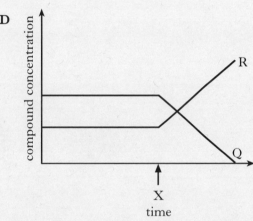

25. The table shows the results of an experiment carried out to study the effects of a plant growth substance on the roots of tomato plants.

Concentration of growth substance		Control 0 mg/litre	10^{-1} mg/litre
Average length of 20 roots	Before treatment	16 mm	16 mm
	After treatment	24 mm	20 mm

Which of the following states the effect of the plant growth substance on the lengths of the roots compared to the control treatment?

A 25 percent stimulation

B 50 percent stimulation

C 25 percent inhibition

D 50 percent inhibition

26. A short day plant is one which

A will flower only if the night length is less than the critical value

B will flower only if daylight is less than 12 hours

C will flower only if the hours of daylight are less than a critical value

D flowers only if the hours of daylight are more than a critical value.

27. A plant becomes etiolated when it

A grows in poor soil

B grows in the dark

C is treated with gibberellin

D has the apical bud removed.

28. If the concentration of glucose in the blood of a healthy man or woman rises above normal, the pancreas produces

   A   more insulin but less glucagon

   B   more insulin and more glucagon

   C   less insulin but more glucagon

   D   less insulin and less glucagon.

29. If body temperature drops below normal, which of the following would result?

   A   Vasodilation of skin capillaries

   B   Vasoconstriction of skin capillaries

   C   Decreased metabolic rate

   D   Increased sweating

30. The diagram below represents a sandy coastal area. The sand deposits support various communities of plants.

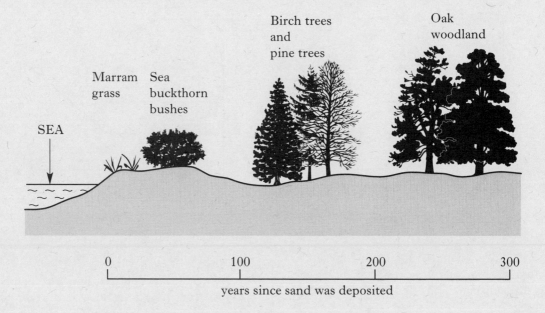

What term is used to describe the sequence of communities shown?

   A   Colonisation

   B   Climax

   C   Progression

   D   Succession

Candidates are reminded that the answer sheet MUST be returned INSIDE the front cover of this answer book.

[Turn over for Section B on *Page ten*

DO N
WRIT
TH
MAR

Marks

SECTION B

All questions in this section should be attempted.

1. The diagram shows a mitochondrion from a human muscle cell.

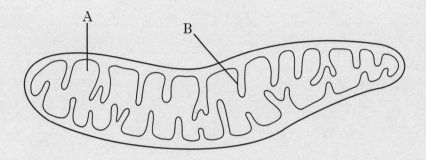

    A

            B

(a) Name regions A and B.

    A _____

    B _____   1

(b) The table shows some substances involved in respiration.

    (i) Complete the table by inserting the number of carbon atoms present in each substance.

Substance	*Number of carbon atoms present*
Pyruvic acid	
Acetyl group	
Citric acid	

      2

    (ii) To which substance is the acetyl group attached before it enters the citric acid cycle?

      _____   1

Marks

1. **(continued)**

(c) In region B, hydrogen is passed through a series of carriers in the cytochrome system as shown in the diagram below.

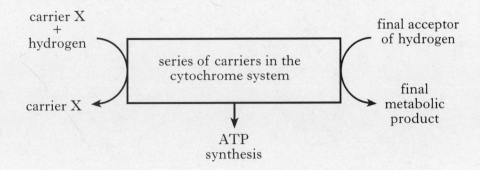

(i) Name carrier X.

_____ 1

(ii) Name the final acceptor of hydrogen.

_____ 1

(iii) Describe the importance of ATP in cells.

_____

_____ 1

(iv) The quantity of ATP present in the human body remains relatively constant yet ATP is continually being broken down.

Suggest an explanation for this observation.

_____

_____

_____ 1

(d) Name the final metabolic product of **anaerobic** respiration in a muscle cell.

_____ 1

[Turn over

2. The diagram shows two different types of blood cell involved in the defence of the human body.

Marks

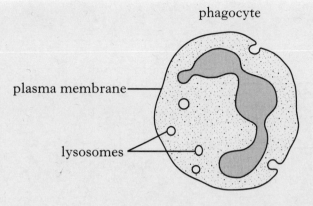
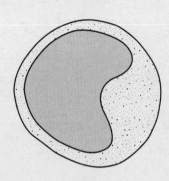

phagocyte   cell X

plasma membrane

lysosomes

(a) Describe how the plasma membrane and the lysosomes of phagocytes are involved in helping to destroy bacteria.

   (i) plasma membrane _____

_____ 1

   (ii) lysosomes _____

_____ 1

(b) (i) Name cell X.

_____ 1

   (ii) Explain how cell X may be involved in tissue rejection following a transplant operation.

_____

_____

_____ 1

   (iii) What treatment is given to prevent tissue rejection?

_____ 1

Marks

3. In Dachshund dogs, the genes for hair texture and hair length are located on different chromosomes.

The allele for wire hair (**A**) is dominant to the allele for smooth hair (**a**).
The allele for short hair (**B**) is dominant to the allele for long hair (**b**).

Wire hair is **always** short so dogs with allele **A** are **always** short haired.

Two Dachshunds with the genotype **AaBb** were crossed.

(*a*) State the phenotype of the parents in this cross.

_____ 1

(*b*) The grid shows all the genotypes of the offspring that may arise from this cross.

Complete the grid by adding the genotypes of the male and female gametes.

Male gametes

	¹ AABB	**AABb**	**AaBB**	**AaBb**
Female gametes	**AABb**	**² AAbb**	**AaBb**	**Aabb**
	AaBB	**AaBb**	**³ aaBB**	**aaBb**
	AaBb	**Aabb**	**aaBb**	**⁴ aabb**

1

(*c*) Complete the table below to give the phenotypes of the offspring indicated by the shaded boxes numbered 1 to 4 on the grid.

Box	*Phenotype*
1	
2	
3	
4	

2

(*d*) From the grid, calculate the expected ratio of the phenotypes of **all** the offspring from this cross.

Space for working

_____ wire short hair : _____ smooth short hair : _____ smooth long hair   1

DO N
WRIT
TH
MAR

Marks

4. (*a*) The diagram shows the amino acid sequences of a fish hormone and two human hormones which may have evolved from it.

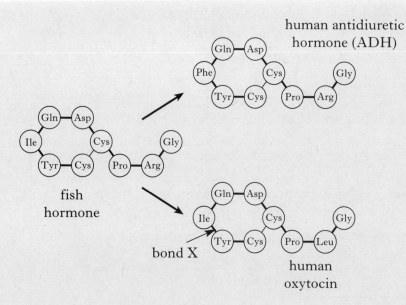

human antidiuretic
hormone (ADH)

fish
hormone

bond X

human
oxytocin

Amino acid key

Arg	arginine
Asp	aspartic acid
Cys	cysteine
Gln	glutamine
Gly	glycine
Ile	isoleucine
Leu	leucine
Phe	phenylalanine
Pro	proline
Tyr	tyrosine

(i) Name the type of bond represented by X.

_____

1

(ii) In the evolution of human oxytocin from the fish hormone, a gene mutation resulted in the amino acid arginine being replaced by leucine.

The table shows four of the mRNA codons for the amino acids arginine and leucine.

Codons for arginine	Codons for leucine
CGU	CUU
CGC	CUC
CGA	CUA
CGG	CUG

Name the type of gene mutation that occurred and justify your answer.

Type of gene mutation _____ 1

Justification _____

_____ 1

(iii) Describe the change in protein structure that occurred in the evolution of human antidiuretic hormone (ADH) from the fish hormone.

_____

_____ 1

Marks

4.   (continued)

    (*b*)   Antidiuretic hormone (ADH) is involved in osmoregulation in humans.

        (i)   Name the gland that releases ADH.

                                                             1

        (ii)   The graphs show the effects of increasing blood solute concentration and increasing blood volume on the plasma ADH concentration.

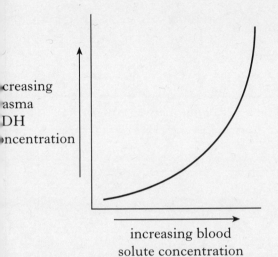

increasing plasma ADH concentration

increasing blood solute concentration

increasing plasma ADH concentration

increasing blood volume

        Use the information in the graphs to complete the table by using the terms "increases", "decreases" or "stays the same" to show the effect of various activities on the plasma ADH concentration.

        Each term may be used **once**, **more than once** or **not at all**.

Activity	Effect on plasma ADH concentration
Drinking fresh water	
Sweating	
Eating salty food	
Severe bleeding	

2

       (iii)   Describe the effect that an increase in plasma ADH concentration has on the activity of kidney tubules.

1

[Turn over

DO N
WRIT
TH
MAR

Marks

5. The diagram shows how an isolating mechanism can divide a population of one species into two sub-populations and then act as a barrier to prevent gene exchange between them.

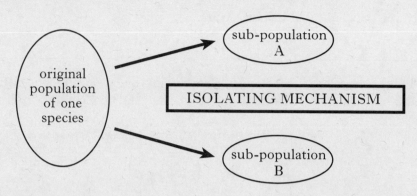

(*a*) Name **one** type of isolation that could prevent gene exchange between the two sub-populations.

_____ 1

(*b*) Over a long period of time, the gene pools of sub-populations A and B become different from each other.

(i) Explain how mutations and natural selection account for the differences.

1. Mutations _____

_____

_____ 1

2. Natural selection _____

_____

_____

_____ 2

(ii) Eventually, sub-populations A and B may become two different species. What evidence would confirm that this had happened?

_____

_____ 1

Marks

6. The list below contains terms related to genetic engineering and somatic fusion.

   List of terms:

   > cellulase
   > gene probe
   > ligase
   > plasmid
   > protoplast
   > restriction endonuclease.

   (a) Complete the table to match **each** of the following descriptions to the correct term from the above list.

Description	Term
Contains bacterial genes	
Cuts DNA into fragments	
Locates specific genes	
Removes plant cell walls	

   2

   (b) State the problem in plant breeding that is overcome by using the technique of somatic fusion.

   _____

   1

   [Turn over

DO
WRI
TH
MAR

Marks

7. (a) The diagram represents a plant with two regions magnified to show tissues involved in transport.

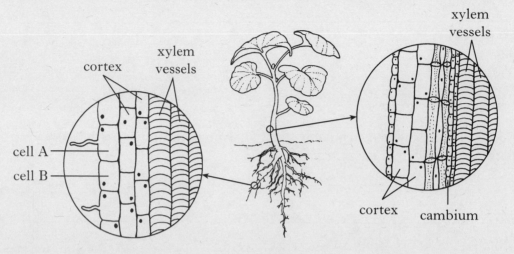

(i) Describe the process by which water moves into cell A.

_____

_____

_____ 1

(ii) Cells A and B have a similar function.
Explain how the structure of cell A makes it better adapted to its function than cell B.

_____

_____

_____ 1

(iii) Name the force that holds water molecules together as they travel up the xylem vessels.

_____ 1

(iv) Cell division in the cambium produces new cells which then elongate and develop vacuoles.

Describe **two** further changes that take place in these cells as they differentiate into xylem vessels.

1 _____

_____ 1

2 _____

_____ 1

DO NOT
WRITE IN
THIS
MARGIN

Marks

7.   **(continued)**

(b)   The diagrams show stomata in the lower epidermis of a leaf.

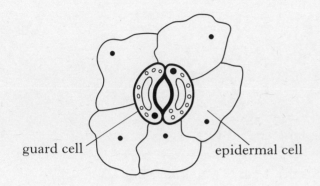
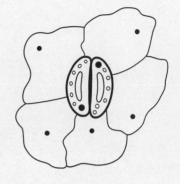

guard cell   epidermal cell

open stoma   *closed stoma*

(i)   In the following sentence, **<u>underline</u>** one of the alternatives in each pair to make the sentence correct.

Stomata close when water moves $\begin{Bmatrix} \text{into} \\ \text{out of} \end{Bmatrix}$ the guard cells

and they become $\begin{Bmatrix} \text{more} \\ \text{less} \end{Bmatrix}$ turgid.   1

(ii)   What is the advantage to plants in having their stomata closed at night?

_____ 1

(c)   The grid shows factors affecting the rate of transpiration from leaves.

A increased temperature	B increased wind speed	C increased humidity
D decreased temperature	E decreased wind speed	F decreased humidity

(i)   Which **three** letters indicate the changes that would result in a decrease in the rate of transpiration?

Letters _____ , _____ and _____.   1

(ii)   The transpiration stream supplies plant cells with water for photosynthesis.

Give **one** other benefit to plants of the transpiration stream.

_____ 1

8. **Figure 1** shows how glycerate phosphate (GP) and ribulose bisphosphate (RuBP) are involved in the Calvin cycle.

Figure 1

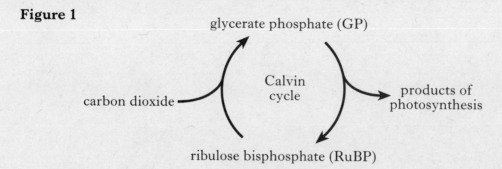

An investigation of the Calvin cycle was carried out in *Chlorella*, a unicellular alga.

Graph 1 shows the concentrations of GP and RuBP in *Chlorella* cells kept in an illuminated flask at 15 °C. The concentration of carbon dioxide in the flask was 0·05% for the first three minutes, then it was reduced to 0·005%.

Graph 1

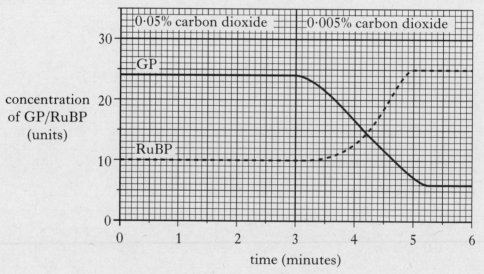

Graph 2 shows the rate of carbon dioxide fixation by *Chlorella* cells at various carbon dioxide concentrations.

Graph 2

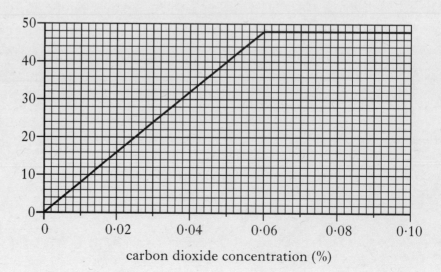

Marks

8.   (continued)

(a)   (i)   Use values from **Graph 1** to describe the changes in the RuBP concentration over the first six minutes.

   _____

   _____

   _____   2

   (ii)   Use the information in **Figure 1** to explain the increase in RuBP concentration shown in **Graph 1** when the carbon dioxide concentration is decreased.

   _____

   _____

   _____   2

(b)   From **Graph 1**, calculate the percentage decrease in the concentration of GP from three to six minutes.

Space for calculation

                                            _____ %   1

(c)   Use the terms "increase", "decrease" or "stay the same" to complete the sentence below. Each term may be used **once**, **more than once** or **not at all**.

If the carbon dioxide concentration was returned to 0·05% at 6 minutes,

the concentration of RuBP would _____

and the concentration of GP would _____ .   1

(d)   From **Graph 2**, state the rate of carbon dioxide fixation by *Chlorella* at a carbon dioxide concentration of 0·01%.

                                      _____ mmol h^{-1} 1

(e)   How many times greater is the rate of carbon dioxide fixation from 0 to 3 minutes compared with 3 to 6 minutes?

Space for calculation

                                            _____ times   1

Marks

9. African wild dogs are social animals that hunt in packs. They rely on stamina to catch grazing prey such as wildebeest.

    The table shows the effect of wildebeest age on the average duration of successful chases and the percentage hunting success.

Wildebeest age	Stage	Average duration of successful chases (s)	Hunting success (%)
up to 1 year	calves	20	75
from 1 – 2 years	juveniles	120	50
over 2 years	adults	180	45

(a) Describe the effect of wildebeest age on the average duration of successful chases.

_____

_____ 1

(b) How many times longer does it take the wild dogs on average to successfully hunt adult wildebeest rather than calves?

Space for working

_____ times 1

(c) Suggest a reason why hunting success is greatest with calves.

_____

_____ 1

(d) Wild dogs kill a greater number of adult wildebeest than calves.

Explain this observation in terms of the economics of foraging behaviour.

_____

_____

_____ 1

(e) State an advantage of cooperative hunting to the wild dogs.

_____ 1

(f) Following a successful hunt, wild dogs may be displaced from their kill by spotted hyenas. What type of competition does this show?

_____ 1

Marks

10. (*a*) Fulmars and Common Terns are seabirds that breed in large social groups.

The table compares features of breeding in these birds.

Feature of breeding	Fulmar	Common Tern
nest distribution and location	crowded on cliff ledges	scattered on pebble beaches
egg number and colour	single white egg	three speckled eggs
chick behaviour	remains in nest until able to fly	can move short distances from nest soon after hatching

(i) Use information in the table to explain why Fulmars are less vulnerable to predation than Common Terns.

_____

_____

_____   1

(ii) Suggest how features of Common Tern eggs and chicks may increase their survival chances.

1 Eggs _____

_____

_____   1

2 Chicks _____

_____

_____   1

(*b*) Explain how living in large social groups may help animals in defence against predators.

_____

_____

_____   1

[Turn over

Marks

11. An investigation was carried out into the effect of lead ethanoate and calcium ethanoate on the activity of catalase.

Catalase is an enzyme found in yeast cells. It acts on hydrogen peroxide to produce oxygen gas.

The stages in the investigation are outlined below.

1   Three yeast suspensions were made by adding 100 mg of dried yeast to each of the following.

- 25 cm^3 of 0·1 M lead ethanoate solution
- 25 cm^3 of 0·1 M calcium ethanoate solution
- 25 cm^3 of water

2   The suspensions were stirred and left for 15 minutes.

3   Separate syringes were used to add 2 cm^3 of each yeast suspension to 10 cm^3 of hydrogen peroxide in 3 identical containers.

4   The volume of oxygen produced in each container was measured at 10 second intervals.

The results are shown in the table.

Time (s)	Volume of oxygen produced (cm^3)		
	yeast suspension + lead ethanoate	yeast suspension + calcium ethanoate	yeast suspension + water
0	0	0	0
10	6	32	38
20	10	62	56
30	14	74	78
40	15	88	86
50	16	90	88
60	17	90	90

(a) Why was it good experimental procedure to leave the yeast suspensions for 15 minutes at stage 2?

_____

_____   1

(b) Why was a separate syringe used for each yeast suspension at stage 3?

_____

_____   1

(c) Identify **one** variable, not already described, that should be kept constant.

_____   1

11. (continued)

(d) The results for the yeast suspensions in 0·1 M calcium ethanoate and in water are shown in the graph.

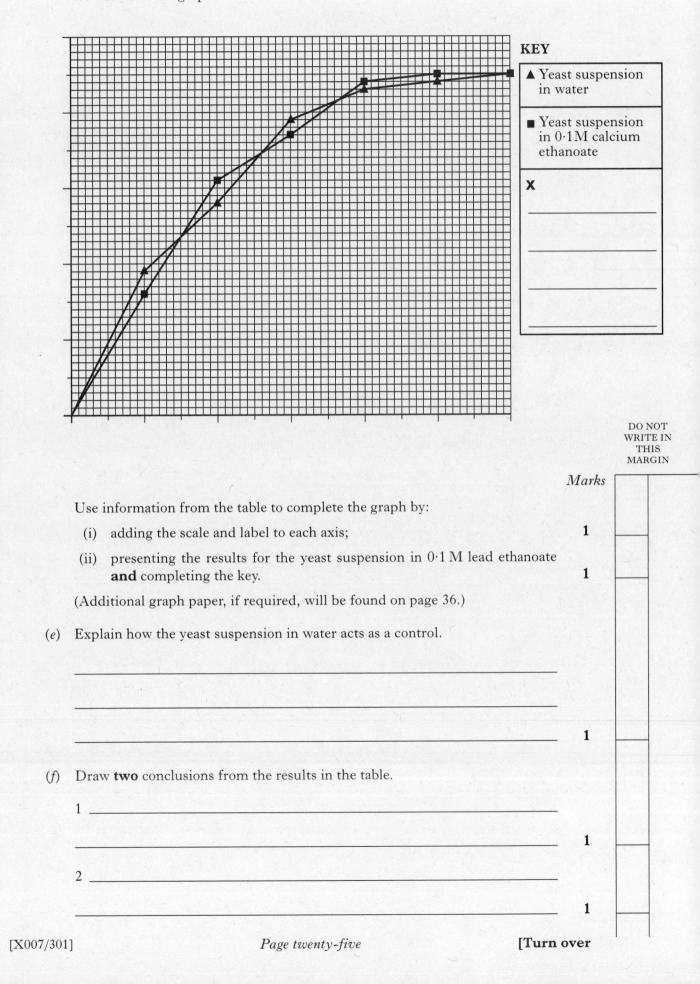

KEY

▲ Yeast suspension in water

■ Yeast suspension in 0·1 M calcium ethanoate

X

_____

_____

_____

DO NOT WRITE IN THIS MARGIN

Marks

Use information from the table to complete the graph by:

(i) adding the scale and label to each axis; **1**

(ii) presenting the results for the yeast suspension in 0·1 M lead ethanoate **and** completing the key. **1**

(Additional graph paper, if required, will be found on page 36.)

(e) Explain how the yeast suspension in water acts as a control.

_____

_____

_____ **1**

(f) Draw **two** conclusions from the results in the table.

1 _____

_____ **1**

2 _____

_____ **1**

Marks

12. (a) The diagram shows a section through a barley grain.

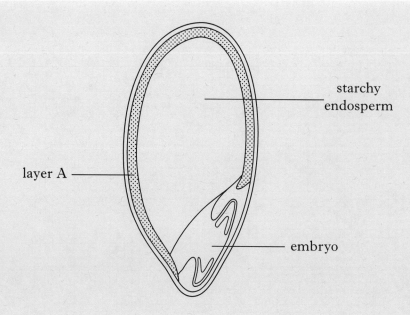

starchy
endosperm

layer A

embryo

Layer A produces α-amylase.

(i) Name layer A.

_____   1

(ii) What substance made by the embryo induces α-amylase production?

_____   1

(iii) Explain the role of α-amylase in the process of germination.

_____

_____

_____   2

(b) Give **one** practical application of a plant growth substance.

_____   1

Marks

13. The graph shows the results of an investigation into the relationship between environmental temperature and body temperature for a bobcat and a rattlesnake.

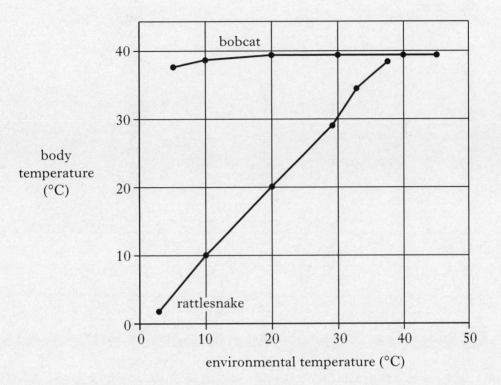

(a) Using information from the graph, **<u>underline</u>** one of the alternatives in each pair to make the sentence correct.

The rattlesnake is an $\begin{Bmatrix} \text{ectotherm} \\ \text{endotherm} \end{Bmatrix}$ because the results show that it $\begin{Bmatrix} \text{can} \\ \text{cannot} \end{Bmatrix}$ control its body temperature.

1

(b) Describe a rattlesnake behaviour pattern that is likely to raise its body temperature above the surrounding air temperature.

_____

_____

1

(c) What evidence from the graph suggests that the bobcat has mechanisms to prevent overheating?

_____

_____

1

(d) Explain why the bobcat's metabolic rate is greater at 10 °C than at 30 °C.

_____

_____

_____

2

DO
WR
T
MA

Marks

SECTION C

Both questions in this section should be attempted.

Note that each question contains a choice.

Questions 1 and 2 should be attempted on the blank pages which follow.

Supplementary sheets, if required, may be obtained from the invigilator.

Labelled diagrams may be used where appropriate.

1. Answer **either** A **or** B.

    A. Give an account of populations under the following headings:

    (i)   the importance of monitoring wild populations;   **5**

    (ii) the influence of density-dependent factors on population changes.   **5**

    (10)

    OR

    B. Give an account of growth and development under the following headings:

    (i)   the influence of pituitary hormones in humans;   **4**

    (ii) the effects of Indole Acetic Acid (IAA) in plants.   **6**

    (10)

In question 2, ONE mark is available for coherence and ONE mark is available for relevance.

2. Answer **either** A **or** B.

    A. Give an account of the absorption of light energy by photosynthetic pigments and the light-dependent stage of photosynthesis.   **(10)**

    OR

    B. Give an account of the structure of RNA and its role in protein synthesis.   **(10)**

[END OF QUESTION PAPER]

SPACE FOR ANSWERS

SPACE FOR ANSWERS

DO NOT
WRITE IN
THIS
MARGIN

SPACE FOR ANSWERS

[Turn over

SPACE FOR ANSWERS

SPACE FOR ANSWERS

SPACE FOR ANSWERS

SPACE FOR ANSWERS

DO N
WRIT
TH
MAR

SPACE FOR ANSWERS

ADDITIONAL GRAPH PAPER FOR QUESTION 11(*d*)

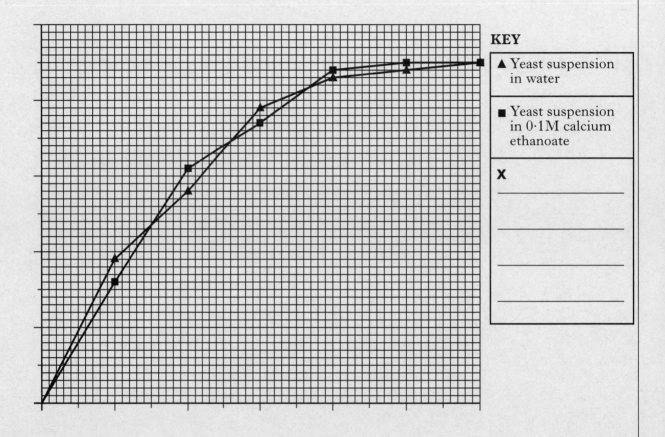

KEY

▲ Yeast suspension in water

■ Yeast suspension in 0·1M calcium ethanoate

X

2006 | Higher

[BLANK PAGE]

FOR OFFICIAL USE

Total for
Sections
B and C

X007/301

NATIONAL
QUALIFICATIONS
2006

TUESDAY, 23 MAY
1.00 PM – 3.30 PM

BIOLOGY
HIGHER

Fill in these boxes and read what is printed below.

Full name of centre

Town

Forename(s)

Surname

Date of birth
Day Month Year

Scottish candidate number

Number of seat

SECTION A—Questions 1–30 (30 marks)

Instructions for completion of Section A are given on page two.

For this section of the examination you must use an **HB pencil**.

SECTIONS B AND C (100 marks)

1 (a) All questions should be attempted.

(b) It should be noted that in **Section C** questions 1 and 2 each contain a choice.

2 The questions may be answered in any order but all answers are to be written in the spaces provided in this answer book, **and must be written clearly and legibly in ink**.

3 Additional space for answers will be found at the end of the book. If further space is required, supplementary sheets may be obtained from the invigilator and should be inserted inside the **front** cover of this book.

4 The numbers of questions must be clearly inserted with any answers written in the additional space.

5 Rough work, if any should be necessary, should be written in this book and then scored through when the fair copy has been written. If further space is required a supplementary sheet for rough work may be obtained from the invigilator.

6 Before leaving the examination room you must give this book to the invigilator. If you do not, you may lose all the marks for this paper.

SCOTTISH
QUALIFICATIONS
AUTHORITY

Read carefully

1   Check that the answer sheet provided is for **Biology Higher (Section A)**.

2   For this section of the examination you must use an **HB pencil**, and where necessary, an eraser.

3   Check that the answer sheet you have been given has **your name**, **date of birth**, **SCN** (Scottish Candidate Number) and **Centre Name** printed on it.

    Do not change any of these details.

4   If any of this information is wrong, tell the Invigilator immediately.

5   If this information is correct, **print** your name and seat number in the boxes provided.

6   The answer to each question is **either** A, B, C or D. Decide what your answer is, then, using your pencil, put a horizontal line in the space provided (see sample question below).

7   There is **only one correct** answer to each question.

8   Any rough working should be done on the question paper or the rough working sheet, **not** on your answer sheet.

9   At the end of the exam, put the **answer sheet for Section A inside the front cover of this answer book**.

Sample Question

The apparatus used to determine the energy stored in a foodstuff is a

A   calorimeter

B   respirometer

C   klinostat

D   gas burette.

The correct answer is **A**—calorimeter. The answer **A** has been clearly marked in **pencil** with a horizontal line (see below).

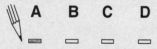

Changing an answer

If you decide to change your answer, carefully erase your first answer and using your pencil fill in the answer you want. The answer below has been changed to **D**.

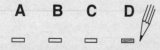

SECTION A

All questions in this section should be attempted.

Answers should be given on the separate answer sheet provided.

1. The diagram below represents a highly magnified section of a yeast cell.

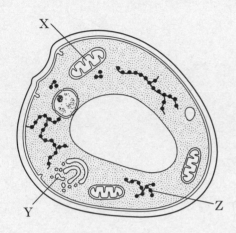

Which line of the table below correctly links each cell structure with its function?

	Aerobic respiration	Protein synthesis	Packaging materials for secretion
A	X	Y	Z
B	Y	Z	X
C	X	Z	Y
D	Z	X	Y

2. The action spectrum in photosynthesis is a measure of the ability of photosynthetic pigments to

   A   absorb red and blue light

   B   absorb light of different intensities

   C   carry out photolysis

   D   use light of different wavelengths for synthesis.

3. The diagram below shows the energy flow in an area of forest canopy during 1 year.

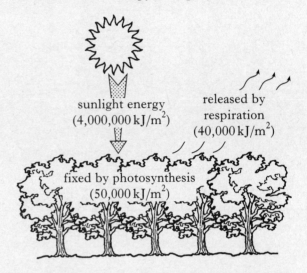

What percentage of available sunlight energy is fixed by the trees?

   A   0·25%

   B   1·00%

   C   1·25%

   D   2·25%

[Turn over

4. Photosynthetic pigments can be separated by means of chromatography as shown in the diagram below.

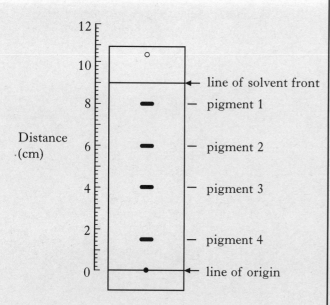

A pigment can be identified from its R_f value which can be calculated as follows:

$$R_f = \frac{\text{distance travelled by pigment from origin}}{\text{distance travelled by solvent from origin}}$$

Which line of the table correctly identifies the R_f values of pigments 2 and 3 on the above chromatogram?

	Pigment 2	Pigment 3
A	0·44	0·17
B	0·67	0·44
C	0·44	0·67
D	0·67	0·89

5. The diagram below shows a mitochondrion surrounded by cytoplasm.

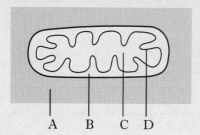

Where does glycolysis take place?

6. Which of the following statements refer to glycolysis?

1   Carbon dioxide released.

2   Occurs during aerobic respiration.

3   The end product is pyruvic acid.

4   The end product is lactic acid.

A   1 and 3

B   1 and 4

C   2 and 3

D   2 and 4

7. During anaerobic respiration in muscle fibres what is the fate of pyruvic acid?

A   It is converted to lactic acid.

B   It is broken down by the mitochondria.

C   It is broken down to carbon dioxide and water.

D   It is converted to citric acid.

8. Which of the following proteins has a fibrous structure?

A   Insulin

B   Pepsin

C   Amylase

D   Collagen

9. If ten percent of the bases in a molecule of DNA are adenine, what is the ratio of adenine to guanine in the same molecule?

A   1:1

B   1:2

C   1:3

D   1:4

10. In the life cycle of a bacterial virus which of the following sequences of events occurs?

A   Lysis of the cell membrane, synthesis of viral DNA, replication of viral protein

B   Lysis of cell membrane, synthesis of viral protein, replication of viral DNA

C   Replication of viral DNA, synthesis of viral protein, lysis of cell membrane

D   Synthesis of viral protein, replication of viral DNA, lysis of cell membrane

11. The table below shows some genotypes and phenotypes associated with forms of sickle-cell anaemia.

Phenotype	Genotype
unaffected	$Hb^A Hb^A$
sickle-cell trait	$Hb^A Hb^S$
acute sickle-cell anaemia	$Hb^S Hb^S$

A woman with sickle-cell trait and a man who is unaffected plan to have a child.

What are the chances that their child will have acute sickle-cell anaemia?

A   None

B   1 in 1

C   1 in 2

D   1 in 4

12. The following cross was carried out using two pure-breeding strains of the fruit fly, *Drosophila*.

P straight wing   curly wing
                    +   ×   +
                 black body   grey body

F_1 All straight wing + black body

The F_1 were allowed to interbreed

F_2 straight wing   curly wing
                    +   ×   +
                 black body   grey body

F_2 Phenotype
Ratio   3   :   1

In a dihybrid cross the typical F_2 ratio is $9 : 3 : 3 : 1$.

An explanation of the result obtained in the above cross is that

A   crossing over has occurred between the genes

B   before isolation F_1 females had mated with their own type males

C   non-disjunction of chromosomes in the sex cells has taken place

D   these genes are linked.

13. The recombination frequency obtained in a genetic cross may be used as a source of information concerning the

A   genotypes of the recombinant offspring

B   diploid number of the species

C   fertility of the species

D   position of gene loci.

14. Red-green colour deficient vision is a sex-linked condition. John, who is affected, has the family tree shown below.

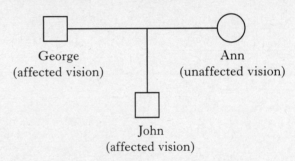

George
(affected vision)   Ann
                              (unaffected vision)

John
(affected vision)

If b is the mutant allele for the condition, which of the following could be the genotypes of George's parents and Ann's parents?

	George's parents		Ann's parents	
A	$X^B X^b$	$X^B Y$	$X^B X^B$	$X^B Y$
B	$X^B X^B$	$X^b Y$	$X^B X^B$	$X^B Y$
C	$X^B X^b$	$X^B Y$	$X^B X^b$	$X^B Y$
D	$X^B X^B$	$X^b Y$	$X^B X^B$	$X^b Y$

15. Klinefelter's syndrome is caused by the presence of an extra X chromosome in human males. Affected individuals are therefore XXY.

This syndrome is caused by

A   recombination

B   sex-linkage

C   crossing-over

D   non-disjunction.

[Turn over

16. The table refers to the mass of DNA in certain human body cells.

Cell type	Mass of DNA in cell ($\times 10^{-12}$ g)
liver	6·6
lung	6·6
R	3·3
S	0·0

Which of the following is the most likely identification of cell types R and S?

	R	S
A	ovum	mature red blood cell
B	mature red blood cell	sperm
C	nerve cell	mature red blood cell
D	kidney tubule cell	ovum

17. The following steps are involved in the process of genetic engineering.

1 Insertion of a plasmid into a bacterial host cell

2 Use of an enzyme to cut out a piece of chromosome containing a desired gene

3 Insertion of the desired gene into the bacterial plasmid

4 Use of an enzyme to open a bacterial plasmid

What is the correct sequence of these steps?

A	4	1	2	3
B	2	4	3	1
C	4	3	1	2
D	2	3	4	1

18. Osmoregulation in bony fish is achieved by a variety of strategies, depending on the nature of the environment.

Strategies

1 Large volume of dilute urine produced.

2 Small volume of concentrated urine produced.

3 Kidneys contain many large glomeruli.

4 Kidneys contain few small glomeruli.

Which of these strategies are employed by a freshwater bony fish?

A 1 and 4

B 2 and 4

C 1 and 3

D 2 and 3

19. The list below shows benefits which an animal species can obtain from certain types of social behaviour.

1 Aggression between individuals is controlled.

2 Subordinate animals are more likely to gain an adequate food supply.

3 Experienced leadership is guaranteed.

4 Energy used by individuals to obtain food is reduced.

Which statements refer to co-operative hunting?

A 1 and 2 only

B 1 and 3 only

C 2 and 4 only

D 3 and 4 only

20. The rates of carbon dioxide exchange by the leaves of two species of plants were measured at different light intensities.

   The results are shown in the graph below.

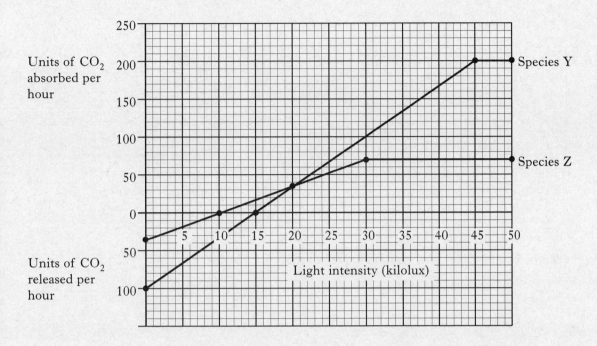

   By how many kilolux is the compensation point for species Y greater than the compensation point for species Z?

   A   5

   B   10

   C   15

   D   130

21. A feature of phenylketonuria in humans is

   A   the synthesis of excess phenylalanine

   B   an inability to synthesise phenylalanine

   C   the synthesis of excess tyrosine from phenylalanine

   D   an inability to synthesise tyrosine from phenylalanine.

22. Plant ovary wall cells develop differently from plant phloem cells because of

   A   random assortment in meiosis

   B   genes being switched on and off during development

   C   their having different numbers of chromosomes

   D   their having different sets of genes.

[Turn over

23. An investigation was carried out into the germination of barley seeds.

The concentration of amylase and the rate of breakdown of starch was measured over 15 days.

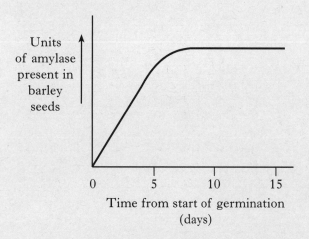

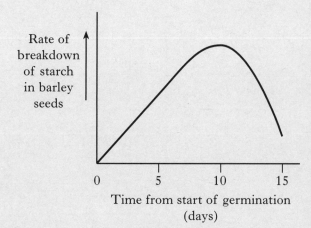

From the graphs it can be seen that after 10 days

A   the production of gibberellin has ceased

B   the rate of starch digestion decreases

C   the barley is synthesising its own starch

D   the amylase is becoming denatured.

24. The graph below contains information about fertiliser usage.

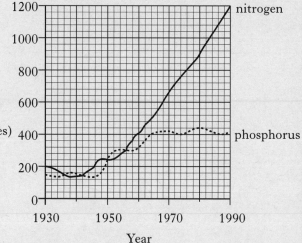

Which of the following statements about nitrogen usage between 1930 and 1990 is correct?

A   It increased steadily.

B   It increased by 500%.

C   It increased by 600%.

D   It always exceeded phosphorus usage.

25. Dietary deficiency of vitamin D causes rickets.

This effect is due to

A   poor uptake of phosphate into growing bones

B   low vitamin D content in the bones

C   poor calcium absorption from the intestine

D   loss of calcium from the bones.

26. Which of the following would result from an increased production of ADH?

A   The production of urine with a higher concentration of urea

B   Decrease in the permeability of the kidney collecting ducts

C   A decrease in the rate of glomerular filtration

D   An increase in the rate of production of urine

27. The graph below records the body temperature of a woman during an investigation in which her arm was immersed in water.

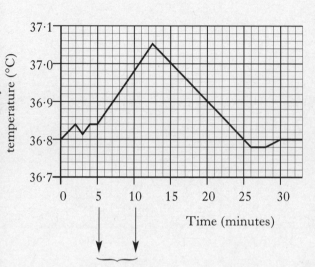

Arm immersed
in water during
this period

By how much did the temperature of her body vary during the 30 minutes of the investigation?

A   2·7 °C

B   0·27 °C

C   2·5 °C

D   0·25 °C

28. The graph below contains information about the birth rate and death rate in Mexico.

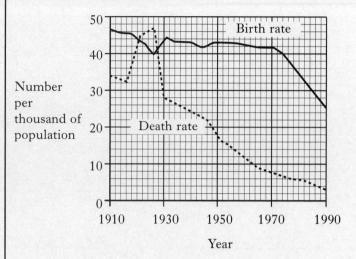

Which of the following conclusions can be drawn from the graph?

A   At no time during the century has the population of Mexico decreased.

B   The greatest increase in population occurred in 1970.

C   The population was growing faster in 1910 than in 1990.

D   Birth rate decreased between 1970 and 1990 due to the use of contraception.

[Turn over

29. The bar chart below shows the percentage loss in yield of four organically grown crops as a result of the effects of weeds, disease and insects.

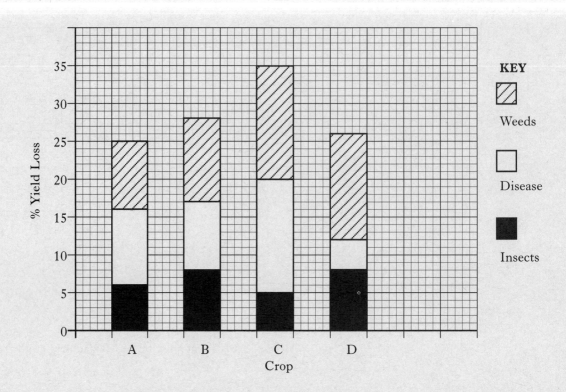

Predict which crop is most likely to show the greatest increase in yield if herbicides and insecticides were applied.

30. During succession in plant communities a number of changes take place in the ecosystem. Which line of the table correctly describes some of these changes?

	Species diversity	Biomass	Food web complexity
A	rises	rises	rises
B	rises	falls	rises
C	falls	rises	rises
D	rises	rises	falls

Candidates are reminded that the answer sheet MUST be returned INSIDE the front cover of this answer book.

[Turn over for Section B on *Page twelve*

Marks

SECTION B

All questions in this section should be attempted.

All answers must be written clearly and legibly in ink.

1. (a) The grid contains information about the plasma membrane and the cell wall.

A contains phospholipid	B fully permeable	C made of fibres
D contains cellulose	E selectively permeable	F made up of two layers

(i) Two of the boxes contain information about the **structure** of the plasma membrane.

Identify these **two** boxes.

Letters _____ and _____   1

(ii) One of the boxes contains information that relates to the role of the cell wall in the movement of water into a cell.

Identify this box.

Letter _____   1

(b) The table shows the percentage change in mass of apple tissue after immersion in sucrose solutions of different concentrations.

Concentration of sucrose solution (M)	Change in mass of apple tissue (%)
0·00	+22·0
0·10	+13·0
0·15	+8·5
0·20	+4·0
0·25	−0·5
0·30	−5·0
0·40	−14·0
0·50	−23·0

Marks

1. **(b)** **(continued)**

(i) Using values from the table, plot a line graph to show the percentage change in mass of the apple tissue against the concentration of sucrose solution.

Use appropriate scales to fill most of the grid.

(An additional grid, if required, may be found on page 40.)

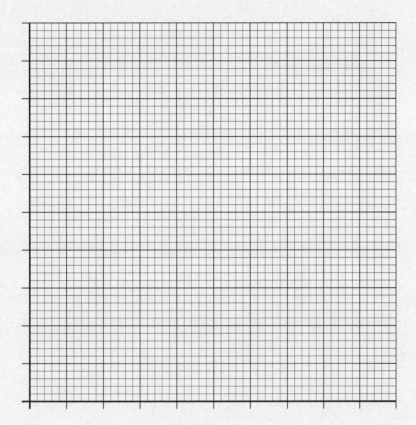

2

(ii) Complete the following sentences by underlining **one** of the alternatives in each pair.

The 0·1 M sucrose solution is $\begin{Bmatrix} \text{hypotonic} \\ \text{hypertonic} \end{Bmatrix}$ to the apple tissue.

Apple cells immersed in this solution may become $\begin{Bmatrix} \text{plasmolysed} \\ \text{turgid} \end{Bmatrix}$. **1**

[Turn over

Marks

2. The diagram shows an outline of the stages in photosynthesis.

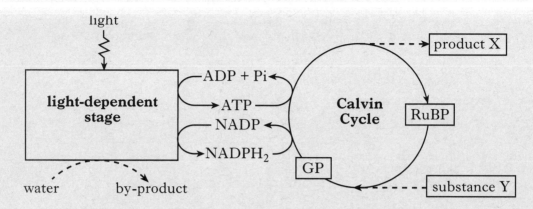

(a) (i) Name the by-product produced by the light-dependent stage.

_____ 1

(ii) Name product X and substance Y.

Product X _____

Substance Y_____ 1

(iii) State the number of carbon atoms in RuBP and GP.

RuBP _____ GP _____ 1

(b) (i) Describe the role of ATP in photosynthesis.

_____

_____

_____ 1

(ii) Explain why hydrogen from the light-dependent stage of photosynthesis is needed by the Calvin cycle.

_____

_____

_____ 1

Marks

2. **(continued)**

(c) The graph shows the absorption spectra of three photosynthetic pigments.

Pigments P and Q were extracted from a hydrophyte with leaves that float on the water surface.

Pigment R was extracted from a species of photosynthetic algae that lives in the water below the hydrophyte.

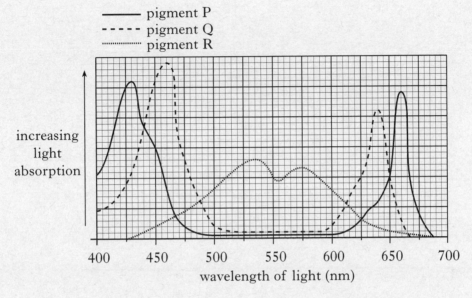

—— pigment P
- - - - pigment Q
·········· pigment R

increasing
light
absorption

wavelength of light (nm)

(i) Tick (✓) **one** box to identify the wavelengths of light at which pigment P shows greatest absorption.

425–450 nm	450–475 nm	525–550 nm	625–650 nm	650–675 nm

1

(ii) Explain why it is an advantage to the hydrophyte to have more than one pigment.

_____

_____

_____   1

(iii) Give **one** adaptation of hydrophyte leaves and state its effect.

Adaptation _____

Effect _____

_____   1

(iv) From the information given, explain how the algae from which pigment R was extracted are adapted to photosynthesise in their environment.

_____

_____

_____   1

DO
WRI
TH
MAI

Marks

3. Experiments were carried out to investigate the hypothesis that the uptake of ions into mammalian cells takes place by active transport.

(a) The concentrations of potassium ions and chloride ions inside and outside a mammalian cell were measured.

The table shows the results obtained at an oxygen concentration of 4·0 units.

Ion	Ion concentration inside cell (mM)	Ion concentration outside cell (mM)
Potassium	140	5
Chloride	10	110

(i) Describe the information shown in the table that supports the original hypothesis.

_____

_____

_____ 1

(ii) From the table, calculate the simplest whole number ratio of potassium ions to chloride ions outside a mammalian cell.

Space for calculation

_____ potassium ions : _____ chloride ions   1

Marks

3. **(continued)**

(b) The graph shows the effect of changing oxygen concentration on the concentration of potassium ions inside a mammalian cell.

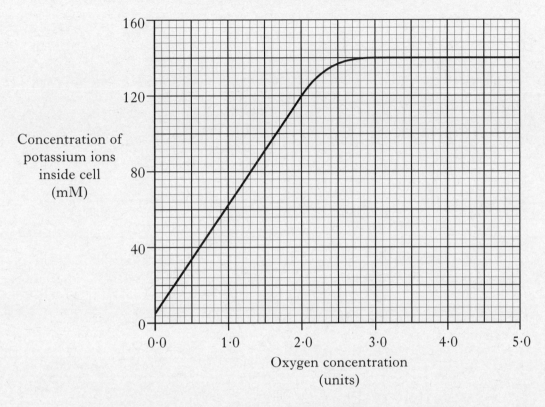

(i) Explain the shape of the graph between oxygen concentrations of 1·0 and 2·0 units.

_____

_____

_____ ,

_____ 2

(ii) Suggest a reason why the graph levels off at oxygen concentrations above 3·0 units.

_____

_____ 1

[Turn over

Marks

4. Yeast is a micro-organism capable of both aerobic and anaerobic respiration.

(*a*) Describe the role of oxygen in aerobic respiration.

_____

_____ 1

(*b*) The diagrams represent a mitochondrion from a normal yeast cell and one from a mutant yeast cell.

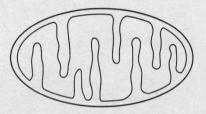 

mitochondrion from   mitochondrion from
normal yeast cell   mutant yeast cell

(i) Name the structures that are absent from the mitochondrion of the mutant yeast cell.

_____ 1

(ii) An experiment was carried out to investigate the effect of oxygen on the growth of normal and mutant yeast cells.

The method used in the experiment is outlined below.

- Three normal yeast cells were placed on agar growth medium containing glucose in a petri dish.

- Three mutant yeast cells were placed on the same agar growth medium containing glucose in a second dish.

- The dishes were then incubated at 30 °C for four days in aerobic conditions to allow the cells to multiply and produce colonies of yeast cells.

- The above three steps were repeated and the dishes were incubated this time in anaerobic conditions.

The sizes of the colonies produced are shown in the following diagrams.

Marks

4. (*b*) **(ii)** **(continued)**

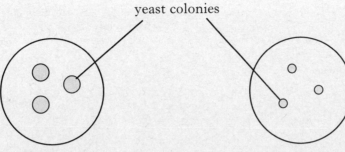

yeast colonies

normal yeast
grown in aerobic conditions

mutant yeast
grown in aerobic conditions

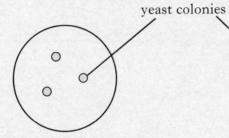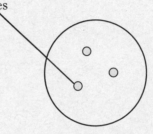

yeast colonies

normal yeast
grown in anaerobic conditions

mutant yeast
grown in anaerobic conditions

1. Suggest a possible improvement to the experimental method, other than repeating the experiment, that would increase the reliability of the results.

_____

_____ 1

2. Give an explanation for the difference in colony size observed for the normal yeast grown in aerobic and anaerobic conditions.

_____

_____

_____ 2

3. Suggest why there was no difference in colony size when the mutant cells were grown in aerobic and anaerobic conditions.

_____

_____ 1

[Turn over

Marks

DO
WRI
TI
MA

5. The diagram shows translation of part of a mRNA molecule during the synthesis of a protein.

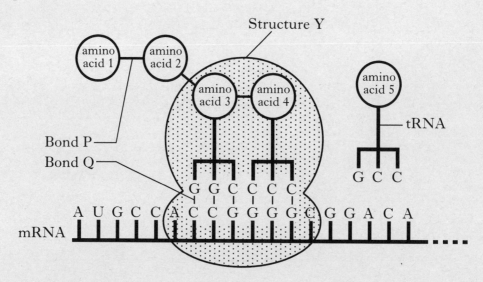

(a) Name structure Y.

_____ 1

(b) Name the types of bond shown at P and Q.

Bond P _____

Bond Q _____ 1

(c) Give the anticodon for the tRNA for amino acid 1.

_____ 1

(d) Describe **two** functions of tRNA in protein synthesis.

1 _____

_____ 1

2 _____

_____ 1

(e) Genetic information for protein synthesis is in the form of a triplet code. Explain what is meant by this statement.

_____

_____

_____ 1

Marks

6. Patients who have had tissue transplants may be treated with a drug that suppresses the immune system.

The table shows the number of lymphocytes in the blood of a patient before and after treatment.

Number of lymphocytes before treatment (cells per mm^3)	Number of lymphocytes after treatment (cells per mm^3)
7500	3000

(a) Calculate the percentage decrease in the number of lymphocytes following treatment with the suppressor drug.

Space for calculation

_____ %   1

(b) Explain why there is a risk of rejection when tissues are transplanted.

_____

_____

_____

_____   2

(c) Some suppressor drugs act by binding to DNA molecules in such a way that the separation of the two DNA strands is prevented.

Predict **one** possible consequence of the use of this type of suppressor drug on the normal functions of DNA.

_____

_____

_____   1

[Turn over

Marks

7. (*a*) The letters A – E represent five statements about meiosis.

Letter	Statement
A	haploid gametes are produced
B	chiasmata are formed
C	chromatids separate
D	gamete mother cell is present
E	homologous chromosomes form pairs

(i) Use **all** the letters from the list to complete the table to show the statements that are connected with the first and the second meiotic divisions.

First meiotic division	*Second meiotic division*

2

(ii) Independent assortment of chromosomes during meiosis is a source of genetic variation.

Describe the behaviour of chromosomes during the first meiotic division stage that results in independent assortment.

_____

_____

_____ 1

Marks

7. (continued)

(b) Duchenne muscular dystrophy (DMD) is a recessive, sex-linked condition in humans that affects muscle function.

The diagram shows an X-chromosome from an unaffected individual and one from an individual with DMD.

X-chromosome from unaffected individual

X-chromosome from individual with DMD

    (i) Using information from the diagram, name the type of chromosome mutation responsible for DMD.

_____   1

    (ii) **On the diagram** of the chromosome from the **unaffected individual**, put a **cross (X)** on the likely location of the gene involved in DMD.   1

    (iii) Males are more likely to be affected by DMD than females.

Explain why.

_____

_____

_____

_____   1

    (iv) A person with DMD has an altered phenotype compared with an unaffected individual.

Explain how an inherited chromosome mutation such as DMD may result in an altered phenotype.

_____

_____

_____

_____   1

[Turn over

Marks

8. Three species of small bird, the Blue Tit, the Great Tit and the Marsh Tit, forage for caterpillars in oak woods in early summer.

    Investigators observed each bird species for ten hours. They recorded the percentage of time each species spent foraging in different parts of the trees. The results are shown in the **Bar Chart**.

    Table 1 shows the percentage of the birds' diet that came from different caterpillar size ranges.

    Table 2 shows the beak size index calculated for each species using the following formula.

    $$beak\ size\ index = average\ beak\ length\ (mm) \times average\ beak\ depth\ (mm)$$

Bar Chart

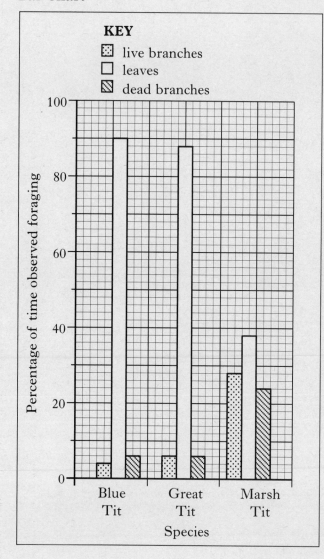

Table 1

caterpillar size range (mm)	% of diet from each size range		
	Blue Tit	Great Tit	Marsh Tit
1–2	63·6	18·2	18·1
3–4	24·3	20·4	60·6
5–6	10·0	27·2	12·1
7–8	2·1	34·2	9·2

Table 2

species	beak size index (mm^2)
Blue Tit	40·3
Great Tit	67·6
Marsh Tit	44·2

(a) Calculate the number of minutes the Blue Tits were observed foraging on live branches.

Space for calculation

_____ mins   1

8. (continued)

Marks

(b) What evidence from the **Bar Chart** suggests that Marsh Tits forage on tree parts other than those shown?

_____

_____ **1**

(c) Calculate the average percentage of the birds' diets in the 1–2 mm caterpillar size range.

Space for calculation

_____ % **1**

(d) Describe the relationship between beak size index and caterpillar size range eaten.

_____

_____ **1**

(e) The average beak length of Great Tits is 13 mm.

Calculate their average beak depth.

Space for calculation

_____ mm **1**

(f) From the information given, describe all of the ways by which interspecific competition for caterpillars is reduced between the following pairs of bird species.

(i) Blue Tits and Great Tits _____

_____

_____ **1**

(ii) Blue Tits and Marsh Tits _____

_____

_____ **1**

(g) Each bird species must forage economically.

Explain what is meant by this statement in terms of energy gain and loss.

_____

_____

_____ **1**

DO N
WRIT
TH
MAR(

Marks

9. The ancestor species of the modern tomato produces small fruits but can grow in soils with low nitrogen levels.

The modern species of tomato has been selectively bred to produce large fruit but requires soil rich in nitrogen to grow well.

(a) (i) Give **one** reason why nitrogen is important for plant growth.

_____

_____ 1

(ii) Give **one** symptom of nitrogen deficiency in plants.

_____ 1

(b) The diagram represents steps in a technique used by tomato breeders to combine characteristics of these two species.

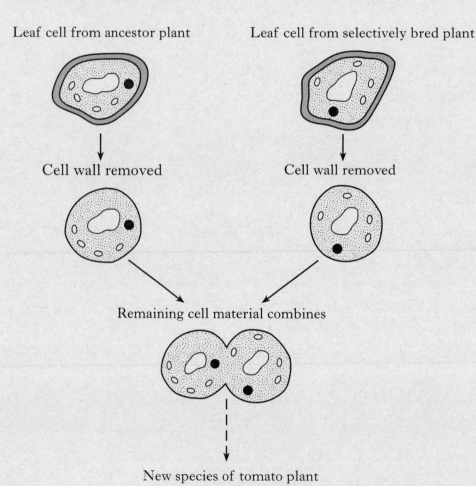

[X007/301]

DO NOT WRITE IN THIS MARGIN

Marks

9. (*b*) (continued)

(i) Give the name of the technique shown in the diagram.

______________________________ **1**

(ii) Name the enzyme that is used to remove the cell walls from the leaf cells.

______________________________ **1**

(iii) Explain why cultivation of the new species of tomato could lead to a reduction in the use of nitrogen fertiliser.

____

____

______________________________ **1**

[Turn over

DO N
WRIT
TH
MAR

Marks

10. An investigation was carried out to compare the growth of *Escherichia coli* (*E. coli*) bacteria in different nutrient solutions.

    E. coli were grown in a glucose solution for 24 hours. Two 50 cm³ samples were transferred to two identical containers each with different sterile nutrient solutions as shown in the table.

Container	Nutrient solution
X	0·5 mM glucose
Y	0·5 mM lactose

    One container is shown in the diagram.

    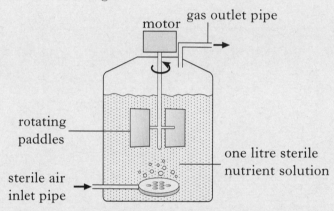

    The pH and temperature were kept constant.

    Every 30 minutes, a 2 cm³ sample was taken from each container.

    An instrument was used to measure the number of bacteria present. The higher the instrument reading, the more bacteria.

    (a) (i) Suggest a reason for having rotating paddles.

    _____

    _____ 1

    (ii) Explain why a gas outlet pipe is needed in the apparatus.

    _____

    _____

    _____ 1

    (b) Identify **two** variables not already mentioned that would have to be controlled in both containers to make the procedure valid.

    1 _____ 1

    2 _____ 1

Marks

10. (continued)

(c) The results of the investigation are shown in the graph.

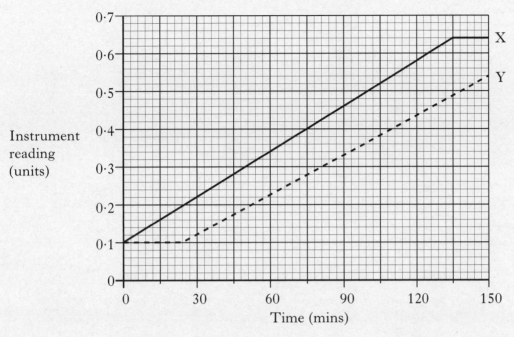

E. coli only produces the enzyme to metabolise lactose when there is no glucose available to the cells.

(i) Use information from the graph to state the time taken for the bacterial cells to produce the enzyme needed to metabolise lactose.

Justify your answer.

Time _____ minutes

Justification _____

_____

_____   1

(ii) Explain how lactose acts as an inducer of this enzyme.

_____

_____

_____   2

(iii) Predict the instrument reading at 150 minutes if a third container had been used with nutrient solution containing 0·25 mM glucose.

_____ units   1

DO
WRI
TH
MAF

Marks

11. In seed pods of garden pea plants, smooth shape (T) is dominant to constricted shape (t) and green (G) is dominant to yellow (g).

The genes are not linked.

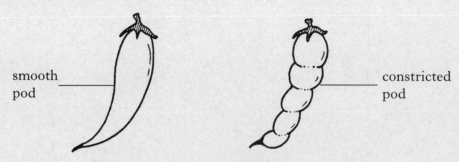

smooth
pod _____

constricted
pod

(*a*) In an investigation, a pea plant heterozygous for both smooth and green pods was crossed with a pea plant with constricted, yellow pods.

Complete the table to give the genotypes of the parent plants and **all** of their possible gametes.

Phenotype of parent	*Genotype of parent*	*Genotype(s) of gamete(s)*
Smooth green pod		
Constricted yellow pod		

1

1

(*b*) In a second investigation, two pea plants heterozygous for both seed shape and seed colour were crossed. This produced 112 offspring.

(i) Calculate the **expected** number of offspring that would have yellow pods.

Space for calculation

_____ 1

The actual phenotypes obtained did not occur in the expected numbers.

(ii) Suggest **two** reasons why the **actual** numbers observed may differ from the **expected** numbers in a dihybrid cross.

1 _____

_____ 1

2 _____

_____ 1

Marks

12. A potato tuber is a swollen underground stem.

Two similar tubers, each with one apical bud and four lateral buds were treated as shown in the diagram. Their appearance after being kept in the dark for three weeks is also shown.

Apical buds produce the plant growth substance IAA.

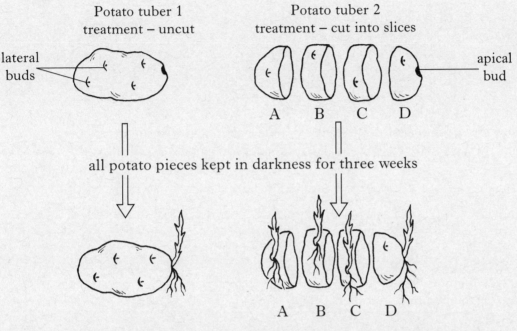

Potato tuber 1
treatment – uncut

Potato tuber 2
treatment – cut into slices

lateral
buds

apical
bud

A   B   C   D

all potato pieces kept in darkness for three weeks

A   B   C   D

(a) Name the effect of IAA that is shown by potato tuber 1 after three weeks.

_____ 1

(b) Explain why the lateral buds on slices A, B and C produced shoots.

_____

_____

_____ 1

(c) Potato tuber 1 was then exposed to light from one direction for a further three days. The shoot showed phototropism.

Explain the role of IAA in phototropism.

_____

_____

_____ 2

(d) Potatoes are long day plants. In terms of changing photoperiod, describe what is meant by "long day plant".

_____

_____ 1

DO N
WRIT
TH
MAR

Marks

13. The table shows the mass of salmon caught in coastal waters around Scotland.

Year	Scottish catch (tonnes)
1973	1300
1980	1200
1988	900
1998	200

(a) By how many times was the 1973 catch greater than the 1998 catch?

Space for calculation

_____ times   1

(b) Scientists monitoring the salmon have suggested the following four possible factors for the decline in numbers.

- Predation by seals

- Food shortage

- Rising sea temperature

- Infection by sea louse parasites

Underline the factor(s) that would have had a density-independent effect on the salmon population.   1

(c) Populations of North Atlantic salmon are monitored because they are a food species.

Give **one** other reason for monitoring animal populations.

_____

_____   1

Marks

14. The table shows how two structures in mammalian skin respond to a drop in the surrounding air temperature from 20 °C to 5 °C.

Structure	Air temperature	
	20 °C	5 °C
hair erector muscles	relaxed	contracted
blood vessels	dilated	constricted

(a) (i) Name the temperature monitoring centre in the body of a mammal.

_____   1

(ii) State how messages are sent from the temperature monitoring centre to the skin.

_____   1

(b) Explain the advantage to the organism of constriction of skin blood vessels when the air temperature drops from 20 °C to 5 °C.

_____

_____

_____

_____   1

(c) Give the term that describes an animal that obtains most of its body heat from its own metabolism.

_____   1

[Turn over for Section C on *Page thirty-four*

DC
WR
T
MA

SECTION C

Marks

Both questions in this section should be attempted.

Note that each question contains a choice.

Questions 1 and 2 should be attempted on the blank pages which follow.

Supplementary sheets, if required, may be obtained from the invigilator.

All answers must be written clearly and legibly in ink.

Labelled diagrams may be used where appropriate.

1. Answer **either** A **or** B.

    A. Give an account of transpiration under the following headings:

        (i) the effect of environmental factors on transpiration rate; **5**

        (ii) adaptations of xerophyte plants that reduce the transpiration rate. **5**

        (10)

    OR

    B. Give an account of how animals and plants cope with dangers under the following headings:

        (i) behavioural defence mechanisms in animals; **5**

        (ii) cellular and structural defence mechanisms in plants. **5**

        (10)

In question 2, ONE mark is available for coherence and ONE mark is available for relevance.

2. Answer **either** A **or** B.

    A. Give an account of the principle of negative feedback with reference to the maintenance of blood sugar levels. **(10)**

    OR

    B. Give an account of the role of the pituitary gland in controlling normal growth and development and describe the effects of named drugs on fetal development. **(10)**

[END OF QUESTION PAPER]

SPACE FOR ANSWERS

[Turn over

SPACE FOR ANSWERS

SPACE FOR ANSWERS

SPACE FOR ANSWERS

DO NOT
WRITE IN
THIS
MARGIN

SPACE FOR ANSWERS

SPACE FOR ANSWERS

ADDITIONAL GRAPH PAPER FOR QUESTION 1(*b*)(i)

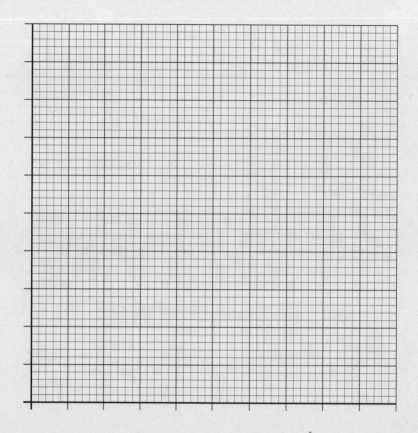

2007 | Higher

[BLANK PAGE]

FOR OFFICIAL USE

Total for
Sections
B and C

X007/301

NATIONAL
QUALIFICATIONS
2007

MONDAY, 21 MAY
1.00 PM – 3.30 PM

BIOLOGY
HIGHER

Fill in these boxes and read what is printed below.

Full name of centre

Town

Forename(s)

Surname

Date of birth
Day Month Year   Scottish candidate number   Number of seat

SECTION A—Questions 1–30 (30 marks)

Instructions for completion of Section A are given on page two.

For this section of the examination you must use an **HB pencil**.

SECTIONS B AND C (100 marks)

1   (a)   All questions should be attempted.

(b)   It should be noted that in **Section C** questions 1 and 2 each contain a choice.

2   The questions may be answered in any order but all answers are to be written in the spaces provided in this answer book, **and must be written clearly and legibly in ink**.

3   Additional space for answers will be found at the end of the book. If further space is required, supplementary sheets may be obtained from the invigilator and should be inserted inside the **front** cover of this book.

4   The numbers of questions must be clearly inserted with any answers written in the additional space.

5   Rough work, if any should be necessary, should be written in this book and then scored through when the fair copy has been written. If further space is required a supplementary sheet for rough work may be obtained from the invigilator.

6   Before leaving the examination room you must give this book to the invigilator. If you do not, you may lose all the marks for this paper.

SCOTTISH
QUALIFICATIONS
AUTHORITY

Read carefully

1   Check that the answer sheet provided is for **Biology Higher (Section A)**.

2   For this section of the examination you must use an **HB pencil**, and where necessary, an eraser.

3   Check that the answer sheet you have been given has **your name**, **date of birth**, **SCN** (Scottish Candidate Number) and **Centre Name** printed on it.

    Do not change any of these details.

4   If any of this information is wrong, tell the Invigilator immediately.

5   If this information is correct, **print** your name and seat number in the boxes provided.

6   The answer to each question is **either** A, B, C or D. Decide what your answer is, then, using your pencil, put a horizontal line in the space provided (see sample question below).

7   There is **only one correct** answer to each question.

8   Any rough working should be done on the question paper or the rough working sheet, **not** on your answer sheet.

9   At the end of the exam, put the **answer sheet for Section A inside the front cover of this answer book**.

Sample Question

The apparatus used to determine the energy stored in a foodstuff is a

A   calorimeter

B   respirometer

C   klinostat

D   gas burette.

The correct answer is **A**—calorimeter. The answer **A** has been clearly marked in **pencil** with a horizontal line (see below).

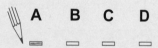

Changing an answer

If you decide to change your answer, carefully erase your first answer and using your pencil fill in the answer you want. The answer below has been changed to **D**.

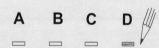

SECTION A

All questions in this section should be attempted.

Answers should be given on the separate answer sheet provided.

1. Which line in the table identifies correctly the two cell structures shown in the diagram?

	X	*Y*
A	Golgi body	Vesicle
B	Golgi body	Ribosome
C	Endoplasmic reticulum	Vesicle
D	Endoplasmic reticulum	Ribosome

2. The phospholipid molecules in a cell membrane allow the

   A free passage of glucose molecules

   B self-recognition of cells

   C active transport of ions

   D membrane to be fluid.

3. Red blood cells have a solute concentration of around 0·9%.

   Which of the following statements correctly describes the fate of these cells when immersed in a 1% salt solution?

   A The cells will burst.

   B The cells will shrink.

   C The cells will expand but not burst.

   D The cells will remain unaffected.

4. Which graph best illustrates the effect of increasing temperature on the rate of active uptake of ions by roots?

A
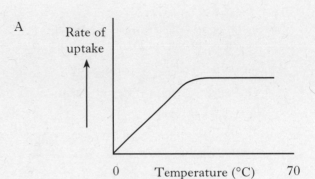

B
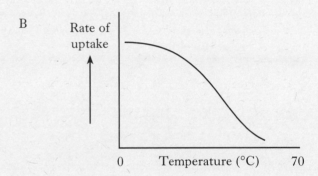

C
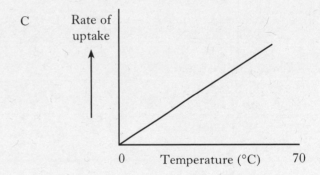

D
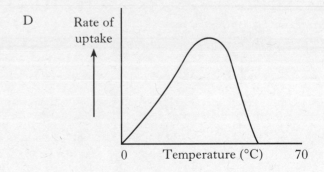

5. Which substances must be provided by host cells for the synthesis of viruses?

   A   Proteins and nucleotides

   B   Amino acids and DNA

   C   Proteins and DNA

   D   Amino acids and nucleotides

6. The action spectrum of photosynthesis is a measure of the ability of plants to

   A   absorb all wavelengths of light

   B   absorb light of different intensities

   C   use light to build up foods

   D   use light of different wavelengths for synthesis.

7. The diagram shows DNA during replication. Base H represents thymine and base M represents guanine. Which letters represent the base cytosine?

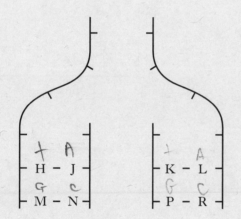

   A   J and K

   B   J and L

   C   N and P

   D   N and R

8. The graph below shows the effect of light intensity on the rate of photosynthesis at different temperatures.

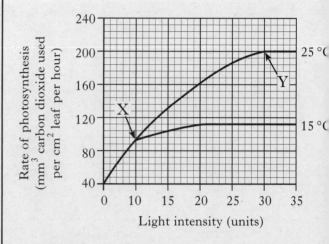

Which of the following conclusions can be made from the above data?

   A   Only at light intensities greater than 20 units does temperature affect the rate of photosynthesis.

   B   At point Y, the rate of photosynthesis is limited by the light intensity.

   C   Temperature has little effect on the rate of photosynthesis at low light intensities.

   D   At point X, temperature limits the rate of photosynthesis.

9. The cell structures shown below have been magnified ten thousand times.

Mitochondrion   Chloroplast

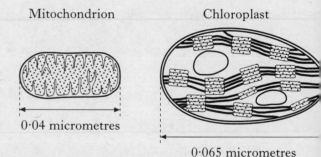

0·04 micrometres   0·065 micrometres

Expressed as a simple whole number ratio, the length of the mitochondrion compared to that of the chloroplast is

   A   8 : 13

   B   13 : 8

   C   40 : 65

   D   65 : 40.

10. A section of a DNA molecule contains 300 bases. Of these bases, 90 are adenine. How many cytosine bases would this section of DNA contain?

   A   60

   B   90

   C   120

   D   180

11. What information can be derived from the recombination frequencies of linked genes?

   A   The mutation rate of the genes

   B   The order and location of genes on a chromosome

   C   Whether genes are recessive or dominant

   D   The genotype for a particular characteristic

12. The diagram shows a family tree for a family with a history of red-green colour deficiency.

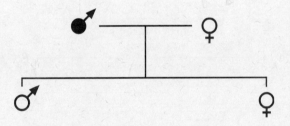

 Unaffected male

 Affected male

 Unaffected female

 Affected female

The allele for red-green colour deficiency is sex-linked.

Which of the following statements is true?

   A   Only the son is a carrier.

   B   Only the daughter is a carrier.

   C   Both son and daughter are carriers.

   D   Neither son nor daughter is a carrier.

13. Apple crop yields have been increased by plant breeders selecting for

   A   disease resistance

   B   flavour

   C   resistance to bruising

   D   sugar content.

14. Human insulin can be produced by the bacterium *E. coli* using the following steps.

   1   Culture large quantities of *E. coli* in vats of nutrients.

   2   Insert human insulin gene into *E. coli* plasmid DNA.

   3   Cut insulin gene from human chromosome using enzymes.

   4   Extract insulin from culture vats.

The correct order for these steps is

   A   3, 2, 1, 4

   B   3, 1, 2, 4

   C   1, 4, 3, 2

   D   1, 2, 3, 4.

15. In a desert mammal, which of the following is a physiological adaptation which helps to conserve water?

   A   Nocturnal foraging

   B   Breathing humid air in a burrow

   C   Having few sweat glands

   D   Remaining underground by day

16. The following factors affect the transpiration rate in a plant.

   1   increasing wind speed

   2   decreasing humidity

   3   rising air pressure

   4   falling temperature

Which two of these factors would cause an increase in transpiration rate?

   A   1 and 2

   B   1 and 3

   C   2 and 4

   D   3 and 4

[Turn over

17. When first exposed to a harmless stimulus, a group of animals responded by showing avoidance behaviour. When the stimulus was repeated the animals became habituated to it.

    What change in response would have shown that habituation was taking place?

    A   An increase in the length of the response

    B   A decrease in the time taken to respond

    C   An increase in response to other stimuli

    D   A decrease in the percentage of animals responding

18. In tomato plants, the allele for curled leaves is dominant over the allele for straight leaves. The allele for hairy stems is dominant over the allele for hairless stems. The genes for curliness and hairiness are located on different chromosomes.

    If plants heterozygous for both characteristics were crossed, what ratio of phenotypes would be expected in the offspring?

    A   All curly and hairy

    B   3 curly and hairy: 1 straight and hairless

    C   9 curly and hairy: 3 curly and hairless:
        3 straight and hairy: 1 straight and hairless

    D   1 curly and hairy: 1 curly and hairless:
        1 straight and hairy: 1 straight and hairless

19. The bar graph below shows changes in the DNA content per cell during stages of meiosis.

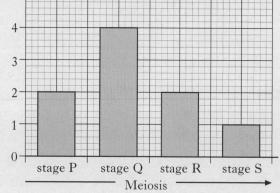

    When do the homologous pairs of chromosomes separate?

    A   Before the start of stage P

    B   Between stages P and Q

    C   Between stages Q and R

    D   Between stages R and S

20. The genes for two different characteristics are located on separate chromosomes.

    In a cross between individuals with the genotypes AaBb and aabb, what is the chance of any one of the offspring having the genotype aabb?

    A   0

    B   1 in 2

    C   1 in 4

    D   1 in 8

21. Which line in the table identifies correctly the main source of body heat and the method of controlling body temperature in an endotherm?

	Main source of body heat	Principal method of controlling body temperature
A	Respiration	Behavioural
B	Respiration	Physiological
C	Absorbed from environment	Behavioural
D	Absorbed from environment	Physiological

22. The following four statements relate to meristems.

    1   Some provide cells for increase in diameter in stems

    2   Some produce growth substances

    3   They are found in all growing organisms

    4   Their cells undergo division by meiosis

    Which of the above statements are true?

    A   1 and 2 only

    B   1 and 3 only

    C   2 and 3 only

    D   2 and 4 only

23. The diagram below shows a transverse section of a woody stem.

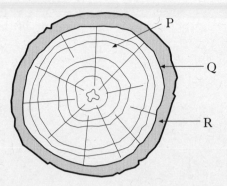

Which line of the table identifies correctly the tissues P, Q and R?

	P	Q	R
A	cambium	xylem	phloem
B	phloem	xylem	cambium
C	xylem	phloem	cambium
D	xylem	cambium	phloem

24. The graph below shows changes which occur in the masses of protein, fat and carbohydrate in a girl's body during seven weeks of starvation.

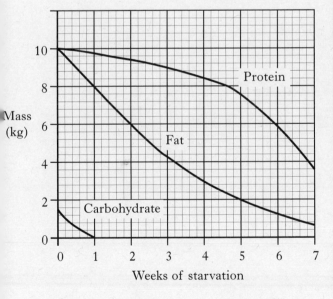

The girl weighs 60 kg at the start. Predict her weight after two weeks without food.

A   43 kg

B   50 kg

C   54 kg

D   57 kg

25. Which of the following is triggered by the hypothalamus in response to an increase in the temperature of the body?

A   Contraction of the hair erector muscles and vasodilation of the skin capillaries

B   Relaxation of the hair erector muscles and vasodilation of the skin capillaries

C   Contraction of the hair erector muscles and vasoconstriction of the skin capillaries

D   Relaxation of the hair erector muscles and vasoconstriction of the skin capillaries

26. Plants require macro-elements for the synthesis of various compounds. Identify which macro-elements are required for synthesis of the compounds shown in the table below.

	Chlorophyll	Protein	ATP
A	phosphorus	magnesium	nitrogen
B	phosphorus	nitrogen	magnesium
C	magnesium	nitrogen	phosphorus
D	magnesium	phosphorus	nitrogen

27. The following are events occurring during germination in barley.

1   The embryo produces gibberellic acid (GA)

2   α-amylase is produced

3   Gibberellic acid (GA) passes to the aleurone layer

4   α-amylase converts starch to maltose

5   Maltose is used by the embryo

Which of the following indicates the correct sequence of events?

A   1 2 4 5 3

B   1 3 2 4 5

C   3 2 1 4 5

D   5 1 3 2 4

[Turn over

28. The table shows the masses of various substances in the glomerular filtrate and in the urine over a period of 24 hours.

Which of the substances has the smallest percentage of reabsorption from the glomerular filtrate?

	Substance	Mass in glomerular filtrate (g)	Mass in urine (g)
A	Sodium	600·0	6·0
B	Potassium	35·0	2·0
C	Uric acid	8·5	0·8
D	Calcium	5·0	0·2

29. An investigation was carried out into the effect of indole acetic acid (IAA) concentration on the shoot growth of two species of plant. The graph below shows a summary of the results.

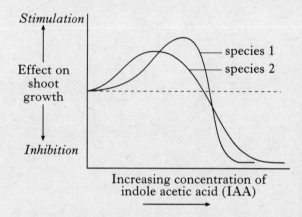

Which one of the following conclusions is justified?

A   Species 1 shows its maximum stimulation at a lower IAA concentration than species 2.

B   Species 2 is more inhibited by the highest concentrations of IAA than species 1.

C   Species 2 is stimulated over a greater range of IAA concentrations than species 1.

D   Species 1 is stimulated by some IAA concentrations which inhibit species 2.

30. An enzyme and its substrate were incubated with various concentrations of either copper or magnesium salts.

The time taken for the complete breakdown of the substrate was measured.

The results are given in the table.

Salt Concentration (M)	Time needed to break down substrate (s)	
	Copper salts	Magnesium salts
0	39	39
1×10^{-8}	42	21
1×10^{-6}	380	49
1×10^{-4}	1480	286

(increasing concentration →)

From the data, it may be deduced that

A   high concentrations of copper salts promote the activity of the enzyme

B   high concentrations of copper salts inhibit the activity of the enzyme

C   low concentrations of magnesium salts inhibit the activity of the enzyme

D   high concentrations of magnesium salts promote the activity of the enzyme.

Candidates are reminded that the answer sheet MUST be returned INSIDE the front cover of this answer book.

[Turn over for Section B on *Page ten*

DO WRIT TH MAR

Marks

SECTION B

All questions in this section should be attempted.

All answers must be written clearly and legibly in ink.

1. (*a*) The diagram contains information about light striking a leaf.

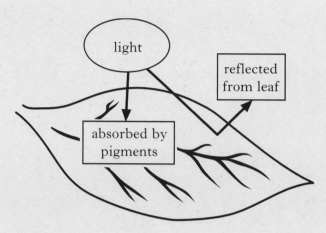

    (i) Apart from being absorbed or reflected, what can happen to light which strikes a leaf?

    _____   1

    (ii) Pigments that absorb light are found within leaf cells.

    State the exact location of these pigments.

    _____   1

(*b*) The diagram below shows part of the light dependent stage of photosynthesis.

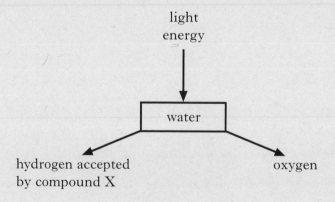

    (i) Name this part of the light dependent stage.

    _____   1

    (ii) Name compound X.

    _____   1

Marks

1. (continued)

(c) The following sentences describe events in the carbon fixation stage of photosynthesis.

Underline one alternative in each pair to make the sentences correct.

The $\left\{ \begin{array}{c} \text{three} \\ \text{five} \end{array} \right\}$ carbon compound ribulose bisphosphate (RuBP) accepts

$\left\{ \begin{array}{c} \text{carbon dioxide} \\ \text{hydrogen} \end{array} \right\}$.

$\left\{ \begin{array}{c} \text{Carbon dioxide} \\ \text{Hydrogen} \end{array} \right\}$ is accepted by the $\left\{ \begin{array}{c} \text{three} \\ \text{five} \end{array} \right\}$ carbon compound

glycerate phosphate (GP).

2

[Turn over

DC
WR
T
MA

2. The diagram shows apparatus set up to investigate the rate of respiration in an earthworm. After 10 minutes at 20 °C the level of liquid in the capillary tube had changed as shown.

Marks

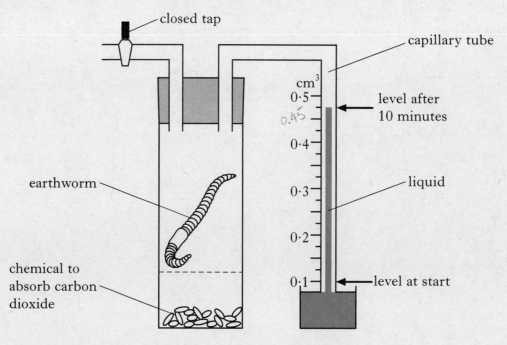

(*a*) (i) What volume of oxygen is used by the earthworm during the 10 minute period?

_____ cm^3 1

(ii) Describe a suitable control for this experiment.

_____

_____   1

(*b*) In a second experiment, a worm of 5 grams used 0·5 cm^3 of oxygen in 10 minutes.

Calculate its rate of respiration in cm^3 per minute per gram of worm.

Space for calculation

_____ cm^3 per minute per gram of worm   1

[Turn over for Question 3 on *Page fourteen*

DO
WRI'
TI
MAI

Marks

3. (*a*) Samples of carrot tissue were immersed in a hypotonic solution at two different temperatures for 5 hours. The mass of the tissue samples was measured every hour and the percentage change in mass calculated.

The results are shown on the graph.

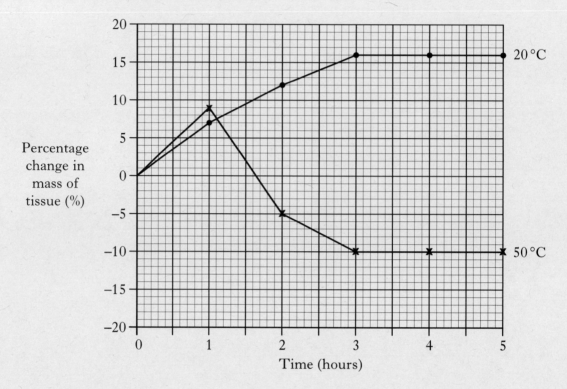

    (i) Explain the results obtained at 20 °C from 0 to 3 hours and from 3 hours to 5 hours.

       0 to 3 hours _____

       _____ **1**

       3 to 5 hours _____

       _____ **1**

    (ii) Explain the change in mass of the carrot tissue between 1 and 3 hours at 50 °C.

       _____

       _____

       _____ **2**

Marks

3. (continued)

(b) The chart shows the concentration of ions within a unicellular organism and in the sea water surrounding it.

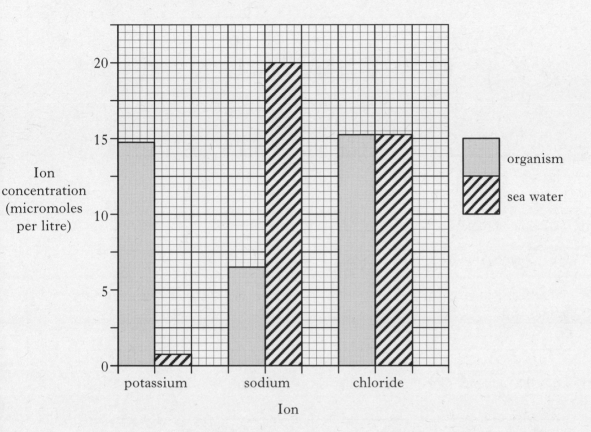

(i) From the information given, identify the ion which appears to move between the organism and the sea water by diffusion.

Justify your choice.

Ion _____

Justification _____

_____   1

(ii) When oxygen was bubbled through a tank of sea water containing these organisms, the potassium ion concentration within the organisms increased.

Explain this effect.

_____

_____

_____   2

[Turn over

4. The diagram shows events occurring during the synthesis of a protein that is secreted from a cell.

Marks

(a) (i) Name molecule X. _____ **1**

(ii) Name bond Y. _____ **1**

(b) What name is given to a group of three bases on mRNA that codes for an amino acid?

_____ **1**

(c) Give the sequence of DNA bases that codes for amino acid Z.

_____ **1**

(d) Describe the roles of the endoplasmic reticulum and the Golgi apparatus between the synthesis of the protein and its release from the cell.

Endoplasmic reticulum _____

_____ **1**

Golgi apparatus _____

_____ **1**

(e) The table contains some information about the structure and function of proteins.

Add information to the boxes to complete the table.

Protein	Structure (Globular or Fibrous)	Function
Cellulase		
Collagen		Structural protein in skin

2

Marks

5. (*a*) The graph shows the relationship between plant species diversity in grassland and grazing intensity by herbivores.

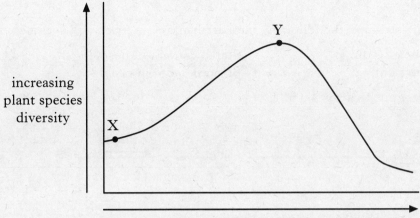

increasing plant species diversity

increasing grazing intensity by herbivores

(i) Explain the effect on plant species diversity of increased grazing intensity by herbivores between X and Y on the graph.

_____

_____

_____   2

(ii) What evidence is there that grassland contains plant species tolerant of grazing?

_____

_____   1

(*b*) State **one** feature of some plant species that allows them to tolerate grazing by herbivores.

_____

_____   1

[Turn over

6. Norway Spruce (*Picea abies*) is an evergreen species of tree with needle-like leaves, found in regions with extremely cold winters.

The rate of photosynthesis of the species is at its maximum during spring then decreases from June to December.

In an investigation, a sample of one-year-old seedlings was collected in each month from June to December.

For each sample of seedlings, the following measurements were made and averages calculated.

- Dry mass of whole seedlings
- Dry mass of roots only
- Starch content in needles
- Sugar content in needles

The results are shown in **Graphs 1** and **2**.

Graph 1

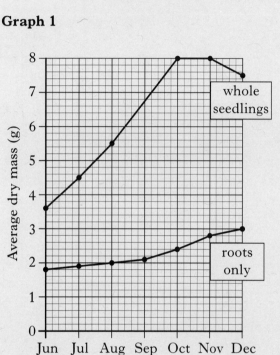

Graph 2

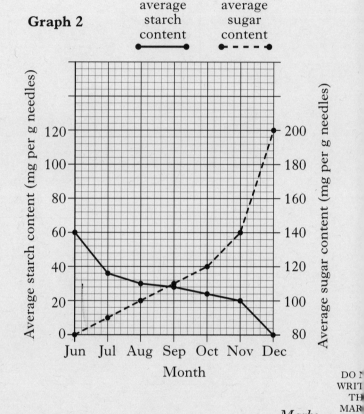

Marks

(a) (i) **Use values from Graph 1** to describe the changes in average dry mass of whole seedlings from June to December.

_____

_____   2

(ii) Between which two months was there the greatest increase in average dry mass of the seedlings' roots only?

Tick (✓) **one** box.

Jun–Jul   Jul–Aug   Aug–Sept   Sept–Oct   Oct–Nov   Nov–Dec

☐   ☐   ☐   ☐   ☐   ☐   1

(iii) **From Graph 2**, calculate the ratio of average starch content to average sugar content in the needles in November.

Space for calculation

_____ Starch: _____ Sugar   1

Marks

6. (a) (continued)

   (iv) **From Graph 2**, calculate the percentage decrease in average starch content in the needles between June and October.

   Space for calculation

   _____ % decrease   1

(b) Explain the decrease in average starch content in the needles between June and December.

   _____

   _____   1

(c) Raffinose is a sugar that prevents frost damage to needles.

   The table shows the raffinose content of needles from the seedling samples.

Month	Raffinose content (mg per g of needles)
June	0
July	1
August	2
September	3
October	9
November	30
December	50

   (i) What evidence is there that raffinose is not the only sugar present in the needles of Norway Spruce?

   _____

   _____   1

   (ii) Suggest how the changing raffinose content of needles from June to December is of survival value to Norway Spruce.

   _____

   _____   1

   [Turn over

Marks

7. The diagram shows stages in meiosis during which a mutation occurred and the effect of the mutation on the gametes produced.

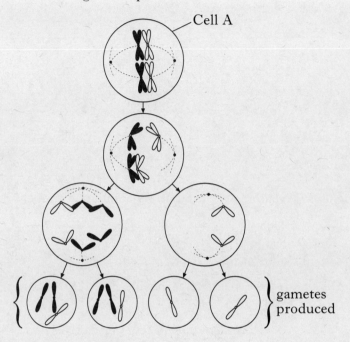

Cell A

gametes
produced

(a) (i) What name is given to cells such as cell A, that undergo meiosis?

_____ 1

(ii) Cell A contains two pairs of homologous chromosomes.

Apart from size and shape, state **one** similarity between homologous chromosomes.

_____ 1

(iii) This mutation has resulted in changes to the chromosome numbers in the gametes.

Name this type of mutation.

_____ 1

(iv) State whether the mutation has occurred in the first or second meiotic division and justify your choice.

Meiotic division _____

Justification _____

_____ 1

(v) State the expected haploid number of chromosomes in the gametes produced if this mutation **had not occurred**.

_____ 1

7. (continued)

Marks

(b) The diagram represents the sequence of bases on part of one strand of a DNA molecule.

Part of DNA molecule   T   G   A   A   C   T   G

The effects of two different gene mutations on the strand of DNA are shown below.

Gene mutation 1   T   T   G   A   A   C   T   G

Gene mutation 2   T   G   A   C   C   T   G

Complete the table by naming the type of gene mutation that has occurred in each case.

Gene Mutation	Name
1	
2	

2

[Turn over

Marks

8. The table shows information about three species of oak tree that have evolved from a common ancestor.

	Oak Species		
	Sessile Oak	Kermes Oak	Northern Red Oak
Leaf Shape	Rounded lobes	Sharp spines	Lobes with sharp spines
Growing Conditions	Mild and damp	Hot and dry	Cool and dry

(a) (i) The Oak species have evolved in ecological isolation.

State the importance of isolating mechanisms in the evolution of new species.

_____ 1

(ii) Use the information to explain how the evolution of the Oak species illustrates adaptive radiation.

_____

_____ 2

(b) The Kermes Oak grows to a maximum height of one metre.

Explain the benefit to this species of having leaves with sharp spines.

_____

_____ 1

(c) To maintain genetic diversity, species must be conserved.

State **two** ways in which species can be conserved.

1 _____

2 _____ 1

Marks

9. (*a*) The graph shows the body mass of a human male from birth until 22 years of age.

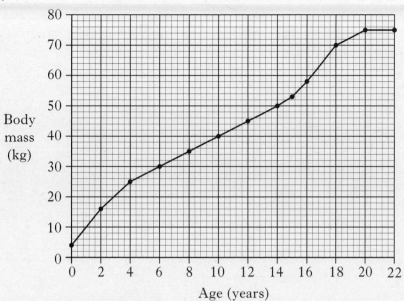

Body mass (kg) vs Age (years)

(i) Calculate the average yearly increase in body mass between age 6 and age 14.

Space for calculation

_____ kg   **1**

(ii) Explain how the activity of the pituitary gland could account for the growth pattern between 15 and 22 years of age shown on the graph.

_____

_____

_____   **2**

(*b*) The diagram shows the role of the pituitary gland in the secretion of a hormone from the thyroid gland.

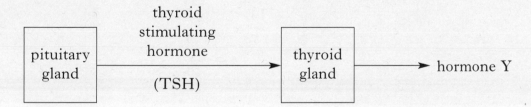

Name hormone Y and describe its role in the control of growth and development.

Hormone Y_____   **1**

Role _____   **1**

Marks

10. An experiment was carried out to investigate the effect of gibberellic acid (GA) on the growth of dwarf pea plants. GA can be absorbed by leaves.

Six identical pea plants were placed in pots containing 100 g of soil. The leaves of each were sprayed with an equal volume of water containing a different mass of GA. The soil in each pot received 20 cm³ water each day and the plants were continuously exposed to equal light intensity from above.

After seven days the stem height of each plant was measured and the percentage increase in stem height calculated.

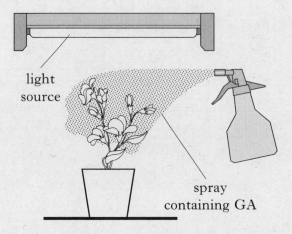

light source

spray containing GA

(a) (i) Identify **two** variables, not already mentioned, that should have been controlled to ensure the experimental procedure was valid.

Variable 1 _____ 1

Variable 2 _____ 1

(ii) State **one** way in which the experimental procedure could be improved to increase the reliability of the results.

_____

_____ 1

(b) The results of the experiment are shown in the table.

Mass of GA applied (micrograms)	Percentage increase in stem height (%)
0·01	90
0·03	120
0·05	160
0·08	240
0·10	320
0·11	350

Marks

10. (b) (continued)

    (i) On the grid provided, complete the line graph to show the percentage increase in stem height against the mass of GA applied.

        Use an appropriate scale to fill most of the grid.

        (Additional graph paper, if required, will be found on page 36.)

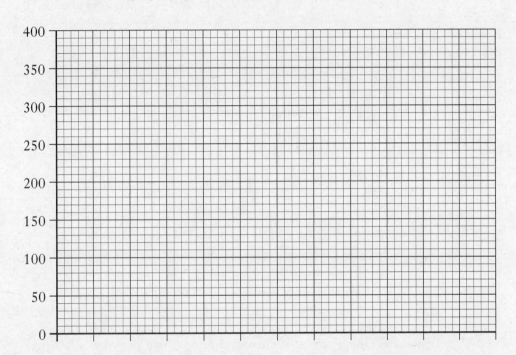

2

    (ii) Another pea plant was treated in the same way, using a water spray containing 0·12 micrograms of GA. Predict the percentage increase in stem height of this plant after seven days.

        _____ percentage increase   1

  (c) Explain why the method of application of GA could lead to errors in the results.

    _____

    _____   1

[Turn over

Marks

11. (*a*) The bacterium *Escherichia coli* can control its lactose metabolism.

Complete **all** boxes in the table to show whether each statement is true (T) or false (F) if lactose is present or absent in the medium in which *E. coli* is growing.

Statement	Lactose present	Lactose absent
Regulator gene produces the repressor molecule		
Repressor molecule binds to inducer		
Repressor molecule binds to operator		
Structural gene switched on	T	F

2

(*b*) Part of a metabolic pathway involving the amino acid phenylalanine is shown in the diagram.

digestion of protein in diet → **phenylalanine** —enzyme A→ **tyrosine** —enzyme B→ **other compounds**

Phenylketonuria (PKU) is an inherited condition in which enzyme A is either absent or does not function.

(i) Predict the effect on the concentrations of phenylalanine and tyrosine if enzyme A is absent.

Phenylalanine _____ 1

Tyrosine _____ 1

(ii) PKU is caused by a mutation of the gene that codes for enzyme A.

Explain how a mutation of a gene can cause the production of an altered enzyme.

_____

_____

_____ 2

Marks

12. An experiment was set up to investigate the effect of photoperiod on flowering in *Chrysanthemum* plants. Four plants A, B, C and D were exposed to different periods of light and dark in 24 hours. This was repeated every day for several weeks and the effects on flowering noted.

The periods of light and dark and their effects on flowering are shown in the diagram.

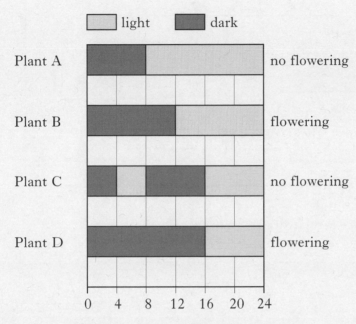

Periods of light and dark (hours)

(a) From the information given, identify the conditions required for flowering in *Chrysanthemum* plants. Justify your answer.

Conditions _____

Justification _____

_____   1

(b) Flowering in response to photoperiod ensures plants within a population flower at the same time. Explain how this enables genetic variation to be maintained.

_____

_____   1

(c) Mammals also show photoperiodism.

Describe how one type of mammal behaviour can be affected by photoperiod.

_____

_____   1

[Turn over

Marks

13. The homeostatic control of blood glucose concentration carried out by the human liver is shown on the diagram.

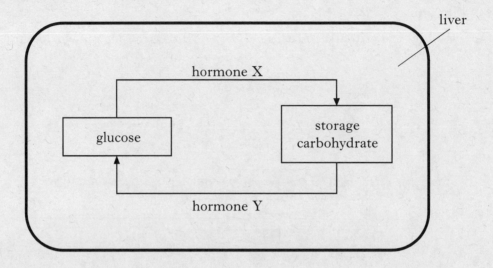

(a) Name the storage carbohydrate found in the liver.

_____   1

(b) (i) Name hormones X and Y.

Hormone X _____

Hormone Y _____   1

(ii) Name the organ that produces hormones X and Y.

_____   1

(iii) Explain how negative feedback is involved in the homeostatic control of blood glucose concentration.

_____

_____

_____   2

14. (*a*) The diagram shows some plant communities present at various time intervals on farmland cleared of vegetation by a fire.

Plant communities	Grass	Shrubs	Pine wood	Oak forest
Time after fire	1–3 years	15–20 years	25–100 years	150–200 years

(i) State the term used to describe this sequence of plant communities.

_____ 1

(ii) Give a reason to explain why the shrub community is able to replace the grass community after 15 years.

_____ 1

(iii) Oak forest is the climax community in this sequence.
Describe a feature of a climax community.

_____ 1

(*b*) The grid shows factors that can influence population change.

A competition	B predation	C rainfall
D disease	E temperature	F food supply

(i) Use **all** the letters from the grid to complete the table to show which factors are density dependent and which are density independent.

Density dependent	*Density independent*

2

(ii) **Underline** one alternative in each pair to make the sentences correct.

As population density $\left\{ \begin{array}{l} \text{increases,} \\ \text{decreases,} \end{array} \right\}$ the effect of density dependent factors increases.

As a result, the population density then $\left\{ \begin{array}{l} \text{increases} \\ \text{decreases} \end{array} \right\}$. 1

[Turn over for Section C on *Page thirty*

DO N
WRIT
TH
MAR

Marks

SECTION C

Both questions in this section should be attempted.

Note that each question contains a choice.

Questions 1 and 2 should be attempted on the blank pages which follow.

Supplementary sheets, if required, may be obtained from the invigilator.

All answers must be written clearly and legibly in ink.

Labelled diagrams may be used where appropriate.

1. Answer **either** A **or** B.

    A. Give an account of respiration under the following headings:

        (i)   glycolysis;   **5**

        (ii) the Krebs (Citric acid) cycle.   **5**

                                                                                    (10)

    OR

    B. Give an account of cellular defence mechanisms in animals under the following headings:

        (i)   phagocytosis;   **4**

        (ii) antibody production and tissue rejection.   **6**

                                                                                     (10)

In question 2, ONE mark is available for coherence and ONE mark is available for relevance.

2. Answer **either** A **or** B.

    A. Give an account of the problems of osmoregulation in freshwater bony fish and outline their adaptations to overcome these problems.   **(10)**

    OR

    B. Give an account of obtaining food in animals by reference to co-operative hunting, dominance hierarchy, and territorial behaviour.   **(10)**

[END OF QUESTION PAPER]

SPACE FOR ANSWERS

[Turn over

SPACE FOR ANSWERS

SPACE FOR ANSWERS

DO N
WRIT
TH
MAR

SPACE FOR ANSWERS

SPACE FOR ANSWERS

SPACE FOR ANSWERS

ADDITIONAL GRAPH PAPER FOR QUESTION 10(*b*)

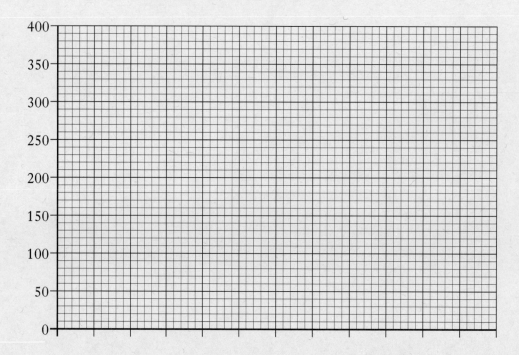

[BLANK PAGE]

[BLANK PAGE]

[BLANK PAGE]

[BLANK PAGE]

[BLANK PAGE]

Acknowledgements

Leckie and Leckie is grateful to the copyright holders, as credited, for permission to use their material.

The following companies have very generously given permission to reproduce their copyright material free of charge:
Advanced Human Biology © (2007) Simpkins, HarperCollins Publishers Ltd (2003 paper p 14)

Pocket answer section for
SQA Higher Biology
2003–2007

© 2007 Scottish Qualifications Authority, All Rights Reserved
Published by Leckie & Leckie Ltd, 3rd Floor, 4 Queen Street, Edinburgh EH2 1JE
tel: 0131 220 6831, fax: 0131 225 9987, enquiries@leckieandleckie.co.uk, www.leckieandleckie.co.uk

Higher Biology 2003

Section A

1.	C	16.	B
2.	A	17.	C
3.	A	18.	B
4.	B	19.	A
5.	D	20.	C
6.	D	21.	B
7.	C	22.	D
8.	A	23.	A
9.	A	24.	A
10.	D	25.	B
11.	C	26.	D
12.	B	27.	D
13.	C	28.	A
14.	B	29.	C
15.	C	30.	B

Section B

1. (a) (i)
   - **E**   Transport
   - **A**   Mitochondrion
   - **B**   Packaging / Processing / Modifying / Adding carbohydrate to proteins / secretions / enzymes
   - **C**   Nucleus

   (ii) Increased/Large surface area
   More rapid/Faster/More efficient diffusion/uptake/absorption

   (b) (i) X is NADPH/$NADPH_2$/reduced NADP
   Y is glucose

   (ii) Granum/grana

   (iii) Calvin/carbon fixation

   (iv) Cellulose

2. (a) To prevent entry of other light
   OR
   So discs only receive green light/light from lamp

   (b) Increase reliability/Minimise error due to chance/ Reduce the effect of an atypical result

   (c) Leaf discs:
   same size/diameter/mass/weight/leaf used/thickness/surface area

   Solution that provided carbon dioxide:
   same concentration/temperature/volume

   (d) Gas/Oxygen made so discs are more buoyant/less dense/lighter

2. (e) They/Nettles can use green light for photosynthesis
   Shade plants/forest floor receives green light/light not absorbed by sun plants/light transmitted by canopy.

   (f) Compensation point

   (g)
   Rate of photosynthesis by nettle leaf discs (units)

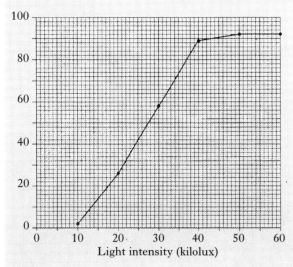

Light intensity (kilolux)

   (h) Effect: increase/rise
   Justification: CO_2 limiting OR
   Effect: stay the same
   Justification: temperature limiting/CO_2 not limiting.

3. (a) Stage 2:
   Viral nucleic acid/DNA/RNA takes over/alters cell metabolism
   Stage 5:
   Nucleic acid/DNA/RNA enters/joins with viral/protein coats

   (b) Ribosome

   (c) (i) Lymphocyte

   (ii) Surface protein/foreign protein/antigen

   (iii) Antibodies/They are specific
   OR other viruses not recognised
   OR antigen is different
   OR antigen does not match antibody

Higher Biology 2003 (cont.)

4. (a) ATP

   (b) (i) Lactic acid
       (ii) Ethanol/alcohol and carbon dioxide

   (c) NAD/NADH/NADH$_2$/Reduced NAD

   (d) No oxygen available as (final) hydrogen acceptor

   (e) 40·6%

   (f) Cytochrome system/Hydrogen transfer system

5. (a) Ovarian/Ovary

   (b) 4

   (c) Same genes/Genes for same characteristics

   (d) Increases variation/Produces recombinants /
       Produces new allele combinations / Increases
       genetic diversity

6. (a) (i) X^BX^b

       (ii) X^bY

   (b) 100%/1 in 1/certainty/ He will have it

   (c) R received X^b/the recessive allele from both
       parents and mother is a carrier

7. (a) (i) Beaks different so birds eat different foods/
           have different feeding methods

       (ii) Descended from/Fossil evidence of/Share a
            common ancestor

   (b) Reproductive OR Ecological

8. (a) (i) Avoidance/escape

       (ii) Defence against predators/protection/avoid
            injury/less likely to be eaten

   (b) (i) Habituation

       (ii) Saves/Conserves – energy
            OR
            Does not use energy responding to a
            harmless stimulus
            OR
            can continue feeding

9. (a) 25 g per m^2

   (b) 10–20

   (c) 5 g

   (d) (1) As population density increases the total
           biomass increases
       (2) Up to a population density of 40 per m^2
       (3) At a total biomass of 125g per m^2
       (4) After this the total biomass stays constant
       All four points = 2 marks
       Any three points = 1 mark

   (e) At high population density/As population
       density increases, there is greater competition
       between limpets so (average) shell length
       decreases OR converse

   (f) (i) 56 and 30·5/31

       (ii) Ratio 3:2

       (iii) Shore B
             Justification: shell index shows it came
             from a region with strong wave action

10. (a) (i) C D F

        (ii) A E

    (b)

Adaptation	Behavioural	Physiological
High level of blood ADH		✓
Lives in underground burrow	✓	
Nocturnal foraging	✓	
Absence of sweating		✓

All correct = 2 marks
2 or 3 correct = 1 mark

11. (a) (i) S

        (ii) Division/Mitosis/Elongation/Vacuolation

    (b) Insect moults/Skin is shed/Exoskeleton is shed
        at A allowing growth/increase in body length
        Skin/Exoskeleton hardens preventing further
        growth/increase in length

12. (a) Same set up/Similar container with all elements
        present/no elements missing

    (b) Algae may use same resources/minerals/
        nutrients

12. (*c*)

Element	Symptoms of deficiency	
	Leaf bases red	Chlorotic leaves
Magnesium		✓
Phosphorus	✓	
Nitrogen	✓	✓

All correct = 2 marks
2 or 3 correct = 1 mark

(*d*) Chlorophyll/Chlorophyll a/Chlorophyll b

(*e*) Oxygen needed for respiration to release energy/make ATP
Active transport/Uptake of elements requires energy/ATP

13. (*a*) Pituitary

(*b*) (i) Group B have more thyroxine than Group A and this increases their metabolic rate and Group B have a higher oxygen consumption
OR Group A have more thyroxine than Group C and this increases metabolic rate Group A have higher oxygen consumption

(ii) They/Group A have a higher O_2 consumption than rats with the thyroxine inhibitor/Group C

(iii) (Group A will produce) less/lower (TSH than C)
OR Group C make more TSH than Group A

(iv) 25

(v) Compared with the rats in group B, the rats in group C have a <u>lower</u> metabolic rate and show <u>constriction</u> of skin blood vessels.

The behaviour of rats in group C allows them to <u>conserve</u> body heat

SECTION C

1. A. (i) **Occurrence of mutant alleles and the effect of mutagenic agents**

1. Random/spontaneous/by chance
2. Low frequency/rare
3. One type of mutagenic agent eg chemicals or named chemical such as mustard gas
4. A second type of mutagenic agent eg radiation or named type of radiation

1. A. (i) continued

5. as X-rays, gamma rays, UV light Mutagenic agents cause or induce mutations/increase mutation rate/increase chance of a mutation occurring/increase frequency of mutation
Maximum three marks

(ii) **Types of gene mutation and how they alter amino acid sequences**

6. Gene mutation is a change in the bases/base types/base sequence/base order (Note: this must be stated, and cannot be shown in a diagram. Also, **nucleotide** can be taken as equivalent to **base**.)
7. Substitution: base/bases – replaced with another/others
8. Inversion: order of bases reversed/bases turned round
9. Substitution/Inversion may change base order of codon
OR Substitution/Inversion is a point mutation
10. Substitution/Inversion may change only one/two amino acid(s)
11. Deletion: base/bases – deleted from chromosome / removed / taken out
12. Insertion: base/bases – inserted into chromosome/added/put in
12a. Substitution, inversion, deletion and insertion ALL named
13. Deletion/Insertion changes codons/triplets after the mutation
OR Deletion/Insertion is a frameshift mutation
14. Deletion/Insertion changes all amino acids <u>after the mutation</u>
15. Protein made (following substitution or inversion) will work/will be unaffected OR Protein made (after deletion or insertion) will not function/will not work/is the wrong protein/enzyme.
Maximum 7 marks
Maximum total 10 marks

1. B. (i) **The transpiration stream**

1. Water enters root <u>hairs</u>
2. Water moves from a high water concentration/from HWC down/along a concentration gradient
OR Water moves from a hypotonic solution/moves by osmosis (accept anywhere but only **once**)

Higher Biology 2003 (cont.)

1.B (i) continued

3. Water moves across the <u>cortex</u>
4. Water moves through cells / through cell walls / through intercellular spaces
5. Continuous/Unbroken column/thread of water in the xylem/the vessels/the stem/the plant
6. Root pressure helps move water up xylem/up stem/up plant
7. A force /An attraction between water molecules (cohesion)
8. A force/An attraction between xylem/vessels and water molecules (adhesion)
8a. Cohesion and adhesion both named
9. Transpiration draws/pulls water up xylem/up stem/up plant
10. Water evaporates into air spaces of leaf
11. Water (vapour) diffuses out through stomata/through pores
12. Transpiration rate can be increased by – increase in temperature/increase in wind speed/increase in light intensity/decrease in humidity/decrease in air pressure – or any converse

     Maximum 8 marks

(ii) **Importance of the transpiration stream**

13. Uptake/Transport of minerals / nutrients/nutrient ions/salts/a named ion e.g. nitrate
14. Cooling effect
15. Provides water for photosynthesis/turgidity/support

     Maximum 2 marks
     Maximum total 10 marks

2. A.   **Mechanisms:**

1. Temperature regulation controlled by negative feedback
2. Hypothalamus monitors blood temperature **OR** Hypothalamus is the temperature detecting centre/temperature monitoring centre/temperature control centre
3. Hypothalamus sends out nerve messages to effectors/to skin
4. Vasodilation (or description) occurs in response to temperature rise/to hot conditions
5. Heat lost/Heat radiated from skin

2.A. continued

6. Sweating in response to temperature rise/to hot conditions
7. Heat lost by evaporation of water/sweat
8. In response to drop in temperature /In cold conditions – hair erector muscles contract/erector muscles make hairs stand up/erector muscles raise hairs
9. Trapped air gives insulation / Trapped air reduces heat loss
10. In response to drop in temperature/In cold conditions – increase in metabolic rate/increased movement / shivering

     Maximum 7 marks

Importance:

11. Chemical reactions/Metabolism controlled by enzymes
12. Enzymes have an optimum temperature/have a temperature at which they work best/do not work well at low temperatures/do not work well at high temperatures

     Maximum 1 mark
     Maximum Knowledge and Understanding 8 marks

1 mark for coherence + 1 mark for relevance

Coherence
• 1   The writing must be under sub headings or divided into paragraphs. A sub heading/paragraph for 'Mechanisms' and a sub heading/paragraph for 'Importance'.
• 2   Related information should be grouped together.

Information on 'Mechanisms' should be grouped together and at least 4 points must be given.
Information on 'Importance' should be grouped together and at least 1 point must be given.

Both must apply correctly to gain the Coherence mark.

2. A. continued

Relevance

- 1   Must not give details of ectotherms or any other homeostatic system e.g. blood glucose level or water content of blood.
- 2   Must have given at least four relevant points from 'Mechanisms' and at least one relevant point from 'Importance'.

Both must apply correctly to gain the Relevance mark

2.   B.   Shoot growth and development:

(i) 1.   Plants/Shoots show phototropism **OR** shoots <u>grow</u> towards light

2.   Greater concentration of auxin/IAA on dark side **OR** Less auxin/IAA on light side **OR** Auxin/IAA moves to dark side

3.   Greater elongation of cells on dark side **OR** Less elongation of cells on light side

4.   Etiolation in absence of light/in the dark

5.   Description of etiolation: small leaves; yellow/chlorotic leaves; long internodes/long and thin stems (Any 2 for 1 mark) **OR** Description of appearance of plant in light: large leaves; green leaves; short internodes/short and thick stems (Any 2 for 1 mark)

Maximum 3 marks

Timing of flowering in plants

6.   Plants show photoperiodism OR Flowering is affected by the photoperiod

7.   Photoperiod is the number of hours of light in a day/in 24 hours

8.   Long-day plants flower when: Either the photoperiod reaches/is above a critical level/a certain number of hours OR hours of darkness below a critical level/below a certain number of hours

9.   Short-day plants flower when: Either the photoperiod is below a critical level/is below a certain number of hours OR hours of darkness above a critical level/above a certain number of hours

Maximum 3 marks

2.B. continued

Timing of breeding in animals

10.   Long day breeders/Birds/Small mammals/Named example – breed in spring as photoperiod increases

11.   Short day breeders/Large mammals/Named example – breed in autumn as photoperiod decreases

12.   Young are born when conditions favourable/when food abundant OR Young have long period of growth before winter/before unfavourable conditions

Maximum 2 marks
Maximum Knowledge and Understanding 8 marks

1 mark for coherence + 1 mark for relevance

Coherence

- 1   The writing must be under sub headings or divided into paragraphs.

There should be a sub heading/paragraph for each of 'Shoot growth and development', 'Timing of flowering in plants' and 'Timing of breeding in animals'.

- 2   Related information should be grouped together.

Information on each of 'Shoot growth and development', 'Timing of flowering in plants' and 'Timing of breeding in animals' should be grouped together. There must be a minimum of 5 points with at least 1 point given for each group.

Both must apply correctly to gain the Coherence mark.

Relevance

- 1   Must not give details of any other effects of IAA or any effects of GA.
- 2   Must have given a minimum of 5 relevant points with at least 1 point from 'Shoot growth and development' plus at least 1 point from 'Timing of flowering in plants' plus at least 1 point from 'Timing of breeding in animals'.

Both must apply correctly to gain the Relevance mark.

Higher Biology 2004

Section A

1.	B	11.	D	21.	D
2.	C	12.	A	22.	B
3.	B	13.	C	23.	D
4.	A	14.	A	24.	B
5.	C	15.	D	25.	B
6.	C	16.	B	26.	B
7.	A	17.	A	27.	A
8.	D	18.	C	28.	C
9.	D	19.	D	29.	C
10.	A	20.	C	30.	A

Section B

1. (a) (i) 1. Phospholipid, 2. Protein
   (ii)

Process	Letter
Glycolysis	D
Transcription	F

   (b) Golgi (apparatus)/ Golgi (body)/ (Secretory) vesicles

   (c) All of:
   - Can detect light/Has a light detector
   - Can move to the light/Has flagellum to move nearer light
   - Has chloroplasts/grana/chlorophyll/ structure E (for photosynthesis).

2. (a)

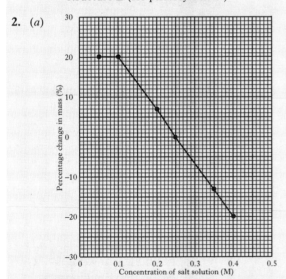

   (b) (i) 0·35 OR 0·40
         Mass has decreased due to water leaving cells/due to water moving from sap to solution/due to osmosis/due to water moving from HWC to LWC.
      (ii) Plasmolysed/Flaccid

   (c) Starting masses different
       OR
       Difficult to get starting masses the same

   (d) −26 to −27

   (e) (Salt solutions): Volume/Temperature/Same salt/pH
       (Beetroot tissue): Same beetroot/surface area/shape/blotting dry/plant/age

3. (a) (i) Cristae of mitochondria
          OR
          Folded inner membrane of mitochondria
      (ii) NAD/NADH/NADH$_2$/reduced NAD/ FAD
      (iii) X = ADP/Adenosine diphosphate
            Y = Pi/phosphate/PO$_4$ (or converse)
            Z = Oxygen/O$_2$

   (b) (i) To make amino acids/proteins/enzymes/ bases/nucleotides/nucleic acids/DNA/ RNA/chlorophyll/NAD/NADP/ATP/ADP /IAA
      (ii) Oxygen needed to make ATP in respiration/to release energy in respiration
           OR
           Aerobic respiration gives more energy/more ATP
           AND
           Uptake of nitrate/Uptake of elements/ Active transport requires energy/ATP
      (iii) Inhibits/Denatures/Poisons/Damages/ Destroys enzymes
            AND
            Enzymes involved in/regulate/control respiration/ATP production/active transport/uptake of nitrate/uptake of minerals

4. (a) (i) R = Deoxyribose
            S = Thymine
      (ii) Hydrogen

   (b) To make a copy of chromosomes/of genetic information/of DNA.
       AND
       Daughter cells receive one copy/one set/correct information

   (c) (i) Proline-Glycine-Serine-Alanine
      (ii) Gene/Allele

   (d) Transfer RNA/tRNA

   (e) (fibrous:) collagen/keratin/actin/myosin/elastin
       (cellulase:) globular

5. (a) (i) Translocation
      (ii) Radiation/UV/X-rays/gamma rays
           OR
           Chemicals/mustard gas
           OR
           High temperature

   (b) (Partial) Non disjunction
       OR
       Failure of homologous chromosomes/pairs to separate
       OR
       Spindle failure

   (c) (i) Deletion/Insertion
      (ii) Enzyme would not work/Wrong enzyme made/ Enzyme not made
           AND
           (Metabolic) pathway would be blocked/would not work/ would stop

   (d) 64

Official SQA Answers to Higher Biology 7

6. (a) (i) Gene probe/Gene probing/Chromosome mapping/Gene mapping/Banding (patterns)/Crossover values/Recombination frequencies
    (ii) 1. Restriction enzyme/Endonuclease
        2. Ligase

   (b) Insulin/Somatotrophin/Growth hormone/GH

7. (a) (i) Drinking water/Drinking watery liquids/Increased water intake/High water content of food eaten
    (ii) 1. Antidiuretic hormone/ADH
        2. Pituitary
    (iii) Blood/Bloodstream
    (iv) Increase permeability to water
        OR
        Increase water absorption
    (v) Decrease/Lower/Fall/Less

   (b)

Statement	Sea Water	Fresh Water
Salmon drinks a large volume of water	✓	
Salmon produces a large volume of urine		✓
Chloride secretory cells pump out ions	✓	
Salmon gains water by osmosis		✓

8. (a) (i) 3
    (ii) Day 10–15
    (iii) Decrease due to food used/respiration of stored food
        Increase due to food made/photosynthesis
        [Starch or energy store are equivalent to food]
    (iv) Variable mass/Variable width of shoots
        OR
        Other parts of plant may grow at a different rate/No account taken of root/leaf/fruit/lateral growth
        OR
        Water content of shoot cells is variable/may mask dry mass changes
    (v) 0.025

   (b) (i) less – **no** photosynthesis
    (ii) greater – plants would become etiolated
        OR
        plants trying to reach light

   (c) (i)

Effects caused by IAA	Effects caused by GA
B, C, D, E	A, F

    (ii) Herbicide/Weedkiller/Rooting powder/Seedless fruits/Parthenocarpy/Prevention of fruit fall

9. (a) Cambium
   (b) Has a large diameter/Is wide
   (c) Annual ring

10. (a)

Adaptation	Effect
Many large air spaces	For buoyancy OR Allow leaf-like structure/leaf/plant to float
Stoma on upper surface	Allows exchange of gases OR Allow CO_2 to diffuse in/ Allows O_2 to diffuse out

   (b) Xerophyte

11. (a) From 10 to 30 (beetles) by 50 days
        Then to 15 (beetles) by 300 days
   (b) 2:5
   (c) 250
   (d) Parasite/Disease has a greater effect on T. *castaneum*
        OR
        T. *castaneum* less resistant to parasite/disease
        AND
        More food available for T. *confusum*/Less competition for food
        OR
        Parasite/Disease has less effect on T. *confusum*
        OR
        T. *confusum* more resistant to parasite/disease
        AND
        Get more food/Compete better for food
   (e) Start with same number of both species
        OR
        Each species on its own for comparison/as controls
   (f)

Factors	Density-dependent	Density-independent
Presence of parasites	✓	
Availability of food	✓	
Temperature		✓

12. (a) True
        False
        True
        False
   (b) Lactose
   (c) Saves energy/Conserves resources/Does not make enzyme when no substrate present/Does not make enzyme when lactose absent/Does not make enzyme when it is not needed
        OR
        Converses of the 'Does not' statements

Higher Biology 2004 (cont.)

Section C

1. A. Meiosis

(i) First meiotic division:
1. start with a gamete mother cell/diploid cell
2. each chromosome made up of two chromatids
3. **homologous** chromosomes pair up
4. crossing over may occur
5. at chiasmata
6. **nuclear** membrane disappears OR spindle forms
7. independent assortment occurs OR (homologous) chromosomes line up on equator
8. homologous chromosomes/pairs are pulled apart
9. new **nuclear** membrane formed OR division of cytoplasm.

        Maximum 6 marks

(ii) Second meiotic division:
10. chromosomes line up on equator and **chromatids** pulled apart
9. new **nuclear** membrane formed OR division of cytoplasm (include point 9 once only - EITHER in context of first OR second meiotic division)
11. four cells produced.

        Maximum 2 marks

(iii) Importance of meiosis:
12. produces haploid gametes/cells OR chromosome number halved
13. crossing over gives recombination/variation/diversity
14. independent assortment gives variation/diversity.
15. meiosis/it gives variation/diversity (this is alternative to 13 + 14)

        Maximum 2 marks

B. Evolution of new species

(i) Isolating mechanisms:
1. a species is a group of organisms interbreeding to produce fertile offspring
2. common gene pool
3. a species/a population separated into two by an isolating mechanism/barrier
4. prevents gene exchange/gene flow/interbreeding between populations/groups
5. two types of isolation given (eg geographical/ecological)
6. third type of isolation given (eg reproductive).

        Maximum 4 marks

(ii) Effects of mutations and natural selection:
7. mutations occurring in each population/group will be different OR mutation occurs in one group
8. (mutation) gives variation/different phenotypes/new genes/new alleles/alters gene pool
9. different environments
10. selection is different for each population/group

1. B. (ii) continued
11. best adapted/best suited survive OR survival of the fittest OR converse
12. (they/best adapted/best suited/fittest) pass on favourable characteristics/genes/alleles to offspring/next generation OR less well adapted/less suited/less fit do not pass their characteristics/genes/alleles to offspring/next generation
13. many generations/long period of time
14. new species formed when populations/groups can no longer interbreed.

        Maximum 6 marks

2. A. Structure of chloroplast:
1. double outer membrane
2. grana are stacks of membranes
3. grana contain photosynthetic pigments/chlorophyll
4. light-dependent stage/photolysis in grana
5. stroma is fluid/liquid region surrounding grana
6. carbon fixation stage/Calvin cycle in stroma

        Maximum 4 marks

Separation of Pigments:
7. grind/mash leaves with acetone/solvent
8. filter/centrifuge to remove cell debris/to obtain extract
9. repeat applications/spots on chromatography paper/thin layer (gel)
10. allow solvent time to run
11. pigments travel different distances/pigments travel at different rates/pigments have different solubilities
12. pigments are – Carotene, Xanthophyll, Chlorophyll a, Chlorophyll b.

        Maximum 4 marks
       Maximum KU – 8 marks
1 mark for coherence and 1 mark for relevance.

Coherence
1. The writing must be under **sub-headings** or divided into **paragraphs**.
   A sub-heading/paragraph for each of 'Structure of chloroplast' and 'Separation of pigments'.

2. Related information should be **grouped together**.
   Information on 'Structure of chloroplast' should be grouped together with at least **two** points given.
   Information on 'Separation of pigments' should be grouped together with at least **two** points given.
   There must be a minimum of **five correct** points (the fifth mark may come from either group)

Both must apply correctly to gain the **Coherence** mark.

Relevance

1. **Must not** give details of other organelle structure.

2. **Must** have given at least **two** relevant points from 'Structure of choloroplast' and at least **two** relevant points from 'Separation of pigments' and at least **five** correct points overall.

   Both must apply correctly to gain the **Relevance** mark.

B. Nature of viruses:

1. very small/not cellular
2. reproduce inside cells/cannot reproduce outside cells
3. attack/infect specific (host) cells
4. nucleic acid/DNA/RNA surrounded by protein/protein coat/capsid.

Maximum 2 marks

Production of more viruses:

5. virus attaches to (host) cell
6. virus/nucleic acid/DNA/RNA enters cell
7. virus/nucleic acid/DNA/RNA takes over control of cell/alters metabolism
8. copies of viral nucleic acid/viral DNA/viral RNA made OR viral nucleic acid/viral DNA/viral RNA replicates
9. viral protein made/protein coat made/capsid made
10. (host) cell nucleotides/amino acids/ATP/enzymes used
11. viruses/virus particles assembled OR equivalent
12. viruses/virus particles released.

Maximum 6 marks
Maximum KU – 8 marks
1 mark for coherence and 1 mark for relevance.

Coherence

1. The writing must be under **sub-headings** or divided into **paragraphs**.
   A sub-heading/paragraph for each of 'Nature of viruses' and 'Production of more viruses'.

2. Related information should be **grouped together**.
   Information on 'Nature of viruses' should be grouped together with at least **one** point given. Information on 'Production of more viruses' should be grouped together with at least **four** points given.

   Both must apply correctly to gain the **Coherence** mark.

Relevance

1. **Must not** give details of cellular defence mechanisms in animals or plants.

2. **Must** have given at least **one** relevant point from 'Nature of viruses' and at least **four** relevant points from 'Production of more viruses'.

   Both must apply correctly to gain the **Relevance** mark.

Higher Biology 2005

Section A

1.	A	11.	B	21.	D
2.	A	12.	B	22.	B
3.	D	13.	C	23.	C
4.	A	14.	B	24.	C
5.	B	15.	A	25.	D
6.	C	16.	C	26.	C
7.	D	17.	D	27.	B
8.	D	18.	B	28.	A
9.	A	19.	A	29.	B
10.	C	20.	C	30.	D

Section B

1. (a) A (Central) matrix
   B Crista(e)

   (b)　(i)

Substance	Number of carbon atoms present
Pyruvic acid	2x3 OR 3
Acetyl group	2
Citric acid	6

   (ii) Coenzyme A/CoA

   (c)　(i) NAD
   (ii) Oxygen/O_2
   (iii) Transfer of chemical energy
   or
   Immediate/Instant source of energy
   or
   Energy for enzyme controlled reactions/for metabolic reactions/for chemical reactions
   or
   Energy for DNA synthesis/DNA replication/protein synthesis/glycolysis/active transport/muscle contraction/cell division/mitosis/meiosis/Calvin cycle
   (iv) ATP is made at the same rate as it is broken down
   or
   ATP is continually/continuously/constantly/always made/synthesised/regenerated
   or
   As ATP is broken down, more is produced
   or
   ATP made to replace ATP broken down/used

   (d) Lactic acid/lactate

2. (a)　(i) Engulf or description of engulfing, e.g. flows around/surrounds
   (ii) Join to vacuole/vesicle and add digestive enzymes

Higher Biology 2005 (cont.)

2. (b) (i) Lymphocyte
(ii) Transplant recognised as foreign **or**
Transplant has foreign antigens/proteins
and Cell X will make antibodies against
it/them
or
Produces antibodies that react with foreign
antigens/foreign proteins/antigens on
transplanted tissue
(iii) Immunosuppressor drugs/suppressor
drugs
or
Drugs that suppress the immune system

3. (a) Wire, short OR Short, wire

(b)

		Male gametes		
	AB	Ab	aB	ab
AB	¹ AABB	AABb	AaBB	AaBb
Ab	AABb	² AAbb	AaBb	Aabb
aB	AaBB	AaBb	³ aaBB	aaBb
ab	AaBb	Aabb	aaBb	⁴ aabb

(Female gametes — rows: AB, Ab, aB, ab)

(c)

Box	Phenotype
1	wire short
2	wire short
3	smooth short
4	smooth long

(d) 12 : 3 : 1

4. (a) (i) Peptide
(ii) Type of gene mutation: Substitution
Justification: Middle (base) G (for arg
codon) replaced by (base) U (for leu)
(iii) Ile/Isoleucine replaced by
phe/phenylalanine
or
Phe/phenylalanine used instead of
ile/isoleucine

(b) (i) Pituitary
(ii) Drinking fresh water = Decrease
Sweating   = Increase
Eating salty food   = Increase
Severe bleeding   = Increase
(iii) Increases permeability to water
or
Increases absorption/reabsorption of water

5. (a) Geographical/ecological/reproductive

(b) (i) 1 They/Mutations are different in each
sub-population **or**
Mutation in one sub-population but not in
other
2 Best adapted survive/Survival of the
fittest **or** converse

5. (b) (i) continued
or
Organisms with favourable
characteristics/genes/alleles/mutations
survive/are selected for **or** converse

(Favourable) characteristics
/genes/alleles/mutations passed on (to
offspring/next generation) OR converse
or
(both ideas in one sentence, e.g.)
Organisms with favourable characteristics
survive and pass them on.
(ii) They cannot interbreed/crossbreed/
hybridise.
They cannot breed together/with each
other.

6. (a)

Description	Term
Contains bacterial genes	plasmid
Cuts DNA into fragments	(restriction) endonuclease
Locates specific genes	gene probe
Removes plant cell walls	cellulase

(b) Sexual incompatibility **or**
Two species cannot interbreed/hybridise

7. (a) (i) Down a concentration gradient
From a high to a low water concentration
From hypotonic to hypertonic solution.
(ii) Large surface area for greater/better/more
absorption/water uptake/osmosis.
or
Greater/Larger/Bigger surface area for
absorption/water uptake/osmosis.
(iii) Cohesion
(iv) Any 2 from:
Nucleus/Cytoplasm/Contents of cell break
down/disintegrate/disappear/are destroyed.
Forms tube/End walls break down/
disintegrate/disappear/are destroyed.
Lignin formed/deposited.

(b) (i) out of, less
(ii) Stops/Reduces/Prevents water loss **or**
No water lost **or**
To conserve/save water/moisture

(c) (i) C, D, E (all three needed)
(ii) Provides/Supplies water for turgidity/for
support
or
Provides/Supplies/Transports
minerals/nutrients/ions (or named
example)
or
Cooling/heat loss

8. (*a*) (i) At 3 minutes concentration is 10 units
At 5 minutes/2 minutes later, concentration is 25 units/increased by 15 units.
(ii) Less RuBP is changed to GP
GP continues to be changed to RuBP.

(*b*) 75

(*c*) Decrease, Increase

(*d*) 8

(*e*) 10.

9. (*a*) As it/age increases, duration (of chase) increases **or** converse.

(*b*) 9

(*c*) Slower **or** less experienced **or** tire more quickly **or** have less stamina **or** are weaker **or** less able to defend themselves.

(*d*) Net energy gain is greater **or** description.

(*e*) Hunting success is greater
or
Can hunt for larger prey
or
Individual energy output is less
or
More food gained than hunting alone
or
Can tire out prey
or
Can protect kill better.

(*f*) Interspecific.

10. (*a*) (i) Crowded for increased protection by neighbours/other birds
or
Nest on cliff ledges where predators can't reach them
or
Chicks remain in nest and get protection.
(ii) 1. Three/More (eggs) so increased chance of one surviving
or
Speckled eggs so are difficult to see/are camouflaged
2. Can move short distances/away from nest/soon after hatching to escape from/hide from predators/danger.

(*b*) Description of group behaviour in response to presence of predator so predator is discouraged from attacking/attack repelled **or**
More eyes on the lookout so alarm raised earlier **or**
Confuse predator so harder to catch one/pick one off.

11. (*a*) Allow/Let/Time for the solutions/chemicals to have an effect
or
Allow/Let/Time for (dried) yeast to become active/produce enzyme/catalase.

11. (*b*) Prevent cross contamination/contamination with other solutions/suspensions
or
Prevent mixing of solutions/suspensions.

(*c*) Temperature/type of yeast/concentration of hydrogen peroxide/pH.

(*d*) (i) and (ii)

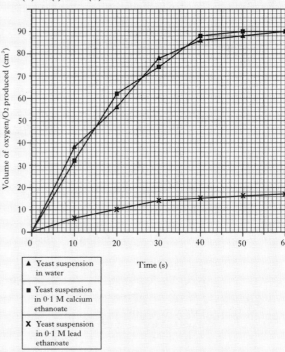

▲ Yeast suspension in water

■ Yeast suspension in 0·1 M calcium ethanoate

X Yeast suspension in 0·1 M lead ethanoate

(*e*) Allows a comparison to be made with other results/when no chemical is added
or
Shows activity of catalase without chemicals/solutions.

(*f*) Any two from:
1. Calcium does not inhibit/has no effect on yeast activity/enzyme/catalase
or
Calcium has no effect on oxygen production
2. Ethanoate does not inhibit/has no effect on yeast activity/ enzyme/catalase
or
Ethanoate has no effect on oxygen production
3. Lead inhibits yeast activity/enzyme/catalase
or
Lead reduces oxygen production.

12. (*a*) (i) Aleurone
(ii) Gibberellic acid/GA
(iii) Breaks down starch into maltose
Used as energy source for growth/for germination/by embryo.

(*b*) Herbicide/weed killer/rooting powder **or**
To produce seedless fruits/parthenocarpy **or**
To prevent/delay fruit fall/fruit abscission **or**
To promote fruit development.

Higher Biology 2005 (cont.)

13. (a) Underline: <u>ectotherm</u> and <u>cannot</u>.

(b) Lying in the sun
or
Lying on a hot surface/hot sand/hot rock
or
Basking.

(c) As environmental temperature rises above body temperature it stays constant
or
Body temperature stays below 40°C when environmental temperature is greater than 40°C.

(d) At 10°C, greater heat loss.
Metabolic reactions/Metabolism/Respiration provides heat.

Section C

1. A (i) **The importance of monitoring wild populations**
1. food species plus a strategy for management, e.g. prevent overfishing/set quotas
2. raw material species **or** species used in medicine plus strategy for management, e.g. avoid over-harvesting
3. pest species plus reason for monitoring, e.g. control of pest
4. indicator species plus reason for monitoring, e.g. to assess levels of pollution
5. endangered species plus reason for monitoring, e.g. to prevent extinction **or** a consequential strategy, e.g. protection/conservation (or named example)
6. one named example from any of 1–5 above
7. one different named example from another of 1–5 above.

(ii) **The influence of density-depenent factors on population changes**
8. effect of density-dependent factor increases as density increases (or converse)
9. two density-dependent factors named from <u>List</u>
10. a third density-dependent factor named from <u>List</u>
    List
        Disease/Parasites/Infection
        Food supply/availability
        Predation
        Competition for food/space/territory
        Toxic waste made by organisms
11. relate population change to <u>Effect</u> of two factors

12. relate population change to <u>Effect</u> of a third factor
    Effect
        if population increases then increase in disease/in spread of disease/parasites/infection
        if population increases then decrease in food available to individuals
        if population increases then increase in predation
        if population increases then increase in competition for food
        if population increases then increase in competition for space/territory
        if population increases then increase in production of toxic waste.
    (converses of the above are also acceptable)
13. (linked to 11 and 12) relate any of the above effects to a subsequent decrease in population
    or
    (if converses given in 11 and 12) relate any of the above effects to subsequent increase in population
14. population returns to a size that the environment can sustain/to a stable level.

B (i) **The influence of pituitary hormones in humans**
1. pituitary makes GH/growth hormone/somatotrophin
2. GH promotes growth of bones **or** GH increases transport/uptake of amino acids
3. pituitary makes TSH/thyroid stimulating hormone
4. TSH affects/controls/stimulates regulates activity of thyroid gland/thyroxine production
5. increase in TSH results in increase in thyroxine **or** converse
6. thyroxine affects metabolic processes/metabolism/rate of chemical reactions.

(ii) **The effects of Indole Acetic Acid (IAA) in plants**
7. promotes cell division/mitosis
8. leads to cell elongation
9. inhibits development/growth of lateral buds **or** leads to apical dominance
10. causes fruit formation
11. low levels lead to leaf abscission
12. leads to phototropic response/phototropism
13. in directional light, IAA accumulates on dark side/side away from light
14. greater/more elongation on dark side **or** less elongation on light side.

2. A **Absorption of light energy**
1. chlorophyll a and b, xanthophyll and carotene named
2. chlorophyll absorbs red and blue light/colours/wavelengths
3. xanthophyll and carotene/accessory pigments absorb light from other regions of spectrum/of other colours/of other wavelengths
4. light absorption occurs over a wide range of spectrum/wider range of colours/more wavelengths
5. energy absorbed by xanthophyll/carotene/ accessory pigments is passed on to chlorophyll
6. occurs in the grana.

Light-dependent stage
6. occurs in the grana
7. light energy converted to chemical energy
8. regenerate ATP from ADP and Pi
9. split water **or** energy used in photolysis of water
10. hydrogen combines with NADP **or** NADPH2/NADPH/reduced NADP formed
11. oxygen is a by-product **or** oxygen diffuses/ passes/goes out of cells/leaf
12. NADPH2 and ATP diffuse/pass/go to stroma/are used in Calvin cycle.

Coherence
1. The writing must be under **sub-headings** or divided into **paragraphs**.
   A sub-heading/paragraph for each of 'Absorption of light energy' and 'Light-dependent stage'.
2. Related information should be **grouped together**.
   Information on 'Absorption of light energy' should be grouped together with at least two points given.
   Information in 'Light-dependant stage' should be grouped together with at least two points given.
   There must be a minimum of **five correct** points.
   Both must apply correctly to gain the **Coherence mark**.

Relevance
1. **Must not** give details of the carbon fixation stage of photosynthesis.
2. **Must** have given at least **two** relevant points from 'Absorption of light energy' and at least **two** relevant points from 'light-dependent stage' and at least **five** correct points overall.
   Both must apply correctly to gain the **Relevance mark**.

2. B **Structure of RNA**
1. single stranded
2. made of nucleotides
3. has a base, ribose (sugar) and a phosphate
4. bases are guanine, cytosine, adenine and uracil. (not letters A,U,G,C)

Role in protein synthesis
5. mRNA carries information/code (for protein) from nucleus/from DNA
6. mRNA attaches to ribosome
7. three bases on mRNA is a codon
8. tRNA transport amino acids to ribosome
9. tRNA transports specific amino acids
10. three bases on tRNA is an anticodon
11. codons match/pair with their anticodons
12. joins/adds correct amino acid onto growing protein/polypeptide.
13. sequence of bases/codons on mRNA gives sequence of amino acids.

Coherence
1. The writing must be under **sub-headings** or divided into **paragraphs**.
   A sub heading/paragraph for each of 'structure of RNA' and 'Role in protein synthesis'.
2. Related information should be **grouped together**.
   Information on 'Structure of RNA' should be grouped together with at least **two** points given.
   Information on 'Role in protein synthesis' should be grouped together with at least **three** points given.
   Both must apply correctly to gain the **Coherence mark**.

Relevance
1. **Must not** give details of DNA structure, DNA replication, protein transport, protein secretion (allow only **ONE** reference to DNA but don't count a reference to DNA in a description of transcription).
2. **Must** have at least **two** relevant points from 'Structure of RNA' and at least **three** relevant points from 'Role in protein synthesis'.
   Both must apply correctly to gain the **Relevance mark**.

Higher Biology 2006

Section A

1.	C	2.	D	3.	C
4.	B	5.	A	6.	C
7.	A	8.	D	9.	D
10.	C	11.	A	12.	D
13.	D	14.	C	15.	D
16.	A	17.	B	18.	C
19.	C	20.	A	21.	D
22.	B	23.	B	24.	B
25.	C	26.	A	27.	B
28.	B	29.	D	30.	A

Section B

1. (a)   (i) A and F
           (ii) B

     (b)   (i) 1.Correct scale and label added to both
              axes as follows:
              Y axis
              Scale: from − 25 to +25 in steps of
              5%/10% including 0
              Label: Change in mass of apple tissue (%)
              X axis
              Scale: 0 to 0.5 in steps of 0.05 or 0.1
              Label: Concentration of sucrose solution
              (M)
              2. All points correctly plotted and straight
              line drawn through all points
           (ii) hypotonic and turgid

2. (a)   (i) Oxygen /O_2
           (ii) Product X: Glucose
              Substance Y: Carbon dioxide/CO_2
          (iii) RuBP: 5, GP: 3 OR 2x3C

     (b)   (i) Transfer/Carry/Take (chemical) energy
              (from the light-dependent stage) to Calvin
              cycle/carbon fixation/light-independent
              stage/ stroma
              OR
              Provide energy for
              Calvin cycle/carbon fixation/light
              independent stage/synthesis of
              glucose/synthesis of product X/converting
              GP to glucose/converting GP to product
              X
          (ii) For reduction of GP/substance Y/carbon
              dioxide/CO_2 (to glucose/product X/
              carbohydrate)
              OR
              Glucose/Product X/Carbohydrate is a
              reduced form of GP/substance Y/carbon
              dioxide/CO_2

2. (c)   (i) Tick box: 425–450 nm
           (ii) To absorb (energy/light/colours) from
              more regions of the spectrum/from more
              wavelengths/from a greater/wider/bigger
              range/variety of wavelengths
              OR
              To allow photosynthesis over more regions
              of the spectrum/from more
              wavelengths/from a greater range of
              wavelengths/from a greater range of
              colours
              OR
              Absorb greater spectrum of light
              OR
              Broaden the absorption spectrum/action
              spectrum
          (iii) *Any one from:*

	Adaptation	Effect
1.	air/gas spaces	For buoyancy/to float OR storage of air/gas/oxygen
2.	stomata absent OR stomata reduced	gases exchanged direct with (leaf) cells
3.	stomata on (upper) surface	for gas exchange OR example eg absorb CO_2, release oxygen
4.	narrow/rolled/finely divided (leaves)	prevent damage
5.	flat (leaves)	can float
6.	flexible (leaf) stalk/leaf stem	prevent damage in moving water
7.	long (leaf) stalk/leaf stem	(leaf) can vary in height with water
8.	reduced xylem	water absorbed directly into cells
9.	cuticle reduced/thin/ absent	no need to prevent water loss
10.	xylem centred in leaf stem	flexibility

          (iv) (Algae/They) can use
               energy/light/colours/green
               light/wavelengths
               transmitted by/passing through/not
               absorbed by/not used by the
               hydrophyte/plants above/other
               plants/pigments P&Q

3. (a)   (i) Higher concentration of/More potassium
              ions inside cell
              OR
              Potassium ions 140mM inside cell and
              5mM outside.
          (ii) 1 : 22

3. (b) (i) (As oxygen concentration increases from 1.0 to 2.0 units/as graph rises)
   1. More oxygen is available for respiration
   2. More ATP/energy made
   3. Ion uptake/active transport/active uptake requires ATP/energy
   OR converse (but must state for decreasing oxygen concentration)
   (ii) Respiration/ATP production/Enzymes/ Active transport/Potassium ion uptake at maximum
   OR
   Oxygen (concentration) is not/is no longer the limiting factor (for ion uptake)
   OR
   A factor other than oxygen/Another factor is limiting (the ion uptake)
   OR
   Temperature/Glucose (availability) may be the limiting factor
   OR
   Glucose/Energy source used up

4. (a) Accepts/Removes hydrogen from cytochrome system
   OR
   Final hydrogen acceptor
   OR
   To combine with hydrogen and form water

   (b) (i) Cristae
   (ii) 1. Start with/Add/Use more (yeast) cells (per dish/per plate)
   OR
   More dishes/plates for each set of conditions
   2. Aerobic respiration/Aerobic conditions gives more ATP/energy
   AND
   (This/More ATP/More energy) gives more growth/more cell division/larger colonies
   OR
   Anaerobic respiration/Anaerobic conditions gives less ATP/energy
   AND
   (This/Less ATP/Less energy) gives less growth/less cell division/smaller colonies
   3. In aerobic conditions –
   only 2 ATP made
   only ATP/energy from glycolysis made
   less ATP/energy made
   OR
   In both conditions –
   Same ATP/energy made
   Only 2 ATP made
   Only ATP/energy made in glycolysis
   Only glycolysis carried out
   Only anaerobic respiration carried out

5. (a) Ribosome

   (b) P = peptide (bond)
   Q = hydrogen (bond)

   (c) UAC

5. (d) *Any two from*
   1. Collects/Picks up/Binds to specific amino acid
   2. Take/Carry/Transport amino acids to ribosome/site of translation/site of protein synthesis
   3. Join to/Pair with/Match with/Recognise correct codon (on mRNA)
   OR
   Brings amino acid to the correct position

   (e) A triplet of/Three nucleotides/bases code for one amino acid

6. (a) 60

   (b) 1. Transplants/Tissues/They have different proteins (acceptable equivalents to 'different' are 'foreign'/'non-native'/'non-self')
   (acceptable equivalent to 'proteins' is 'antigens')
   2. (Different proteins are) detected by/recognised by the immune system/lymphocytes
   OR
   Response made by the immune system/lymphocytes
   3. (Response is) antibodies made (against transplant)

   (c) (DNA) cannot replicate/make copies (so no cell division)
   OR
   No more chromosomes can be made (so no cell division)
   OR
   (DNA) will not be able to make mRNA (so no protein synthesis)
   OR
   Transcription not possible (so no protein synthesis)

7. (a) (i) First meiotic division: B,D,E
   Second meiotic division: A,C
   (ii) 1. Homologous pairs (of chromosomes)
   OR
   Homologous chromosomes
   2. Line up/(across cell/on equator/before separation)
   3. Independently
   OR
   Without reference to other pairs
   OR
   In one of two different ways
   OR
   On their own
   OR
   Randomly

Higher Biology 2006 (cont.)

7. (*b*) (i) Deletion

(ii) X should be centred on fourth bar in from right of upper diagram

(iii) Males (are XY so) only need one copy of the gene/allele/mutation (for it to show/to be affected)
And
females (are XX so) need two copies
OR
Y chromosome cannot mask the condition in males but second X chromosome in females could

(iv) Correct/Important/Essential/Particular/Certain protein is not made
OR
Incorrect/Wrong/Different/Another/No protein is made
(accept enzyme as equivalent to protein)
OR
Protein/Enzyme/Amino acid sequence is changed

8. (*a*) 24

(*b*) Foraging shown accounts for part/90% of time observed
OR
Foraging shown is not 100% of time observed
OR
Some/10% of foraging time not recorded

(*c*) 33.3

(*d*) The bigger the beak size, the more of the larger caterpillars eaten OR converse
OR
The bigger the beak, the larger the proportion of large caterpillars eaten OR converse

(*e*) 5.2

(*f*) (i) Eat different caterpillar sizes/size ranges OR description with correct values

(ii) Eat different caterpillar sizes/size ranges OR a description with correct values
AND
Forage in different parts of trees OR a description with correct values (both required)

(*g*) Energy gain from food (found) must be greater than energy lost/used in finding it
OR
There must be an overall/a net energy gain from food/from foraging

9. (*a*) (i) For synthesis of/To make/Essential for amino acids/proteins/enzymes/nucleic acids/bases/DNA/RNA/chlorophyll/NAD/NADP/ATP/ADP/auxins/IAA

(ii) Slow/Reduced/Stunted growth
OR
Plants/Leaves chlorotic/pale (green)/yellow
OR chlorosis
OR
Leaf bases red
OR
Roots long/thin

(*b*) (i) Somatic fusion OR Protoplast fusion
(ii) Cellulase
(iii) (New tomato species/It)can grow in soils with low nitrogen

10. (*a*) (i) Mix contents OR Get even distribution of contents/conditions

(ii) Prevent build up of pressure/air/gas
OR
Let air/gas flow through container
OR
Allow escape of excess gas (made by cells)
OR allow CO_2 out

(*b*) *Any 2 from*
1. Speed of paddles/Stirring speed/Stirring rate/Motor speed
2. Air flow rate/Inlet flow rate
3. Composition of sterile/inlet air OR Oxygen concentration
4. Method of sampling
5. Volume of air/gas in
6. Concentration of nutrients other than glucose and lactose
7. Time that motor/paddles work for

(*c*) (i) (Time:) 24 OR 25 (minutes)
(Justification:)
It/Graph (Y) starts to rise then/at this time/at 24 minutes
OR
Growth (in Y) starts then/at this time/at 24 minutes
OR
No growth (in Y) till then/till this time/till 24 minutes
OR
Reading/Number of cells stays constant till then/stays at 0·1 till then

(ii) 1. It/Lactose binds to repressor (protein/molecule)
2. Repressor can't bind to operator
OR Operator not inhibited
OR operator free
3. Structural gene/Gene coding for enzyme is switched on/transcribed

(iii) 0.37

11. (*a*)

Smooth green pod: $\boxed{TtGg}$ + $\boxed{TG, Tg, tG, tg}$

Constricted yellow pod: $\boxed{ttgg}$ + $\boxed{tg}$

(*b*) (i) 28

(ii) *Any two from*
1. Fertilisation/Fusion of gametes is random/is chance event
2. Not enough/Too few offspring examined OR sample size too small
3. Gene/Sex linkage OR Crossing over OR Recombination
4. Mutation OR correctly named chromosome/gene mutation

12. (*a*) Apical dominance

(*b*) They/Lateral buds receive no IAA so growth is not inhibited
OR
IAA cannot reach them/lateral buds to inhibit growth
OR
Slicing prevents IAA reaching them/lateral buds to inhibit growth
OR
Concentration of IAA has dropped, so no apical dominance
Note: Auxin is equivalent to IAA

(*c*)
1. IAA stimulates cell division/cell elongation
2. More IAA on dark side OR Less IAA on light side OR IAA moves to the dark side OR IAA destroyed on light side
3. Plant/Shoot/Stem grows towards light or more elongation/cell division on dark side

(*d*) Flower when photoperiod reaches/is above a certain number/a minimum number of hours
OR
Flower when photoperiod reaches/is above a critical level

13. (*a*) 6.5

(*b*) Rising sea temperature

(*c*) (Provide data to:)
Help protect/conserve/preserve an endangered species
OR
Assess levels of pollution OR If they are pollution indicators
OR
Control pest species
OR
Prevent over-harvesting of a raw material

14. (*a*) (i) Hypothalamus
(ii) Nerves OR Nerve impulses

(*b*) No/Less blood flow to skin/surface
AND
Less heat lost/Heat not lost (by radiation/to the environment)

(*c*) Endotherm

Section C

1. A (i) **The effect of environmental factors on transpiration rate**
1. Temperature
2. Wind (speed)
3. Light intensity
4. Availability of soil water
Increase in any of 1, 2, 3 or 4 may increase transpiration rate (or converse)
5. Humidity
6. Air pollution/Blocked stomata
7. Air pressure
Increase in any of 5, 6 or 7 may decrease transpiration rate (or converse)

(ii) **Adaptations of xerophyte plants that reduce the transpiration rate**
8. Small leaves OR Reduced size of leaves OR Reduced number of leaves OR Leaves reduced to spines OR Shedding of leaves so reduction in leaf area (through which water lost.)
9. Reduced number of stomata OR Reduced stomatal density OR Fewer stomata so reduction in (stomatal pore) area (through which water lost.)
10. Waxy/Thick cuticle so there is a physical/waterproof barrier (to water loss) OR Waxy/Thick cuticle prevents/reduces water loss
11. Rolled leaves so moisture/humid air trapped (round stomata).
OR stomata less exposed to air.
OR reduced air movement.
12. Hairs on leaf so moisture/humid air trapped (round stomata).
OR stomata less exposed to air.
OR reduced air movement.
13. Stomata sunk in pits/Sunken stomata so moisture/humid air trapped (round stomata).
OR stomata less exposed to air.
OR reduced air movement.
14. Reduction in the water concentration gradient/diffusion rate of water.
15. Reversed stomatal rhythm so stomata closed in middle part of day

B (i) **Behavioural defence mechanisms in animals**
1. Avoidance behaviour/Escape response.
2. Gives defence against predator/unpleasant stimulus OR Allows animals to avoid/escape a predator/unpleasant stimulus OR Description of an example eg Snail retreating into shell
3. One example of individual behavioural defence from the lists below
4. A second example of individual behavioural defence from the lists below
5. One example of social defence from the lists below
6. A second example of social defence from the lists below

Higher Biology 2006 (cont.)

<u>**Individual** behavioural defence responses:</u>

animal fights back	eg cat fights back when attacked by a dog
animal flees	eg gazelle flees from cheetah attack
animal stays motionless	eg young roe deer lies still when fox nearby
animal takes cover/hides	eg sparrows fly into hedge when sparrow hawk nearby
animal produces foul smell/chemical substance/poison	eg skunk sprays an attacker with foul smelling chemical
animal displays diversion activity	eg bird feigning injury to take predator away from eggs
threat display (in defence)	eg baring teeth when attacked

<u>**Social/collective/cooperative/group** behavioural defence responses:</u>

schooling in fish	eg herring group together in large numbers
herding in mammals	eg wildebeest group together in large numbers
formation of protective group	eg wild oxen form ring with horned males on outside
mobbing of a predator	eg several crows mobbing a single buzzard
rapid movement to confuse predator	eg group of pigeons taking off in all directions when disturbed
alarm calls	eg blackbird alarm call given when predator nearby
lookouts	eg meerkat standing upright

(ii) **Cellular and structural defence mechanisms in plants**

7 Have/Make toxic compounds/toxins/poisons
8 Any two examples from tannins/cyanide/nicotine
9 Unpleasant taste discourages animals from eating the plant
10 Isolate injured area with resin OR Resin seals wound
11 This prevents disease spread (through the plant)
12 Any two examples of structural mechanisms from stings/thorns/spines
13 These give unpleasant experience that discourages animals from eating the plant

2. A **Principal of negative feedback**
1. Negative feedback maintains constant internal conditions in the body/homeostasis
2. A change from the normal level/set point is detected
3. A corrective mechanism is switched on/activated
4. When condition returns to its normal level/set point, corrective mechanism switched off.
(Maximum 2 marks)

Maintenance of blood sugar levels
5. Blood sugar/glucose level (BSL) detected by the pancreas
6. If BSL increases, (more) insulin is made
7. Insulin increases permeability of cells to glucose OR Insulin increases uptake of glucose by cells
8. Liver/Muscle cells convert glucose to glycogen OR Glucose converted to glycogen and stored in liver/muscle
9. BSL returns to its normal/set point
10. If BSL decreases, (more) glucagon is made
11. Glucagon causes conversion of glycogen to glucose
12. Glucose released into blood
13. BSL returns to normal/set point
(Maximum 6 marks)

Coherence
1. The writing must be under **sub-headings** or divided into **paragraphs** with a sub-heading/paragraph for each of 'Principle of negative feedback' and 'Maintenance of blood sugar levels'.
2. Information on 'Principle of negative feedback' should have at least **one** point given.
Information on 'Maintenance of blood sugar levels' should have at least **four** points given.
Both must apply correctly to gain the **Coherence** mark.

Relevance
1. **Must not** give details of control of water balance or temperature regulation
2. **Must** have given at least **one** relevant point from 'Principle of negative feedback' and at least **four** relevant points from 'Maintenance of blood sugar levels'.
Both must apply correctly to gain the **Relevance** mark.

2. B **Role of pituitary**
   1. Pituitary makes growth hormone/GH/somatotrophin
   2. GH promotes growth of bone/muscle
      OR GH increases protein synthesis
      OR GH increases transport/uptake of amino acids by cells/tissues
   3. Pituitary makes thyroid stimulating hormone/TSH
   4. TSH controls/stimulates/regulates activity of thyroid (gland)/thyroid production
   5. Increase in TSH causes thyroid to make more thyroxine
      OR Decrease in TSH causes thyroid to make less thyroxine
   6. Thyroxine affects metabolism/metaolic process/chemical reactions in cells
      (Maximum 4 marks)

Effects of named drugs on fetal development
   7. Thalidomide may cause limb deformities
   8. Nicotine may restrict growth
      OR Nicotine may cause lower birth weights
   9. Nicotine may cause abnormal brain development/learning difficulties
   10. Alcohol may restrict growth
       OR Alcohol may cause lower birth weights
       OR Alcohol may cause facial abnormalities/heart defects
   11. Alcohol may cause abnormal brain development/learning difficulties
       (Maximum 4 marks)

Coherence
   1. The writing must be under **sub-headings** or divided into **paragraphs**.
      There must be a sub-heading/paragraph for each of 'Role of pituitary' and 'Effects of named drugs on fetal development'.
   2. Related information should be **grouped together**.
      Information on 'Role of the pituitary' should be grouped together with at least **two** points given.
      Information on 'Effects of named drugs on fetal development' should be grouped together with at least **two** points given.
      There must be a minimum of **five correct** points.
      Both must apply correctly to gain the **Coherence** mark.

Relevance
   1. **Must not** give details of other pituitary hormones eg ADH or details of other factors that can affect normal growth and development eg vitamin or mineral deficiency, lead.
   2. **Must** have at least **two** relevant points from 'Role of the pituitary' and at least **two** relevant points from 'Effects of named drugs on fetal development'.
      There must be a minimum of **five correct** points overall.
      Both must apply correctly to gain the **Relevance** mark.

Higher Biology 2007

SECTION A

1. A	**2.** D	**3.** B
4. D	**5.** D	**6.** D
7. D	**8.** C	**9.** A
10. A	**11.** B	**12.** B
13. A	**14.** A	**15.** C
16. A	**17.** D	**18.** C
19. C	**20.** C	**21.** B
22. A	**23.** D	**24.** C
25. B	**26.** C	**27.** B
28. C	**29.** D	**30.** B

SECTION B

1. (*a*) (i) Transmitted (through leaf)/ transmission/transmittance
       (ii) granum/grana (of chloroplast)/thylakoids

   (*b*) (i) photolysis/photolytic splitting of water (in granum)
       (ii) NADP

   (*c*) five
        carbon dioxide
        hydrogen
        three

2. (*a*) (i) $0 \cdot 375 \text{ cm}^3$
       (ii) Identical/same apparatus with no/dead worm or glass beads/plasticene (instead of worm)

   (*b*) $0 \cdot 01$

3. (*a*) (i) *0–3 hours*
          (Mass increases as) water enters/is gained/absorbed by osmosis.
          OR Water diffuses into cell/enters from more dilute solution.
          OR Water enters/moves from HWC to LWC.
          OR Water moves from higher water concentration/hypotonic (to hypertonic) region/solution.
          OR Osmosis from HWC to LWC.
          OR Water moves down a concentration gradient

          3–5 hours
          Cells/tissue/carrot turgid/isotonic with the solution.
          OR (Cell) wall (pressure) stops more water entering/osmosis.
          Wall has reached limits of elasticity

Higher Biology 2007 (cont.)

3. (a) (ii) Temperature/heat denatures/destroys/
damages protein in membrane.
Making (the membrane) fully
permeable/no longer selectively permeable.
AND This allows cell contents/water to
escape/leak out/be lost (giving a decrease
in mass)

  (b) (i) Ion: chloride/chlorine
Justification: concentration (of chloride) is
equal/the same (inside and outside the
organism)

     (ii) Oxygen/aerobic conditions allows
increased (aerobic) respiration which
provides more ATP/energy, so increasing
active transport (of potassium).

4. (a) (i) Transfer RNA/tRNA/TRNA
     (ii) Hydrogen (bond)

  (b) Codon

  (c) TTA

  (d) • Endoplasmic reticulum carries/transports/
transfers/sends/passes (protein) to the
Golgi (apparatus).
    • Golgi apparatus processes/packages/
modifies/adds carbohydrate to protein (for
secretion).
OR packages secretion
OR produces vesicles containing protein

  (e)

Protein	Structure	Function
Cellulase	globular	Breaks down/ degrades/digests/removes/destroys/gets rid of cell walls/cellulose OR Makes protoplasts
Collagen	fibrous	structural protein in skin

5. (a) (i) At higher grazing intensity graph does not
fall to zero/some species survive/are not
extinct.
     (ii) *Any one from:*
       • Low/basal/underground/close to ground
meristems
       • Low/basal growing points
       • Underground stems/rhizomes
       • Deep root (systems) OR roots lower in
ground
       • Low apical meristems

  (b) Dominant/more competitive/faster-growing/
prolific grasses/plants/species are eaten
more/kept in check/prevented from taking over
so other grasses/plants/species can grow

6. (a) (i) From June to October, mass increases
from 3·6 g to 8·0 g/by 4·4 g.
From October to November, mass remains
constant/does not change/levels off.
From November to December, mass
decreases/reduces to 7·5 g/by 0·5 g.
     (ii) Oct to Nov
    (iii) 1:7
    (iv) 60%

  (b) Photosynthesis decreases/less starch made and
starch used as an energy source/in respiration/as
food/converted to raffinose/ used in growth

  (c) (i) Raffinose concentration is less than the
total sugar concentration
     (ii) Temperatures drop/winters are extremely
cold/frost is likely and raffinose increases
to prevent frost damage/freezing of
sap/needles
OR Higher concentration in winter/colder
months helps to prevent frost damage (to
needles)

7. (a) (i) Gamete mother (cells)
     (ii) Same genes/order of genes/gene sequence/
gene loci/position of genes/alleles/genes
for same characteristics
OR match each other gene for gene/same
banding pattern
    (iii) (Partial) non-disjunction
    (iv) First meiotic division
Justification: (this is when) homologous
chromosomes pair/are separating/fail to
separate
OR Homologous pairs form/separate/fail
to separate.
OR Does not involve separation of
chromatids.
     (v) 2

  (b) 1. Insertion
     2. Substitution

8. (a) (i) Barriers to gene exchange/gene flow/
interbreeding/spreading of mutations
between groups/sub groups/populations
OR Splits the gene pool/creates two gene
pools/prevents mixing of gene pool
     (ii) They have/share a common ancestor.
Leaves are selected for/adapted to/suited
to/developed for different/their growing
conditions/environment/niche/climate.

  (b) Spines/they/it give protection
from/discourage/reduce/stop grazing by
herbivores/predators AND
reference to low growing

  (c) *Any two from:*
    • Wildlife/Nature/Game reserves
    • captive breeding
    • breeding programmes
    • cell/seed/gene banks
    • hunting/fishing quotas
    • poaching bans
    • being made a protected species
    • breeding in zoos
    • only being allowed to hunt at certain times
of the year

9. (*a*) (i) 2·5kg
    (ii) Increased/more growth hormone/GH
         (causes a growth spurt/rapid increase in
         growth) between 15 and 20 years/up to 20
         years/through the teenage years.
         Decrease/less/no/cessation of growth
         hormone/GH (causes growth to cease)
         after 20 years/between 20 and 22 years.

   (*b*) Hormone Y: Thyroxine
        Role: It controls/regulates (the rate of)
        metabolism/ metabolic rate

10. (*a*) (i) *Any two from:*
         • temperature
         • type of soil
         • pH
         • mineral content of soil
         • fertility of soil
         • nutrients (availability) in soil
         • carbon dioxide conc./availability/level (in
           atmosphere)
         • distance/position/angle of spray from plant
    (ii) Use more pea plants at each
         concentration/mass of GA./Use more
         replicates at each conc/mass of GA

   (*b*) (i)

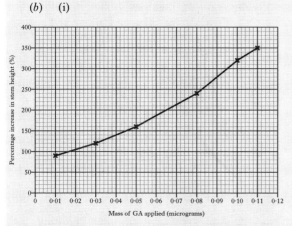

    (ii) 370–380% increase

   (*c*) Some spray may miss the plant AND so less/
        unknown/inaccurate mass of GA applied.

11. (*a*)

Statement	Lactose present	Lactose absent
Regulator ... molecule.	T	T
Repressor ... inducer.	T	F
Repressor ... operator	F	T

11. (*b*) (i) Phenylalanine: increases/builds
              up/rises/higher/more
              Tyrosine - decreases/falls/goes down/lower
              (to zero)/less
        (ii) (Mutation) changes order/sequence of
             bases/nucleotides (in a gene)
             OR bases altered
             OR Change to DNA code/sequence,
             mRNA code/sequence
             OR Change to codon/codons/codon
             sequence
             (Leading to) change in (order/sequence of)
             amino acids
             Order/sequence of amino acids determines
             the (shape/function/structure of) protein/
             enzyme

12. (*a*) Condition: continuous/uninterrupted/constant
        period of darkness must be 12 hours or more
        Justification: if dark period too short/less than
        12 hours or interrupted then flowering does not
        occur

   (*b*) Enables/allows sexual reproduction/cross
        pollination/interbreeding/cross-breeding
        OR Pollen able to fertilise/be carried to other
        plants

   (*c*) Changing photoperiod can affect timing of/
        cause breeding/mating
        OR Small mammals/example breed when
        photoperiod increasing/during spring
        OR Large mammals/example breed when
        photoperiod decreasing/during autumn

13. (*a*) Glycogen

   (*b*) (i) X: insulin
             Y: glucagon
        (ii) Pancreas
       (iii) Raised/High blood sugar/glucose level
             causes release of insulin/hormone X.
             Insulin stimulates conversion of glucose to
             glycogen/storage carbohydrate. This moves
             blood sugar/glucose level back to
             normal/set point.
             OR
             Reduced/Low blood sugar level causes
             release of glucagons/hormone Y. Glucagon
             stimulates conversion of glycogen to
             glucose. This moves blood sugar level
             back to normal/set point.
             OR
             A change is detected, so the appropriate
             corrective mechanism switched on. The
             glucose level returns to set point/normal
             and so corrective mechanism is switched
             off.

Higher Biology 2007 (cont.)

14. (*a*) (i) Succession
       (ii) Grass alters/modifies the habitat/soil so
            that it is more suitable/favourable for
            shrubs.
            OR Grass increases humus/water
            retention/soil fertility/nutrient level/depth
            of soil
      (iii) Diverse/high biomass/contains complex
            food webs

    (*b*) (i) Density dependent - competition,
          predation, disease, food supply (A, B, D
          and F)
          Density independent - rainfall,
          temperature (C, E)
      (ii) increases
          decreases

SECTION C

1A (i) Your answer should include at least five points
    from the following:
1. Occurs in cytoplasm
2. Glucose broken down to/converted to/
   reduced to/oxidised to (two molecules of)
   pyruvic acid
3. C6 compound broken down to 2 X C3
4. Step by step breakdown by enzymes OR
   series of enzyme controlled reactions
5. Net gain/production of ATP/explanation
   of net gain of ATP
6. NAD accepts hydrogen/NADH produced
   and transferred to cytochrome system/
   cristae/electron transfer system
7. Oxygen not required/anaerobic./Occurs in
   aerobic and anaerobic conditions

  (ii) Your answer should include at least five points
    from the following:
8. Occurs in the mitochondrion matrix
9. Requires oxygen OR aerobic phase
10. C2 acetyl group produced from pyruvic
    acid
11. Acetyl group joins with CoA
12. Acetyl CoA reacts/combines with a C4
    compound to form C6 compound/citric
    acid
13. Cyclical series of reactions back to the C4
    compound
14. Carbon dioxide produced/given off/
    released
15. NAD accepts hydrogen/NADH produced
    and transferred to cytochrome system
16. Krebs cycle needs/requires/is controlled by
    enzymes

1B (i) Your answer should include at least four points
    from the following:
1. Carried out by phagocytes/monocytes/
   macrophages
2. Non-specific nature of process
3. Bacteria/foreign material/virus
   engulfed/enveloped OR description/
   diagram
4. Into a vacuole/vesicle
5. Lysosomes fuse/join to vacuole AND add
   enzymes to vacuole
6. Bacteria/foreign material/virus digested/
   destroyed/broken down by enzymes

  (ii) Your answer should include at least four points
    from the following:
7. Antibodies are proteins
8. They are produced by lymphocytes
9. Production stimulated by/in response to
   foreign/non-self antigens/proteins
10. Antibodies are specific/match the shape of
    antigens OR lock and key diagram
11. Antibody renders harmless/destroys/
    attacks/combats/neutralises/combines with
    antigen

Your answer should also include at least two
points from the following:
12. Transplanted tissues are antigenic/have
    foreign antigens/proteins recognised as
    foreign/non-self
13. Will be rejected/attacked by patient's
    antibodies
    OR antibodies made against transplant
    tissue
14. Risk of rejection is reduced by
    suppressors/immunosuppressors/drugs
    which suppress/inhibit immune system OR
    repressors which inhibit/suppress the
    immune system

2A Your answer should include any two points from
the following:
1. Fish (tissues)/body fluids hypertonic to
   surroundings OR converse
2. Water enters fish through gills and/or mouth by
   osmosis
3. Potentially leading to bursting of/damage to
   cells
   OR dilutes cytoplasm/increases water content of
   cells
   OR excess water must be removed
   OR water must be removed to keep water
   balance
4. Salts lost in urine/through mouth linings/gills

Your answer should also include any six points
from the following:
5. Kidneys have many glomeruli
6. Kidneys have large glomeruli
6a. Have many large glomeruli
7. Filtration rate of kidneys/glomeruli/blood is
   high
8. Urine produced is dilute
9. Large volume/amount/quantity of urine
   produced

2A 10. Chloride secretory cells present in gills absorb salts
11. Against the concentration gradient/by active transport/uptake/actively

In question 2A, one mark is available for coherence and one mark is available for relevance.

2B Your answer should include at least two points from the following:
1. Co-operative hunting means animals hunting in a social group/pack/team
   OR means working together in hunting/to get food
2. Advantage eg larger prey/more successful, less energy used/pursuit time per individual, net gain of energy is greater than by foraging alone
3. Another different advantage from list

Your answer should also include at least three points from the following:
4. Dominance hierarchy is a rank/pecking order within a social group
5. Consists of dominant/alpha and subordinate individuals
6. In feeding dominant/alpha individuals eat first (followed by subordinate)
   OR dominant get bigger share of food
   OR converse
7. Ensured survival of dominant when food scarce
8. Subordinate animal may gain more food than by foraging alone

Your answer should also include at least three points from the following:
9. Territory is (an area) marked/defended for feeding/hunting
10. Ensures a food supply/must contain enough food
    OR the more food available the smaller the territory
    OR converse
11. Territorial behaviour reduces competition
12. Energy expended in marking/patrolling/defending (territory)
14. Gain of energy increased by lack of competition
    OR foraging made more economical

In question 2B, one mark is available for coherence and one mark is available for relevance.